SPECIAL

CIRCUMSTANCES

ALSO BY SHELDON SIEGEL

SPECIAL

CIRCUMSTANCES

A Mike Daley/Rosie Fernandez Thriller

SHELDON SIEGEL

Sheldon M. Siegel, Inc.

ISBN (Ingram): 978-0-9996747-9-6
Original ISBN: 0-553-80141-4
eBook ISBN: 978-0-9913912-1-9
ISBN: 978-0-9913912-0-2

1. Daley, Mike (Fictitious Character) – Fiction.
2. Fernandez, Rosie (Fictitious character) – Fiction.
3. San Francisco (California.) – Fiction. 4. Attorney and Client- Fiction. 5. Trials (Murder) – Fiction.

For Linda, Alan, Stephen and Charlotte.

CHAPTER 1

A LICENSE TO PRINT MONEY

"Founded in 1929 and headquartered in San Francisco, Simpson and Gates is the largest full-service law firm based west of the Mississippi. With over nineteen hundred attorneys in eighteen offices on four continents, Simpson and Gates is recognized as an international leader in the legal profession."
— Simpson and Gates Attorney Recruiting Brochure.

"For seven hundred and fifty dollars an hour, I'd bite the heads off live chickens."
— J. Robert Holmes, Jr., Chairman, Simpson and Gates Corporate Department. Welcoming remarks to new attorneys.

For the last twenty years, being a partner in a big corporate law firm has been like having a license to print money. At my firm, Simpson and Gates, we've had a license to print *a lot* of money.

At six-fifteen in the evening of Tuesday, December 30, the printing press is running at full speed forty-eight floors above California Street in downtown San Francisco in what our executive committee modestly likes to call our world headquarters. Our 420 attorneys are housed in opulent offices on eight floors at the top of the Bank of America Building, a fifty-two-story bronze edifice that takes up almost an entire city block and is the tallest and ugliest testimonial to unimaginative architecture in the city skyline.

Our two-story rosewood-paneled reception area is about the size of a basketball court. A reception desk that is longer than a Muni bus sits at the south end of the forty-eighth floor, and I can see the

Golden Gate Bridge, Alcatraz Island and Sausalito through the glass-enclosed conference room on the north wall. The gray carpet, overstuffed leather chairs and antique coffee tables create the ambiance of a classic men's club, which is entirely appropriate since most of our attorneys and clients are white, male and Republican.

Even in the evening of the customarily quiet week between Christmas and New Year's, our reception area is buzzing with a higher level of activity than most businesses see in the middle of the day. Then again, most businesses aren't the largest and most profitable law firm on the West Coast.

Tomorrow is my last day with the firm and I am trying to shove my way through three hundred attorneys, clients, politicians and other hangers-on who have gathered for one of our insufferable cocktail parties. I hate this stuff. I guess it's appropriate that I have to walk the gauntlet one last time.

In the spirit of the holiday season, everybody is dressed in festive dark gray business suits, starched monogrammed white shirts and red power ties. A string quartet plays classical music in front of the blinking lights of our twenty-foot Christmas tree. The suits have gathered to drink chardonnay, eat hors d'oeuvres and pay tribute to my soon-to-be ex-partner, Prentice Marshall Gates III, the son of our late founding partner, Prentice Marshall Gates II. Prentice III, one of many lawyers in our firm with Roman numerals behind his name, is known as Skipper. He is also sailing out of the firm tomorrow. The circumstances of our respective departures are, shall I say, somewhat different.

After my five years as an underproductive partner in our white-collar criminal defense department, our executive committee asked me to leave. I was, in short, fired. Although the request was polite, I was told that if I didn't leave voluntarily, they would invoke Article Seven of our partnership agreement, which states, and I quote, that "a Partner of the Firm may be terminated by the Firm upon the affirmative vote of two-thirds (2/3) of the Partners of the Firm, at a duly called and held meeting of the Partners of the Firm." In the last three years, fourteen of my partners have been Article Sevened. I have graciously agreed to resign. On Monday, I'll open the law offices of Michael J. Daley, criminal defense attorney, in a subleased office in a walk-up building in the not-so-trendy part of San Francisco's South of Market area. Welcome to the modern practice of law.

Skipper's story is a little different. After thirty years as an underproductive partner in our real estate department, he spent three million dollars of the money he inherited from his father to win a mean-spirited race for district attorney of San Francisco, even though he hasn't set foot in a courtroom in over twenty years. My partners are thrilled. They have never complained about his arrogance, sloppy work and condescending attitude. Hell, the same could be said about most of my partners. What they can't live with is his six-hundred-thousand-dollar draw. He has been living off his father's reputation for years. That's why all the power partners are here. They want to give him a big send-off. More important, they want to be sure he doesn't change his mind.

The temperature is about ninety degrees, and it smells more like a locker room than a law firm. I nod to the mayor, shake hands with two of my former colleagues from the San Francisco Public Defender's Office, and carefully avoid eye contact with Skipper, who is working the room. I overhear him say the DA's office is his first step toward becoming attorney general and, ultimately, governor.

In your dreams, Skipper.

I'm trying to get to our reception desk to pick up a settlement agreement. Ordinarily, such a document would be delivered by one of our many in-house messengers. Tonight, I'm on my own because the kids who work in our mailroom aren't allowed to come to the front desk when the VIPs are around. I sample skewered shrimp provided by a tuxedoed waiter and elbow my way to the desk, where four evening-shift receptionists operate telephone consoles with more buttons than a 747. I lean over the polished counter and politely ask Cindi Harris if she has an envelope for me.

"Let me look, Mr. Daley," she says. She's a twenty-two year-old part-time art student from Modesto with long black hair, a prim nose and a radiant smile. She has confided to me that she would like to become an artist, a stock-car driver or the wife of a rich attorney. I have it on good authority that a couple of my partners have already taken her out for a test drive.

A few years ago, our executive committee hired a consultant to spruce up our image. It's hard to believe, but many people seem to perceive our firm as stuffy. For two hundred thousand dollars, our consultant expressed concern that our middle-aged receptionists didn't look "perky" enough to convey the appropriate image of a law firm of our stature. In addition, he was mortified that we had two receptionists who were members of the male gender.

At a meeting that everyone adamantly denies ever took place, our executive committee concluded that our clients—the white, middle-aged men who run the banks, insurance companies, defense contractors and conglomerates that we represent—would be more comfortable if our receptionists were younger, female, attractive, and, above all, perkier. As a result, our middle-aged female and male receptionists were reassigned to less-visible duties. We hired Cindi because she fit the profile recommended by our consultant. Although she's incapable of taking a phone message, she looks like a Victoria's Secret model. S&G isn't a hotbed of progressive thinking.

Don't get me wrong. As a divorced forty-five-year-old, I have nothing against attractive young women. I do have a problem when a firm adopts a policy of reassigning older women and men to less-visible positions just because they aren't attractive enough. For one thing, it's illegal. For another, it's wrong. That's another reason I got fired. Getting a reputation as the "house liberal" at S&G isn't great for your career.

Cindi's search turns up empty. "I'm sorry, Mr. Daley," she says, batting her eyes. She flashes an uncomfortable smile and looks like she's afraid I may yell at her. While such wariness is generally advisable at S&G, it shows she doesn't know me very well. Jimmy

Carter was in the White House the last time I yelled at anybody. "Let me look again."

I spy a manila envelope with my name on it sitting in front of her. "I think that may be it."

Big smile. "Oh, good."

Success. I take the envelope. "By the way, have you seen my secretary?"

Deer in the headlights. "What's her name again?"

"Doris."

"Ah, yes." Long pause. "Dooooris." Longer pause. "What does she look like?"

I opt for the path of least resistance. "I'll find her, Cindi." I start to walk away, but she stops me.

"Mr. Daley, are you really leaving? I mean, well, you're one of the nice guys. I mean, for a lawyer. I thought partners never leave."

Cindi, I'm leaving because I have more in common with the kids who push the mail carts than I do with my partners. I was fired because my piddly book of business isn't big enough.

I summon my best sincere face, look her right in her puppy eyes and pretend that I'm pouring out my heart. "I've been here for five years. I'm getting too old for a big firm. I've decided to try it on my own. Besides, I want more time for Grace."

My ex-wife has custody of our six-year-old daughter, but we get along pretty well, and Grace stays with me every other weekend.

Her eyes get larger. "Somebody said you might go back to the public defender's office."

I worked as a San Francisco PD for seven years before I joined S&G. The *State Bar Journal* once proclaimed I was the best PD in Northern California. Before I went to law school, I was a priest for three years. "Actually, I'm going to share office space with another attorney." Without an ounce of conviction, I add, "It'll be fun." I leave out the fact I'm subleasing from my ex-wife.

"Good luck, Mr. Daley."

"Thanks, Cindi." It's a little scary when you talk to people at work in the same tone you use with your first-grade daughter. It's even scarier to think that I'll probably miss Cindi more than I'll miss any of my partners. Then again, she didn't fire me.

I know one thing for certain. I'll sure miss the regular paychecks.

* * *

I push my way toward the conference room in search of Doris when I'm confronted by the six-foot-six-inch frame of Skipper Gates, who flashes the plastic three-million-dollar smile that graces fading campaign posters nailed to power poles across the city. He is inhaling a glass of wine. "Michael," he slurs, "so good to see you."

I don't want to deal with this right now.

At fifty-eight, his tanned face is chiseled granite, with a Roman nose, high forehead and graceful mane of silver hair. His charcoal-gray double-breasted Brioni suit, Egyptian cotton white shirt and striped tie add dignity to his rugged features. He looks like he is ready to assume his rightful place on Mount Rushmore next to George Washington.

As an attorney, he's careless, lazy and unimaginative. As a human being, he's greedy, condescending and an unapologetic philanderer. As a politician, however, he's the real deal. Even when he's half tanked and there's a piece of shrimp hanging from his chin, he exudes charisma, wealth and, above all, style. It's some sort of birthright of those born into privilege. As one of four children of a San Francisco cop, privilege is something I know little about.

He squeezes my hand and pulls me uncomfortably close. "I can't believe you're leaving," he says. His baritone has the affected quality of a man who spent his youth in boarding schools and his adulthood in country clubs. As he shouts into my ear, his breath confirms he could launch his forty-foot sailboat with the chardonnay he's consumed tonight.

His speech is touching. It's also complete crap. Instinctively, I begin evasive maneuvers. I pound him a little too hard on his back and dislodge the shrimp from his chin. "Who knows, Skipper?

Maybe we'll get to work on a case together."

He tilts his head back and laughs too loudly. "You bet."

I can't resist a quick tweak. "Skipper, you *are* going to try cases, right?"

District attorneys in big cities are political, ceremonial and administrative lawyers. They don't go to court. The assistant DAs try cases. If the ADA wins, the DA takes credit. If the ADA loses, the DA deflects blame. The San Francisco DA has tried only a handful of cases since the fifties.

He turns up the voltage. Like many politicians, he can speak and grin simultaneously. He hides behind the cocoon of his favorite sound bite. "Skipper Gates's administration is going to be different. The DA is a law enforcement officer, not a social worker. Skipper Gates is going to try cases. Skipper Gates is going to put the bad guys away."

And Mike Daley thinks you sound like a pompous ass.

He sees the mayor and staggers away. I wish you smooth sailing, Skipper. The political waters in the city tend to be choppy, even for well-connected operators like you. Things may be different when your daddy's name isn't on the door.

* * *

A moment later, I find my secretary, Doris Fontaine, standing outside our power conference room, or "PCR." Doris is a dignified fifty six-year-old with serious blue eyes, carefully coiffed gray hair and the quiet confidence of a consummate professional. If she had been born twenty years later, she would have gone to law school and become a partner here.

"Thanks for everything, Doris," I say. "I'll miss you."

"I'll never get another one like you, Mikey."

I hate it when she calls me Mikey. She absentmindedly fingers the reading glasses hanging from a gold chain. She reminds me of Sister Eunice, my kindergarten teacher at St. Peter's. She looks at the chaos in the PCR through the glass door and shakes her head.

The PCR houses an eighty-foot rosewood table with a marble top, matching credenza and fifty chairs, a closed-circuit TV system connecting our eighteen offices and a museum-quality collection of Currier and Ives lithographs. Six presidents, eight governors and countless local politicians have solicited campaign funds in this very room. Thirty expandable aluminum racks holding hundreds of carefully labeled manila folders containing legal documents cover the table. The room is littered with paper, coffee cups, half-eaten sandwiches, legal pads, laptops and cell phones. It looks like mission control before a space shuttle launch. The grim faces of the fifty people in the PCR are in contrast to the forced smiles at Skipper's party outside. Nobody is admiring the lithographs.

"How is Bob's deal going?" I ask.

"Not so well," Doris says.

Ever the diplomat. She's worked for Bob Holmes, the head of our corporate department, for about twenty years. In every law firm, there's one individual with a huge book of business and an even bigger ego whose sole purpose is to make everyone miserable. Bob is our nine-hundred-pound gorilla. His eight-million-dollar book of business lets him do whatever he wants. For the most part, he's content to sit on our executive committee, torture his associates, and whine. Last year he took home two million three hundred thousand. Not bad for a short kid from the wrong side of the tracks in Wilkes-Barre. Although my partners find it difficult to agree on anything, they're willing to acknowledge that Bob is a flaming asshole.

Whenever a big deal is coming down at S&G, the PCR is the stage, and Bob plays the lead. At the moment, he's screaming into a cell phone. He hasn't slept in three days, and it shows. He's in his late forties, but with his five-seven frame holding 230 pounds, his puffy red face and jowls make him look at least sixty. Although some of us remember when his hair was gray, it's now dyed an unnatural shade of orange-brown that he combs over an expanding bald spot. On his best days, he storms through our office with a pained expression suggesting a perpetual case of hemorrhoids. Tonight the grimace is even more pronounced.

I share Doris with Bob and a first-year associate named Donna Andrews, who spends her waking hours preparing memoranda on esoteric legal issues. It may seem odd that a heavy hitter like Bob has to share a secretary. However, by executive committee fiat, every attorney (including immortals) must share a secretary with two others. This means Bob gets ninety-nine percent of Doris's time, I get one percent and Donna gets nothing. From the firm's perspective, this allocation is entirely appropriate. Bob runs the firm, I'm on my way out the door and Donna is irrelevant.

I ask Doris if she can take the day off tomorrow.

"Doesn't look good. I was hoping for some time with Jenny." She's a single mom. Never been married. Her daughter is a senior at Stanford.

"I saw her earlier today. Sounded like she had a cold."

"You know how it is. Spend your whole life worrying about your kids."

I know. "Any chance you got my bills out?" Ordinarily, I don't sweat administrative details like bills and timesheets. However, if my bills are late, the firm will withhold my paycheck. It's our only absolute rule. No bills—no paycheck—no exceptions. Doris has long been convinced that my lackadaisical attitude would do irreparable harm to S&G's finely tuned money machine.

"I got them into the last mail run," she says.

Relief. "You're still the best. Are you sure you won't come work for me?"

"You can't afford me, Mikey."

The door to the PCR opens and a blast of stale air hits me. Joel Friedman, a harried corporate associate, steps outside. His collar is unbuttoned and the bags under his eyes extend halfway down his cheeks. "Doris, are you going to be here for a while?"

"Just for a few more minutes."

Joel is sort of a Jewish Ward Cleaver. He's an excellent attorney with a terrific wife and twin six-year-old boys. He's thirty-eight, a trim five-nine. His father is the rabbi at Temple Beth Sholom in the Richmond District. Joel left the yeshiva after two years and went to my alma mater, UC-Berkeley's Boalt Law School. He graduated second in his class and joined S&G seven years ago. His brown hair is graying, the bald spot he tries to hide is getting larger and his tortoiseshell glasses give him a rabbinical look which, in the circumstances, is entirely appropriate. In Yiddish, he would be described as a mensch, which means an honorable man. He's also my best friend.

"Is your deal going to close?" I ask.

He's up for partner this year. If his deal closes, he's a shoo-in. He modestly describes his job as thanklessly walking behind Bob Holmes and sweeping up the debris. In reality, he does all the work and Bob takes the credit. Frankly, he's the last line of defense between Bob and our malpractice carrier.

"It's fucked up," he says. Like many attorneys, he holds the misguided belief that he's more convincing if he peppers his speech with four-letter words. Very unbecoming for the rabbi's son. He nods at our client, Vince Russo, an oily man about Joel's age who has jammed his Jabba-the-Hutt torso into a chair next to Holmes. "The closing depends on Vince. He's selling his father's business, but he's having second thoughts. He thinks he can get a higher price if he can find another buyer."

I've never had the pleasure of meeting Russo. From what I've read, he's run his father's real estate conglomerate into the ground. "Why doesn't he pull out?"

"His creditors will force him into bankruptcy. They aren't going to wait another year or two."

I gaze at the frenzy in the PCR. "Looks like you could use some help."

"As usual, I'm not getting much." He glances at Diana Kennedy, a glamorous twenty-nine-year-old associate with deep blue eyes, stylish blond hair and a figure that reflects a lot of time at the gym. She's a rising star. "Things might go a little faster if Diana would focus a little more on work."

Doris looks away. If you believe the firm's gossip mongers, Bob Holmes and Diana Kennedy have been sleeping together for the last year or so. I don't know for sure.

Joel shakes his head. "To top everything off, Beth showed up an hour ago and served Bob with divorce papers."

I can't help myself and I grin. Beth is Bob's soon-to-be-fourth ex-wife. It's twisted, but I silently rejoice at his latest marital failure. I'm sorry I won't be around to witness the fallout. His last divorce was spectacular.

Instinctively, Doris comes to Bob's defense. "She could have waited."

It's funny. Bob has been treating Doris like dirt for twenty years. They fight like cats and dogs all day, yet she's always the first to defend him. I change the subject. "Why doesn't Bob get Russo to take his chances in bankruptcy?"

Joel's eyes twinkle. "Because we won't get paid. Do you know how much Russo owes us?"

"A million bucks?"

"Try fifteen million."

I'm stunned.

His grin widens. "If you're going to start your own firm, you should learn a little about this financial stuff. We're doing this deal for a contingency fee. We get paid only if it closes. It's in the escrow instructions. We get twelve million at the closing."

"I thought you said he owes us fifteen."

"He does."

"But you said we're getting only twelve."

"We are."

"Who gets the other three?"

"Guess."

"I don't know."

Doris answers for him. "Bob does."

What the hell? "No way. He can't siphon off a three-million-dollar personal gratuity. It's against firm policy. The fees belong to the firm. Some of that money belongs to *me*."

Joel chuckles. "It's been approved by the executive committee. That's why Bob will pull every string to get this deal to close."

As he says the word "close," I see Russo's face turning bright crimson.

"Stand back," Joel says. "Mount Russo is about to erupt."

Russo clumsily squeezes out of his chair and storms toward us. He slams his three-hundred-pound frame against the glass door. When he's halfway out, he turns around and faces the roomful of apprehensive eyes. "Another forty million? How am I supposed to afford another forty million? Why do I pay you lawyers?"

The party outside goes silent. Skipper looks mortified. Russo waddles down the hall.

I look at Doris. "What was that all about?"

She shrugs and says she has to go back to work.

Joel winks. "It seems there's been a modest reduction in the purchase price. It's such a pleasure working with our highly sophisticated, state-of-the-art corporate clients." He arches an eyebrow. "I think we could use a glass of wine."

CHAPTER 2

"WE MAY HAVE A LITTLE PROBLEM WITH THE CLOSING"

"People think being administrative partner is a boring, thankless job. I disagree. The administrative partner is the glue that holds the firm together as an institution."
— Simpson and Gates administrative partner Charles Stern. Welcoming remarks to new attorneys.

A few minutes later, I'm sitting in a sterile conference room on the forty-fifth floor, where my partner, Charles Stern, has called a meeting of our associates. For the last ten years, Charles has held the boring, thankless job of serving as our administrative partner, a position for which he is uniquely suited. A terminally morose tax attorney, his unnaturally pasty complexion, pronounced widow's peak and emaciated physique make him look considerably older than fifty-five. He views the Internal Revenue Code as akin to the Bible. He always refers to it as the Good Book. Likewise, he calls the 1986 Tax Act the Satanic Verses, because it took away many of his favorite tax-avoidance schemes. At S&G, we call what he does creative tax planning. Out there in the real world, most people would say he helps his clients engage in varying degrees of tax fraud.

In addition to his modest tax practice, he devotes most of his time to serving on virtually every firm committee, thereby bringing order to the chaos that would ensue without his steady hand. He has also appointed himself the financial conscience of the firm, and reviews each and every expense report before any of our hard-earned cash goes out the door. He handles personnel matters and insists on being present when anyone is fired. He seems to take particular pleasure in this aspect of his job. He's known as the Grim Reaper.

Except for light reading of the *Daily Tax Report*, the only joy in his life seems to be the production of an endless stream of e-mails on every imaginable administrative subject, and some that are unimaginable. My life would be a hollow, empty shell without at least one missive every day about procedures, timesheets and expense reimbursements.

He insists that everyone call him Charles. Not Charlie. Not Chuck. Charles. An unseemly hazing ritual takes place every year when Bob Holmes sends an unsuspecting new associate to visit "Charlie." Last year, I had to intervene to prevent Stern from firing an associate on her third day.

A couple of years ago, in a meeting with the associates, my mouth shifted into gear while my brain was still idling, and I sarcastically dubbed him Chuckles. Naturally, everyone now refers to him by that name.

I have been invited because I have served as the liaison partner for five years, and Chuckles wants to make a presentation to our associates. As liaison partner, I have had the joyous task of addressing the concerns of our associates. It's the second-most-thankless job at the firm, behind administrative partner. The title of liaison partner goes to the most junior partner who doesn't have the practice or the balls to say no. If there's a shoe with dog crap on it, I always seem to be wearing it.

Everybody hates the liaison partner. The associates hate me because they think I'm a toady for the partners. They're right. The partners hate me because starting salaries are more than a hundred and sixty thousand dollars. Nice piece of change for a kid right out of law school. It isn't their fault that they're being overpaid. In fairness to yours truly, I didn't create this problem. Our salaries are exactly the same as every other big firm in town. The managing partners get together every year to decide how much money the new attorneys will make. In other industries, this would be called price-fixing. It isn't fair to blame me because the managing partners have had a collective brain cramp for the last ten years and decided to grossly overpay baby lawyers. Nobody said life is fair.

Our offices are hooked up by conference telephone call, so this meeting is a bad sign. Good news is communicated by closed-circuit TV. The lack of refreshments is even more ominous. We're incapable of holding a meeting without sodas, bottled water, cheese, crackers and fruit. On extraordinarily festive occasions, we get cookies.

Of the hundred associates, only five are women and just one is black. Although Chuckles doesn't know it, the African-American associate has accepted a job at another firm, and will give notice after he gets his bonus tomorrow. The seating is always the same. Chuckles sits at one end of the table and everybody else (including me) sits as far away from him as possible. He looks sad and lonely at the other end of the table. Joel slides into the seat to my immediate right.

Chuckles clears his throat. "May I have your attention, please?" He's wearing his gray Men's Wearhouse suit, and his blue polka dot tie has a stranglehold around his neck. The room becomes silent. He glances uncomfortably over the top of his reading glasses. He looks my way and his thin lips contort to form a pained expression that suggests he's trying to smile. He takes off his reading glasses with uncharacteristic animation. "Before we start, I want to thank Mike Daley for his hard work on associate issues."

Relief, followed by acute embarrassment.

Chuckles is looking at me. "As you know, Mike's last day is tomorrow. On behalf of everybody in this room, I want to wish him the very best."

My face is red and my neck is burning. I nod as the associates dutifully pat their hands together in quiet applause.

Chuckles puts his reading glasses back on. His eyes never leave his legal pad. "The partners asked me to update you on certain issues considered by the executive committee. After discussion with our consultant, we have made some important decisions. I want to assure you we have reviewed these issues very carefully, and acted fairly and in the best interests of the firm as an institution."

I love it when he refers to the firm as an institution. I've placed a legal pad between Joel and me. I jot a note that says, "Hold on to your wallet."

Stern's eyes are glued to his notes. "Effective immediately, associates will be considered for election to the partnership after eight and a half years at the firm, instead of seven years, as is current policy." He looks up for a fraction of a second to see if an insurrection is brewing.

Joel writes "BS" on the pad and interrupts him. "Excuse me, Charles. May we assume that those of us who are up for partner this year will be grandfathered in under the old rules?"

Chuckles closes the small lizard-like slits he uses for eyes. He takes off his glasses. "Did Bob talk to you?"

"No."

Chuckles twirls the glasses. The telltale "oh shit" expression. "Joel, let's talk about this after the meeting."

It's fun to watch Chuckles tap-dance.

Joel's eyes light up. "Let's talk about it now. Am I up for partner or not?"

Chuckles sighs. "You're not. And Bob was supposed to talk to you."

Chuckles usually doesn't have to face the music from the associates.

Joel isn't backing off. "Well, he didn't. This stinks. We *will* talk after the meeting. Before we do, maybe you should explain why the associates shouldn't have their resumes out on the street tomorrow morning."

We've always had great finesse with these touchy-feely human-relations issues.

On go the glasses. Chuckles finds his place and continues reading. "In addition, the firm will not be in a position to pay associate bonuses this year."

There's an audible gasp. The more-senior associates are expecting bonuses in excess of thirty thousand dollars.

Chuckles is astute enough to realize he's in trouble. He makes the correct move and returns to the script. "I want to assure you these decisions were made after careful deliberation and represent the unanimous view of the executive committee as to what is fair and what constitutes the best interests of the firm as an institution."

At times like this, I've tried to defuse the tension with a wisecrack. Tonight, Chuckles is working without a net. I write another note to Joel. "Now, the explanation."

"By way of explanation," Chuckles continues, "the partners wanted me to make it clear that these decisions were not made for economic reasons. The financial health of the firm is excellent."

Bad move. If we're doing so great, it means the partners have decided to keep more money for themselves. I don't necessarily have a problem with this because it means my last draw check will be a little bigger. On the other hand, if we aren't doing great, he's lying. Either way, the associates are getting screwed. And they know it.

Chuckles drones on. "With respect to the partnership track, we have decided it would be beneficial to give each associate additional time to work with as many partners as possible."

It's not like we're just pulling up the ladder.

"With respect to bonuses, we have expended substantial sums to upgrade our computers, a decision made in response to concerns expressed by our younger attorneys. We believe it is in the firm's long-term financial interests to pay for our new equipment as soon as possible. We realize this may not be the most popular decision, but we believe the computer enhancement is in the best interests of the firm as an institution."

Especially if the associates pay for it.

The associates turn toward Joel, who has been their spokesman for the last few years. He glares at Chuckles and keeps his tone even. "You realize, Charles, that what you just said is complete and utter bullshit?" Without waiting for a response, he pushes his chair back and calmly walks out of the room.

Chuckles senses that the mood isn't good. He gathers his notes and practically sprints from the room. The meeting lasted less than five minutes.

* * *

When I return to my office, the gruff voice of Arthur Patton, our managing partner and chairman of the three-man star chamber we call our executive committee, summons me from my voicemail. "Michael, Arthur Patton. Come to the executive conference room ASAP."

It would never occur to him that I may not be available. I walk downstairs to our "executive" conference room on the forty-sixth floor in an office that once belonged to Skipper's father. When he died, Skipper laid claim to the office by birthright. Bob Holmes said he was entitled to it because he had the biggest book of business. Arthur Patton said he should get it just because he's Patton. After three weeks of backbiting, Chuckles Stern implemented what is now known as the "Great Compromise," and the office was converted into a conference room. My suggestion of a "one-potato, two-potato" marathon was dismissed.

The room has a marble conference table, ten black leather chairs and a view of the Golden Gate Bridge. Portraits of our founding partners hang on the west wall, and portraits of our current X-Com—Patton, Chuckles and Holmes—hang on the east wall. Patton and Chuckles are glum as they sit beneath the smiling pictures of themselves. Mercifully, Holmes is nowhere to be found. The usual assortment of cheese and fruit is on a silver platter.

On December 30th of each year, X-Com meets to give themselves a collective pat on the back and to determine "the Estimate," which is their best guess of firm profits for the year. More important, they allocate each partner's percentage interest in the profits of the firm, or "points," for the upcoming year. The Estimate will be announced with great ceremony at a partners' meeting at eight o'clock tomorrow morning. I've always thought we could streamline the process by putting a tote board in our reception area. This suggestion has not been well received over the years. At the meeting, each partner will receive a check and a memo indicating his points. Theoretically, everybody will begin the new year in a good mood. Unless you're like me, and your points have been reduced in each of the last four years.

I'm not sure why I've been summoned on the night of all nights. I'm pretty sure they can't fire me again. I take a seat beneath the portraits of Leland Simpson and Skipper's dad. I feel like I'm surrounded.

"We wanted to discuss your departure," Patton says.

Uh-oh.

Patton's bald head, Nixon-like jowls and Brezhnev-like eyebrows overwhelm the rest of his tiny face. His red suspenders strain to hold his ample gut. At sixty-two, his gravel baritone is commanding, but its forcefulness has been tempered by forty years of cigars and single-malt scotch. At times, he's capable of playing the role of the genial grandfather. Last year, he was Santa at our Christmas party. The next day, he fired his secretary because there was one typo in an eighty page brief. That's part of his charm. You never know if you'll get the puppy or the pit bull.

In law-firm-lingo, he handles complex civil litigation. I've never met a lawyer who admits he handles litigation that's anything less than "complex." In reality, he represents defense contractors who get sued when their bombers don't fly. To Art, every case is a holy war of attrition where he showers the other side with paper. Fortunately, his clients have the resources to wear down their opponents. He responds to every letter with his own version that rearranges the facts in his favor. He follows up every phone call with a letter that bears only passing resemblance to the matters that were discussed. Around the firm, he's known as the Smiling Assassin.

He stares over my right shoulder and begins with the grandfatherly tone. "I know we have had our disagreements, but I would like to think we can work things out and remain friends."

As if. I look right through him and remain silent. Let him talk. Don't react.

His condescending smirk makes its first appearance. "Here is our proposal. If anyone asks, we will portray your departure as voluntary. You will agree not to say anything bad about us. We will return your capital contribution tomorrow."

When you're elected to the partnership, you have to make a capital contribution. The amount is based upon the number of your points. Baby partners like me contribute ninety grand. Power partners like Patton pony up a half a million bucks.

"That's it?" I ask.

"That's it. Except for one thing. As a matter of good practice, we need you to sign a full release of the firm. We ask all departing partners. Just housekeeping."

Keep the tone measured. "Let me see if I have this straight. I won't piss on you, and you won't piss on me. That's fair. And that's the way it will work because we're smart enough not to say nasty things about each other. San Francisco is a small town. And you will pay me back my capital."

"Yes."

"Good. Because our partnership agreement says you have to pay me back whether or not I agree to say nice things about you, and even if I don't sign your release. I have no intention of suing you, but if I change my mind, I don't want you waving a release in my face."

Gotcha. If I were in his shoes, I'd ask for the release. If he were in mine, he'd say no. I'm glad Joel showed me the section in our partnership agreement that says they have to return my capital.

He shifts to the half grin. "We figured you might say that. We are therefore prepared to make a one-time offer of twenty thousand dollars for your cooperation. Take it or leave it."

Visions of paying off my Visa bill and a year of rent dance in my head. "Not enough. Make it a hundred and we may have something to talk about."

Chuckles shakes his head. "Too much, Mike. No can do."

Patton trots out his "mad dog" persona for a preemptive strike. His act loses some of its impact when you've seen it as many times as I have. "If it had been up to me, I would have thrown your sorry ass out of here at least two years ago."

For an instant, I think Leland Simpson's picture is going to spring to life. "Yeah," he'd say, "I would have thrown your sorry ass out of here at least *three* years ago. Hell, I never would have hired you in the first place."

Patton isn't finished. "Use your head for once and take the money."

I place my fingertips together in my best Mother Teresa imitation. "Arthur, if you're going to lose your temper, you're going to have to go to your office and take a time-out." I've been waiting five years to say that to him. I head toward the door. As I'm about to leave the room, I turn and face them. "Gentlemen, I'll see you in the morning. I wouldn't want to miss the reading of the Estimate."

* * *

When I arrive at the office at seven the next morning, I have voicemail messages from five associates who are furious about the decision on bonuses. Three ask me to be a reference. As always, the first person I see is Anna Sharansky, a Soviet refugee who begins every day by brewing enough Peet's coffee to fill the sixty coffeepots placed around the firm. S&G spends over a quarter of a million bucks a year on coffee. We exchange pleasantries. She never complains. I'll miss her.

At seven-forty-five, I walk to a utilitarian conference room on the forty-sixth floor to get a seat for the reading of the Estimate. The ceremony usually takes place in the PCR. We're downstairs because Bob Holmes won't move the documents for Russo's deal. It smells like a French pastry shop. Croissants, muffins, scones and fruit are lined up in neat rows on silver platters. Anna has filled the coffeepots and set out the bone china bearing the S&G logo. In the center of the table sit ninety envelopes, each bearing a partner's name. They look like seating assignments at a wedding.

By 7:55, the room is full. I pour myself a cup of coffee and take a croissant with the sterling-silver tongs. The blue sky frames the Golden Gate Bridge. Let the exercises begin.

Patton always wears his tuxedo to the reading of the Estimate. He seems to think this lends a festive mood to the occasion. I think he looks like a maître d'. At precisely eight o'clock, he makes his grand entrance, his face glowing. For fifteen minutes a year, we're everything described in our recruiting brochure: a big, collegial family of highly trained professionals who admire, respect and trust one another.

He beams at the head of the table. "Thank you for coming at this early hour. I know how hard it is for some of you to get here when you've been out partying all night." Forced laughter. "I want to get Bob Holmes down here to report on Vince Russo's deal. We will start in a few minutes."

He asks Chuckles to find Bob. Chuckles seems pleased he won't have a speaking role today, and he darts out. The sound of clinking china resumes. Several partners take calls on their cell phones. I focus on the envelope in the middle of the table with my name.

Ten minutes pass. Chuckles and Joel appear outside the glass door. Chuckles looks more gaunt than usual. Joel looks distraught.

Chuckles opens the door and speaks in a barely audible voice. "Art, can I see you outside for a minute?"

The room goes silent. Patton motions Chuckles in. Chuckles tries to convince him to step outside. After a moment's hesitation, Chuckles comes in and whispers into Patton's ear. Patton's eyes get larger. I hear him mutter, "Geez."

Patton turns, strokes his jowls, and addresses nobody in particular. "It is my unhappy responsibility to make a sad announcement. Bob Holmes and Diana Kennedy were found dead in Bob's office a few minutes ago. I have no other information. The police have been called."

We sit in stunned silence.

"Obviously, we may have a little problem with the closing of the Russo deal. Any discussion of the firm's results for this year would be premature. I will provide further information later today. Meeting adjourned."

More silence.

After a moment, I hear Patton whisper to Chuckles, "He couldn't have killed himself. We're completely screwed. He had a fiduciary duty to us to close the deal"

Leave it to Art Patton to try to explain a man's death by citing a legal doctrine.

As always, Chuckles is more practical. He says to Patton, "I suspect Bob wasn't thinking about his fiduciary duties last night."

Without another word, we file out, pausing to pick up our envelopes.

CHAPTER 3

"HE KEPT A LOADED GUN AT HIS DESK"

"The managing partner of Simpson and Gates has issued a statement reassuring the firm's clients that the situation is completely under control."
— KCBS NEWS RADIO. 8:40 A.M. Wednesday, December 31.

By eight-thirty, the firm is in chaos. Every thirty seconds or so, a voice on the emergency intercom announces that there has been an incident and we shouldn't use the elevators. Word spreads quickly, and people gather in the corridors.

My office is on the forty-seventh floor, between Joel's small office and Bob's palatial northwest corner. Joel is talking on the phone as I walk past his doorway. He's trying to find Vince Russo. A policeman is unrolling yellow tape outside Bob's office.

I walk into my office and sit down. The room is empty except for a few last boxes and my coffee cup with Grace's picture on it. I listen to the sirens forty-seven floors below. It sounds as though every police car in the city is heading toward our building.

Doris comes in a moment later. "Is it true?"

"Yes. Patton said Bob and Diana are dead. Chuckles and Joel broke up the partners' meeting. I don't know any details."

Tears well up in her eyes. "I can't believe it."

I give her a hug. She starts sobbing into my shoulder. "It'll be all right," I say feebly.

"It finally got to him. The divorce, the deal, the money. And Diana, too. Why Diana?"

"These things happen for a reason." I realize this line from my religious training never rang very true. It was one of the reasons I left the priesthood. I had trouble saying the party line toward the end.

She wipes her eyes and sits down. I absentmindedly turn on my computer. It's funny how you revert to habit. I have two e-mails. The second is from Patton, advising that there will be an emergency meeting at nine o'clock. The other is from Bob Holmes. It was sent at 1:20 this morning. I get chills.

"Look at this," I say to Doris.

She comes around behind my desk and reads over my shoulder. Bob's final words are concise. *"To everyone. I am sorry for the pain I have inflicted. I hope you will find it in your hearts to forgive me. I cannot go on. I wish you the best. Bob."*

I read it again. "An e-mail suicide note. This is weird, even for Bob." I get a sour feeling in my stomach. His body is still in the office next door.

My phone rings and I pick up. My mother is calling from home. "Mickey, I'm watching TV. They said somebody at your office got shot. Are you okay?"

"I'm fine, Mama."

"Thank God. Did you know them?"

"Yeah, I knew them."

"Mickey, be careful."

"I will. I'll call you back later, okay?"

I open the Channel 4 website and turn on the live feed. A reporter is standing in the plaza outside the California Street entrance to our building. She's in front of the huge black polished-granite sculpture designed by Masayuki Nagare that the late Herb Caen, the immortal *San Francisco Chronicle* columnist, dubbed the Banker's Heart.

"This is Rita Roberts. We are live in San Francisco, where police are reporting an incident at Simpson and Gates, the city's largest law firm. Details are sketchy, but it appears that two Simpson and Gates attorneys have been killed by gunshots. Newly elected San Francisco District Attorney Prentice Gates III was a partner at the firm. Mr.

Gates and the mayor were in the firm's office last night. Moments ago, a spokesman told us that the mayor left the Simpson and Gates suite about nine o'clock last night and arrived at his office this morning at his usual time. We haven't been able to confirm the whereabouts of Mr. Gates. Rita Roberts for NewsCenter 4."

I'm turning down the sound when a young policeman knocks on my open door. "I'm Officer Chinn. We're asking everyone to return to their desk."

"We understand, Officer." He walks down the hall.

Doris is offended.

"He's just following procedure," I tell her. "He's supposed to secure the scene and wait for help." In reality he's also supposed to separate us so we can't compare stories. She heads out the door.

* * *

My phone keeps ringing. My younger brother, Pete, a former San Francisco cop who works as a private investigator, gets through on the first try. "You okay, Mick? I heard it on the box."

"I'm fine."

"You talk to Ma?"

"Yeah. Told her I'm okay. Mind giving her a call? She'll feel better if she hears from you."

"No problem, Mick. Gotta go. I'm working."

I pity the unfaithful husband he's tailing. What he lacks in finesse he makes up for in tenacity.

* * *

"Que pasa, Miguel? You all right?" My ex-wife, Rosita Carmela Fernandez, doesn't speak Spanish, except to me.

"I'm fine, Rosie."

Rosie grew up in the Hispanic enclave in the Mission District. Her dad was a carpenter. Her mom babysits Grace when Rosie's in trial. Rosie was the first member of her family to go to college. She worked her way through San Francisco State and Hastings Law School. We used to work together at the PD's office. We were married for about three years. We were a lot better at trying cases than we were at being married.

Her tone is businesslike. "I was worried my new tenant wasn't going to move in."

That was part of the problem when we were married. Among other things, Rosie is good at keeping track of money, I'm not. She's organized. I'm flexible. It used to drive her nuts. We got along great until we got married. Then all of my faults came to light. After a couple of years of ceaseless sniping, we finally split up after Grace turned one. Once the divorce messiness was over, we started to get along a lot better.

"I'm moving in just the way we planned," I say.

"Good man. I'll call you later. *Adios.*"

Rosie, you're the best ex-wife a man could have. Damn shame we couldn't stand living together.

* * *

Joel pokes his head in while I'm on the phone with my baby sister, Mary, a first-grade teacher in L.A. His hair is disheveled. His eyes are puffy. I motion for him to sit down. I say good-bye to Mary.

His voice is a hoarse whisper. "Long night, Mike."

"I'll bet. What can I say?"

"I've never seen a dead body before. Jews don't do open caskets." He tries to compose himself. "He practically blew the side of his head off."

"Do you have any idea what happened?"

He holds up his hands. "We finished negotiations about nine. We gave the documents to the word processors. Diana and I went to Harrington's for a quick bite. She went home. I got back around eleven-fifteen. We finished signing papers by twelve-thirty. Everybody left. I went down to the lunchroom for a Coke. I read documents for two or three hours and I took a nap down there. I got up around six and went back to my office. I thought Bob had gone home. Next thing I knew, it was eight o'clock and Chuckles asked me for the keys to Bob's office. That's when we found them."

"Did Russo kill the deal?" I realize that my choice of words could have been more discreet.

"I don't know. I can't find him. Last time I saw him was when he signed the papers. He said he was going back to the Ritz. He stays there so he doesn't have to drive all the way down to his house in Hillsborough. He wasn't sure if he'd authorize the wire transfers to close the deal. He said he was going to sleep on it. He said he might have to go to his backup plan."

"What's that?"

"A flying leap off the Golden Gate Bridge. I called the hotel. They said he didn't sleep in his bed last night." He sighs. "I can't believe Bob killed himself, even if Vince decided to pull out. Bob's seen deals go south before."

"The police are going to want to talk to you. I'll drive you home when you're done."

"Thanks, Mike."

This is going to be tough on Joel.

* * *

At five after nine, Arthur Patton is still wearing his tuxedo when he convenes an all-hands meeting in the reception area. Thankfully, somebody had the good judgment to turn off the lights on the Christmas tree. Patton speaks in an even tone. "As many of you are aware, Bob Holmes and Diana Kennedy were found dead in Bob's office this morning. The police have indicated they died of gunshot wounds. Bob's wounds may have been self-inflicted.

"This is Inspector Roosevelt Johnson of the SFPD, who is in charge of the investigation. I would ask each of you to assist the police. Our office is closed until Monday, and you are free to go home as soon as the police say you may do so."

Roosevelt Johnson was my father's first partner. Every time I see him, I think of my dad. I've known Roosevelt since I was a kid. He worked his way up the ranks and made homicide inspector. Dad stayed on the street. Although Roosevelt is in his early sixties, at six-four and 235 pounds, he still looks like he can play linebacker at Cal. His ebony skin, gray mustache, bald dome and gold wire-rimmed glasses command the attention of everyone in the room.

He speaks in an eloquent baritone. "Ladies and gentlemen, I promise to get you home as soon as possible. We need to obtain a statement from each of you. If you didn't see or hear anything, I would ask you to write a note to that effect and give it to one of our officers. I would appreciate it if you would return to your office or workstation. I must ask you not to discuss this matter with each other. Please stay away from Mr. Holmes's office while we gather evidence. I apologize for the inconvenience, and I thank you for your cooperation."

Doris raises her hand. "Inspector, can you give us any information about the circumstances surrounding Bob's and Diana's deaths?"

"It appears they were victims of gunshot wounds."

"Were they self-inflicted?"

"We don't know yet. A handgun was found at the scene. We will provide additional information as soon as possible."

* * *

At ten o'clock, I'm on the phone when a subdued Chuckles walks into my office. I hold my thumb and forefinger a quarter of an inch apart, signaling I'll only be a minute. He sits down. I reassure my mother for the third time today and hang up.

Chuckles pushes out a sigh. "I haven't seen so much blood since I was in the service."

To Chuckles, the service usually means the IRS. I realize he's talking about the military. "You were in the army, Charles?"

"Marines. Vietnam. I've got a bum shoulder to show for it."

I never would have figured. Although it's entirely inappropriate, I imagine Chuckles and his platoon lobbing copies of the Internal Revenue Code toward the Vietcong. "I lost a brother over there near the end of the war."

"I didn't know. I'm sorry, Mike.

"Thank you." Tommy's death was one of the reasons I became a priest. My family was seriously Catholic. I was better at it than either of my brothers. Although the church had a lot of rules, it was a truly spiritual place for me when I was growing up. The spirituality disappeared when I became a priest. I decide it isn't a great time to mention my participation in the antiwar protests in Berkeley.

Chuckles is more somber than usual. "I know we have other things on our minds, but I wanted to let you know we decided to give you your capital back. We aren't going to insist that you sign a release." He pulls a check out of his jacket pocket and hands it to me.

"Thanks, Charles. That's very decent of you."

"Sometimes you make decisions because it's the right thing to do."

And sometimes you fire your partners because they don't have enough business. I expect him to leave, but he doesn't. "You knew Bob for a long time. Do you have any idea what this is all about?"

"I don't know. We weren't close. I'm not sure he had any close friends."

The same could be said about you, Chuckles.

He keeps talking. "Art knew him the best. They used to talk about stocks. They invested in a restaurant together. That fancy place in Palo Alto. Bob called it his private black hole for money. Bob and I just used to talk about firm business. He was having his biggest year ever. I can't believe he'd kill himself the night before the deal was going to close. Confidentially, he was going to get a big bonus today."

I feign surprise. "I didn't realize that, Charles."

"That's why it doesn't make sense. You know Bob. Or knew him, I guess. He'd never turn down a check. Maybe it was the divorce." He pauses. "You heard he used his own gun."

"He brought a gun to the office?"

"He *kept* it at the office, Mike. At his desk. I thought everyone knew."

Not everyone. "Loaded?"

"Yep."

"What for?"

"You were here when that lunatic killed all those people at 101 California."

In July of 1993, a crazed former client walked into the offices of a prominent San Francisco law firm and opened fire with an arsenal of semiautomatic weapons. He killed eight people and wounded a dozen others before he killed himself. The firm closed its doors two years later. "I knew some people over there," I tell him. "Good lawyers. Nice people."

"Yup. Every firm has a security system. We spent a quarter of a million on ours. Each receptionist has a panic button. If they see trouble, they punch it. The doors lock and a light goes on in personnel and at the security desk. Thank goodness we've never had to use it."

"Brave new world."

"No kidding. After the incident at 101 Cal, Bob said he wasn't going to let the same thing happen to him. He kept a loaded gun at his desk. He didn't make a big deal about it. We'd like to try to keep it out of the papers if we can."

"Not a bad idea." What's next? Metal detectors? I can see the headlines. *"Prominent San Francisco Attorney Kills Himself with Loaded Piece He Kept at His Desk."*

Chuckles shakes his head. "Now we have a big problem. We were counting on the fees from the Russo deal to make our year-end numbers. Art's beside himself. I think he may retire and move to Napa fulltime. I'm thinking about getting out, too. I don't know if the firm can survive."

There's the Chuckles I know and love. Two hours after he finds his partner's body, he's already worried about his draw.

* * *

Doris is back in my office at ten-fifteen. "Those police inspectors are really pushy. They treated me like a criminal."

"I did my five minutes with Officer Chinn. He was okay."

"Maybe to you. The cop I talked to acted like I was a murder suspect."

"I know this is tough. They're just doing their job."

"They were rude. And they asked a lot of questions about Diana's personal life."

"Like what?"

"Like whether she was sleeping with Bob."

"Was she?" I've always wondered.

"It's none of your business. And it sure as hell is none of theirs."

"Doris, this is tough on all of us. Give yourself a little space."

She starts to cry. I get up and put my arm around her. "It's such a waste," she says.

CHAPTER 4

THE LEGEND

"When I started working Homicide, there was no such thing as affirmative action. I'm not saying it was right. It's just the way it was."

— Inspector Roosevelt Johnson. *San Francisco Chronicle.*

At ten-thirty I'm at my desk watching Skipper being interviewed on TV. He mentions the shootings briefly, then he moves straight into his campaign speech.

Roosevelt Johnson's commanding presence fills my doorway, and the familiar baritone resonates off the walls. "Hello, Michael. This is a far cry from the PD's office."

"It's been a long time, Roosevelt."

He's a legend. He and his partner, Marcus Banks, are SFPD's most senior homicide team. They handle all the high-profile cases.

He closes my door. "How's your mama?"

"On good days she's ornery. On bad days, she doesn't say much. She's in the early stages of Alzheimer's. It isn't going to get better, but we're hoping it won't get worse too soon. She's still at home. Pete's living with her. He never moved out."

"Your mom and dad were never the same after Tommy died."

My older brother was one of the last MIAs in Vietnam. They never found his body. He was an all-city quarterback at St. Ignatius and all-conference at Cal. Tommy had another year of eligibility. He could have gotten deferred. He volunteered for the Marines. I tried to talk him out of it, but Dad told him it was the right thing to do. He never forgave me for trying to talk Tommy out of going, and he never forgave himself when Tommy died. Then he got sick. My dad worked his ass off for thirty years for his city pension. He died five years ago, about a year after Grace was born. At least he got to see his first grandchild.

Roosevelt takes a seat. "It's hard to bury your children, Mike." He knows. His son was nineteen when he was killed in a drive-by shooting near Candlestick Park. "Did you decide to become a priest after Tommy died?"

"In part." Unlike most of my friends, I loved going to church when I was a kid. It gave me time with my mom and dad. It gave my life structure. And it had lots of rules. I was always good at rules. It wasn't until I was in college that I started questioning them. I'll never forget the look of pride on my dad's face when I told him I was going to the seminary, or the look of disdain when I told him I was leaving the priesthood to become a lawyer. He hated lawyers. "When Tommy died, I went to the church to try to find some answers."

"What happened?"

"I guess it didn't have the answers I was looking for." He looks uncomfortable. "I didn't do anything terrible, Roosevelt. It just didn't work out." The rules that seemed so meaningful when I was a kid seemed prehistoric by the time I was a priest.

"Why did you end up in law school?" he asks.

"The church doesn't have an outplacement service for downsized priests. I figured I might be able to make a living helping people who got screwed. Lawyers can do a lot of things nobody else can do. Besides, I didn't have any better ideas." This is clearly more than he'd bargained for, so I change the subject. "How's your family?"

"Janet has good days and bad days, too. Arthritis. My daughter is an OB-GYN at San Francisco General. My granddaughter is at UCLA Law School. With my luck, she'll end up a public defender like you did."

"She'll probably end up at some Wall Street firm making two hundred thou a year."

He chuckles. "How are Rosie and the baby?"

"Complicated subject. Rosie and I split up about a year after

Grace was born. We couldn't figure out a way to work out the little stuff. And if you can't deal with the little stuff, you can't deal with the big stuff. Things are better now. Grace is in first grade. She lives with Rosie, but I'm a couple of blocks away. She stays with me every other weekend."

"How did you end up in a place like this?"

"I needed the money when we got divorced. This firm was starting a white-collar criminal defense practice. I was the best guy at the PD's office, so they hired me. Made me a partner. Doubled my salary."

He glances around my stripped office. "I take it you're leaving?"

"It didn't work out. The big-time white-collar practice didn't happen. The guy with the big book of business left after a year. I started bringing in DUI and robbery cases. Firms like S&G don't like to have real criminals roaming around the office. It scares the corporate clients. I'm going out on my own. I'm renting space on Mission."

"Sounds good."

"I hope so. Rosie's my landlord."

"You've always had a flair." He turns serious. "I know we didn't always see eye to eye when you were at the PD's office, but I'd like to think it was because we were on opposite sides of a few cases."

"It was never personal, Roosevelt."

"I'd like your help in sorting out this case. Off the record, if you'd like. Professional courtesy."

"I'll do anything I can to help you."

"I'd appreciate it if you'd keep our discussion confidential for the time being."

"Of course."

He skims his notes. "So far, we know that Holmes and Kennedy died of gunshot wounds. His to the head, hers to the chest. His wound looks self-inflicted. Your colleagues Charles Stern and Joel Friedman found the bodies and a Smith and Wesson thirty-eight-caliber revolver on the floor. Friedman said he last saw Holmes about twelve-thirty this morning. He had dinner with Kennedy about ten last night. He said she went home from the restaurant. We don't know when she came back. Our people are dusting the office and the gun. If I had to guess, it looks like he killed her and then killed himself. We've seen the e-mail message sent from his computer. But it's too soon to tell. You know me. I do it by the numbers."

"I know. Have you been able to impart your way of thinking upon your partner?"

"Marcus is a good cop. He doesn't always handle things the way I would. He's kept his nose clean the last few years. What can you tell me about Holmes? Was anything bothering him? Was anybody angry at him?"

"A lot was bothering him. And everybody in the city was angry at him." I tell him what I know about Bob. How my partners hated his guts. About his acrimonious divorces. About the divorce papers his wife served on him last night.

"Anybody else mad at him?"

"He was working on a big deal. Everybody was unhappy. There was quite a scene last night. His client, Vince Russo, was screaming at him. I presume it isn't going to close now." I ponder how much I can and should tell Roosevelt about Joel's description of the deal.

"Russo seems to have dropped off the face of the earth. What's his story?"

I describe how Russo inherited his father's business and ran it into the ground. I explain that Russo's creditors were forcing him to sell. "I hear he's a tough guy to like."

"Where does Ms. Kennedy fit in?"

He knows more than he's letting on. "She was Bob's star associate and a real go-getter. She was on the fast track."

"What about their personal relationship? Anything out of the ordinary? Any hanky-panky?"

"Purely professional, as far as I know. But some people think there was more to it."

"Were they sleeping together?"

"Don't know." He gives me a skeptical look. "Honest, Roosevelt. If there were something I'd promised to keep quiet, I'd tell you that much. The fact is, I just don't know."

He bores in. "Was she sleeping with anybody else?"

"I don't know. She didn't have a boyfriend. She always had a date for the Christmas party. I'm not tuned in to firm gossip."

"Fair enough. Who is tuned in?"

Before I can catch myself, I blurt out, "Joel."

He chuckles. "I figured that out already. There are still a few instincts left in this old carcass."

"Did you ask him?" I'm as curious as the next guy.

"Yeah. He said he wasn't sure. He's heard the rumors. Who else should I talk to?"

"Charles Stern knows about the firm's finances. Arthur Patton is the managing partner."

"I've talked to them. They think Holmes wouldn't have killed himself. Patton said Holmes was up for a big bonus."

"I've heard that."

"What about his secretary?"

"Doris? She's a gem. She can give you the skinny on Bob's divorces. She's very discreet, though. And very protective of him. By the way, if you get any dirt on his divorces, I'll buy you a steak at any restaurant in town to hear about it."

"Deal. What about Mr. Gates?"

"Our district attorney wore out his welcome years ago. Between us, they couldn't wait to get him out the door."

"Doesn't surprise me." He wipes his glasses. "Mike, do you think Holmes was the kind of guy who would have killed himself?"

I answer him honestly. "I don't know. A few days ago, I would have said no way. On the other hand, his deal may have been cratering. His wife served him with divorce papers. Now, I'm not sure."

"I'll call you when I have a better handle on things. In the meantime, say hi to your mama for me."

* * *

Joel is standing in my doorway at twelve-thirty. "You ready to get out of here?"

"Yes." I pick up my coffee mug. As we walk out my door I see a police officer standing outside Bob's office. A team from the medical examiner's office is inside. As we're heading into the elevator lobby, I ask Joel if he found Russo.

"Nope. Never showed up. Never called. Won't respond to texts or e-mails. We had a ten o'clock deadline for the wire transfers. We didn't make it. The buyer's attorney said he'd call me Monday. As far as he's concerned, the deal is off. I guess we'll deal with bankruptcy if and when Vince surfaces."

We reach the lobby and head down the escalators toward the underground garage. We stop on the intermediate level so I can drop off announcements for my new office in our mailroom, which is in a windowless suite next to the health club. In a cost-saving exercise a few years ago, we moved our mailroom, copy center and accounting department to this subterranean vault everyone calls the Catacomb. I feel sorry for these poor people who never see the daylight.

I bang on the heavy steel door. Virginia Wallace, the manager of our accounting department, opens the door. A ghoulish, gray-haired woman of indeterminate age, she started as a file clerk about thirty years ago. I've always been terrified of her. True to form, she's waiting to see if any of our clients send us any money before the stroke of midnight and our fiscal year turns into a pumpkin.

"Hi, Virginia. You holding up okay?"

"As well as can be expected."

"Good. Could you do me a favor and leave these envelopes for the guys in the mailroom? I was hoping they might be able to get these out to the post office in the last run."

Big sigh. "Just this once because it's your last day."

"Thanks, Virginia." I'll never impose upon you again. I look over her shoulder and see Mark Jenkins, our head delivery person, getting out of the freight elevator that connects the Catacomb with our offices upstairs. I've always liked Mark, an African-American man from Hunters Point who's worked his way out of the projects and spends his days riding up and down the freight elevator and putting up with Virginia. He's finishing up at San Francisco State this year. I'm hopeful he'll find something better suited to his talents after he graduates. Mark agrees to send out my announcements, and I wish him well. Virginia glares.

The steel door slams, and Joel and I head to the garage. With a little coaxing, my nine-year-old Corolla turns over. I pay the kid with monster headphones in the booth, and we head west on Pine. The street is littered with paper. I remind myself that it's New Year's Eve. In San Francisco, the people who don't work in hermetically sealed high-rises traditionally toss their obsolete calendar pages out their windows. The city pays a fortune in overtime to clean up the mess.

Traffic is light as we drive past the Ritz and the back of the Stanford Court toward Joel's house in the Richmond District. When we reach Van Ness, he says, "I can't believe it. Yesterday, I was getting ready to close a huge deal and to celebrate my election as a partner. Today, two people are dead, the deal is off and my career is in limbo."

"You'll be okay They need you to service Bob's clients."

"I guess. I still can't figure it out. He waits another day and he gets three million bucks."

"There's more to it."

"The cops sure think so."

"They're just doing their jobs."

"Spoken like the son of a cop. The head guy, Johnson, thinks there's more to it than suicide."

"He was my father's partner. He's a good man."

We drive in silence across Fillmore through a neighborhood that once was known as the Western Addition, but with gentrification was rechristened Lower Pacific Heights. As we're passing the dim sum restaurants on Clement Street. Joel says, "I know Bob was going through another divorce and this deal was all messed up. But I don't see him killing himself. And I don't see him taking Diana with him."

"Johnson asked me if Bob and Diana were sleeping together. You know anything?"

"I've heard the same stuff everybody's heard."

"Just between us. You think they were getting it on?"

"Wouldn't surprise me."

"While we're speculating, let's suppose they were sleeping together. And she broke up with him. And Vince told Bob the deal's off. And Bob was really mad about the divorce. Maybe you've got a scenario where he decided to end it."

Joel isn't buying it. "I just can't see it. Bob's been divorced three times. He's seen deals go down."

"You think somebody killed him?"

He shrugs. "Russo really wanted out of the deal. For that matter, so did the buyer."

"Why?"

"Continental Capital Corporation is the fourth-largest public company in the world. Their mergers and acquisitions stud, Jack Frazier, convinced them to buy Vince's business. Frazier's one of those young MBAs who figured this deal was the next step up the ladder. He convinced the suits at CCC to pay nine hundred million for a company that's worth a lot less. By the time Golden Boy Frazier figured out he was buying a pig in a poke, it was too late. The boys at headquarters in Stamford won't be happy."

"Why didn't they pull out?"

"Do you know what a breakup fee is?"

I shake my head.

"It's a payment a buyer has to make if it backs out of a deal for no reason. It's supposed to keep the buyer serious and cover the seller's legal fees if the deal craters."

"Why didn't CCC pay the fee and walk?"

"Because the fee is fifty million dollars. It's a lot of money for nothing, even for CCC. If they paid it, Frazier would be working on one of their oil rigs off the coast of Siberia by the end of the week. There was no breakup fee if Vince killed the deal. Frazier's been trying to get Vince to pull the plug for two weeks."

"What about the guy from the mayor's office, Dan Morris? What was he doing there?"

"You'll never believe this. When it looked like Vince's business was going down in flames, the mayor appointed one of those blue-ribbon task forces because he didn't want three thousand jobs moving to CCC's western headquarters in Dallas. Bad optics. It's one thing for the Niners to lose a game to the Cowboys. It's another thing for three thousand jobs to go to the land of George W. Bush. So the mayor got CCC to agree to keep Russo International's headquarters here by providing a hundred million in financing. Pretty slick, eh? If the deal closes, the mayor can take credit for saving a bunch of jobs."

"So the city wanted the deal to close?"

"Actually, no. Turns out the city didn't have the money to make the loan. Cash-flow problems. The city was going to have to borrow the money at loan-shark rates. The mayor figured it out last night. He decided he'd rather lose the jobs. He figures the voters will forget about the jobs, but they'll never forgive a budget deficit. He sent his political fixer over here to kill the deal, but make it look like somebody else's fault. The city was going to use tax dollars to finance a deal that was so screwed up, nobody, including our own client, wanted it to close."

"Looks like everybody is going to get their wish."

"Looks that way."

As always, the weather in the Richmond is cooler and foggier than downtown. We pass Park Presidio Boulevard and drive past Temple Beth Sholom, where Joel's father holds court. I turn right onto Sixteenth Avenue and drive halfway up the block of tightly packed bungalows. I stop in front of Joel's modest gray house, around the corner from his father's.

"Happy New Year," he says as he gets out.

"I'll talk to you next week."

I hope you still have a career.

CHAPTER 5

THE LAW OFFICES OF MICHAEL J. DALEY, ESQ.

"Michael J. Daley, formerly of the San Francisco Public Defender's Office and formerly a partner at Simpson and Gates, announces the opening of the Law Offices of Michael J. Daley, Esq,. at 553 Mission Street, San Francisco, California. Mr. Daley will continue to specialize in criminal defense practice in state and federal court."
 — San Francisco Legal Journal. Monday, January 5.

"Now," I say to Rosie, "all I need are a couple of paying clients, a secretary and a functional telephone, and I'm on my way back to the big time."

"At least your computer is working." She chuckles as I unpack boxes at nine-fifteen in the morning on Monday, January 5. "Looks like the grand opening of the Law Offices of Michael J. Daley, Esq." is going to be somewhat less than auspicious," she says.

True. My new office is in the basement of the two-story 1920s building on Mission Street, down the block from the Transbay bus terminal. I'm renting space from the Law Offices of Rosita C. Fernandez in a neighborhood that was fashionable seventy years ago. After decades of neglect, the sprawl of downtown has given the area new life. Nevertheless, by six o'clock every evening, a group of homeless people gather in front of the building. I look up at the side of a Chinese restaurant called Lucky Corner No. 2 through the metal bars that protect my small window. The name is misleading. The restaurant isn't located on a corner. We'll see whether it will be lucky for me.

"Give it time," Rosie says. "We had to move a lot of files to set this up."

"This was your file room?"

"Yeah. It looks much nicer now. Rolanda can help you get settled."

"Thanks." I look at the metal desk, mismatched chairs and stained file cabinet. "I didn't bring much. Just my computer, some books and a few files."

"Good. Rent is due the first of the month."

"You won't need to remind me." I'm already beginning to feel like we're married again. It was much more fun when we were first dating and we didn't have to worry about rent, car payments and, later, diapers. We started going out when we worked at the PD's office. Rosie was spinning out of a bad marriage. I was coming off a long-term relationship with a law school classmate. We found each other on the rebound. She liked me because I was funny. I liked her because she was direct. And Lord knows, we knew each other's work schedules. "By the way, my highly generous former partners gave me a substantial check for my capital on my way out the door."

"Excellent. Any more on the incident at S&G?"

Interesting choice of words. I guess "incident" sounds better than "suicide," "shooting" or the more generic "tragedy." "Not much. I haven't talked to Roosevelt since Wednesday."

"I saw your pal Skipper Gates on the tube. He seems to think there's more to it."

"He's trying to keep his name in the papers. He's called a press conference at nine-thirty. Want to watch?"

"Sure."

I pull up the Channel 4 website. I can make out the faces of Skipper and Roosevelt standing in a briefing room.

"This is Rita Roberts of NewsCenter 4 reporting from San Francisco police headquarters. District Attorney Prentice Gates and Homicide Inspector Roosevelt Johnson are about to begin a press briefing concerning the incident at the Simpson and Gates law firm last week. Mr. Gates will speak first."

"Incident" seems to be the word of choice. Skipper and Roosevelt are standing behind a table on which the obligatory assortment of evidence is laid out in clear plastic bags: bullet casings, a computer keyboard, a telephone answering machine and several printouts. Skipper steps to the microphone. Cue the lights. He works without notes.

"Thank you for coming this morning. First day on the job and already I have a major case. As you know, sometime between the hours of eleven-thirty p.m. on Tuesday, December thirtieth, and eight a.m. on Wednesday, December thirty-first, my friend and former partner, Bob Holmes, and my former associate, Diana Kennedy, were killed by gunshots. We are investigating this tragedy, and we will have further details for you as they become available. I will now call upon Inspector Roosevelt Johnson, who is in charge of the investigation."

Roosevelt steps to the microphone. "Ladies and gentlemen, we are continuing our investigation. We will have more for you as the situation develops."

Skipper returns to the microphone. He doesn't realize he's smiling. "We have time for just a few questions."

The silver-haired anchor of Channel 5 Eyewitness News is first. "Mr. Gates, is it true the gun belonged to Mr. Holmes?"

"Yes. It was registered to Mr. Holmes."

"How did the gun get to the S&G office?"

Skipper doesn't want to admit his partner kept a loaded piece at his desk. "Somebody brought it to the office."

Not a bad response. I'm convinced.

"One of the lawyers at the firm said Holmes kept a loaded gun at his desk."

"You have good sources. I would like to talk to that person." Laughter. "The answer, by the way, is I don't know. But we are looking into it."

Roosevelt moves to the microphone. "We are checking everything out."

Skipper is annoyed. "Obviously, we wouldn't want to encourage people to keep concealed weapons at their desks."

A reporter from Channel 7 shouts, "We understand there was a suicide note."

Roosevelt shakes his head. "No comment."

"Are you treating this case as a homicide or a suicide?"

Roosevelt answers again. "Ms. Kennedy's death appears to be a homicide. The investigation is ongoing."

The blonde from Channel 2 who used to work at NBC pushes her way to the front. "Mr. Gates, what's your gut feeling? Was it a suicide?"

Roosevelt tries to intercept Skipper, but Skipper elbows his way to the mike. "Young lady, Bob Holmes was my partner and my friend. I must rely on the SFPD and experienced homicide investigators like Inspector Johnson. They will gather the evidence and I will ultimately decide whether there is any basis to prosecute anyone. That's all I have for today."

"Well, what do you think?" Rosie asks.

"Not a bad performance for his first press conference."

"Not Skipper. The killings. What do you think?"

"They're holding stuff back. Vince Russo disappeared. Skipper didn't even mention his name. There was nothing about the deal or the divorce."

* * *

At twelve-fifteen the same day, Doris is getting her first look at my new office. "Geez, Mikey, this isn't an office, it's a closet." She gives me a hug. "What's that smell?"

"Moo shu pork." Seems my office starts to smell like the Chinese place next door by mid-morning.

"You'll get used to it, Mikey. How's Grace?"

"Fine. And Jenny?"

"So-so. Boyfriend trouble. You know how it is."

We exchange small talk. She tells me things are starting to calm down at S&G. She's been reassigned to another attorney. She says she's going to take a few weeks off for a trip to the Bahamas.

She opens a shopping bag and takes out a small plant. "I thought you might like something to brighten up your office."

"Thanks. It could use a little help."

She glances at Grace's picture. "I was hoping you'd do me a favor." She takes a manila envelope out of her purse and hands it to me. "Open it."

Inside I find a check made out to me for a hundred dollars. The memo says "retainer." There is a form letter saying that she's engaging the law office of Michael J. Daley to represent her on all legal matters. There is a copy of her will.

"Doris—,"

"How many clients do you have, Mikey?"

I look down.

"Well, now you have one."

"Look, Doris, I can't . . ."

"Yes, you can. This isn't charity. I need you to review my will."

"There are people at S&G who could help you."

"If I wanted somebody at the firm to represent me, I wouldn't be here. How many arguments did we have during the five years we worked together?"

"A few."

"And how many did I win?"

"All of them."

"And I'm going to win this one, too." She smiles. "You don't have to cash the check."

"I think I'll frame it."

"That's fine. The Law Offices of Michael J. Daley are now officially open for business."

"Can I buy you lunch?"

"Absolutely. The moo shu pork smells pretty good."

CHAPTER 6

"A GREAT HUMANITARIAN"

"HOLMES, John Robert, Jr." died suddenly on December 31, at age 48. Beloved husband of Elizabeth, father of seven. A respected partner at the international law firm of Simpson and Gates. Services will be held at Grace Cathedral, San Francisco, on Tuesday, January 6, at 10:00 a.m. Donations in his memory may be made to the Legal Community Against Violence."

— Obituary Notice, *San Francisco Chronicle,* Tuesday, January 6.

Rosie and I are standing on the front steps of Grace Cathedral when Art Patton approaches us.

"Did you read Bob's obit, Mike?" he says. "You'd have thought he was fucking Mother Teresa."

I keep my voice measured. "Well, Art, I guess it depends on how you're using the word 'fucking' in this context."

Rosie stifles a chuckle. Patton's second trophy wife, Shari, a former S&G receptionist, smiles politely. Art and Shari head inside. You'd never guess they're going through a nasty divorce.

"They never knew what hit them," Rosie says.

Bob had told me a few months ago he wanted a funeral just like Princess Di's, except Bruce Springsteen would sing "Born to Run" instead of Elton John singing "Candle in the Wind." As it turns out, the funeral Beth Holmes has arranged isn't far from Bob's wish.

The front steps of Grace Cathedral look like the Academy Awards. The TV cameras, news vans and A-team reporters are here. The service is going to be streamed live. Two news choppers hover overhead. A thousand people are expected.

Rosie is a good sport. Funerals are difficult in the best of circumstances. Funerals for assholes in your ex-husband's former law firm are really tough. Even during the darkest times of our marriage and divorce, we always went to funerals together. It's our unspoken pact.

I've never been very good about funerals. It goes back to my days as a priest. When you're the low priest on the totem pole, you get a lot of funeral duty. I remember doing four in one day for people I'd never met. I felt bad for the families. I did my standard spiel, said a few words to the families and left. Tough gig.

The paparazzi remain at a respectful distance, and I have hopes that this will not turn into a circus. Then Skipper's black Lincoln arrives and the frenzy begins. The cameramen jockey for position as the reporters shove microphones into his face. His longsuffering wife, Natalie, a society matron, looks embarrassed. Skipper mouths appropriate sentiments about attending his partner's funeral. He says the DA's office is working day and night to solve the case. To his credit, he resists the urge to turn Bob's funeral into a press conference.

My former partners file past without saying much. Chuckles tries to ignore me, but his wife stops to chat. I've always liked Ellen. For the life of me, I can't figure out how an outgoing interior decorator who serves on the symphony and opera boards has managed to stay married to Chuckles for thirty-two years. Maybe she's a closet tax-code junkie.

Doris arrives with her daughter, Jenny. I hug them and they shake hands with Rosie. Jenny's pretty face is pale, and she looks sad in her dark dress. She's taking this harder than I would have thought. Doris never warmed up to Rosie. It goes back to the bad old days after we got divorced. Things were pretty acrimonious between us when I first started working at S&G. We had a big fight over custody. If I had a chance to do anything over again, I would have let Rosie have custody from the beginning. It's amazing how otherwise rational people can turn into jerks when emotions run amok. We finally called a truce when Rosie's mom and my mom got together and told us we were going to screw up Grace's life if we didn't stop acting like idiots. I'm glad we finally listened to them.

"Pretty rough time, Doris," I say. I turn to Jenny. "How are things at Stanford?"

"One more semester."

"Are you still thinking about law school?"

"I'm not sure. I applied to UCLA, Hastings and Boalt. We'll see. I have a lot on my mind."

I'd like to be twenty-two again.

Joel and Naomi Friedman arrive by cab and join us. Joel has been asked to speak, and he looks nervous. Naomi is a petite brunette with curly hair who teaches nursery school at the JCC. She's a ball of fire. Perfect for Joel.

We head inside and pay our brief respects to Bob's widow, Beth, and her three children, ages two to five, all of whom are sitting in the front row. The second row is reserved for Bob's three ex-wives and their current spouses and significant others and Bob's four children from his previous marriages.

The S&G contingent occupies about twenty rows on the left side of the cathedral. We find seats across the aisle. I'm in no mood to sit with my former colleagues. The back of the house is packed. The legal community has turned out. So have the politicians and the upper crust of Pacific Heights. Somber organ music emanates from the front of the cathedral. I never had a chance to work such a big crowd when I was a priest.

At ten-fifteen, the organist plays a chord, signaling the service is about to begin. A young minister welcomes us and says a few perfunctory words about Bob's life and career. He clearly never met him. He introduces Art Patton, who tries to appear respectful, but looks like David Letterman preparing to deliver a monologue as he saunters to the front. Rosie is thinking the same thing and she whispers to me, "He thinks it's the firm Christmas party."

Art tries for a somber expression. "Thank you for coming. Bob would have been pleased to see such a large turnout. It's sad that it takes a great tragedy to bring us together. I hope we will have a chance to meet on a happier occasion." He takes a deep breath. It's hard to look serious with a smirk plastered on your face. "Bob Holmes was a great lawyer and my best friend."

Murmurs from the S&G section. Art's taking some license. He and Bob hated each other's guts.

"He was also a great humanitarian."

Someone in the S&G section laughs out loud.

"It's appropriate that we gather to celebrate his life and pay our respects to his memory." He describes Bob's humble beginnings in Wilkes-Barre, his education at Penn and Harvard Law School, his admission to the partnership at thirty-two. He says Bob was a loving father, but doesn't linger on his four marriages. Bob's eldest son once told me that the children from his first three marriages stopped speaking to him years ago.

After a description of Bob's achievements, he introduces Joel, who walks slowly to the lectern, a faraway look in his eyes.

"My name is Joel Friedman. Bob Holmes was my colleague, my mentor and my friend. This is the most difficult thing I've ever had to do."

Easy, Joel.

"Bob taught me how to be a lawyer. And, despite what some people may think, he taught me how important it is to treat everyone with respect. He was a fine man whose legacy is in this room. He leaves his family, colleagues and friends with memories of a man who worked hard, loved his family and loved his job. I will miss him."

Well done. He steps away from the podium to compose himself. The minister comforts him.

Skipper's up next. Rosie whispers, "This should be a beaut."

Skipper faces the TV camera and tries to look serious. "I knew Bob for twenty-two years. He was one of the finest lawyers I've ever met. Bob built Simpson and Gates into a powerhouse. More important, I want to say a few words about Bob, the man. He was sometimes difficult to get along with. That's the price you pay for dealing with genius. He never demanded more from his colleagues than he expected from himself. Yes, he was a perfectionist. Yes, he was driven. Yes, he screamed at times. It was never out of malice. He simply wanted to be the best he could be, and he expected the same from his colleagues."

More coughing from the S&G section. Rosie whispers, "This is really getting thick."

"It is tragic that Bob won't have an opportunity to see his children grow up. It is sad that he won't have a chance to fulfill his dreams. A great life. Cut short." He stops to wipe away a tear that isn't there. "His legacy is great. In his honor, I promise each of you, and Bob, that I will not rest until I find out the circumstances surrounding his death. It is my solemn pledge."

Doris nudges me and whispers, "For God's sake, he's making a campaign speech at a funeral."

Skipper finishes his remarks with a tribute to Bob's distinguished record as a husband and as a father, which brings audible laughter from several members of the firm. Two of Bob's college friends say a few words about his achievements. A neighbor reads a poem. The minister reads two psalms and a small choir sings "Amazing Grace." Finally, the organist plays "Born to Run." At eleven-thirty, we file out.

The TV cameras jockey for the standard shot of the pallbearers bringing the casket down the steps. Bob would have loved the fact that the pallbearers include Skipper, the two surviving members of X-Com and three of his partners. I gaze around and my eyes meet those of Roosevelt Johnson, who is standing on the sidewalk, a respectful distance away. He is looking discreetly through the crowd. It is common practice for a homicide inspector to attend the funeral of the subject of his investigation, but somehow, I didn't expect to see him today.

Joel and Naomi find us, and we watch the pallbearers load the casket into the hearse. I say good-bye to Doris and Jenny. Skipper's Lincoln pulls up behind the hearse and the reporters surround him.

"Mr. Gates," a reporter calls out, "any new information on the case?"

He takes the high road. "This is an inappropriate time to discuss the investigation. I will talk to you at the office."

The hearse pulls away and begins the long drive to the town of Colma, just south of the city, where San Franciscans bury their dead.

* * *

You won't find Bill's Place in *Gourmet* magazine. Housed in a single story building at Twenty-fifth and Clement, it was a diner before it became fashionable, and it served comfort food four decades before food critics coined the term. The long counter, huge chandeliers and Formica tables are a throwback to simpler times. The waitresses have hair in varying shades of blue and orange and call their customers "honey." It's still the best place in the city to take screaming children for hamburgers and milk shakes. It may never be the subject of an American Express commercial, but it's been one of my favorite places since my dad took me here when I was a kid.

Naomi Friedman is eating a French fry. "Mike, I'm worried about Joel," she says.

"What's up?" I ask.

"He was at police headquarters all day Sunday. They asked him a lot of questions."

Rosie, Joel, Naomi and I are eating a quick lunch before we head south on the 280 freeway to Colma for our second funeral of the day. Diana's funeral is going to be a graveside affair for immediate family and friends. I've been asked to say a few words. At the moment, Joel is in the restroom.

I take a bite of my cheeseburger. "I'm sure they're just trying to be thorough. This is a high-profile case."

Joel returns and there's an uncomfortable silence. "What?" he asks.

"Nothing," Naomi says.

"Come on."

"I was just telling them about your glorious Sunday."

"I already told you. It's nothing to worry about."

She gives him a sharp look. "It's a lot to worry about. Why did they talk to you for so long?"

I sense that they've been through this already, and Joel doesn't want to replay it in front of Rosie and me.

He picks up his burger and turns to me. "I don't know how you eat this stuff. It'll kill you."

"My grandfather ate this stuff every day for eighty-seven years."

"Imagine how long he would have lived if he had taken better care of himself."

Naomi is annoyed. "Can you guys stop it? This is serious. Mike, why do you think they're giving Joel the third degree?"

Joel answers her. "They're just trying to figure out what happened. That's it. It's not like I'm a suspect. Two people are dead, and the cops are just doing their job. They said they'd probably declare it a suicide in the next couple of days."

"What about Russo?"

"No word."

I ask if the police had told him anything more about what had happened.

"Not much. The bullets came from Bob's gun."

Naomi loses interest in her French fries. "Do we have to talk about this at lunch?"

"Sorry." I turn to Joel. "Which cops did you talk to?"

"Your buddy, Roosevelt Johnson, and his partner, Marcus Banks."

"Johnson's a good man."

"He's a suspicious man. And his partner isn't a nice guy."

"Marcus is a little heavy-handed. He beat a confession out of a man for the murder of a prostitute. Turns out the guy really did it, but they had to turn him loose because of the coerced confession. A week later, the guy woke up dead."

"Not good."

"Nope. Don't underestimate them, Joel."

Rosie has heard enough. "Can we change the subject now?"

Naomi looks relieved.

Joel finishes his burger. "My dad is doing Diana's service."

"I didn't know she was Jewish."

"Yeah. Well, sort of. She grew up in our neighborhood and went to our temple. Except back then, her name was Debbie Fink, her hair was dark brown, her nose was longer than mine and she weighed about two hundred and fifty pounds."

"What happened to Debbie Fink?"

"Between her senior year in college and her first year in law school, she spent a summer at a fat farm, had her hair dyed and got her nose fixed. Lord knows what else she had taken in. Her personal trainer was a guy named Billy Kennedy. The marriage lasted about six months, but the remake stuck. Debbie Fink became Diana Kennedy."

"Sounds like quite a transformation. "Who else knows about this?"

"Everybody at the firm except you, of course."

Rosie tosses her head back and laughs. "I just figured out the inscription on your tombstone. 'Michael Daley. Priest. Lawyer. He was always the last to know.' "

We pay the bill and drive south through Golden Gate Park to Nineteenth Avenue. It's about twenty minutes to Colma.

* * *

It's drizzling when we reach the old Jewish cemetery at three o'clock. The crowd numbers only about thirty, and we stand under umbrellas on an artificial turf mat next to the gravesite. Joel's father is standing under a black umbrella. Next to him is a woman I assume is Diana's mother.

I've known Rabbi Neil Friedman for years. He's an older, huskier version of Joel, with an eloquent, stained-glass voice with the hint of a New York accent. "Michael, I haven't seen you in a while," he says. He introduces us to Diana's mother, Ruth Fink. She's polite, but brief.

Doris and Jenny Fontaine join us. Skipper, Art Patton and Charles Stern arrive as the service is beginning. A TV cameraman stands about a hundred yards away near the gate. No reporters or news vans this afternoon.

As Rabbi Friedman begins the service, I see Roosevelt standing near the gate. He nods. The rain becomes heavier, and Mrs. Fink loses her composure. The rabbi intones the Kaddish, the Jewish prayer of mourning.

It's been a helluva week.

CHAPTER 7

"I HAVE TO GO BE A LAWYER FOR A COUPLE OF HOURS"

"We are looking forward to the new year with great optimism."
— Simpson and Gates managing partner Arthur Patton.
San Francisco Legal Journal. Friday, January 9.

"The firm is starting to implode," Joel tells me. "Twenty labor lawyers announced they're leaving. They're talking about staff layoffs and big cutbacks."

He's describing the state of the firm three days later, at six o'clock on Friday evening. We're having a beer on his back porch as mist covers the bungalows in the Richmond. He's throwing me a modest going-away party from S&G. Rosie, Grace and my mom are here. So are Doris and Jenny Fontaine, along with Wendy Hogan, a part-time tax attorney at S&G, and her six-year-old son, Danny. Joel's parents are supposed to stop by on their way to temple for Friday-night services.

"Sounds like I got out just in time," I say.

"The firm must be in worse shape financially than anybody let on. I guess we really needed the cash from Russo's deal. I've heard First Bank may foreclose on our equipment loans. They may hit up the partners. It may turn out to be a good thing I didn't make partner."

"Joint and several liability is a nasty thing." Although most states now permit law firms to be organized as "professional corporations" or "limited liability partnerships," many firms, S&G among them, are still set up as general partnerships, which means each partner is fully responsible for firm debts even if the partner didn't incur the debt on behalf of the firm. Professional service firms are the only large businesses still organized as partnerships. General Motors wouldn't be structured in a similar way. "I heard they found Russo's car."

"Along with his keys and wallet in the parking lot at the north end of the Golden Gate Bridge. They think he may have jumped. Nobody saw him."

"Any chance he's still alive?"

"Don't know. He could have planted the car and driven away in another one. He could have taken a cab. Hell, somebody could have driven him to the airport. It wouldn't surprise me if he's sipping a fruity drink by a beach."

"Did he stash any cash?"

"He probably had some money in a foreign bank account."

My mom comes in from the kitchen. She's having a good night. "Have things settled down at the office, Joel?"

"We're hoping things will get back to normal soon."

Joel's son Alan marches outside with the bravado of a six-year-old and gives my mom a hug. Little kids can spot a grandmother a hundred yards away. He is holding a piece of challah in his right hand. "Uncle Mike, Mommy says it's time for you and Daddy to come inside for dinner."

"Okay. Tell Mommy we'll be right there. Can I sit next to you?"

"Sorry, Uncle Mike. I always sit next to Daddy."

* * *

An oak table overwhelms the cramped dining room. Alan and his twin brother, Stephen, are impressively well-behaved as they sit on opposite sides of the table, at right angles to their father. Joel sits at the head. Grace sits between Rosie and me. My mom is next to me. Doris and Jenny are across from us. Naomi sits at the foot of the table.

Wendy Hogan is next to Doris. Her son, Danny, sits next to her.

Wendy and her husband split up a couple of years ago. She went through the mother of all custody battles. I can relate. She keeps her sad brown eyes hidden behind wire-rimmed glasses. Her frizzy hair and mousy demeanor belie the fact that she's a terror in negotiations with the IRS. I like her. We divorced, recovering Catholics have a lot in common. And S&G treats her like dirt. Someday, I'm going to summon the courage to ask her out. She's a little gun-shy around men.

Wendy's expression is serious. "I think I may get laid off."

"No way," I say. "They need you."

"Every department is making a hit list. They won't keep any of us part-timers. My billables aren't good enough."

She may be right. She works four days a week, but she's paid only about 60 percent of what a fulltime associate makes. According to the firm, if a lawyer works four days a week, you still have to pay rent and a secretary five days a week. As a result, it's unfair to pay the attorney a straight prorated salary. Most people think it's just another way to screw the part-timers.

Rosie pipes up. "Don't worry, Wendy. You'll find something."

"It doesn't make things easier. Whenever my finances change, Andy tries to break up our custody and child-support deal."

Danny frowns. He's a good kid. He's watched his parents fight over custody his entire life. I don't say it out loud, but I'm betting he's on his way to years of therapy.

* * *

The kids finish first and they wander to the den in the back of the house to do what children do these days—watch videos and play games on their tablets. As we're clearing the table, there's a knock at the door. Joel looks up. "Mom and Dad are here early."

Alan comes bouncing down the hall. "Grandma and Grandpa!" he shrieks with six-year-old glee. He runs through the dining room and down the stairs to open the door. His brother is a step behind him. Naomi smiles.

A moment later, Stephen comes back upstairs, a troubled look on his face. "Daddy, there's a policeman downstairs. He wants to talk to you."

Joel freezes. Naomi looks alarmed.

Joel holds up a hand. "Okay, Steve. Daddy will go down and see what this is all about. Don't worry."

Stephen goes over to his mother and grabs her hand. Joel walks downstairs.

A moment later, we hear agitated voices at the bottom of the stairs. Rosie and I go to the living room and look out the windows. She turns to me and says, "This doesn't look good."

I see two police cars in the driveway. My stomach tightens. There are four policemen. One is having a heated discussion with Joel.

Grace comes up to us. "Is something wrong. Daddy?"

I keep my tone calm. "No, sweetie. It looks like the policemen want to talk to Uncle Joel. I'll find out what's going on." She moves closer to Rosie.

I reach the bottom of the stairs and open the door. I'm stunned to see a middle-aged policeman, whose face I remember, but whose name escapes me, putting handcuffs on Joel.

"You have the right to remain silent."

I try to keep my tone non-confrontational. "Excuse me, Officer. May I ask what's going on?"

"You have the right to an attorney."

The cop looks at me. "Please step back, sir. This matter does not concern you."

"Anything you say can be used against you in a court of law."

"Officer, Mr. Friedman's wife asked me to find out what's going on."

"If you cannot afford an attorney, one will be appointed for you."

Naomi is coming out the door as the policeman says, "Mr. Friedman is being arrested for the murders of Robert Holmes and

Diana Kennedy. We have a warrant for his arrest, and we're taking him into custody. Please step aside."

Skipper's pulling a publicity stunt.

Naomi screams. Joel tries to calm her down. "It's okay. We'll get this straightened out."

Although Naomi doesn't realize it, her kids have followed her. They start to cry.

My tone is perfectly even. "Naomi, let me handle this. Take the kids back upstairs."

She nods and takes them upstairs. She returns without them a moment later.

Joel is trying to reason with the policeman when a black Lincoln drives up and Skipper steps out. The pieces are starting to fit together.

Skipper looks triumphant as he speaks to Joel. "Well, young man, I knew you had a temper, but I didn't think you'd kill two people."

A white Channel 4 news van pulls up behind Skipper's car. Rita Roberts and her cameraman leap out.

Joel is furious. "Are you out of your mind, Skipper? You think I'd kill two people because I didn't make partner?"

"There's a lot more to it. You'll have your day in court."

I try to interject before things deteriorate further. I point at the handcuffs. "Officer, you don't need those. Mr. Friedman is a respected attorney. He's not a threat."

"Standard procedure, sir."

I turn to Skipper. "What kind of stunt is this?"

"Look who's here. My favorite ex-partner. The one who just got fired. Always spend your free time with murderers?"

"For God's sake, Skipper, if you wanted to arrest him, you could have called. He would have surrendered without all the theatrics. He isn't a flight risk."

"Stay out of this, Mike."

"And I suppose it's just a coincidence that the TV stations

arrived now?"

"They must have heard it on the police band."

"Bullshit, Skipper."

"Fuck you, Mike. This doesn't have anything to do with you, so stay out of it."

I don't retort. Joel is in enough trouble without my getting into hand-to-hand combat with Skipper on the front steps of Joel's house.

Joel's mother and father arrive. They look startled. Joel's mother, Mollie, is a heavyset woman with a knack for saying the right thing. She elects to remain silent.

Joel's father speaks in an even voice. "Is there a problem, Officer?"

Skipper answers him. "Rabbi, I'm sorry to be the bearer of bad news, but your son is under arrest for the murder of two people."

"There's been a mistake."

"I'm afraid there's no mistake, Rabbi. Now, if you'll excuse us."

Rabbi and Mrs. Friedman huddle with Naomi, who is standing behind me. I turn around to face them. "I'll figure out what's going on. You guys stay put."

The uniforms push Joel toward one of the squad cars. "For God's sake," I say, "take off the handcuffs."

Skipper can't resist. "Bob and Diana would have wished he'd been in handcuffs the night he killed them."

Asshole.

One of the uniforms says they're taking Joel to the Hall of Justice. Before they put him in the car, I say to him, "Joel, I'll be right behind you. Be cooperative and above all, don't talk to anyone. These people are not your friends. Got it?"

He nods, but I see him biting back panic. "You've got to take care of this, Mike."

"I will. Right now, you have to do what I say."

The uniform shoves me out of the way. "Who the hell are you, anyway?"

Joel answers. "He's my lawyer. I'm not saying a word to you unless he's present."

I look directly into Rita Roberts's camera and summon an authoritative tone. "May I have your attention, please? My name is Michael Daley. I am Mr. Friedman's attorney. I have instructed Mr. Friedman not to talk to any of you outside of my presence. Rabbi and Mrs. Friedman are witnesses." I turn to Skipper. "If you talk to my client, I'll have you brought up before the state bar."

He turns away. My little speech was just beamed live to households all over the Bay Area. A media star is born.

The two police cars pull away and head down Sixteenth. The Lincoln follows them. I turn to Rabbi and Mrs. Friedman. "We need to talk."

* * *

Upstairs, Naomi has sent the children to watch TV under my mother's watchful eye. Naomi, Rosie, Wendy, Doris, Jenny and I gather in the living room with Rabbi and Mrs. Friedman.

"What happens now?" Naomi asks me.

"I'll go down to the Hall of Justice and ask for bail. He may have to spend the night. They arrested him late on a Friday because it's tough to find a judge right before the weekend."

"He didn't do it, Mike."

"I know. I'll call you as soon as I can." I ask Rosie to call Pete to take my mother home. She agrees.

I walk to the back of the house where the kids are gathered with my mother. I give Grace a hug. "I have to go out for a while," I tell her. "You're going to have to stay with Mommy tonight."

"Is Uncle Joel in trouble?"

"Yeah, sweetie. But it's a big mistake. I'm going downtown to straighten it out. You look after Mommy and Grandma, okay?"

"I will, Daddy. I love you."

"I love you, too."

I turn to my mother. For the first time in five years, her eyes are truly clear. Before I can say anything, she says, "They arrested him."

"Yeah."

I see the look that I saw so many times when my dad got a call at home from his sergeant. For a moment, she's thirty years younger, and her blue eyes are steel. "Do what you have to do to help him, Michael."

"I have to go be a lawyer for a couple of hours."

"I know. You take good care of him."

"I will. Pete's going to come over and take you home."

"I'll be up late, Michael. Call me when you know what's going on."

"I will."

After all these years, Margaret Murphy Daley is still the wife of a cop.

CHAPTER 8

THE HALL OF JUSTICE

"The Hall of Justice is an expensive homeless shelter, detox center and drug treatment facility, and an utterly inept way to handle social problems."
— Director of Inmate Release Program. *San Francisco Examiner.*

In San Francisco, the DA's office, criminal courts and city jail are located in a Stalinesque seven-story structure at Seventh and Bryant known as the Hall of Justice. Although a fifty-million-dollar jail wing was added in the early nineties, the Hall hasn't lost any of its charm. The new jail was built to ease overcrowding in the system, which has been under a federal court consent decree since the eighties because of poor conditions. The north wall of the new jail almost touches the 101 freeway, and prisoners sleep less than fifty feet from the slow lane.

At seven-thirty, the traffic on Van Ness is heavy as I weave southbound through a driving rain. Surprisingly, I find a parking place on Seventh between two squad cars. I grab my briefcase and try to look lawyerly in my jeans and polo shirt.

I'm soaked as I run up the front steps of the Hall and explain to the guard at the metal detector that I'm here to see my client, Mr. Friedman. He motions me through, and I detour around the tortoise-slow Depression-era elevators and head for the stairs.

In 1996, a new intake center was opened in the new wing of the Hall. County Jail 9 is a far cry from the chaos that reigned at the raucous booking hub on the sixth floor of the old Hall, which resembled an overcrowded zoo on a busy night. The old jail is now used primarily for high-security housing.

In contrast to traditional "linear" jails where the cells line a central corridor, the holding cells in the antiseptic-clean new booking hub are in a circle around a deputies' workstation. The prisoners are housed in well-lighted cells behind glass doors. There are no clanking iron doors or shouts of inmates. As usual, the parade of humanity is awaiting processing.

Whenever I'm in the Hall, I think of my dad. I always expect to see him walking down the corridors, bearing erect, chest out, a cigarette hanging from his lips. He was so proud to be a cop. He put the bad guys away.

Although the Hall serves as the city jail, for bureaucratic reasons, it's run by the County Sheriff's Department. I survey the deputies working behind the desk, and I recognize the pockmarked face of Sergeant Philip Ramos.

I hand him my driver's license, my state bar card and one of my new business cards. "Good evening, Sergeant Ramos."

He glances at my card, then surveys me up and down. Ten years ago, Phil Ramos found himself on the wrong side of a gang fight. A bullet wound in his left thigh moved him behind a desk. He's never been happy about it. "Mike Daley. I thought you moved downtown. May I assume your visit this evening is not entirely social?"

"That would be correct."

"And may I ask which one of our guests will have the pleasure of your company?"

"Joel Friedman. They just brought him in."

"Excuse me, Mr. Big Time. A murder rap. He's being processed. Gonna be a few minutes." He picks up his phone and asks someone to bring Joel to the interview room adjacent to his desk. "Do me a favor and keep it short. They haven't finished booking him." He looks at his computer screen. "What's this about?"

"You heard about the shootings at Simpson and Gates?"

"Yeah."

"I worked there. Friedman still works there. Skipper's trying to pin the shootings on him."

"I thought it was a suicide."

"Something's going on. Skipper's calling the shots. There's no way this guy did it."

He gives me the "I've heard it a million times" look. "I just process them. Roosevelt wouldn't have charged him if he didn't have a solid case."

"Do me a favor, Phil. If he has to stay the night, put him in his own cell, okay? If you put him in with everybody, he'll get eaten alive."

"I'll see what I can do. We have a full house. Fridays are always busy."

"Thanks, Phil."

Two deputies lead Joel into the consultation room behind the intake desk. I used to meet with my clients in similar rooms when I was a PD. The lucky ones got five minutes of my time. I'd try to come up with a workable deal and move to the next case.

Joel keeps his head down. Intake isn't fun. First you get fingerprinted. Then you have a medical interview. In some cases, you get strip-searched. Finally, you're issued an orange jumpsuit and assigned to a cell.

Ramos presses a button and the door opens. The deputies have taken off Joel's handcuffs. He slumps into a chair. I ask the deputies to wait outside.

There's desperation in Joel's voice. "You've got to get me out of here."

"We need to talk fast. First, I'll try to find a judge to set bail. It may be hard at this hour."

"You can't let them keep me here."

"The desk sergeant is going to get you your own cell." I don't know this for sure, but I'm hoping Ramos will keep his word. "Don't talk to anybody. Everybody will lie about you. They'll say you confessed to something. Even the ones you don't talk to will lie. Got it?"

"Got it."

"They're going to finish your paperwork and they'll take you to a holding cell."

"What am I going to tell Naomi and the kids?"

"I'll take care of that. We'll take this one step at a time. Rosie's at your house. So are your mom and dad. We'll get through this. For now, I need you to stay calm and be smart."

The deputy opens the door. "Time to go."

"Just one more minute," I say. He steps back outside. "Joel, one other thing. I'll do everything I can to help you if you want me to represent you. But I don't want you to feel obligated to hire me. You don't have to tell me tonight. But you're going to have to decide soon."

"I wouldn't trust anybody else."

"Good. Now do what the deputies say. I'll take care of everything else."

He looks back at me as they lead him out the door. He mouths the word "Thanks."

* * *

At ten-fifteen, I'm in the lobby of the Hall. I punch in Joel and Naomi's number on my cell. Rosie answers.

"No bail," she says.

"How did you know?"

"We saw it on the news. Skipper said he's charging Joel with first-degree murder. I didn't think they'd let him out tonight. Here's Naomi."

Her voice cracks. "Hi, Mike."

"I just talked to Joel. He's doing okay." A small lie. "I know the desk sergeant. He's going to put Joel in his own cell. He'll be all right for the night."

"What am I supposed to tell the boys?"

What *is* she supposed to tell the boys? "The legal system works slowly, so we have to stay calm." Easy for me to say. "I'll be right over. Have Rosie screen any calls. And don't talk to the press."

* * *

The kids are asleep at eleven-thirty when Rosie, Naomi and I meet in the dining room where we'd eaten Naomi's chicken a few hours earlier. The news vans are gone. Rabbi and Mrs. Friedman have gone home. Pete picked up my mom an hour ago.

Naomi's eyes are puffy. "What do we do now?"

I take her hand. "I'll talk to another judge. It would help if you have access to some money."

"We'll find it. The news said they might not grant bail."

I look at Rosie. If Skipper goes for special circumstances (that is, the death penalty), there will be no bail. Not even for a pillar of the legal community. Not even for the rabbi's son.

"Naomi," Rosie says, "sometimes they don't set bail. It depends on the charge."

Naomi is holding back tears. "You guys are the lawyers. What happens next?"

I squeeze her hand. "He'll probably be arraigned on Monday." We lawyers often forget how Byzantine the legal system appears to civilians. "We go to court and formal charges are read. Joel pleads not guilty. It takes five minutes. Then I'll go have a big fight with the DA."

"And if they don't drop the charges?"

"We'll get ready to go to trial, if we have to."

"I see." It's sinking in. "When will that be?"

"Technically, we can demand a trial within sixty days, but almost everybody agrees to a delay to have more time to prepare." She's starting to lose it. "One other thing. You and Joel may decide to let somebody else handle the case. If you do, I'll understand."

Rosie looks at me as if I've lost my mind.

Naomi exhales heavily. "I'll talk it over with Joel. I'm sure he'll want you. I do."

"Thanks, Naomi. We'll call you in the morning."

* * *

I carry Grace to Rosie's car. She's getting heavy. "Rosie," I say, "mind if I stop by for a few minutes on my way home?"

"Just business tonight, Mike."

"Understood. Seems I might have to prepare for a murder case."

"We'll do crisis sex another time."

"Thanks." I give her a thoughtful look. "One of these days, you're going to find a guy you really like, and we're going to have to shut this down."

"We'll see. In the meantime, this works for me."

"Me too. I'll see you at home."

CHAPTER 9

LARKSPUR

"You're moving to Larkspur? Marin County? You're a city boy, Mike. The fresh air will kill you."
— Joel Friedman.

Rosie and I live about three blocks from each other in Marin County in Larkspur, which is about ten miles north of the Golden Gate Bridge. Larkspur's eleven thousand residents live in well-tended houses on the flatlands between the 101 freeway and Mount Tamalpais. In Marin, the single folks live in Sausalito, the artists and writers live in Mill Valley, the nouveau riche live in Tiburon and the old money lives in Ross. The few working stiffs tend to congregate in Larkspur and its sister city, Corte Madera, although housing prices are getting so high that only the truly affluent will be living there soon.

Moving to Marin was one of many compromises. We never would have made the move if Grace hadn't been born. If it had been up to me, we'd have moved back to Berkeley. If Rosie had had her way, we wouldn't have left the city. Kids change things, and I like where we are. Maybe you don't have to make a political statement with every aspect of your life.

It's a few minutes after midnight now, and I've just crossed the Golden Gate Bridge. My Corolla strains up the Waldo Grade above Sausalito. If it weren't raining so hard, I'd have a great view of the city.

As usual, I'm listening to KCBS, the all-news station. Joel is a hot topic. "In tonight's headlines, Joel Mark Friedman was arrested for the murder of two attorneys at the Simpson and Gates law firm."

Randy Short, my mentor at the PD's office, used to say that you know your client is in big trouble when they use all three of his names on the news.

"District Attorney Prentice Gates will hold a press conference Saturday morning. KCBS will cover it live. KCBS news time is twelve-ten." I switch to jazz.

I take Paradise Drive west past the upscale Corte Madera mall. I head north on Magnolia, Larkspur's main street. A mile later, I turn right onto Alexander Avenue, and pull into the narrow driveway of Number 8, across from the Twin Cities Little League field. Because of its proximity to the ballpark, it's known as the hey-batter-batter house. Rosie has been renting the white bungalow since Grace started school last year. Many homes in Larkspur were built as temporary housing after the 1906 earthquake. Rosie's was built in 1925 for a local schoolteacher, who paid twenty-five hundred dollars for it. Today, the seven-hundred-square-foot house would set you back a million bucks.

Rosie is watching the rebroadcast of the news. I knock on the door and let myself in. It's a good sign when your ex-wife lets you have your own key. She holds a finger to her lips and motions me into the living room. Grace is asleep.

"Joel's the lead story. They got your speech in front of his house on camera. They got another shot of you walking out of the Hall."

"Nike will be calling tomorrow to offer me a sneaker contract. The 'Air Daley' line."

She's heard this one before. "They said you had no comment."

"That would be correct."

"You could have said he was innocent."

"I'm saving my best lines for Anderson Cooper."

We stare at the TV. NewsCenter 4 loves to send its news vans all over the Bay Area to do live "team coverage." TV news directors seem to think we want to see their reporters catching pneumonia. Rita Roberts is standing in the rain on the empty street in front of Joel's house. As she gets soaked, they show videos of the arrest. They cut to a second reporter who is getting drenched on the empty street in front of the Hall. They show videotape of Joel being escorted into the building.

Rosie turns off the TV. "Joel has a big problem."

"What else did they say on the news?"

"The usual blather about incontrovertible evidence placing Joel at the scene. Inconsistencies in his story. They claim he's been uncooperative and tried to flee." She pauses. "Oh, one more thing. One station quoted 'reliable sources' saying Joel was having an affair with Diana."

"It had to be Skipper."

"It's a DA's wet dream. First week on the job and he's got a high-profile murder case."

Rosie has such a delicate way with words. "Did they interview Roosevelt?"

"Briefly. He said they have solid evidence."

I look at the fire in her fireplace. "Joel has a big problem."

The dancing light reflects off her eyes. "My little rainmaker. First week on the job and you land a high-profile murder case for a paying client. Not bad."

"It's a standard marketing technique. You go to dinner at your best friend's house and hope he gets arrested for murder between the salad and the entree. All those marketing seminars at S&G finally paid off."

She turns serious. "First things first. You're going to do this by the book. I have a standard retainer letter on my laptop. We're going to put one together right now. Joel has to sign a retainer letter. And you have to talk to him about what this is going to cost."

I nod.

She takes my hand. "I know you hate this stuff, but you're running a business now. You're going to take this case to the finish line, Mike. I don't want you to suggest to Joel or Naomi that they hire another lawyer. This is your case. Period. And if you're the attorney of record, you need a retainer letter."

"Understood." She's right, of course. Rosie used to lecture me a lot when we were married. More often than not, she had good reason.

"I think you should spend tomorrow with your new client."

"I will. Unless I can pull a rabbit out of my hat, he isn't going anywhere any time soon."

* * *

At one-fifteen A.M, I arrive at my one-bedroom apartment in a walk-up building behind the Larkspur fire station. I climb up the short flight of steps and fumble for my keys in the dark. The building is vintage fifties, and it's showing its age. My apartment consists of a small living room, a tiny bedroom, a dining area barely big enough for a dinette set and a kitchen big enough for one. It's cramped when Grace stays here. The furniture is Scandinavian teak, with a few bookcases built of bricks and boards. The only modern technology is a laptop on the kitchen table. Forty-five years old and I'm still living like a college student. It's the price you pay when you have alimony, child support and an ex-wife who wants nice stuff for our daughter. Rosie probably doesn't need the money from me, but she's right to demand it. Given my propensity for frittering it away, it's better that I have a legal obligation to pay it to her. It doesn't help that I have a sixty-eight-year-old mother who isn't in the greatest of health.

I grab a Diet Dr. Pepper from the fridge and I look at my reflection in the mirror. My thick light brown hair is matted to my head. There are a few flecks of gray in the sideburns. The crow's-feet around my eyes remind me that I'm no longer in my thirties. My face is a little rounder than it used to be. I still have the lean legs from my days as a back-up running back at St. Ignatius. Rosie says I look like a middle-aged Irishman: a combination of boiled potatoes and beer. I realize that I'm beginning to look more and more like my dad.

There are two messages when I plug in my cell and start recharging the battery. The first one surprises me. "Mike, this is Roosevelt Johnson. I'd appreciate it if you would call me as soon as you can."

The second is from Rabbi Friedman. "Michael, please call me on Saturday afternoon after services. There are a few things I'd like to discuss with you."

I close my eyes and wonder if Rabbi Friedman is calling to ask why Joel is still in jail.

Let the second-guessing begin.

CHAPTER 10

"FIRST, YOU HAVE TO TELL ME EVERYTHING"

"In our top story this morning, District Attorney Prentice Gates said attorney Joel Mark Friedman will be charged with first-degree murder in the shootings of two colleagues."
— NewsCenter 4 Daybreak. Saturday, January 10.

At eight-thirty the next morning, Joel's unshaven face has a look of desperation as we meet in an airless consultation room. "Did you find a judge yet, Mike? When the hell am I getting out of here?"

"Rosie's calling in some favors. The duty judge said we'd have to wait till Monday."

"Dammit."

"It's an old trick. They haul you in on Friday night so you have to spend the weekend. They think it'll soften you up."

"For what? They think I'm gonna confess to something?"

"I assume you have nothing to confess to."

"You got that right."

"Good. How did you make it through the night?"

"Like a night at a fine hotel."

"Joel. Did they give you your own cell?"

"For a couple of hours. Then they put me in with a guy who was arrested for beating up a hooker. The cops said he wasn't dangerous. He scared the hell out of me."

Thanks a lot, Sergeant Ramos.

His tone turns somber. "What happens next?"

"First, you have to tell me everything. Then you have to tell me what you told the police. Then I'll try to find a judge who's willing to set bail. And I'll have a little talk with Inspector Johnson. And with

Skipper."

"I don't trust either of them."

"The only person you should trust is me."

He gives me a weak smile. "Do I get to talk to the judge anytime soon?"

Corporate attorneys haven't a clue about criminal procedure. "You don't talk to the judge. I do. On Monday, we'll go to court for an arraignment. They'll charge you. You'll plead not guilty. The judge will schedule a preliminary hearing. It'll be over in five minutes. It's as exciting as watching grass grow."

"Can you get me out of here on Monday?"

"Maybe. If we can't get a judge to set bail over the weekend, we'll ask at the arraignment."

"What are the chances?"

"Depends on the charge. If they go murder one, bail may be tough." If they ask for the death penalty, there's no way.

He's crushed. It's a shock when somebody first says aloud you're being charged with murder.

"I need to know all the details from you so I can do my job. I need the story straight. Don't embellish. Don't sugarcoat. Just tell me everything that happened." This is standard defense attorney jargon. I don't want to ask him flat out if he did it. If he lies to me, I'll have perjury issues. I'm not supposed to let him lie. It happens all the time, of course, but I try to avoid it. If he didn't do it, which I assume, and, coincidentally, I believe, I need his story to put together his defense.

He figures out where this is heading. "I want to get this right out on the table. I didn't do it. And it is absolutely imperative not only that I be found not guilty, but also that I am fully exonerated. Are we clear?"

"Joel, I need you to understand a few things. First, I believe you. I don't think you're capable of killing two people. I've known you for a long time, and I'm a very good judge of people."

I get the hint of a smile.

"But I don't do absolutions anymore. I'll give you the best defense I can, twenty-four/seven. My job is to try to get you off. I'll do everything I can to do that. If you need more, you'll need to go to your rabbi or another lawyer."

He looks away.

"You can still find another lawyer," I say.

"You're my lawyer. One more thing. How much do you think this is going to cost?"

"If we go to trial, at least a hundred and fifty thousand—probably more. If we need a lot of experts, double it. If you want jury consultants and mock trials, figure a half a million."

"I thought corporate lawyers were expensive."

"Trials have a life of their own. And Grace has to eat."

"What's your billing rate?"

I stop cold. The fact is, I haven't decided. "Two-ninety an hour plus expenses."

"Weren't you four-ninety at S&G?"

"Yeah. You're getting the deal of the century."

"You need a retainer?"

"Let's say forty thousand."

He doesn't blink. "All right. And if you get the charges dropped on Monday?"

"Your money will be cheerfully refunded, and you can buy me lunch at Bill's."

"Naomi will get you a check. We may need to borrow some money."

"Your credit is good."

"All right, Counselor, where do we start?"

"From the beginning. Tell me everything that happened, minute by minute, on the evening of December thirtieth."

* * *

Joel is working on his second cup of coffee. "Right after the meeting with Chuckles, I went back to the PCR and reviewed the final documents."

"That was around seven-fifteen?"

"Right. We were waiting for a call from CCC's board in Stamford. They were meeting to approve the deal. We got the go-ahead at eight-thirty. The deal was still on track, except, of course, for Vince. He said he wasn't sure he'd close."

"Who else was working on the deal?"

"Bob, Diana and the usual army of secretaries and paralegals. Jack Frazier from CCC. His lawyer, Martin Glass. Dan Morris, the political fixer. Ed Ehrlich from the city attorney's office."

"Who else was around?"

"The word processors and a couple of file clerks. And some of the people from Skipper's party."

"Like who?"

"The mayor stopped by and talked to Morris. Neither of them looked happy."

"Was Doris around?"

"No. She went home around eight. A few of the partners were still there, too. Patton stopped by. Chuckles was around. I talked to him after the meeting with the associates. Gave him a little more grief. You have to keep them honest."

"Were you really surprised by the decision to extend the partner track?"

"Not entirely. Still, they didn't handle it right. Bob should have told me."

He's right. On the other hand, it's hard to tell whether his speech to Chuckles at the associates' meeting was genuine or an act. I asked him what happened next.

"We gave some documents to the word processors around nine-thirty. Everybody went out to eat. Diana and I went to Harrington's. We finished around ten-fifteen. She went home. I came back upstairs. She lives over in Golden Gateway."

The Golden Gateway apartments are a high-rise complex a couple of blocks north of the Embarcadero Center towers. It's a five-minute walk from downtown.

Joel is still talking. "Bob took Vince to Tadich's, and Frazier and Morris went to Michael Mina. I think the mayor went with them."

Tadich Grill opened in 1849 and serves traditional fish in a paneled dining room on California Street. On a good night, you can get a private booth and a great piece of petrale sole. Michael Mina is two doors down and a hundred and fifty years removed from Tadich's. Its namesake celebrity chef appears regularly in food magazines. I've eaten there only once. The crab cakes are out of this world. So are the prices.

Joel stands to stretch his legs. "I got back first. Everybody else got back by eleven. We signed the papers by twelve-fifteen. I had a few cleanup things to go through, so I went back to my office. We agreed to meet at eight-thirty the next morning for the closing. I worked on the escrow instructions and gave the mark-up to word processing. I walked by Bob's office around twelve-thirty. He was arguing with Vince, so I poked my head in and told him we were ready. We barely said three words."

"So by twelve-thirty, the deal was set to close?"

"Right. Except everything depended on Vince. He had to give the final go-ahead in the morning to authorize the wire transfers."

"And at twelve-thirty, he still wasn't prepared to close?"

"He said he had to sleep on it. I went to my office, got my closing checklist and went down to the lunchroom for a soda."

"You were ready to close?"

"Yeah. In big deals like this, you sign all the documents the day before. The closing is usually a nonevent. Everybody drinks coffee until you get confirmation of the wire transfers."

"What did you do in the lunchroom?"

"I went through the checklist. I pushed three chairs together and took a nap. I woke up around six and went back to my office. I knocked on Bob's door, but it was locked. I figured he'd gone home. I went back to my office. I was there until a little after eight, when Chuckles came by and asked me if I had the keys to Bob's office."

"Did you?"

"No. But I know where Doris keeps an extra set. We let ourselves in."

I take a drink of water from a Styrofoam cup. "What happened when you found them?"

Joel hesitates.

"It's okay. You can tell me."

"I got sick. I . . . well . . .threw up."

"Right there?"

"No. I made it to the bathroom. When I got back, Chuckles was calling nine-one-one. Bob was on the floor. It looked like he shot himself in the temple. Diana was sitting on the floor next to the door. Her clothes were full of blood, and there was blood on the wall behind her. Her eyes were open. It looked like she was calling for help."

This isn't getting easier. "Where was the gun?"

"On the floor next to Bob's chair. It must have fallen out of his hand. It looked like he fell out of his chair."

I'll be able to confirm this from the police reports and the photos. "What did you do?"

"Something stupid, in retrospect. I picked up the gun and took out the bullets."

My first impulse is to scream, "YOU DID WHAT?" I've learned to keep my tone even. "Why did you pick up the gun?"

"I've shot Bob's gun at the range. He was real proud of it. Made everybody do it once or twice. Sort of a rite of passage."

"But why did you pick it up?"

"I wanted to make sure it didn't go off. It's a fussy revolver, Mike. The trigger was sensitive. Once it went off in my hand before it was supposed to. The bullet landed about halfway down the range."

I'm trying not to show it, but this part of Joel's story is sounding a little forced. "So you unloaded the gun?"

"Yes. I wanted to be sure it didn't go off." It's the second time he's mentioned it. "I put the gun on the desk. I put the bullets and the shells next to it."

Swell. "I trust you told the police Bob kept a loaded gun at his desk."

"Yep. They were amazed."

"It's pretty surprising."

"Not if you knew Bob."

"Then what?"

"That's it. We came downstairs to the meeting and we told Art." A look of recognition appears on his face. "I bet they found my fingerprints on the gun."

"Sounds like a good bet." My mind is racing. There has to be more. He has an explanation for his fingerprints on the gun. I need to probe a little more. "What haven't you told me?"

"Nothing. They know I was there. They probably have my fingerprints on the gun. And they seem to think I was really pissed off at Bob about the partner-election stuff."

"What did the police tell you?"

"Nothing. You told me not to talk to them."

"Good boy."

"What do we do now?"

"I'll go see Roosevelt and Skipper. If this is all they've got, we're in good shape." I stand up. As I'm reaching for the handle, I hear Joel's voice from behind me.

"Promise me you'll come back later and tell me what you find out."

"I will."

* * *

At eleven-thirty, my cell phone is pressed tightly against my right ear as I'm standing in the lobby of the Hall. "If Joel is telling the truth, they've got nothing, Rosie. He admitted that he was there all night. He confirmed that he and Chuckles found Bob and Diana. That much we knew. He also told me that he picked up the gun. So now I know how they may have found his fingerprints on it."

Rosie's tone is skeptical. "That's it?"

"Yes."

"Skipper said a lot more at his press conference. They have a witness from Harrington's who says Joel and Diana had a big fight at dinner. A custodian at the B of A Building says he heard Joel and Bob arguing around one o'clock."

"Did he hear gunshots?"

"They're not saying."

"Anything else?"

"They looked at the telephone records. A call was placed from Joel's office phone to Diana's apartment at about ten to one in the morning. They think he lured her back to the office."

I ask her if Skipper said anything else.

"He said he's going to charge Joel with first-degree murder, and he may ask for special circumstances."

Swell. "I'll talk to you later." I head for my car. I want to get to Roosevelt Johnson to get the full story on the evidence And I want to talk to the medical examiner and the evidence techs right away. I begin to outline our requests for access to the evidence in my head. Either Joel neglected to tell me a few important details, or his story has some gaping holes.

Or maybe he's flat-out lying.

CHAPTER 11

"YOUR FRIEND IS IN VERY SERIOUS TROUBLE"

"We're going to charge him with first-degree murder. As long as I'm the DA, we're going to be very aggressive prosecuting violent crimes."
— Skipper Gates. Press conference. Saturday, January 10.

At twelve-thirty on Saturday afternoon, Roosevelt Johnson and I are sitting in a booth at the Tennessee Grill at Twenty-first and Taraval, a couple of blocks from his house in the Sunset. The cop hangout is across McCoppin Square from Taraval Station and around the corner from Lincoln High. He's eating scrambled eggs and toast. I'm nursing a cup of decidedly un-gourmet coffee.

"I tried to reach you yesterday," he says.

"I didn't get the message till I got home late last night. My cell battery ran out. Thanks for trying."

"I didn't like the way it was handled. I know he's your friend. And I didn't realize you'd be representing him."

Neither did I. I watch as he uses his toast to push his eggs onto his fork. He's doing me a favor. I need him make the first move.

He leans forward so nobody can hear us. His gravel voice sounds tired. "We're off the record. Your friend is in very serious trouble. Holmes and Kennedy were killed by shots fired from Holmes's gun. She died from two shots to the chest. He died from one shot to the head. Your guy's fingerprints were on the gun. There were three spent shells and three unused bullets. His fingerprints were on those too."

"It shows that he picked up the gun. It doesn't prove he killed anyone."

"There's more." He clears his throat. "Seems he and Holmes had a big fight. We aren't sure what it was about. The night janitor said they were yelling at each other."

"They could have been talking about business."

"I know. I understand Holmes was a screamer, and Friedman doesn't like being pushed around. They may have been engaged in lawyerly discourse. One of your partners said Friedman was mad about not making partner."

"Who told you that?"

"In due time. Was he mad about not making partner?"

He's going to find out. "Off the record, Roosevelt, you'll find that he was, in fact, angry about not making partner."

"You aren't violating any confidences. He told me so."

He's testing me. "You think he killed Holmes because he didn't make partner?"

Another cold stare. "You know a guy named Rick Cinelli?"

"Yeah. The bartender at Harrington's. He knows more about the firm than most of the partners."

"Friedman and Kennedy had dinner there. Cinelli says they got into a big fight and she left."

I'm beginning to see where this is going. "They were probably talking about business. She wasn't a great legal technician. She probably screwed something up and he laid into her."

He gives me the "nice try" look. "All I know is what Cinelli told me. I don't try the cases. I don't even decide whether to prosecute. I just gather the evidence."

"Anything else?" I half expect him to say he has another janitor who found Joel standing over Bob's body.

"Just one other thing. We're trying to figure out why she came back to the office."

I'm wondering the same thing.

"We checked the S&G phone logs. A two-minute phone call was placed from Friedman's private office line at twelve-fifty-one a.m."

"Let me guess. Somebody called Diana's apartment from Joel's phone."

"Correct. You might want to ask him about it."

"I will." None of this is news to me. I don't want to invite speculation about whether Joel may have tried to lure her to the office. "Do you have the medical examiner's report yet?"

"Not final."

I can't push him. "Thanks for your help. I know you're sticking your neck out."

"You're family. Even if you're a defense lawyer. Besides, you'll get all of this stuff anyway."

He's right. In a few weeks, Skipper will have to present enough evidence at a preliminary hearing to show cause for holding Joel over for trial. He'll undoubtedly use everything Roosevelt just described. This isn't looking good for a quick dismissal.

* * *

Joel is incredulous. "Now they're saying I threatened her at Harrington's, and I lured her back to the office to kill her? What'll they dream up next? That I was sleeping with her?"

At two o'clock on Saturday afternoon, I'm giving Joel a report on my meeting with Roosevelt. "I don't want any surprises," I tell him. "I'm meeting with Skipper in twenty-five minutes. I don't want to hear about any more arguments at restaurants or fights in the office. Am I clear?"

"Yes." He rubs his eyes. "What do you need to know?"

"Everything that happened that night. Good, bad or otherwise. For starters, did you and Diana have an argument at Harrington's?"

"I'd call it a discussion."

I don't have time to play games. "Did you have a fight?"

"All right. Yes. She didn't finish our escrow instructions. I gave her a couple of simple things to do, and she didn't do them. She wasn't a very careful lawyer."

"That's all you were fighting about?"

"Of course."

"Good." I realize I've just congratulated him for making an ass of himself in a public place—for a perfectly legitimate reason. "I need to ask you something else. Was there ever any hanky-panky between you and Diana?"

"Are you asking me if I ever slept with her?"

"In a word, yes."

"The answer, in a word, is no."

"Good." If you're lying to me, I'll rip your lungs out. "Did you call her that night?"

"Yes. Bob told me to tell her to come back to the office. He wanted to talk to her about her closing documents." He pauses. "And I think he just wanted to talk to her."

"Why?"

"They talked a lot."

"Did they talk in bed?"

"I don't know."

"Did you think so?"

He looks away. "Maybe . . . probably. At least I think so."

"Did you and Bob have a fight that night?"

"I wouldn't call it a fight."

"Dammit, Joel. What were you and Bob arguing about?"

"He didn't have the guts to tell me the firm was going to defer all the people up for partner. I told him what I thought."

"One of the custodians heard you."

He closes his eyes. "They're saying I threatened him?"

"That seems to be the jump in their logic."

"And I threatened Diana at Harrington's and lured her back, just so I could kill her?"

"Yeah."

"That's bullshit. You think I'd kill Bob and ruin my life because I didn't make partner? You think I'd kill Diana because she didn't finish a set of escrow instructions? This is preposterous."

"I'm going to meet with Skipper."

"I expect you to get this dismissed by the end of the day."

Not a chance.

CHAPTER 12

"NICE OFFICE, SKIPPER"

"We are going to upgrade our facilities and computers. The San Francisco District Attorney's Office will be state-of-the-art."
— Skipper Gates. Acceptance speech.

The only thing state-of-the-art about the San Francisco District Attorney's Office is the remodeled suite occupied by Skipper Gates. The ADAs still sit in cramped offices behind metal desks with dented olive-green file cabinets. The lucky ones get their own offices. The really lucky ones get windows looking out at the bail bond shops across Bryant Street.

As soon as the election results were in, Skipper began tearing up the third floor of the Hall to make some major capital improvements—for himself. His office has been expanded, and he's built a new area for press conferences. The remodeling hasn't elicited much enthusiasm among the rank and file.

On Saturday afternoon, Skipper's office is a sea of splendor. He's dressed in khaki pants and a light blue polo shirt. His feet are propped up on his desk. I decline a Perrier from his new wet bar.

"Nice office, Skipper," I say. "I don't recall the hardwood floors and paneling when your predecessor occupied this space."

"Thanks. We're trying to upgrade the image of the office."

He's a master at accepting compliments, even when they're given facetiously. Hardwood floors, oak paneling, overstuffed chairs and an antique desk are more than an upgrade. I must admit the large photo of himself with the mayor and the governor hanging behind his desk is very flattering.

"Skipper, if you don't mind my asking, don't you think this might be a little bit much?"

"It's okay. The remodeling's being done on my nickel. It's very important to me to work where I'm comfortable."

"Do you think the new press room is a little overdone?"

"Nonsense. I'm the DA. That makes me the chief law-enforcement officer in the city. If you're going to act the part, you've got to look the part."

I feel like quoting the old Billy Crystal "Fernando" routine on *Saturday Night Live*: "You look mahvalous, Skipper, simply mahvalous."

Sitting quietly and observing this banal exchange is a trim, middle-aged man with short gray hair and thick glasses. Bill McNulty, the ADA in charge of homicide cases, is a native San Franciscan and a career prosecutor. He thought his number had come up last year for the DA job, but there were two problems. First, there isn't an ounce of charisma anywhere in Bill's body. Put him in front of a TV camera and he makes Richard Nixon look photogenic. Second, Skipper tossed his hat into the ring and outspent Bill by about ten to one. Skipper annihilated him in the election in a vicious negative campaign. For twenty-six years, McNulty has been on a mission from God to put the bad guys away. He's good at it. What he lacks in charm, he makes up for by being careful, hard-nosed and meticulous. He has a reputation as a fighter and his nickname around the Hall is Bill McNasty.

Skipper waves a hand at McNulty. "I presume you and Bill have met."

"We've worked on several cases over the years." I turn to McNulty. "Nice to see you again."

He grimaces. A man of few words.

"Are you the ADA assigned to this case?"

He nods.

"Good." Bad, actually. McNasty's good. He's tenacious, and he's prosecuted at least fifty murder cases. He's won most of them. Skipper has made an astute choice for help on his first big case.

McNulty glares at me. "The arraignment is at ten o'clock on Monday. We'll see you there." He stands up.

"Wait a minute, Bill. I thought we might take a few minutes to talk about this."

"There's nothing to talk about. The next step is the arraignment. I assume your guy will plead not guilty, and we'll be on our way."

Skipper holds up a hand. "I've just put Bill on this case. He's understandably reluctant to talk to you before he's been through the file. Isn't that right, Bill?"

McNasty scowls. I can't tell if he's irritated about being here, being put on this case or having to suck up to Skipper. Probably all of the above.

Skipper flashes a phony smile. "Maybe I can answer a few questions. And by the way, I'm sorry about all the hoopla last night. We didn't know you were going to be there. We sure as hell didn't know his kids and parents would be there, too."

Where did you think his kids would be at seven o'clock on a Friday night? "What do you have in mind, Skipper? You can't be serious about charging Joel based upon the skimpy evidence."

"You bet your ass I am."

"Enlighten me. What evidence?" I want to find out everything that I can. And I don't want to give them anything.

Skipper responds with a coy grin. "You can't expect us to tip our hand."

McNulty shakes his head. "You're going to have to tell him sooner or later. Tell him what we've got, or I will."

This is sounding a little rehearsed. "Well, Skipper?"

"We know he was there at the time of the murders."

"Alleged murders."

Eye roll. "Alleged murders. Your client was the only one there. He knew where the gun was. He'd used it at the range. So we've got opportunity."

"Fine. We know he was there. He told you so. And we know about the gun. So what?" I'm tempted to ask Skipper where he was, but I let it go.

"There's physical evidence. His fingerprints were on the gun, the spent shells and the unused bullets. We have direct contact with the murder weapon."

"Not good enough. It shows he disarmed the gun. He told you that. He did it for the safety of the others in the firm. You aren't close to probable cause, let alone a conviction." Actually, he zoomed past probable cause a few minutes ago, and he's about a quarter of the way to a conviction, but he doesn't have to hear that from me.

Skipper takes a drink of Perrier. "Then, of course, we have the question of motive."

I lean back and lock my fingers behind my head. "What motive have you concocted, Skipper?"

"Actually he has motive in both cases. Let's talk about Diana first. He was angry with her. They got into a screaming match at Harrington's The bartender heard it. She tossed a drink at him and stormed out."

"They were fighting about work. She didn't finish some documents. It doesn't mean he killed her."

"That's what your guy is telling you. She went home, had a drink and went to bed. Then around twelve-fifty, after he had a chance to stew about it, he called her and lured her back to the office. He waited for her, then he blasted her. Right there in Bob's office."

"You're dreaming, Skipper. What makes you think he called her?" I know what's coming.

"We have the phone records. A call was placed from his private office line to the land line in her apartment at twelve-fifty-one. It lasted two minutes. She showed up at the office fifteen minutes later at about one-ten. We got the time of her arrival from the building security cameras."

At least the timing of things is becoming clear. We'll subpoena the security videos. "Assuming your records are right, I'll grant you that a call may have been placed from Joel's phone. But it doesn't prove he made the call. Even if he did, he was undoubtedly calling to ask her to come to the office to help with the closing." I'm kind of enjoying the cat-and-mouse aspect of this. It's been a while.

Skipper smiles confidently. "That's where you're wrong. We know exactly what he said to her in that telephone conversation. And it wasn't anything close to the way you described it."

"How's that, Skipper? Are you listening in on Joel's calls? Or did you bug his phone?"

"The conversation was taped on Diana's answering machine."

Uh-oh.

The condescending smirk. "We got this yesterday. She must have been asleep and didn't pick up her phone until the answering machine started taping. She didn't erase the message when she left."

I'm getting a bad feeling about this.

McNulty stands. "While we're being so open about our evidence, let me play something for you." He punches a button on his laptop and turns up the sound.

Beep. "*Wednesday. December thirty-first. Twelve-fifty-one a.m.*" *Beep.* "*Pick up, Diana. God dammit.*"

"*Hello?*"

"*Diana, it's Joel. I was talking to Bob. We need you to come down here right away. We've got a bunch of things to do for the closing.*"

"*Joel? What time is it?*"

"*About ten to one.*"

"*I'm exhausted. Can't it wait until morning?*"

"*No. It can't wait. I've got to see you now.*"

"*I don't want to deal with this now.*"

"*You have to. I need to see you right now. Bob wants to resolve this stuff right now. ASAP. So get your tight little ass over here right away.*"

"*You're a piece of shit.*"

"*So are you. Now get over here or I'll come over there and get you myself.*"

"*All right, asshole. I'll be right there. But this is the last time.*"

We're finished. You understand? You can find somebody else to push around."

"*I wouldn't have it any other way.*"

Beep.

Skipper is triumphant. "Sounds like they were talking about more than business."

"That's what this is all about? A late-night telephone call where he tells her to come back to work? From that you get murder? You're dreaming. This isn't an old episode of *Law & Order*, you know."

Out of the corner of my eye, I think I see McNulty nod, but I'm not sure.

Skipper's tone becomes more strident. "Let me play something else for you." He nods to McNulty, who turns on the audio player on his computer. I recognize the sound of our voicemail prompts.

"*Bob, Joel. I just found out about the new policy on partner elections. I came by your office, but you were with Vince. I want to tell you something. This stinks. You should have told me, but, as usual, you didn't have the balls. I'll get you for this. I'm not gonna take this lying down. Call me right away.*"

I look skeptical. "You're saying this represents a threat?"

"Damn right," Skipper snaps.

I turn to McNulty. "Bill, you know there's no way this will ever add up to a conviction."

McNulty gives Skipper an inquisitive look. Skipper nods.

"What?" I ask.

McNulty turns to me. "It seems that your boy was having an affair with Diana Kennedy. A witness saw the two of them in the same room at your last firm retreat. Let's just say that she wasn't fully clothed."

"No way."

"Yes way," Skipper says. "And that's what ties it all together. Kennedy was sleeping with Friedman. She pulled the plug on him and told him she was sleeping with Holmes. That led to the fight at Harrington's. He came back and confronted Holmes. That led to the phone call to her apartment."

"You're dreaming. Joel wasn't sleeping with her. You can't prove it."

McNulty speaks up. "We've got a witness. There's only one other living person who can rebut his testimony."

"And that would be Joel."

"And that would be correct."

"And who is this honest soul who will step forward and swear my client is an adulterer?"

McNulty stops. "I can't tell you."

"You mean you *won't* tell me."

"Not until I have to."

I turn to Skipper. "Are you prepared to tell me?"

"No. We're only obligated to give you evidence that would exculpate your client. All the evidence we've given you so far points directly toward a conviction."

The key witness has to be an attorney at S&G. "Skipper, you have some shaky circumstantial stuff here, but nothing close to a case."

McNulty looks at me. "There's one more thing."

I'm wondering how many more things. "What is it?"

"She was pregnant."

Hell.

"Before you ask, we don't know who the father is, but we'll find out."

This is going to get messy. "There's a lot of hard evidence this was a suicide. He shot himself with his own gun. He left a suicide note. Before you embarrass yourself on Monday, you ought to wait for the medical examiner's report."

Skipper is enjoying himself. "We got a preview. The cause of Bob's death will be a gunshot wound. But there is evidence that somebody hit him on the head before the shots were fired."

"You're saying somebody tried to make it look like a suicide?"

"Right."

"What about the suicide note, the e-mail?"

"Joel's fingerprints are on Bob's keyboard."

What? How did Joel's fingerprints get on Bob's keyboard? "He could have used Bob's keyboard anytime. It still doesn't show he typed the e-mail."

Skipper finishes his Perrier. "Look, Mike, it's against my better judgment, and Bill is going to kill me for saying it, but I'm prepared to discuss a plea bargain. I'll go down to second-degree murder and recommend a lenient sentence."

Second-degree means at least fifteen years in jail. "No way. You've got no case."

"Yes, we do. I'm going to try it myself."

"You're crazy."

Skipper's eyes gleam. "Tell him we're going to charge him with first-degree murder. We're considering special circumstances. If he's willing to save the taxpayers the cost of a trial, we'll agree to a plea of second-degree with a recommendation of fifteen years. We'll take the death penalty off the table. Our offer is open until the arraignment on Monday. You have an ethical obligation to convey it to your client."

"I won't recommend it. Not in a million years."

"I know you're a little rusty. Bill is my right hand on this case. He hasn't had a chance to study the file in detail, but he's sure we've got a strong case. A very strong case. Right, Bill?"

"Right."

I can't tell if McNulty is sincere or just trying to appease his new boss. "Bill, are you really thinking about going for the death penalty in a circumstantial case in San Francisco? Have you lost your mind?"

He doesn't respond.

CHAPTER 13

"I HAVE TO CONSIDER WHAT'S BEST FOR MY SON"

"Joel Mark Friedman will be arraigned on Monday for double murder. District Attorney Prentice Gates says he may seek the death penalty. In an unusual twist, Gates says he will try the case himself."
— KCBS News Radio. Saturday, January 10.

At three-thirty the same day, I'm in the lobby of the Hall. I'm talking to Rabbi Friedman on my cell.

"How are things going with Joel's case?" he asks.

"As well as can be expected." I describe my meetings with Joel and Skipper, judiciously leaving out any references to Joel's alleged infidelities or Skipper's plea bargain proposal. "It looks like they're going to charge Joel with murder on Monday."

Silence.

"We're doing everything we can. It's going to take some time."

He clears his throat. "That's why I called. I was talking to a couple of my congregants last night. Several lawyers are members of the temple."

"I know." *Probably half your board of directors.*

"This is difficult, so forgive me for being blunt. A couple of members of our board of directors whose judgment I respect suggested you may not be the right person to handle my son's case."

It feels like a piece of sharp glass going through my stomach. "Why did they say that?"

"One of my congregants said you haven't spent a lot of time in court for a few years. He said you may be a little rusty."

"I defended over a hundred murder trials when I was a PD. I've been defending white-collar criminals at the Simpson firm for the last five years. I'm completely current on the law."

"Another attorney suggested that you may have been something of a renegade at the public defender's office."

It's true. My bosses thought I took too many cases to trial. That's bad for business in the PD's office. The supervisors are paid for disposing of cases quickly, not necessarily winning them. "I took a lot of cases to trial when I was at the PD's office. That's what PDs get paid for. I won some cases others would have lost. I won some cases others would have pled out." And, in fairness, I probably lost a few that I could have pled out. "That's what you want from a defense lawyer. You want somebody who will go to bat for your client."

"I have to consider what's best for my son."

"I understand your concerns. This is a very important decision. It's up to Joel. If he wants to hire another lawyer, I'll be disappointed, but I'll understand." And Rosie will kill me.

He pauses. "Maybe there's an alternative. How would you feel about having another lawyer assist you?"

I don't like it. "What do you have in mind?"

"I thought that maybe one of the lawyers from my congregation could help you. I know you don't have a lot of lawyers in your new firm."

This is delicate. "I'm always happy to have help. I figured Rosie would sit second chair. We were a great team at the PD's office."

"I see."

"We criminal defense lawyers are a little protective of our territory. I'd be happy to consider having someone else involved, but only with the understanding that I'd make the final decisions."

He clears his throat. "Michael, let me discuss it with Joel."

* * *

Joel is less than enthusiastic about the possibility of a plea bargain. "Plead guilty to second-degree murder? You've got to be kidding. No way."

"I didn't say you should take it. I just said that they offered it, and I have an obligation to tell you about it. I'm not recommending it."

"Fine. I'm instructing you to reject the plea bargain."

"Good."

"What did you find out from Skipper?"

I tell him about the phone calls, the bartender at Harrington's and the phone messages to Diana and Bob.

"Doesn't mean anything," he insists. "We were working on a deal. Everybody was under a lot of pressure."

Not as much pressure as you're under now. "There's something else. Diana was pregnant."

He responds in a subdued tone. "I know."

"Come again?"

"I knew she was pregnant."

"How did you know?"

"She told me about three weeks ago."

"Did you tell anyone?"

"No. She asked me not to." He looks me in eye. "When people tell me something in confidence, I don't repeat it. I didn't ask to be the father confessor for the firm. It just worked out that way."

I lower my voice to confession-level. "I have to ask."

"I'm not the father. Unless, of course, there was some sort of immaculate conception. You Catholics are more into that stuff than we are."

"There's more."

"What else? Yesterday, I was just a garden-variety killer. Today I'm also an adulterer. Tomorrow, I'll be a sex offender and a child molester, too."

"They have a witness who saw you and Diana together in your room at Silverado at the firm retreat last year. He says she didn't have any clothes on."

"It's Patton. There was a party in his room. Art was drunk. He tried to put the moves on Diana. She blew him off. She went back to her room. He followed her. Depending on who's telling the story, either he asked her nicely to sleep with him, or he attacked her. At two in the morning, she banged on my door. She said Patton tried to rape her. Guess who showed up a minute later? He said he heard some noise. He saw Diana."

"He set you up."

"Yeah. If Diana pursued it, Art could say she was in my room with me. He was protecting himself and the firm from a sexual-harassment suit."

"Can anybody else corroborate any of this?"

"Probably not."

"Diana never pursued it?"

"There was an investigation. As far as I know, she didn't push it. She didn't want to torpedo her career."

"You think Patton is the father?"

"I don't know. It could've been Patton. It could've been Bob. Hell, it could've been anybody."

This is serious. The only person who can contradict Patton's account of the events of that night is Joel. And he isn't going on the stand unless we're desperate. "Does Naomi know about this?"

"No. And she doesn't need to know."

"It's going to come up. I'd rather she heard it from you."

"I'll talk to her."

I hope so.

"What else did you find out from Skipper?" he asks.

"They think Bob was sleeping with Diana."

"I've heard that one many times."

"And they seem to think you were, too."

"Great. Only two people know the truth—Diana and me. Diana is dead. That leaves me. And I presume you don't want me to testify."

"Correct."

"So I'm screwed."

Reality is at hand. "It doesn't look like we'll be able to get the charges dropped on Monday."

He pushes out a heavy sigh. "What's the prognosis on bail?"

"Not great. If Skipper charges you with first-degree, bail will be tough. If he goes for special circumstances, bail's probably out."

He turns white. "The death penalty?"

"We have to be prepared for it. Skipper was talking about it. He may not decide until after the arraignment."

"Dammit."

"One other thing. I talked to your father. Seems he's gotten a few suggestions that I may need a little help on this case."

"Do you?"

"I was planning to have Rosie sit second chair. We were a good team at the PD's office." I explain that murder trials in California are divided into two phases. The first involves a determination of guilt or innocence. If there's a guilty verdict, the trial moves to the so-called penalty phase, where the jury decides whether to impose the death penalty. It's customary for a different attorney to handle the penalty phase so the jury gets to see a new face. In addition, the penalty-phase attorney can argue that the trial attorney was incompetent. The penalty-phase attorney is known as Keenan counsel. I tell him I'll handle the trial phase and Rosie will be Keenan counsel.

He ponders his options for a moment. "I want to think about it. You and Rosie are good, but I want to be sure you have enough firepower. My dad's pretty well-connected. I'll let you know in the next day or so."

* * *

"Rabbi Friedman wants to hire another lawyer as co-counsel?" Rosie asks. She's slicing pizza in her kitchen later the same evening. Grace is watching TV in the living room.

I take a sip of Diet Dr. Pepper. "I'm beginning to see why Joel needed some space from his dad."

"He's worried, Mike. You're going to need some help."

"I know. "I figured I'd take the lead and use Pete as the primary investigator."

"Keep it in the family. I like that. What about Keenan counsel?"

"Joel deserves the best, so I took the liberty of recommending you."

She smiles. "I thought you'd never ask. Do I have to marry you again?"

"No mixing business and pleasure."

"Deal."

"Great. I'll check with Joel." I pause. "And his father, I suppose. One other thing, I get to make all the final decisions in the trial phase."

"Of course."

Joel just hired the best defense team from the PD's office in the last twenty years. Of course, he's also hired two people who reenacted the War of the Roses only five short years ago.

And his arraignment is in two days.

CHAPTER 14

"NOTHING EVER HAPPENS AT AN ARRAIGNMENT"

"Plea bargaining isn't a part of the criminal-justice system—it IS the system."
— Criminal Defense Attorney and Adjunct Professor of Law Morton R. Goldberg. Continuing legal education seminar.

Two days later. Monday, January 12. The TV coverage for every arraignment is always the same. First, there's footage of an unshaven, handcuffed, jumpsuit-clad defendant being led into court looking guilty as hell. Next they show a grim prosecutor (usually a middle-aged white male) marching into court with his minions, uttering platitudes about the strength of his case and his faith in the justice system. Finally, the scene shifts to the steps of the courthouse, where a smarmy defense attorney boldly proclaims his client's innocence and castigates the DA for bringing trumped-up charges against a pillar of the community.

At nine-thirty on Monday morning, the smarmy defense attorney standing in the drizzle in front of the Hall of Justice is me.

I don't particularly care for this sideshow. I'd just as soon avoid becoming a media star. On the other hand, in our media-frenzied culture, you try to make points whenever you can with what we attorneys like to call the potential-juror pool.

An army of reporters and cameramen fight for space. It's a great day for the hair-spray industry. With Naomi standing to my left and Rosie to my right, I speak directly to the cameras. "Ladies and gentlemen, we are shocked and dismayed that Mr. Gates has chosen to proceed with these unsubstantiated charges. We are certain Mr. Friedman will be exonerated."

We push our way through the throng of shouting reporters.

"*Mr. Daley, is it true your client was offered a plea bargain?*"

"*Mr. Daley, is it true your client is going to plead guilty?*"

"*Mr. Daley, is it true your client tried to commit suicide?*"

"*Mr. Daley, is it true your client was having an affair with Diana Kennedy?*"

"*Mr. Daley? Mr. Daley? Mr. Daley?*"

I run interference for Naomi, and Rosie elbows Rita Roberts and her Channel 4 microphone.

"Is it always going to be like this?" Naomi asks.

"Probably for a while," I say. "Rosie will take you to the courtroom. I'm going to see Joel."

* * *

Joel's demeanor is subdued. "Can I talk to you about something for a minute, Mike?"

"Of course."

We're sitting in the holding area behind the courtroom. The arraignment starts in five minutes. I don't want any surprises.

He pushes out a sigh. "I was talking to my dad. He thinks it might be a good idea if we get you some help."

I suspected this was coming. "As I told you on Saturday, I figured I would take the lead and Rosie would sit second chair. Pete will be our investigator." I add halfheartedly, "Of course, we'll do it however you'd like."

"You know Mort Goldberg? He's the president of the temple."

"I've met him." Everyone in town knows Mort Goldberg. Mort the Sport. Smart. Shrewd. Well-connected in the Jewish community. He taught criminal procedure at Hastings. In his day, he was one of the more successful defense lawyers in town. Unfortunately, his day ended about twenty years ago. Now he spends most of his time cutting deals on drunk-driving cases. "He's been at it for years. Solid reputation."

"Dad and I thought Mort might be able to help. Do some

research. Maybe take a few witnesses."

Look over my shoulder. Second-guess every decision. Sounds great. "Let me be honest. He's what we defense lawyers call a pleader. He's not a trial guy. He's a plea-bargain guy."

"Is he good at strategy?"

"Yes, but he's not a strong trial lawyer."

"That's why we have you, right?" He leans back. "I've given this a lot of thought. I want him involved. I thought he could help at the arraignment. He's waiting outside."

"He's here?"

"Yeah. And he's available today."

"Joel, nothing ever happens at an arraignment. You plead not guilty and sit down."

"I need to get bail. You have to get me out of here."

"The arraignment starts in five minutes. We can't talk strategy now."

"I understand. Let me bring him in. I'll tell him he's just going to be an observer today."

"Fine." It's a done deal; what else can I say?

He motions to the deputies, and they bring in Mort and Joel's father. Mort is a stocky sixty-three-year-old with a bald head and thick aviator-style glasses. A natural back-slapper, he shakes hands with Joel and greets me like we've been pals for years. Give him credit. He's an operator.

"Joel," he says, "don't worry about a thing. Mike and I will have you out of here by noon."

Rabbi Friedman beams. Temple board meetings must be a riot.

Mort turns to me. "Glad we'll finally have a chance to work together. I always admired your work at the PD's office. If I knew you were going to leave, I'd have hired you myself."

Smooth. Always start with flattery.

"We're due in court in about thirty seconds," I say.

* * *

In California, criminal arraignments used to be handled in municipal court. In a court reorganization a few years ago, the muni courts were consolidated with the superior courts. As a result, arraignments are now conducted in superior court. Judge Stanley Miller is a dour bureaucrat in his late fifties. In his twenty-one years on the bench, he's worked his way from traffic court down the hall to superior court. He spent the early part of his career defending insurance companies, which gave him tremendous skill in the art of expedience. He's not really a judge. He's more like a legal-system traffic cop. Now semiretired, he found a home hearing motions and setting bail. He keeps the wheels of justice turning. We won't see him again after today. It's probably just as well.

The courtroom is packed. Reporters fill the jury box. Lawyers and police mill around. We aren't the only arraignment on the calendar this morning, but we're the biggest media event. We rise as Judge Miller enters. The case is called. Skipper and I state our appearances.

The judge wastes no time. "Mr. Daley, does your client understand the charges?"

"Yes, Your Honor. We can dispense with a formal reading."

"Good." He turns to Joel. "On the charge of murder in the first degree, how do you plead?"

I nod to Joel, who stands and says in a clear voice, "Not guilty, Your Honor."

"Good." Judge Miller points at me. "By statute, I am required to set a preliminary hearing within sixty days."

The prelim is also held in superior court. The prosecution must show that there is "probable cause" to believe Joel committed a crime. Joel can accelerate the process by demanding a prelim in ten days. Most defendants choose to "waive time," which means they forfeit their right to require the prelim within the ten-day window. Ordinarily, the defense loses little by waiving time, because it gives them additional time to prepare or, in many cases, cut a deal with the DA.

My tone is respectful. "Mr. Friedman chooses not to waive time."

Miller looks at me over the top of his reading glasses. "May I ask why you believe it would be in your client's best interest to proceed so quickly?"

"My client's life has been severely interrupted by these outrageous charges. We are prepared to proceed with his defense as soon as possible to clear his name."

He feigns annoyance as he looks at his calendar and consults with his clerk. They have a brief and testy discussion. "The preliminary hearing will be one week from tomorrow in Judge Kenneth Brown's courtroom."

Not a great draw for us. Brown is a former prosecutor.

Miller turns to Skipper. "Mr. Gates, I trust you're prepared to move forward next week?"

"Let me check my calendar. Your Honor."

"You're supposed to check your calendar before you enter my courtroom, Mr. Gates. I will assume you'll be there." He turns to me. "Mr. Daley, are you prepared to proceed?"

"Yes, Your Honor."

"See you next week." He raises his gavel.

"Your Honor," I say, "we would like to discuss bail."

"Do I understand, Mr. Daley, that no bail has been set?"

"Correct, Your Honor. We request that bail be set. Mr. Friedman is a respected member of the community, and he isn't a flight risk."

Skipper is up like a shot. "Your Honor, the people oppose bail. The defendant is charged with first-degree murder. We may ask for special circumstances. He is dangerous, and bail should not be granted."

"Your Honor," I say, "Mr. Friedman is an attorney with a respected law firm. He has lived here his entire life and has significant community and family ties. He is clearly entitled to bail."

Skipper tries again. "Your Honor, we are considering special circumstances. It would be highly unusual for bail to be set in a capital case. Highly unusual."

My turn again. "With all due respect, Your Honor, the state has not added special circumstances, so this is not a capital case. The judge has discretion to set bail."

Judge Miller flips through the penal code. Without looking up, he says, "Mr. Daley, I realize that you haven't been in my courtroom for a while, so let me give you some advice. When I hear the words 'With all due respect, Your Honor,' I interpret them to mean, 'You doddering old fool, Your Honor.' Let's come up with some authority on this subject."

Touchy, aren't we?

Skipper has prepared a speech and his going to make it. "Your Honor, the defendant is a flight risk. The weekend before he was arrested, he and his wife left town."

"One moment, Your Honor." I ask Joel about it. He whispers that he and Naomi did, in fact, drive up to Mendocino. He says they needed time to talk. I turn back to the judge. "Your Honor, Mr. Friedman and his wife took a drive up the coast for a day. That hardly constitutes flight. He wasn't a suspect at the time."

Judge Miller isn't listening to me. "Mr. Gates, isn't there some statutory authority?"

Skipper shrugs and turns to McNulty, who stands and speaks in a crisp voice. "Your Honor, Section twelve-seventy-five point five of the penal code says, 'A defendant charged with a capital offense punishable by death cannot be admitted to bail when the proof of his guilt is evident or the presumption of guilt is great.'"

Judge Miller is pleased. "That's it. I knew there was something on this."

"But, Your Honor," I say, "this is not a capital offense." At least not yet. "The proof of guilt is not evident, and the presumption is not great in this case." I can recite penal code sections, too.

"Mr. Daley, we can argue all day about whether the proof is evident, and the presumption is great. I'm not going to take the court's time for that."

"Your Honor—,"

"The law is clear. The proof is evident enough for me."

And you have an early tee-off time. He's about to rule when I hear a distinctive nasal voice from behind me.

"Your Honor, may it please the court."

Mort Goldberg is walking through the gate into the well of the courtroom.

Miller smiles. "Why, Mor—Mr. Goldberg, we haven't seen you in this court in some time."

"Thank you, Your Honor. It's nice to see you."

I'm waiting for Mort to ask Miller about his grandchildren. "Your Honor," I say, "may I have a moment with Mr. Goldberg?"

"You have one minute, Mr. Daley."

I pull Mort aside. "What the hell are you doing? He was just about to rule."

"He was about to rule against you. I can help."

"Bad idea."

"I know this guy. We go to the same temple. Besides, you got any better ideas?"

At the moment, no. "You think you can pull a rabbit out?"

"Watch me." He turns back to the judge. "Your Honor, I have just been retained as special counsel to Mr. Friedman. I must confess I haven't read the entire file yet."

And I'm reasonably sure you never will.

"Rather than ask you for a continuance, I have a suggestion as to how the bail issue might be resolved."

Miller is interested. "Go on, Mor—I mean, Mr. Goldberg."

"I understand your concern about bail. The charges are serious."

Skipper is speechless.

"Nevertheless," Mort continues, "I have a creative solution that will ease your concern. I know Your Honor is acquainted with Mr. Friedman's father, Rabbi Neil Friedman, of Temple Beth Sholom."

"Yes, I am."

"I would therefore propose that bail be set for Mr. Friedman, subject to his agreement to remain at all times in the house of Rabbi

Friedman, except when he has to be in court. We would, of course, expect Your Honor to require a fairly substantial bail, and we're prepared to agree to an electronic monitoring device."

Miller looks at Rabbi Friedman. "Is this acceptable to you, Rabbi?"

"Yes, Your Honor."

Skipper leaps up. "The people have utmost respect for Rabbi Friedman, but it's highly unusual for a defendant to be placed in the custody of his own father. Highly unusual."

You're right, Skipper. It's highly unusual.

The judge turns to me. "Is this arrangement acceptable to you, Mr. Daley?"

No. I'd rather let Joel stay in a cell with a pimp. "It's acceptable to us, Your Honor."

"Well, it's highly unusual. On the other hand, this court greatly respects Rabbi Friedman. Bail is set at a million dollars. The defendant will be released to the custody of Rabbi Friedman. He will wear an electronic ankle bracelet and be monitored by the sheriff's department. He is to remain at Rabbi Friedman's house except to appear in court. He may have visits from his attorneys and immediate family only. That's it. We're adjourned."

Joel turns to me. "Am I out?"

"Yeah. We need to post bail. And you have to stay at your dad's house."

"It's better than the place I've stayed the last few nights."

Mort taps me on the shoulder. "What did you think of that one?"

"Pretty smooth, Mort."

"It helps when the judge is on the board of directors at the temple." Mort walks over to Rabbi Friedman. I hear him say he's willing to have the temple building pledged as collateral for Joel's bond.

I glance at Rosie. She's pleased. As we walk out, she whispers, "Do you think we can find a trial judge who's on the temple board, too?"

CHAPTER 15

THE DREAM TEAM

"Hiring Mort Goldberg was brilliant. They should put him in charge."
— NewsCenter 4 Legal Analyst Morgan Henderson. Tuesday, January 13.

"The TV stations have rehired their legal analysts from the O.J. trial," I observe. "I guess they have nothing better to do."

I'm eating a bagel and talking to Joel as we sit in the heavy wooden chairs in his father's dining room at nine o'clock the next morning. Mort nibbles on a sweet roll. Rosie sips a Diet Coke. Pete stands next to Mort. He hates meetings.

I look around the table. Mort is a world-class prima donna. Rosie runs her own cases. Pete works solo. Rabbi Friedman is used to having everybody listen to him. Joel makes all the calls on his deals. Not exactly a roomful of team players.

Showtime. "Let's get started," I say. "We have only a week until the preliminary hearing."

Rabbi Friedman clears his throat. "I'd like to thank Mort for his contribution at the arraignment yesterday."

Mort smiles and waves his unlit cigar. "It was nothing."

I hand out copies of the first police reports. "We should have the medical examiner's report later today." I summarize the evidence. The fingerprints on the gun and the computer keyboard. The phone messages. The fight at Harrington's. The argument in Bob's office. The allegations of an affair. Diana's pregnancy. "They have a week to show they have enough evidence to hold Joel over for trial. We have a week to show they don't. I want to find out as much as we can about Bob and Diana. We need to talk to their friends and relatives.

We need to interview the people at S&G. We have to get a copy of Bob's will and look at his investments. He probably had life insurance."

I turn to Mort. "I'd like your help with legal issues, motions and strategy. We should try to get our hands on every piece of evidence before the prelim."

He's pleased.

Pete looks at me. It's like looking in a mirror. He's a little stockier than I am, and he has a neatly trimmed mustache. His hair is darker. "Where do you want me to start?"

"With the physical evidence and the forensics. I want you to look for holes in the police report and the medical examiner's report." It's nice to have an ex-cop on the team. "And I want you to figure out what happened to Vince Russo. And I have something special for you. I need you to figure out who was sleeping with whom—and when."

His mouth turns up slightly. "Right up my alley."

"I want you to look into Bob's personal life. I want you to see what Bob's widow is up to. And there are some other people I'd like you to watch. They're pretty high up in San Francisco society, so you'll have to be discreet. I want you to tail Arthur Patton."

"What am I looking for?"

"The usual. He's in the middle of an ugly divorce. Evidently, he's had some problems keeping his pants on. And he may have sexually harassed Diana Kennedy."

Mort interrupts. "If you need some help, I can give you the names of a couple of PIs that I've used over the years. They're very good."

Pete stares him down and says, "I'll let you know."

Mort shrugs.

Joel asks, "What can I do?"

"I want you to make a list of everything you saw and everyone who was there."

"I'll put it together right away."

"One other thing. I want you to get on your laptop and look at the corporate filings in every state where Vince Russo had business. Maybe we can find him, if he's still alive. Or maybe we can figure out what happened to him."

"Do we need to worry about the attorney-client privilege?"

It's a legitimate legal question. The correct legal answer is yes. The practical answer is no. "I don't want you to do anything illegal. On the other hand, try to get everything you can. Russo isn't doing you any favors."

Mort holds up his unlit cigar. "The prelim is before Judge Brown. We were law school classmates. Kenny and I play cards at the Concordia Club. It might make sense for me to take a leading role."

Rabbi Friedman nods.

I keep my tone even. "I appreciated your efforts at the arraignment yesterday. But I'm most familiar with the evidence. I'll take the lead in the prelim."

Rabbi Friedman frowns.

Mort looks at his cigar. "It was just a suggestion."

"Let's get one thing straight here, Mort. I'll make the final calls on strategy. Do you understand?"

"Yes, I do."

"Good. It may make sense for you to argue some of the pre-hearing motions. Think you're up to it?"

"Sure, Mike. You're the boss."

"Let's get to work."

* * *

I'm driving Mort toward downtown in the pouring rain later the same morning. "Think we can get this knocked out at the prelim?" he asks.

"It's going to be tough."

He looks out the window. "So the girl was pregnant."

"Yeah."

"You know who the father is?"

For all his idiosyncrasies, at least he doesn't pull punches. "Not yet."

"You thinking what I'm thinking?"

"If Joel is the father, we're screwed. The jury will nail him."

Mort nods. "Just between us, what do you think the chances are that he did it? You know—jealous rage. You've seen it a thousand times."

"Not likely, Mort."

"How well do you know him?"

"Very well."

"Hypothetically, let's suppose he's not quite the Boy Scout you think he is. You suppose it might be a good idea to see what our new DA has up his sleeve?"

His true colors are coming out. "You can't seriously be thinking about a plea. It's way too early. We've had the case for just a few days."

"I know how these guys think. New DA. First big case. Doesn't know what he's doing. Doesn't want to screw up. That's why McNasty's holding his hand. If he can get a guilty plea, he's golden. It's instant political capital. He can say he caught the bad guy and saved the city a ton of money in trial costs."

"I respect your instincts, Mort, but you're way off the mark. I know this guy. He didn't do it. We're going to get this knocked out. Or we're going to beat them at trial."

He gives me a knowing grin. "I'm just saying we should look at our options. I've been doing this for a long time. There are good times and bad times to talk to the DA. For what it's worth, I think now is a good time."

I can't tell if he's exercising cautious judgment, or if he's a tired old man who's lost his nerve. "It's too soon to talk about a plea, Mort," I repeat.

"Would it change your thinking if I told you things haven't always been so great between Joel and Naomi?"

"What are you talking about?"

"You know I'm tight with Joel's dad. Joel and Naomi have had some problems."

"What kind?"

"She had postpartum depression after the twins were born. She's still going through it."

"They're six years old. Nobody has postpartum that long."

"Well, she did. They spent about thirty grand last year on shrinks. That's one of the reasons Joel wanted to make partner—he needs the money."

"Rabbi Friedman told you this?"

"Yeah. In fact, a few years ago, he asked me to recommend a doctor for her."

I watch my windshield wipers swish back and forth as I stop at the corner of Bush and Montgomery to let him out. "What are you saying?"

"I wouldn't rule out the possibility that Joel may have had some extramarital relations. Sometimes, a guy's just got to have it. And I'll bet you anything for the last six years she hasn't been giving it to him very often."

The gospel according to Mort Goldberg. "What would you suggest?"

"I think we ought to feel out the DA."

"We aren't going to consider a plea until we investigate."

He reaches for his umbrella. "You're the boss. But, if we don't get somebody else to confess by Tuesday, they've got enough to bump this case over for trial."

* * *

I have a visitor when I return to my office at eleven o'clock. Naomi looks embarrassed. She's wearing jeans and a plain white cotton blouse, no makeup. "Hi, Mike. I know I should have made an appointment."

"You can come see me anytime."

She declines my offer of water and smiles uncomfortably. "I wanted to talk to you for a few minutes."

"Sure." I don't know why she's here. "How are the kids?"

"They're okay, all things considered. It was difficult at school yesterday, but they're more resilient than we think."

"That's for sure. How are you holding up?"

"Fair."

"Understandable. Naomi, why did you come to see me?"

She looks at her fingernails. "I wanted to see if there's anything I can do to help."

"I need you to take care of the kids and yourself. And I need you to support Joel."

"I figured that much already. I'm not sure I'm up to it."

"Sure you are." I look into the eyes of this decent young woman whose life has been turned upside down. "Why did you really come here, Naomi?"

Her lips form a tight line across her face. "There are a few things I think you should know." She pauses. "Joel doesn't know I'm here. Do you have to tell him I came to see you?"

"Not if you don't want me to." Actually, if she tells me something that will impact the case, I probably have a legal duty to tell Joel. We'll see. "What is it?"

"This isn't easy to talk about."

"Take your time."

"We've had some problems the last few years. Things haven't always been so good between us. When you're the rabbi's son, you don't talk about your problems. You figure everybody at the temple will find out."

"I can relate. My dad was a cop. When other kids got in trouble, it wasn't a big deal. When I got sent home from school, word always got out that Officer Daley's son got in trouble."

"I've had some problems since the kids were born."

"It's tough with little kids. And real tough with twins."

"I've been taking medication for depression, Mike. It started right after the boys were born. And it won't go away."

"A lot of people go through the same thing."

"I know. But I think it bothers Joel." She looks down. "I feel like I've pushed him away."

"The important thing is that you're getting better."

She sighs. "There's been a lot of talk about Joel and Diana. Joel and I don't have any secrets." She's starting to cry. I hand her a tissue. "Joel told me about the incident with Art Patton at Silverado. I don't care what they say. I believe my husband. I came here to tell you that no matter what they say in the papers, my husband wasn't having an affair. I'm sure of it."

I give her a hug. "I believe you." I'm relieved he told her. I wasn't sure he would have.

She buries her head in my shoulder and sobs. A moment later, she lifts her tear-stained face and looks at me. She blurts out emphatically, "My husband isn't a killer, Mike."

* * *

Later the same afternoon, Rosie's secretary and niece, Rolanda, brings in a large manila envelope. It contains police reports, photos and the medical examiner's report.

I always start with the pictures. They put things into perspective. When you put aside the news reports and the lawyerly posturing, the pictures tell the essential story. Two people are dead.

The photos are about what I'd expect. Bob's partially destroyed head. Diana sitting near the door, eyes open, chest covered with blood. A .38-caliber revolver on Bob's desk.

The medical examiner's report is succinct. The time of death was somewhere between one and four a.m. Medical examiners always give themselves a little wiggle room. Diana was killed by gunshots to her lung and heart. Bob died of a single bullet to the head. The wound had the outward appearance of being self-inflicted. Traces of gunpowder were found on his right hand. Powder marks and burns were found on his head at the entrance wound. There was an apparent concussive injury to his head above the exit wound.

Based on what I've seen so far, Mort's probably right. Unless we get a confession from somebody other than Joel by Tuesday, this case is going to trial.

I flip through the police reports. It's all there. The fingerprints. The arguments. The phone messages. The alleged threats. I'm about to pick up the phone when the last police report catches my eye. It's signed by Roosevelt's partner, Inspector Marcus Banks. It describes an interview with Joel at the Hall of Justice on January 8. It contains no new information, except for the last paragraph, which describes some questions Banks asked Joel. It then says, in capital letters, "SUSPECT CONFESSED TO THE MURDERS OF HOLMES AND KENNEDY."

CHAPTER 16

"HOW STUPID DO YOU THINK I AM?"

"It's an open-and-shut case. We will reveal evidence at the preliminary hearing that will cause Mr. Friedman to change his plea to guilty."
— Skipper Gates. CNN. Wednesday, January 14.

"Of course I didn't confess," Joel insists. "For the love of God, Mike, how stupid do you think I am?"

I'm sitting in Rabbi Friedman's living room the following morning, getting Joel's version of the Marcus Banks interview. "Tell me about your interview with Banks."

"I spent about four hours with Banks and Johnson at the Hall. I told them everything. They asked about Diana's sex life. I told them I didn't know who she was sleeping with. They seemed to think she was sleeping with me."

"Where did Banks get the idea you confessed?"

"He made it up."

"You sure?"

"We went over the same stuff about ten times. They said I wasn't a suspect. If I thought I was a suspect, I would have called you. It was about eight at night. I thought we were finished. Johnson left the room for a few minutes. While he was gone, Banks asked me if I did it. I said no. He asked me again. I said no again. He asked me if I was absolutely sure. Finally, I asked him what he wanted me to say. He said he wanted me to say I did it. And I remember exactly what I said. I said the word 'right.' "

"You agreed with him?"

"Of course not. I was being sarcastic. And he knows it."

Joel's his own worst enemy. "He seems to have taken the word 'right' a step farther than you intended."

"Then he's full of shit."

"It's still a problem."

"There's no way they can use it at trial, is there?"

"We'll get it thrown out. Did they read you your Miranda rights?"

"Nobody read me my rights until I was arrested."

"Good. We'll say you weren't properly Mirandized."

"That's not the point. He's lying. I didn't confess."

"I understand. But it's his word against yours. He's going to testify that you did."

"I'm completely screwed."

* * *

I'm in my office at eleven o'clock the same morning, My phone is pressed to my ear as I start with my best source. "Roosevelt, I got the police reports. Your partner seems to think my client confessed."

He clears his throat. "I just got a copy of his report. I didn't know."

"You were there."

"Not when he confessed."

"Allegedly confessed, Roosevelt. We're going to get it knocked out. He didn't confess and Marcus knows it. He wasn't Mirandized. If you guys were going to question him, you should have read him his rights. Judge Brown will never let it in."

"I'll see what I can find out."

"I expected better from you. I don't like being sandbagged."

"I'll see what I can find out," he repeats.

* * *

"Skipper, it's Mike Daley." I could leap through my phone.

"What's up?"

"I just got the police reports."

"So?"

"It seems Marcus Banks claims my client confessed."

"Imagine that."

"Don't play games with me."

"You want me to say that Marcus lied?"

"Yeah."

"He didn't."

"Yes, he did. We're going to the judge. We're going to get this alleged confession kicked out. He'll never let you use it."

"See you at the prelim."

* * *

"Mort," I say, "I'm e-mailing the police report I told you about. I need you to prepare a motion to get this thing tossed. I don't want it to see the light of day. I want it out before the prelim Tuesday."

I can hear the chuckle in his voice. "I'll take care of it. I talked to the judge's clerk. I told him we want to see the judge. He's available right before the prelim."

Mort may be useful after all.

* * *

The phone rings in my office again. "Mr. Daley," the familiar voice sings, "Rita Roberts, NewsCenter 4."

I swear the name on her birth certificate is "Rita Roberts, NewsCenter 4." "I'm a great admirer, Rita."

"Thank you. As you know, I'm covering the Friedman murder case."

I hadn't noticed. "I noticed, Rita."

"We've received a tip from a reliable source that Mr. Friedman confessed. Can you confirm this information?"

"Will you tell me who gave you the tip?"

"You know I can't."

"Sure you can. And if you want anything from me, you'll have to tell me who tipped you."

"I can't do that, Mr. Daley."

I stop to think. If I say there was no confession, I'll sound defensive. If I say no comment, it probably sounds worse. As Mort would say, either way I'm screwed. "For the record, Mr. Friedman did not confess. And if you run a story that suggests that he did, you will be embarrassed, and I will bring legal action against your station."

"You don't really plan to sue us, do you, Mr. Daley?"

No, I don't. "I know you'll do the right thing so it doesn't come to that."

* * *

Late that night, I run my fingers through Rosie's hair as she nuzzles my chest. Sex was always the best part of our marriage. We've come a long way since our first date when she said she wouldn't sleep with me until they took off my training wheels. Rosie taught me everything I know about sex. She was a good teacher. Before we started going out, I had dated only younger women. I had one long-term relationship with a woman in my law-school class. She dumped me as soon as she got a job offer from a Wall Street firm. By the time I started seeing Rosie, I had a lot of catching up to do. Nowadays, we have a workable arrangement. We have recreational sex every few weeks. It isn't ideal, but it's easier than looking online or in bars. Grace is staying at Rosie's mom's house tonight.

She purrs and I kiss the back of her neck. She opens her eyes and looks at me. "So," she says, "do you think Joel really confessed?"

"It's just like when we were married. Can't we forget about business for just a few minutes and focus on high-quality sex? We're consenting adults, after all."

She laughs. "Sorry, Mike. It's just the way I'm drawn."

I kiss her forehead. "That's why I'll always love you, Rosita. Even if you drive me nuts."

"Are you going to answer my question?"

"Yes, Counselor. I don't think he confessed. Marcus lied or rearranged the facts."

"Good answer. Here's your reward." She kisses me softly on the mouth. "Let me ask you another question. After your little talk with Naomi yesterday, how solid do you think their marriage is?"

Interesting question. "Very solid. At least I think so." I smile. "Maybe our marriage wasn't as screwed up as we thought." At least we never cheated on each other.

She kisses me again. "Now for the tough one. Do you think he was sleeping with Diana?"

In this game, the prizes tend to get better as the questions get harder. "I don't think so. He would have told her."

She gives me a cynical look and bites my left ear.

"Then again," I say, "I don't know for sure."

CHAPTER 17

THE MEDICAL EXAMINER AND THE CRIMINALIST

"You have to be curious to be a medical examiner. Your patients can't talk to you."
— Chief Medical Examiner Roderick Beckert. *San Francisco Chronicle*. Thursday, January 15.

"Thank you for seeing me, Dr. Beckert," I say. "I know you're busy."

"Nice to see you again, Mr. Daley," he lies politely.

At eleven o'clock the next morning, I'm meeting with Dr. Roderick Beckert, the chief medical examiner of the city and county of San Francisco, in his modest office on the first floor of the Hall. A stout sixty-two-year-old with a salt-and-pepper goatee and black-framed glasses, he is the dean of big-city coroners. And he knows it. And he'll tell you so. I wouldn't dream of addressing him other than as Dr. Beckert, and he'd never call me Mike. He has been chief medical examiner for almost thirty years. His textbook on autopsy procedures for victims of violent crimes is a seminal work. He is very good at his job.

His neat office smells antiseptic. His bookshelves hold meticulously arranged texts on anatomy and pathology. There are framed pictures of his wife, two grown children and three grandchildren. A model of a skeleton smiles at me from the corner. I've always wondered what medical examiners talk about at the dinner table.

His glasses are perched on his furrowed brow. His thick lips frown. He wears a paisley tie under his white lab coat. A tweed sports jacket hangs on a wooden coatrack in the corner.

"How may I help you, Mr. Daley?" he asks. His voice is the

perfect combination of authority and empathy, with a singsong lilt and hint of a New York accent that's particularly effective at trial. I'll bet his anatomy class at UCSF is terrific.

"Dr. Beckert, you know I'm representing Joel Friedman."

"Of course, Mr. Daley."

"I was hoping we might go through your autopsy reports on Robert Holmes and Diana Kennedy. Maybe you can help us figure out what happened."

He juts out his lower lip in a mock pout. "Mr. Daley, I already know exactly what happened. It's in my report." He knows I'm here to find holes in his work. I have a better chance at winning the lottery. "Where would you like to start?"

"Maybe you can explain how you figured out the time of death."

He flips through his report. It's an act. He can recite verbatim the contents of his reports from twenty years ago. "In both cases, I put the time of death between one and four in the morning."

"I've wondered how you figured that out." Actually, I already know. He knows I know. I still want to hear it from him. It's a free preview of his testimony.

"We look at a number of factors. First, we look at body temperature, which drops by about one and a half degrees per hour after death. Second, we look at lividity. When you die, your blood pressure goes down to zero, and your body begins to discolor. We can calculate the time of death based upon the amount of discoloration. We look at food in the victim's stomach. We see how far the digestive process has gone. We know Mr. Holmes and Ms. Kennedy ate dinner around ten o'clock. There was undigested food in their stomachs. Mr. Holmes had crab cakes. Ms. Kennedy ate a cheeseburger. We do a number of other tests."

I try to sound like an earnest high-school student. "And from this evidence, you concluded the time of death was between one and four in the morning?"

"We always give ourselves a three-hour window."

"Did you find any alcohol in their systems?"

"Mr. Holmes had a couple of glasses of wine with dinner. Ms. Kennedy had consumed a small amount of liquor late in the evening."

I'll bet he knows the type of salad dressing each of them had with dinner. "Perhaps we could look at the pictures."

"Very well."

We start with Diana. He shows me photos of her naked body lying on the stainless-steel autopsy table. I've seen hundreds of similar pictures, but I'm glad I didn't eat a big breakfast.

"Ms. Kennedy died within seconds," he says. "The first bullet pierced her right pulmonary artery and the lung parenchyma, causing a hemopneumothorax. In layman's terms, it went through her right lung, causing a collection of blood and air in the space between the lung and the chest wall. The second bullet penetrated the left ventricle of her heart."

He opens a manila envelope and pulls out three enlarged pictures of what I presume is Bob's head. He clips them to his bulletin board. He uses a gold Cross as a pointer. "Entry was in the right parietal, just above the temple. Exit in the left parietal, above his left ear. Slight upward trajectory."

This may help our suicide argument. Bob was right-handed. His analysis is consistent with a right-handed shooter. "How far was the barrel of the gun from his head when he was shot?"

He's still gesturing toward the photos. "The starburst splitting of the skin indicates it was a contact wound. I found powder marks and burns on his head. In other words, the barrel was placed against the head." His delivery is calm and clinical. He could be reciting baseball scores. He points at the picture on the right. "This is the left side of his head, or, if you'll forgive me, what was left of it. The exit wound was quite dramatic."

I'll say. Everything above the ear line is unrecognizable. "Did you find evidence of gunpowder on his hands?"

"We found gunpowder on his right hand and forearm."

This supports our suicide argument. "Your report suggests the possibility of a concussive wound on his head."

"There *was* a concussive wound, Mr. Daley." He points to the area above Bob's left ear. "Do you see this right here?"

"I'm not sure." It reminds me of the first sonogram of Grace when Rosie was pregnant. The OB could make out a head, a backbone and various organs. It looked like test pattern to me. "I'm sorry. I'm not sure what you're pointing at."

"Right here." He gestures again toward a spot near the edge of the exit wound. "It's as clear as night and day to a trained medical examiner."

I'm not a trained medical examiner.

"It may have been larger," he continues, "but part of it may have been obliterated by the exit wound. What's left is about a quarter of an inch in diameter. There's a small hematoma."

People think lawyers talk in code. Hematoma is doctor-speak for a swelling containing blood. It's hard to see in a flat picture. "How can you tell it wasn't just part of the exit wound?"

"Because the exit wound stops here. The concussive wound is a separate injury."

"How was this wound generated?"

"He must have been struck by a hard object."

I look at the pictures again. "Can you figure out the size or the shape of the object, Doctor?"

"I'm afraid not. It was heavy enough to do some damage, but there were no traces of paint or wood or metal in the skull."

"Is it possible it may have been an old wound? Maybe he bumped his head a few weeks ago."

"No. It was fresh. It's tough to see it in the picture, but if you had the body in front of you, you'd see the bump was just beginning to form. The swelling would have stopped as soon as his heart stopped beating. And if he had been hit after he was shot, there would have been no hematoma because there would have been no blood pumped to the wound."

Too bad. "Doctor, can you tell if he was unconscious when he was shot?"

"Probably."

This isn't helping. On the other hand, a big part of their case may turn on his ability to convince the jury that somebody hit Bob on the head. The gunpowder on Bob's hand is evidence he was holding the gun when it was fired.

"One last question, Doctor. Are you sure somebody hit him on the head?"

"In my best medical judgment, yes."

* * *

Sandra Wilson is the best field-evidence technician, or "FET," in the SFPD. Now in her late thirties, this African-American woman may be the ideal prosecution witness—the voice of authority combined with a tone of reason.

I've left Dr. Beckert and climbed the stairs to Sandra's claustrophobic office on the second floor of the Hall, which she shares with another criminalist. Her pens and paper clips are lined up in front of a photo of her husband. There's a picture of a toddler on the top other computer. Her UCLA diploma hangs on the wall. Her black hair is short, her eyes intense. Her sensible clothing isn't accessorized. Her husband is a cop. They aren't rolling in extra cash.

She smiles. "If my boss finds out I'm fraternizing with the enemy, I'll catch hell."

I like her. "I'll never tell."

"Good. I'm busy. What do you need to know?"

"The usual. Got any nice evidence that will exonerate my client?"

She chuckles. "Of course. We've been sandbagging you." She pulls out a manila folder containing crime-scene photos. Her tone is matter-of-fact. "As you can see, Holmes was on the floor beneath his desk, Kennedy by the door. They were both pronounced dead at the scene at eight-twenty-two. Gun was on the desk. Your client said he found it on the floor and unloaded it." She studies her notes. "Friedman's fingerprints were on the gun, the spent shells and the unused bullets. Also on the computer keyboard, the door handle and the desk."

"He admitted he was at the scene. Got anything to help me prove he didn't fire the gun?"

She hands me a photocopy of a diagram showing exactly where Joel's fingerprints were found on the gun—something she doesn't really have to do. "See for yourself."

I study the drawing. "Did you find Bob's fingerprints on the gun?"

"Several. Just the handle, however."

"What about the trigger?"

"Just an unidentifiable smudged print."

I put the diagram in my pocket. I want Pete's input. "Did you test Joel's hands or clothing for gunpowder residue?"

"No, I didn't. He wasn't a suspect at the scene. By the time he was a suspect, he'd showered and his clothes had been laundered. It would have been too late to get anything."

I appreciate her honesty. "I'll probably have to use that at the prelim."

"I know. I know. You're just doing your job."

"What can you tell me about the gun?"

"It's a Smith and Wesson thirty-eight revolver. Forensics matched the bullets. The blood-spatter analysis indicates that Holmes was sitting in his chair when he was shot."

"What about the keyboard? Skipper thinks Joel typed the suicide e-mail."

"I hope you aren't going to try to come up with some hokey chain-of-custody argument."

"I'm not." Well, I might try. Defense attorneys frequently argue the cops mishandled or even planted evidence. "I know better than to try to nail you on chain of custody. I'm curious, though. Did you find Joel's fingerprints on all the alphabetic keys?"

She glances at her notes. "Yes."

I make a mental note to see if Bob's e-mail used all twenty-six letters in the alphabet. "What about the numeric keys and the function keys?"

"We found your client's fingerprints on all of the numeric keys and three of the function keys."

That's odd. Lawyers use the keyboard to send e-mails and type documents. They rarely touch the function keys. "Did you find Bob's fingerprints on the keyboard?"

"No."

That's really odd. "Let me ask you about the voice messages."

"The message from Friedman to Holmes was recorded at twelve-thirty. We tested the system. We're sure about the time. We'll call an expert if we have to."

It's probably not worth fighting over the time of the call. "What about the call to Diana?"

"Phone company records indicate the call was initiated at twelve-fifty-one a.m. It lasted one minute and thirty-four seconds. We found the message on Diana's home answering machine."

"You're sure of the timing?"

"Yes. We tested the timing mechanism on the answering machine. And don't even think about arguing the tapes were tampered with, Mike."

"You guys aren't doing me any favors."

"This is a high-profile case. Word came from above—no screw-ups. They put the first team on this case. That's why I'm involved. That's why Rod Beckert did the autopsy. That's why Roosevelt is in charge of the investigation. If Skipper loses this case, it won't be because we screwed up."

Swell. "Sandra, do you have anything else that might be useful?"

"I'll send you copies of the security tapes."

"Thanks. Any other fingerprints in Bob's office?"

"We found prints from everybody you'd expect—from his partners to his secretary. We found Vince Russo's fingerprints on his desk. We even found one of your fingerprints on his desk, Mike." She grins. "We'll be keeping an eye on you."

"Rod Beckert seems to think that somebody hit Bob on the side of the head with a heavy object. Did you find any blood or hair on anything in his office that could have been used to knock him out? Maybe a book or a stapler or something?"

"No."

That helps our suicide argument. I thank her for her time. She's going to kill us at the trial.

CHAPTER 18

"NOBODY'S TALKING"

"Simpson and Gates has no comment concerning Mr. Friedman's case. We are confident justice will be served."
— Arthur Patton. *San Francisco Legal Journal.* Friday, January 16

The pretty young woman flashes an uncomfortable smile. "Mr. Patton will see you now, Mr. Daley."

At nine o'clock the next morning, I'm back in familiar territory—the reception area at Simpson and Gates.

Art Patton's secretary ushers me to his museum-like corner office. Like most high-powered civil litigators, there are no files cluttering his office. His slaves handle the grunt work. The Louis-the-something furniture contrasts with the heavy oriental rugs. Several modern sculptures adorn his credenza. The walls are covered with photos of Patton with local politicians. He stands to greet me. Chuckles is sitting in one of Patton's overstuffed chairs. He doesn't get up.

Patton's all smiles. "Good to see you," he lies. He doesn't sit down. If he has his way, this will be a short visit.

"I didn't realize you were going to convene an executive committee meeting."

Not surprisingly, Patton is going to act as spokesman. "When you called, we thought it would be better to do this together. We're extremely busy." His eyes dart toward Chuckles. "I know you want to talk about Joel's case. It's a very serious subject. A great tragedy." He nods solemnly. "We've given our statements to the police. We've put Joel on administrative leave, and we're going to let the justice system take its course. It's all we can do."

Smooth. And carefully rehearsed. "The police reports said you were in the office that night. I was wondering what time you left."

"If you're suggesting somebody in this room was involved, you're mistaken."

"I'm just trying to piece together what happened."

He knows I'm lying, but he'll appear evasive if he doesn't answer. "I left at one-thirty. Charles left a little later. Neither of us saw or heard anything."

It's certainly convenient they can alibi each other. "Thanks. I'm sure your story will be borne out by the security videos." They glance at each other. Let them sweat a little. "Somebody from the firm told the investigating officers that Joel was having an affair with Diana."

"I don't know anything about that. If I did, I'd tell the cops—not you."

"I was hoping you'd confirm that *you* made that accusation."

"We've given our statements to the police."

"I know you told the cops you thought Joel and Diana were having an affair."

"We have given our statements to the police."

He's going to stick to the talking points. "Is it true the firm defaulted on its equipment loans to First Bank?"

"That's absurd. The financial health of the firm is excellent. If I were in your shoes, I would be preparing a defense for my client, not harassing us."

"I can subpoena the firm's financial records."

"This meeting is over, Mike."

* * *

First Bank's general counsel, Jeff Tucker, is a tight-assed little man in his mid-thirties who started his career at S&G. He went to First Bank two years ago when Bob Holmes stabbed him squarely in the back and he didn't make partner. He's still bitter. He works in a ten-by-ten office with a dirt-caked window on the third floor of a boxy seventies office building overlooking an alley on the south side of Market Street. In a cost-cutting move earlier this year, the bank moved from palatial space on the fortieth floor of the Four Embarcadero Center tower to offices formerly occupied by a now-defunct insurance company.

It's a quarter to twelve, and Jeff wants to go to lunch. He squints at me through uncomfortable contact lenses. "I don't know anything that would help you," he says.

When in doubt, try to deflect. "I understand S&G is having some financial troubles."

"You know I can't talk about the bank's customers."

"I'm your customer. I'm a former S&G partner. If the firm goes belly-up, I may have to cough up money to help cover its debts. I can come back with a subpoena, but I'd rather not." A little overbearing, but the tough-guy act usually works with people like Jeff.

"What do you really need to know?"

"Is the firm is in financial trouble."

"Yes."

"Has the firm defaulted on its equipment loans?"

His lips get tighter. "Yes."

"How much were the loans?"

"About twenty million."

"Have you foreclosed?"

"Not yet. My superiors said it would be bad PR to foreclose on the firm right after the tragedy, so we gave them an extension."

Very un-bank-like behavior. "How long?"

"Sixty days. If they don't raise the twenty million by the end of February, we'll foreclose. It'll probably throw the firm into bankruptcy." He stands. "I've told you more than I should have. I'm late for lunch."

* * *

At noon, I'm eating a quarter pounder at the McDonald's on Pine and talking to Rosie on my cell. I ask her if she was able to reach Beth Holmes.

"Yeah. She isn't saying much. She claims she doesn't know anything about Bob's will, life insurance or investments."

"How is that possible?"

"People aren't always as forthcoming with their spouses as we were, Mike. Guess who's the executor of the estate?"

Easy question. "Everybody at the firm uses Chuckles. Dead people feel comfortable around him."

She laughs. "How did your meetings go with your former partners?"

"Lousy. Nobody's talking. Total stonewall."

"No surprise. I gotta run."

* * *

At one o'clock, I'm admiring the view of the Golden Gate Bridge from the thirty-eighth floor of the Transamerica Pyramid. Jack Frazier, Continental Capital Corporation's mergers-and-acquisitions stud, has a corner office that's far too big for a thirty-two-year-old. He's a tall blond with a vacant expression who looks out of place behind his mahogany desk. It's hard to believe this guy persuaded his corporate masters in Connecticut to pay nine hundred million bucks for Vince Russo's company. From what I gather from Joel, he's one of those young MBAs who got out of school at the right time. At the next downturn in the economy, he'll be driving a cab.

Before I can sit down, Frazier announces, "Continental Capital Corporation has no comment with respect to the deaths of Mr. Holmes and Ms. Kennedy."

And that's that.

His ever-present attorney, a dour fiftyish drone named Martin Glass, nods with approval. "Mr. Daley, we have given our statements to the police. We have nothing further to add at this time." He takes off his frameless glasses and puts them on Frazier's desk. It's amazing how everybody clams up when a defense attorney shows up.

Time to play bull in the china shop. "I don't need a lot of your time. I'm just trying to figure out what happened that night. What time did you guys leave?"

Glass responds. "I left a few minutes before ten. Jack left around one-forty-five. We went home."

They've compared notes. "Where do you guys live?"

Again, Glass does the talking. "I live in Seacliff. Jack is on Russian Hill."

I can confirm their departure times from the security videos. "How was the deal going?"

They look at each other. "Fine," says Glass.

Good answer. Says nothing. "Was it going to close?"

"Yes," says Glass, nodding. "All the papers were signed."

"What happened the next morning?"

"I got a call from your client. He told me what happened."

"I understand there was a big breakup fee."

Before Glass can respond, Frazier says, "Yes there was."

I make a mental note that Frazier can be jumpy. If he's as smart as everyone at CCC seems to think he is, he'd shut his mouth. "How much?"

Glass answers again. "That's confidential. Obviously, our client didn't want to pay it. I don't see what this has to do with your client."

"I'm just trying to figure out what was going on." And to see if your client had motive.

"Mr. Daley," says Glass, "we've told you everything we know. I feel badly. I like Joel Friedman. I hope he didn't do it. Of course, if he did, I'm sure he'll get what he deserves."

* * *

At two o'clock, I walk into Assistant City Attorney Ed Ehrlich's windowless office on the fourth floor of a mid-rise fifties office building near Moscone Center. The city can't be criticized for wasting taxpayer funds on opulent offices. The owl-eyed Ehrlich looks at home behind his metal desk. There's no artwork on the walls.

"I'm due at the redevelopment agency," he says as I walk in. "Can we talk later?"

"Sure. Can I ask you a few quick questions before you go?"

"Make it fast."

"How late were you at the S&G offices that night?"

"I went home around ten."

"Was the deal going to close?"

"As far as I knew. It was approved by CCC's board. Everything depended on Russo."

"Was the city happy with the deal?"

"For the most part. Some people were worried about funding for our loan."

"When did Dan Morris leave?"

I see distaste in his eyes. Seems Ed and the mayor's political fixer may not be the best of friends. "I don't know."

"Why did he stay?"

"To work the room. He wanted to suck up to the CCC people. Guys like that are always playing the angles."

"See anything suspicious that night?"

"Nope."

* * *

At two-thirty, I'm walking up Montgomery Street, talking to Pete on my cell. "Find anything we can use? I ask.

"I did a little checking on Russo. He never went back to the Ritz. The cop who found his car at the Golden Gate Bridge didn't see anyone. The car was registered to a limited liability company called Camelot Investments, LLC, which is owned by two trusts in the Bahamas. One is called the International Charitable Trust. The other is the Charitable Trust for Humanity. I'm checking them out."

* * *

My afternoon isn't getting any better. At three o'clock, I'm sitting in Dan Morris's office. The political consultant's office is a monument to his favorite person—himself. Two walls are lined with pictures of Dan grinning with local dignitaries whose political fortunes he's orchestrated. Another wall is adorned with framed political posters for his candidates.

A paunchy redhead, Morris is known as the Chameleon in San Francisco political circles because he'll represent candidates of every political denomination as long as they can come up with the four hundred grand he charges to run a campaign. His candidates win. Lately, he has been running a Senate campaign for Edward Cross, a Republican, and a congressional campaign for Leslie Sherman, a Democrat.

He's been on the phone since I arrived. In the last fifteen minutes, he's raised about a hundred thousand grand for Cross and another fifty for Sherman.

When he finally hangs up, there isn't a hint of remorse in his tone. "Raising money is the shits," he says.

"I understand." Don't feel any obligation to apologize for keeping me waiting.

"I hate to do this to you, but I've got to run. I'm due at the mayor's office in ten minutes."

"Can we reschedule for tomorrow?"

"I'll have to call you. I'm flying to L.A."

"Can't we talk for just a minute?"

"Can't keep the mayor waiting. I'll call you."

* * *

At four-thirty, I walk into Harrington's, a dark wood-paneled pub that's been a workingman's bar on Front Street since 1935— long before it was surrounded by high-rise office buildings.

Rick Cinelli is an olive-skinned man with a raspy voice and a reserved manner. He's been tending bar at Harrington's for twenty years. He could run for mayor. I take a seat at the bar, and he pours me an Anchor Steam.

"Haven't seen you in a while, Mike."

"Been busy, Rick." I sip my beer. "You know I left S&G."

"I heard. Helluva thing about Bob and Diana. I hear you're representing Joel."

"Yeah. Actually, that's why I'm here. I understand Joel and Diana were here that night. Mind if I ask you a few questions?"

"Ask away. I got nothing to hide."

"I heard Joel and Diana had a fight that night."

"They did. One minute they were ordering dinner. The next minute they were arguing. Next thing I know, she storms out. It lasted a minute."

"That's it?"

"That's it."

Now, the important part. "Do you happen to know what they were arguing about?"

"Nope. They were sitting in the corner. As long as they pay for their drinks, I leave them alone. That's why I've been here for so long."

It's what I expected him to say. "Could you tell if they were fighting about work?"

"I couldn't tell."

"Did you hear anything in particular?"

"He said he was going to get her for something. I remember that distinctly. He said it a couple times. "I'll get you for this.""

* * *

"Mr. Kim, may I speak to you for a moment?" I approach Homer Kim, a young custodian, at the employees' entrance to the Bank of America Building. The evening shift is about to start. I introduce myself and hand him a business card. "I wonder if I can ask you a few questions."

"Late for work," he says in broken English.

"It'll take just a minute. I'm Joel Friedman's lawyer. I understand you spoke to the police."

"Yes."

"Did you tell the police Mr. Friedman and Mr. Holmes had a fight that night?"

"Yes. Mr. Friedman was angry at Mr. Holmes." He starts to move away.

"Do you know why?"

"No."

"What did Mr. Friedman say to Mr. Holmes?"

"Don't know. I walked by the office. Mr. Friedman was yelling at Mr. Holmes."

"Mr. Kim, do you know what they were arguing about?"

"Don't know. Late for work."

"Did you hear any shots?"

"No. Late for work."

* * *

At six o'clock, I'm in my office with Rosie when Pete calls in. I put him on the speaker.

"You guys get anything?" he asks.

"Nothing useful," I say. "What about you?"

"I had someone watching Art Patton last night." I can hear the grin in his voice. "You were right about his divorce. He and his wife separated a couple months ago. He's living in an apartment on Russian Hill. Around eight last night, he went over to pay a condolence call to the Widow Holmes. He didn't leave until seven this morning."

If I ever get married again, I'll never cheat as long as Pete is still breathing.

* * *

At seven o'clock in the evening on the following Monday, Rosie, Mort and I meet with Joel and his father in Rabbi Friedman's dining room. The preliminary hearing is set for ten o'clock tomorrow, with motions at nine.

Rabbi Friedman isn't happy. "You're saying you won't be able to get the charges dropped tomorrow?"

"It looks that way, Rabbi. They've probably got enough to take the case to trial."

Mort tries to sound reassuring. "It doesn't prove they have a strong case, Rabbi. It means they have enough to get to trial."

Rabbi Friedman isn't mollified.

Joel is edgy. "So what do you plan to do tomorrow? Roll over?"

"No," I say. "We'll challenge their witnesses, but we won't tip our hand. We don't want to give them anything they can use at the trial."

"You're going to get that so-called confession knocked out, right?"

"That's the first item on the agenda. We're going to talk to the judge in chambers before the hearing. If he lets the confession in, we'll go straight to the appellate court for a writ. I don't want it to see the light of day."

Rabbi Friedman shakes his head.

Joel addresses his father. "They're doing everything they can, Dad. The legal system doesn't work so well sometimes. And it never works very fast."

It's nice when your client defends you. Things usually work better when it's the other way around.

Rosie breaks the silence. "Do you think we should ask for a change in venue? There's been a lot of press coverage. It may be tough to get an unbiased jury."

Mort chimes in first. "I still think we should stay here. San Francisco is a liberal town. I'd rather try a murder case here than almost anywhere else in California."

I agree with him. "You wouldn't want to try this case in Bakersfield or Orange County. I'd take my chances with a San Francisco jury."

Rosie says, "Assuming this moves forward, we need to think about trial dates. We'll need to prepare witnesses, get experts, talk to jury consultants. It could take some time." She turns to Joel. "You'll want to waive the rule that says they have to start the trial within sixty days."

Mort agrees. "I've never had a case where the defendant didn't waive time."

Joel sets his chin. "I'm not going to waive time."

"Can we talk about this, Joel?" I say.

"We can talk all you want. Bottom line, I'm not waiving time. My life has been turned upside down for something I didn't do. My reputation has been destroyed. My wife and kids are going through hell. I don't want to live at my parents' house for a year. This case isn't complicated. I didn't do it. I'm not going to give Skipper more time to practice. Tell the judge tomorrow that I'm not waiving time."

"Joel—," I say.

He stops me. "I'm the client. What I say goes. I'm not waiving time."

CHAPTER 19

THE PRELIMINARY HEARING

NewsCenter 4 has learned from reliable sources that Joel Mark Friedman has confessed to the murders of two colleagues. Judge Kenneth Brown will preside at the preliminary hearing at ten o'clock today."
— Rita Roberts. NewsCenter 4 Daybreak. Tuesday,
January 20.

"Your Honor," Mort begins, "we have three very serious issues."

At nine a.m. on Tuesday, January 20, Rosie, Mort and I sit in Judge Kenneth Brown's cramped chambers. Skipper and McNulty are with us. Brown's desk is littered with files and law books. There's a picture of him shaking hands with the governor.

Judge Brown is late fifties, with a lanky frame and narrow eyes. He's a former prosecutor and political ally of the mayor who is bucking for an appointment to the federal bench. At the moment, he's stuck listening to motions and conducting preliminary hearings. Unlike Judge Miller, Brown actually reads the California statutes from time to time. The scouting report suggests he's never met a prosecutor he didn't like.

He's all business. "What's the problem, Mr. Goldberg?"

This morning's motions will be Mort's show. If he can't convince his poker buddy to exclude the confession, we're in trouble. Mort's actually very good on evidentiary issues.

Mort invokes an even tone. "First, Inspector Marcus Banks has alleged that Mr. Friedman confessed. He didn't. Second, Mr. Friedman wasn't Mirandized when he was questioned. Even if we assume he did, in fact, confess—which he didn't—the confession is inadmissible. Third, somebody from Mr. Gates's office leaked the alleged confession to the press. The potential juror pool has already been irreparably tainted. We have no choice but to move for dismissal."

He'll never dismiss the case. Not a chance.

Skipper clears his throat. "Your Honor—,"

The judge cuts him off. "Mr. Gates, I'll tell you when it's your turn to talk." He turns back to Mort. "Let's take this one step at a time. I've read your motion. I'm not in a position to determine what was said. For purposes of this hearing, I have to let Inspector Banks testify about what he heard—unless I'm pretty sure he's committing perjury."

"But, Your Honor—,"

Brown stops him with an upraised hand. "On the other hand, Mr. Goldberg, your other charges are considerably more serious." He points a pencil at Skipper. "Mr. Gates, was the defendant Mirandized before the interview took place?"

"No, Your Honor. He wasn't Mirandized because he wasn't a suspect at the time."

Brown frowns. "How long was Mr. Friedman questioned?"

"A couple of hours."

I interrupt. "Actually, the interview took four hours. This issue came up at the very end."

"I see." Brown turns back to Skipper. "Did the defendant volunteer the information, or did Inspector Banks ask him if he committed double murder?"

Skipper glances at McNulty before he answers. "I believe he responded to a question."

"Mr. Gates, perhaps we should invite Inspector Banks in so he can tell us exactly what happened."

"Yes, Your Honor."

Judge Brown asks his bailiff to summon Banks, who strolls in confidently. He's sporting a stylish double-breasted gray suit. His French cuffs are accessorized with gold cuff links. He takes a seat in the last empty chair.

Judge Brown is going to ask the questions. "Inspector Banks, we understand you interviewed Mr. Friedman."

"Yes, Your Honor."

"And toward the end of the interview, you claim he confessed to committing the murders of Robert Holmes and Diana Kennedy?"

"Yes, Your Honor. That's correct."

"Was the interview taped?"

"Yes, Your Honor."

"Was this alleged confession taped?"

"Well, no, Your Honor."

Brown opens his eyes wide. "Why not?"

"My partner, Inspector Johnson, and I had concluded the formal part of the interview. We had turned off the recorder."

"And as soon as you turned off the recorder, Mr. Friedman confessed?"

"Yes."

The judge taps his pencil on the desk. "Interesting coincidence. Where was Inspector Johnson when Mr. Friedman allegedly confessed?"

"He went to get Mr. Friedman some water."

"So Inspector Johnson didn't hear this alleged confession?"

"No, he didn't."

"And nobody else heard it?"

"No."

"Your Honor—," I say.

"It will be your turn in a minute, Mr. Daley. Inspector Banks, how long have you been with the department?"

"Thirty years."

"How many murder suspects have you interviewed?"

He thinks about it for a moment. "Hundreds. Maybe thousands."

"You've heard of the Miranda rules?"

He swallows. "Yes, Your Honor."

"Here's my problem. We understand you didn't give Mr. Friedman his Miranda warnings when you questioned him.

Correct?"

"Yes."

I'm impressed with his truthfulness. He could have lied and said he read Joel his rights. It would have been his word against Joel's.

"May I ask why not?"

"He wasn't a suspect at the time of questioning."

"I see. Did Mr. Friedman volunteer this information, or did he respond to a question?"

"I believe I asked him a question."

"Which was?"

Banks looks directly at the judge. "I asked him if he did it."

"But he wasn't a suspect."

"No, Your Honor."

"How did he respond?"

"He responded affirmatively."

"In other words," Judge Brown says, "he said yes."

"That's correct."

Mort interrupts. "Your Honor, in point of fact, Mr. Friedman did not say 'yes.' He said the word 'right' in a sarcastic tone. He was being facetious."

Brown is glaring at Banks. "Is that your recollection of the conversation, Inspector?"

"No, Your Honor. I distinctly asked Mr. Friedman if he did it, and he responded affirmatively."

Nice dance, Marcus. But not good enough. "Your Honor, Mr. Banks did not answer your question." I turn to Banks. "Isn't it true, Inspector Banks, that in response to your question, Mr. Friedman responded by sarcastically saying the word 'right'?"

"That's not the way I remember it."

McNulty leaps in. "Your Honor, even if Inspector Banks asked the defendant if he committed the acts in question, he didn't need to be Mirandized because he wasn't a suspect."

Brown is unhappy. "Mr. McNulty, it seems to me that it's a long stretch to suggest Mr. Friedman wasn't a suspect if Mr. Banks was asking if he committed these crimes." He turns to Banks. "If he wasn't a suspect, Inspector, why did you ask him if he did it?"

I'm trying to find an opportunity to continue my argument that Joel didn't really confess at all. I glance at Rosie, who gives me the signal to keep my mouth shut.

Banks shrugs. "I'm not sure, Your Honor. I guess I just wanted to know."

Judge Brown looks at Skipper. "Mr. Gates, may I assume you have enough evidence to present today without this 'alleged' confession?"

The correct answer is yes.

Skipper hesitates. "Yes, Your Honor," he finally decides. "But it really would help me to get this confession in."

"Then Inspector Banks should have followed the law and read Mr. Friedman his Miranda rights." Judge Brown looks at Banks. "The defense motion is granted. The alleged confession is out."

Round 1 goes to the good guys.

Mort's expression doesn't change. "Your Honor, we have another problem. This bogus confession was leaked to the media. I've already received inquiries from several TV reporters. In fact, I heard about it on the news this morning. The potential juror pool has been irreparably tainted. I have no choice but to ask that the charges be dropped."

It never hurts to ask. The judge will never go for it.

Brown responds with an almost imperceptible grin. "Nice try, Mr. Goldberg. Denied."

Skipper looks pleased.

Judge Brown isn't finished. "I am ordering Mr. Gates to issue a statement saying there was no confession. I will approve its contents. I expect it on my desk by two o'clock."

Skipper is no longer pleased. "I resent the implication that this information was leaked from my office."

"Mr. Gates, I expect the statement on my desk by two o'clock. If it isn't, I'll hold you in contempt."

"Yes, Your Honor."

Mort goes for a gratuitous tweak. "Your Honor, I think Mr. Gates should be sanctioned for this irresponsible leak."

The bull is sprinting at full speed through the china shop. I glance at Rosie. The corners of her mouth turn up slightly.

"Your Honor," Skipper implores, "we didn't leak anything to the press."

Mort turns to him. "Oh, and I suppose you think we did?"

Judge Brown taps his pencil. "Children, please. In the spirit of cooperation, I'm not going to sanction anybody right now."

"Your Honor," I say, "I would ask you to issue an order that would prohibit any such leaks in the future."

"I'll do better than that, Mr. Daley. As of this moment, I am issuing a total gag order. I don't want any of you talking to the press. Do you understand?"

We nod in unison.

"Good. Because if anybody violates the order, I'll put them in jail for contempt. I mean it. Fines don't mean anything to you. I'll put you in jail for a long time. Understood?"

We nod again. It's like kindergarten. When the bell rings, we get to go to recess.

"I'll see you in court," Brown says.

* * *

"Nice work, Mort," I say.

Joel, Rosie, Mort and I are sitting in a consultation room behind Judge Brown's courtroom.

Mort shrugs. "We didn't get everything, but we got the confession out."

Joel's eyes light up. "Can you get the charges dropped?"

Rosie, Mort and I exchange a glance. "It doesn't look good," I say. "They don't have to show very much. They've put you at the scene. Your prints are on the gun and the keyboard. There's the phone messages. That's probably enough to push this to trial."

"But we can explain all that stuff."

"I know. But we don't want to telegraph our defense too soon."

He looks up at the ceiling and says nothing.

* * *

"All rise."

Judge Brown enters his packed courtroom and takes his place on the bench between the Stars and Stripes and the California state flag. Reporters fill the jury box. There's barely enough room for a few courthouse groupies.

Joel sits at the defense table between Rosie and me. Mort is at the end of the table. Rabbi Friedman and Naomi sit behind us in the first row of the gallery. Joel's mother is home watching the children.

The case is called. Skipper and I state our appearances for the record. Judge Brown reads the charges and says the defendant has entered a plea of not guilty. He reminds us that this is a preliminary hearing for the purpose of determining whether there is sufficient evidence to hold the defendant over for trial. Skipper gives a brief opening statement. I give an even shorter one saying, in effect, there are too many holes in the state's case to hold Joel over for trial. Then Judge Brown instructs Skipper to call his first witness.

* * *

Skipper is standing at the lectern. "Please state your name and occupation for the record."

"Dr. Roderick Beckert. Chief Medical Examiner for the City and County of San Francisco."

"How long have you held that position?"

"Thirty years."

Skipper starts to run Beckert through his credentials. Undergrad at Harvard. Medical degree from Stanford. I interrupt and stipulate to his expertise. Skipper is disappointed. He was just getting to the part where Beckert delivered the tablets at Mount Sinai.

Skipper hands Beckert a copy of his autopsy report. Beckert glances at it briefly. He quickly confirms that Bob and Diana died from gunshot wounds. Skipper sits down. He's played just enough cards for a prelim. McNulty has coached him well.

I move to the lectern. "Dr. Beckert, your report says that the wounds to Mr. Holmes may have been self-inflicted."

"Yes, but—,"

"Thank you, Doctor. You've answered my question. I have no further questions."

* * *

Sandra Wilson is next. Skipper quickly walks her through her resume. Undergraduate and master's degrees from UCLA. A nine-year veteran of the SFPD. I'll look like a jerk if I interrupt her.

She calmly walks through the physical evidence. As the sportscasters like to say, we can't stop her—we can only hope to contain her. Skipper takes her through chain-of-custody issues. She leaves no doubt the gun and the other evidence were handled and catalogued appropriately. She says the prints on the gun and the keyboard are a perfect match for Joel's. She introduces the tape from Diana's answering machine and a recording of Joel's voicemail to Bob. Joel leans over and asks whether there's anything we can do. I shake my head. Skipper sits down. He may not need to call any other witnesses.

"Ms. Wilson," I say, "did you test the defendant's hands or clothing for gunpowder residue?"

"No."

"Why not?"

"He wasn't a suspect at the scene. By the time he became a suspect several days later, his hands and clothing would have been cleaned, and the tests wouldn't have shown anything."

"So you can't prove he fired the gun?"

"His fingerprints were on the gun, Mr. Daley."

"I understand. But you can't show that he fired it."

"That's correct."

"Just one more question. Did you find Joel Friedman's

fingerprints on the trigger?"

I'm sure she expected the question. "There were smudged fingerprints on the trigger, Mr. Daley. We were unable to positively identify them."

"So, you can't affirmatively demonstrate that Mr. Friedman pulled the trigger?"

"We could not identify the fingerprints on the trigger."

I argue with the judge that she's being unresponsive. He finally gets her to admit that the physical evidence does not conclusively show that Joel pulled the trigger.

"No further questions," I say.

* * *

Roosevelt takes the stand. He confirms that Joel admitted that he was in the S&G offices the night of the incident. He describes the scene in Bob's office. He provides copies of the phone records showing the call from Joel's office to Diana. His testimony is all factual—and true. I see McNulty's influence. He figures he doesn't need to show very much to get this case to trial. I can't punch a hole in anything Roosevelt says. I'll save it for the trial. I decide not to cross-examine him.

* * *

Skipper trots out Rick Cinelli to provide straightforward testimony about the fight at Harrington's. Then he calls Homer Kim to describe the argument in Bob's office. On cross, I get each of them to admit they didn't know what the arguments were about. I get Cinelli to say that Joel and Diana may have been talking about business. I get nothing out of Kim.

* * *

I figure Skipper is about to wrap up when he calls Art Patton. The courtroom is silent as the Enormous One walks forcefully to the front of the courtroom.

"Mr. Patton," Skipper says, "were you at the Simpson and Gates firm retreat last October?"

"Yes."

"Did you see the defendant and Ms. Kennedy?"

"Several times."

"I would like to ask you about one particular time. Did you see the defendant and Ms. Kennedy at approximately three a.m. on Saturday, October twenty-fifth?"

"Yes."

"Could you describe the circumstances?"

"Objection, Your Honor. Relevance." I'm trying to break up their rhythm.

"I'll allow it," says Judge Brown.

Patton tries to look sincere. "I heard noises from Mr. Friedman's condo. I was concerned, so I knocked on his door. Mr. Friedman answered. I asked him if everything was all right, and he said yes. Then I saw Ms. Kennedy in Mr. Friedman's bed. She didn't appear to have any clothes on."

Murmurs in the gallery. I steal a glance at Naomi, who is looking down.

Skipper is smirking. "What did this lead you to conclude, Mr. Patton?"

"Objection," I say. "Speculative."

"Sustained."

"I'll rephrase," Skipper says. "Did you observe Mr. Friedman and Ms. Kennedy having a physical relationship in his room that night?"

"Objection, relevance."

"Overruled."

Patton tries to look embarrassed. He turns to the judge. "I'm uncomfortable discussing the personal lives of members of the firm."

Bullshit.

Brown says, "Please answer the question, Mr. Patton."

"It appeared that they had been in his bed together."

"No further questions."

It'll be tough to un-ring that bell. I glance at the rabbi, who is frowning. I move right in front of Patton. "Did Mr. Friedman let you into his room?"

"No."

"Did he open the door all the way?"

"No."

"How far did he open the door?"

He glares at me through his tiny glasses. "Maybe halfway."

"Halfway is about a foot, right, Mr. Patton?"

"I guess so."

"I'll bet you couldn't see much of Mr. Friedman's room through that twelve inches."

"I could see most of it."

"How long was the door open?"

"About a minute."

"What was Mr. Friedman wearing?"

"I think it was a sweatshirt and sweatpants."

"Was the light on?"

"No."

"Did you see Mr. Friedman touch Ms. Kennedy?"

"No."

"Was Ms. Kennedy under the covers?"

"I believe so."

"Yet you also testified that Ms. Kennedy appeared to be naked."

"She was."

"But you just said she was under the covers."

"I could still see her."

Sure you could. "You could see through the covers? Do you have X-ray vision?"

"Objection."

"Withdrawn. Mr. Patton, is it possible that Ms. Kennedy may have been wearing clothes or pajamas or a sweat suit, right?"

"I suppose that's possible."

"So it's possible that she wasn't naked as you previously

testified."

"It's possible."

"And you saw all of this while you were looking into a dark room through a twelve-inch gap?"

"Yes."

Now, the kill. "Mr. Patton, did you actually see Mr. Friedman and Ms. Kennedy in bed together that night?"

"No."

"Did you see them have any physical contact that night?"

Skipper's up. "Asked and answered, Your Honor."

"Overruled."

"No," Patton says, "I cannot confirm that they had any physical contact that night."

So far, so good. "Mr. Patton, isn't it true there was a social gathering at your room that same night?"

"I don't recall."

Wake up, Skipper. You should start objecting now. "Mr. Patton, I was there that night. I can provide a copy of the invitation for the party." It's nice of Skipper to let me testify. He should be up on his feet screaming. I glance over and McNulty's whispering frantically into his ear.

Patton nods. "Yes, Mr. Daley. There was a party in my room that night."

"Was Ms. Kennedy there?"

"Yes."

"Ms. Kennedy left the party because she was upset, right?"

"I don't recall."

"Let me refresh your memory. She left the party because she was upset when you demanded that she sleep with you, right?"

The courtroom roars. Judge Brown pounds his gavel.

"Objection," Skipper shouts. "There's no foundation."

Look who woke up.

"Overruled."

Patton's tone is condescending. "I haven't the slightest idea what you're talking about."

"Isn't it true, Mr. Patton, that you followed Ms. Kennedy to her room after she rejected your advances?"

Skipper's up again. "Objection, Your Honor. The witness has indicated that he doesn't know anything about this alleged incident if, in fact, it took place."

"Overruled."

I've moved within two feet of the witness box. "Isn't it true, Mr. Patton, that you attacked Ms. Kennedy in her room, and she went to Mr. Friedman's room for protection? And isn't it true that you went down to Mr. Friedman's room so you could tell everyone you saw Ms. Kennedy and Mr. Friedman in bed together if Ms. Kennedy ever accused you of sexual harassment?"

Skipper's face is red as he screams his objection.

Before the judge can rule, Patton stands up and shouts, "That's a lie!"

Judge Brown slams his gavel on the wooden base. I look at Naomi, who gives me an approving nod. Patton regains his composure and sits down.

Judge Brown looks at me. "The objection is sustained."

"No further questions, Your Honor." If Joel is going on trial, Simpson and Gates is going on trial with him.

* * *

After brief closing arguments, Skipper makes his motion to bind Joel over for trial, and I move for dismissal. Skipper's motion is granted, and mine is denied.

The judge turns to housekeeping. "Mr. Daley, do you wish to move for a change of venue?"

"No, Your Honor. We're happy to stay here in San Francisco."

"May I assume your client will waive time?"

"No, Your Honor. We have a right to a trial within sixty days. We want to go sooner, if possible."

I don't know who looks more dumbfounded—Skipper or the

judge. Skipper stands and says, "Your Honor, we have a very tight schedule at the DA's office. It is highly unusual for a suspect not to waive time in a trial of this complexity. Highly unusual."

"Your Honor," I say, "my client has a statutory right to a trial in sixty days. If Mr. Gates insists on proceeding with this unsubstantiated case, we want to clear Mr. Friedman's name right away. Mr. Gates just started at the DA's office. He couldn't have filled his schedule yet." I get a smattering of chuckles from the gallery.

Judge Brown gives me a skeptical look. "Mr. Daley, are you sure about this?"

No, I think my client is out of his mind. "Yes, Your Honor."

"Very well." He looks at his calendar and confers with his clerk. "I'm setting trial for March sixteenth in superior court before Judge Shirley Chen."

Another lousy draw. Judge Chen was recently appointed. She's another former prosecutor who will be presiding over her first murder trial.

Judge Brown turns off his computer. "Pretrial motions on March ninth. We're done."

CHAPTER 20

MOVIE NIGHT

"We have no intention of discussing a plea bargain."
— Skipper Gates. NewsCenter 4 Daybreak. Wednesday,
January 21.

Lights! Camera! Movie night!

We have gathered in Rabbi Friedman's living room the following evening to view the security videos from the night of the "incident," as we have taken to calling it. True to her word, Sandra Wilson provided six hours of grainy footage. Hopefully, we'll be able to use the fast-forward button liberally. All things considered, I'd rather be over at Joel's house watching *The Lion King* with his kids.

Joel inserts a disc into the DVD player. His father sits in a tall chair in front of the TV, drinking a Sprite. Rosie and I sit on the sofa, notepads poised. Mort is in a side chair near the TV. He won't be taking notes. Joel's mother is watching the kids again, so Naomi has joined us. She sits on the floor in front of the TV, legs crossed. I haven't talked to her since the hearing yesterday. In a modest concession to whimsy, she's made popcorn.

Pete stands behind the sofa, clutching a clipboard with a printout listing all the people who ran their security cards through the scanner to check in or out of the Bank of America Building on the night of December 30. He has a separate list of those who signed in or out by hand. We're trying to confirm what time everybody came and went. And we're looking for inconsistencies between the videos and the lists.

During the evening hours at the Bank of America Building, pedestrian traffic is funneled toward a single exit in the lobby and toward the escalator down to the garage. There are two video cameras in the lobby, one on each side of the guard desk. There's a camera by each of the six elevator banks. A service elevator stops at every floor, but you need a key to use it. There are stairs, of course, but the access doors on the office floors are locked. There are cameras by the entrance and exit to the garage. It would be pretty tough to leave the building undetected. So they say.

Pete's interviews with the security guards revealed there are no cameras in the elevators or stairs. Too expensive. Except for a few acts of vandalism, there isn't much crime in elevators. Nobody uses the stairs.

Joel hits the play button. The quality of the black-and-white video is similar to the videos of convenience store robberies on shows like *America's Most Wanted*. The time stamp is in the lower-left corner. The cameras don't move. It feels like we're eavesdropping.

Pete acts as the master of ceremonies. "The tape starts at eight o'clock. At eight-eleven, Doris Fontaine leaves the building."

We see Doris insert her security card into the scanner at the guard desk at 8:11 and fourteen seconds.

Pete's eyes are glued to the TV. "At eight-thirty-seven, Mike leaves."

I see myself leaving the building at 8:37 and eighteen seconds. Everyone in a security video looks like a criminal.

Mort chirps, "I presume this means we can rule out Mike as a suspect?"

Rabbi Friedman glares at him.

There are no surprises in the first two hours. Most of the people attending Skipper's reception leave by 8:30. The evening word processors show up at 9:00. Skipper and the mayor and their respective entourages leave at 9:15. Everything is just as I'd expect—so far.

At 9:30, the people working on Russo's deal begin to filter out for dinner. I continue to take notes. I want to confirm Joel's time line. Jack Frazier and Dan Morris leave at 9:32, followed almost immediately by Bob Holmes and Vince Russo. At 9:48, Joel and Diana leave. Frazier's lawyer, Martin Glass, and Ed Ehrlich, from the city attorney's office, leave at 10:00.

Pete reminds us Frazier and Morris went to Michael Mina, Holmes and Russo went to Tadich's, and Joel and Diana went to Harrington's. Glass and Ehrlich went home. Pete says he's talked to eyewitnesses and confirmed everybody went where they said they did.

We continue to watch the video. Not much between 10:00 and 11:15, except for Joel's return at 10:25. At 11:15, the rest of the dinner crowd begins to return. Holmes and Russo check in at 11:16. It's hard to tell, but I think Vince is staggering. At 11:18, Frazier and Morris sign in. Nobody looks refreshed after dinner. The video is consistent with the list provided by the security guards.

It's after nine o'clock when we start watching the video showing everything from midnight to two a.m.—the key times.

Our first surprise is at 12:20. Pete looks at his list in disbelief. "He isn't on the list," he mutters, as we stare at the shadowy figure of Skipper Gates passing the guard desk and walking toward the elevators.

I ask Joel to rewind. The NFL isn't the only place where slow-motion instant replays help.

I point at the screen. "Skipper walks past the guard desk, but he doesn't run his card through the scanner. He isn't on the list because the guard let him in."

Pete is irritated by the breach of protocol. "That isn't supposed to happen."

"Happens all the time," I say. "You get to know the guards. They let you in."

"What was Skipper doing there?" Rosie asks.

"We'll find out." I ask Pete if he has a checkout time for Skipper.

"Nope. As far as the guards were concerned, he was never there."

"Either he left without running his card through the scanner, or he didn't leave that night."

Nobody else comes or goes before one o'clock. The rabbi's living room is silent as we concentrate on the black-and-white images. Nobody is eating Naomi's popcorn.

At 1:10, we see the slender figure of Diana Kennedy hurrying toward the guard desk. She's dressed in a sweat suit. At 1:10 and fifteen seconds, she waves to the guard, who lets her in without running her card through the scanner. The building managers will have a fit if they see this tape.

One-fifteen. Skipper saunters past the guard desk. We replay it twice. My heart races. Silently, I hope he'll be spattered with blood. He waves to the guard, but doesn't run his card through the scanner. It confirms that Skipper was in the building after Diana returned. I make a note to figure out how long it takes the elevators to get down from the forty-seventh floor to the lobby. Skipper may have been there when Diana died. I'm not ready to accuse him of anything—yet. On the other hand, I want to keep my options open. At the very least, he has some explaining to do.

At one-thirty, Art Patton lugs his stomach, chins and eyebrows past the guard desk and runs his card through the scanner. Though there's no sound, it's clear that Patton harrumphs at the guard. Even in the middle of the night, Art can find a way to be angry at somebody he barely knows.

Five minutes later, Dan Morris and Jack Frazier walk out together. They're an odd couple—the political fixer and the investment banker. I make a note to check it out.

A morose Vince Russo waddles out on the heels of Morris and Frazier. He scowls at the guard and heads toward the escalator to the garage.

Finally, Charles Stern brings up the rear at five minutes after two, looking, as always, as though he has the weight of the world on his narrow shoulders. He looks even worse in black and white than he does in living color, although there's very little difference.

We quickly fast-forward through the next two hours of video. Except for the departures of the S&G night-shift word processors, nobody comes or goes. It's eleven-fifteen when Pete turns up the lights. Naomi brings in sodas.

Mort excuses himself to use the bathroom for the seventh time. He's gone out to the back porch twice for cigar breaks.

"Michael," Rabbi Friedman says, "is there anything from these videos that may help us?"

"First, we can place everybody at the scene, and we know what time everybody left. Everybody was in the S&G offices after Diana returned from her apartment. Even Skipper was there."

"It doesn't prove any of them did anything. And it doesn't exonerate Joel."

Mort has returned. "Rabbi, it's always good to be in a position to argue that there were other people around. It gives us options. It helps to give the jury an opportunity to blame it on somebody else. Especially if somebody else isn't particularly likable."

Joel is unhappy. "I thought our defense was going to be suicide," he says.

"It is," I say, "but Rod Beckert is going to testify that Bob was knocked unconscious before he was shot. We'll put on our own expert to rebut his testimony. But we also want to keep our options open—and that means we want to identify as many potential suspects as we can. Tonight, we identified a bunch of people who were in the building at the right time—Vince Russo, Jack Frazier, Dan Morris, Arthur Patton and Charles Stern, by my count."

"Don't forget Skipper," Rosie adds. "He was still there when Diana came back."

"I'm meeting with him first thing tomorrow. I'll ask him what he was doing there at one in the morning. The distinguished district attorney of the city and county of San Francisco will be the first name on our witness list."

Under the California rules of criminal procedure, you're required to provide a list of potential witnesses. You can get in trouble if you try to call someone who isn't on the list. You can't get in too much trouble, however, if you put someone on the list and you don't call him or her at trial. Prosecutors and defense attorneys play all sorts of games. If I thought I could get away with it, I would include every name in the San Francisco phone book on ours.

Mort grins. "I like it."

Rosie is more realistic. "They'll never let him testify."

"It'll give them something to think about."

We're gathering our belongings when Joel looks in the Macy's bag in which I brought the discs containing the security videos . "There's one more disc," he says.

Rabbi Friedman wipes his glasses. "It's late. Can't this wait?"

I look at Joel. "Your call. We can come back in the morning."

"You're meeting with Skipper in the morning. We'd better look at this now."

We return to our seats as Joel pops the disc into his laptop. Pete's puzzled. "The inventory says we've seen all the security videos," he says.

We leave the lights on. It's close to midnight.

The video starts. It quickly becomes clear that this isn't a security tape. First we see a black screen. Then we hear a badly dubbed sound track of the theme from *Law & Order*. After about ten seconds, some homemade credits appear. SIMPSON & GATES FIRM RETREAT. The music continues as the scene shifts to the lobby of the S&G offices. The picture is grainy. Somebody did a real hatchet job with a hand-held camera. S&G lawyers are taped as they walk into the reception area. Bob Holmes mugs. Diana Kennedy smiles. Art Patton scowls. Charles Stern says something that I can't make out.

The scene shifts to the Silverado Country Club in Napa. The same S&G lawyers who were shown in their business suits now appear in golf shirts and khaki pants. Some are heading toward the golf course. Others are playing tennis. One big, happy family.

"What's the point of all this?" asks Rabbi Friedman.

Joel answers him. "This was taken at the firm retreat last fall. Why is it here?"

"I can't believe Sandra included this by mistake," I say.

Pete looks intently at his lists. He finds a note from Sandra indicating the package includes one miscellaneous evidence disc in addition to the security videos.

After a few more minutes of well-dressed yuppies butchering the tennis courts, the scene shifts to a swimming pool. I recognize Arthur Patton sitting in a lounge chair.

"The white whale," Rosie says.

The theme from *Law & Order* continues to play as the tape cuts to a dinner party in the Silverado dining room. It looks like a convention for blue blazers. There's a shot of a crowded dance floor. I catch a glimpse of Diana dancing with Patton.

The video cuts to the bar overlooking the golf course. The camera pans across the crowded room. I see myself sitting next to Wendy Hogan at a table in the corner. Bob Holmes and Skipper are sitting near the door. They're surrounded by some of the best wineries in the world, and they're drinking martinis.

Patton is sitting next to Diana at the bar. He's drinking a Manhattan. Two empty glasses sit in front of him. The cameraman circles to his left and focuses on Diana, who winks at the camera. She staggers toward the door. Patton follows her. She gives him a condescending look and says something to him. They continue toward the door. As she passes the table where Joel is sitting, she arches her eyebrows at the camera, leaps into Joel's lap, cups his face in her hands and forcefully kisses him on the mouth. She turns and waves to the camera and struts out of the room.

Patton follows her. The camera pans back to Joel, who smiles sheepishly. The video ends abruptly.

Rabbi Friedman's living room is stone-cold silent. Joel's eyes are closed. The rabbi sits quietly, hands folded. Rosie stares at the screen. Pete looks at his clipboard. Mort looks at his watch. Naomi doesn't take her eyes off Joel.

"Well," I say, "maybe this would be a good time for us to break for tonight."

* * *

"How do you think the scene in the bar will play?" Rosie asks.

We're standing in her kitchen a short time later. "Pretty bad," I say.

"The security videos looked pretty good. At least there were a lot of people there when everything happened."

"Yeah."

"You don't seem convinced."

"The thing at the bar is inflammatory. What are you supposed to think if you're on the jury? We had a decent defense that Joel's an old-fashioned family guy who's been wrongly accused. Now, they'll trot out this cheesy video showing a pretty young woman throwing herself at him. Juries don't like liars. And they really don't like people who cheat on their wives."

She takes a bite of a tuna sandwich. "Do you think you may be overreacting a little bit?"

"Maybe. I just don't like it."

"Maybe we can get it knocked out. You know, that video was edited a lot."

"We'll try."

"You think he was sleeping with Diana?"

"Two weeks ago, I would have said no. Now, I'm not so sure." I look into her dark brown eyes. Rosie and I never cheated on each other. Our breakup was the result of fundamental incompatibility, which we took out on each other. "What do you think, Rosita? You've always had good instincts."

"I wouldn't bet Grace's college fund, if we had one. Do you think Skipper was involved?"

"Hard to say. I can't imagine what motive he had. But he's slippery. I just can't tell."

She kisses me on the cheek. "I guess you'll just have to ask him in the morning."

CHAPTER 21

"WHAT THE HELL WERE YOU DOING THERE, SKIPPER?"

"District Attorney Prentice Gates says he's uncovered new and compelling evidence in the upcoming double-murder trial of accused killer Joel Mark Friedman."
— KCBS NEWS RADIO. Thursday, January 22.

It's ten-fifteen the next morning, a Thursday. After making me cool my heels in his redecorated reception area for fifteen minutes, Skipper grants me an audience. He's brought his faithful companion, Bill McNulty. To even the odds, I've brought Mort, who will play the "bad cop." To his credit, he left his cigars in the car.

Skipper fondles his thousand-dollar MontBlanc pen. He looks great today. He has a press conference at eleven. Turn on the lights.

McNasty left his jacket in his office. He's wearing a light blue shirt with a blue polka-dot tie. Two Bic pens are in his shirt pocket. I can see why Skipper creamed him in the election.

"What the hell were you doing there, Skipper?" I ask. My methods lack a certain degree of finesse.

Skipper's blue eyes sparkle as he smiles broadly. He tilts his head back and laughs loudly. "I take it you've seen the video we asked Sandra to send over?"

"What were you doing in the office that night?"

"I had to get some papers for a meeting the next morning."

"That's it?"

"That's it."

I take a deep breath. "I don't suppose you considered the possibility that you should have reported your presence at the firm at one in the morning to the police?"

"I did."

"Why didn't it find its way into any of the police reports?"

"Ask the cops."

Gimme a break. "You charged a man with double murder. You decide who gets prosecuted."

McNulty makes his presence felt. "He gave his statement to the police. He didn't see anything. He went to his office on forty-six, picked up his briefcase and left."

Mort invokes a condescending tone. "The security tapes show that he was there for almost an hour. What the hell was he doing? And do you plan to testify on his behalf?"

"Don't be ridiculous," McNulty says.

Mort points a stubby finger at Skipper. "You'd better be ready to testify because you're number one on our witness list. You were there, and you're going to have to tell your story. In open court. In front of the jury. For the whole world to hear." He practically spits out the last words.

In the right setting, Mort can still be effective. For ten or fifteen minutes a week, he can still trot out some pretty impressive theatrics.

Skipper's tone is dismissive. "Go ahead and put me on your witness list. Judge Chen will never let me testify. If she does, I'll say exactly what I just told you. I picked up my briefcase. I didn't see anything. End of story."

"You'd better rehearse your lines," I say, "because you're going to have to explain to Judge Chen why you shouldn't be called." I turn to McNulty. "I'm surprised at you. Bill. I thought you knew better."

He does know better. He's playing along with his boss.

Skipper's tone turns smug. "Did you like the video from the retreat? Pretty cute when Diana gave Joel that big kiss."

"It was nothing," I say. "She was drunk."

"Whatever you say."

"Where did you get that video, anyway?"

"One of your former partners shot it."

"Who?"

"Hutch."

I should have guessed. My former partner, Brent "Hutch" Hutchinson, is a remarkable package of blond hair, gleaming teeth and a spectacular line of bullshit. His emotional development came to a screeching halt at a frat party during his sophomore year at USC. After nine years as Art Patton's personal lapdog, he finally sucked his way into the partnership last year. He isn't much of a lawyer, but he'd make a terrific TV game-show host. We're hopeful advances in medical science will someday permit his doctors to surgically remove his lips from their permanent position affixed to Art's bottom. Among his other attributes, Hutch thinks he's Cecil B. DeMille. He's always sticking his video camera in everybody's face.

"They should have confiscated his camera," I say.

Skipper is pleased. "I thought the overdubbing of the theme from *Law & Order* was a nice touch."

Mort growls, "Judge Chen will never let that tape in. It's been edited a million times. It doesn't prove anything."

McNulty's jaw tightens. "We'll get it in."

"The hell you will."

McNulty turns to me. "By the way, we got more video footage last night. We haven't had time to get it copied. If we can get Skipper's TV to work, we'll show it to you."

Skipper pushes a button behind his desk and the opposite wall opens, revealing a sixty-inch flat-screen. I'll bet there aren't any other DAs in California with a moveable wall.

"Impressive," I say. "What's playing today? *Twelve Angry Men*?"

"More footage from the firm retreat. This one's even better."

More highlights from Brent Hutchinson's video library.

Skipper dims the lights. I bet there aren't many DAs with a dimmer switch, either.

The annoying music from *Law & Order* starts again. The footage opens with a shot of a swimming pool near the tennis courts.

Nobody's swimming. The chairs are empty.

The camera pans to the hot tub. There are two people in the water—a man and a woman. The theme from *Law & Order* continues to play. The video is shot from a distance. The camera zooms in on the hot tub. From the rear, I recognize Diana's stylish haircut. She's wearing a string bikini. As the camera focuses in on her, I see the top of her bikini is unfastened.

"I didn't realize Hutch was a Peeping Tom," I say.

Skipper doesn't take his eyes off the screen. McNulty turns my way. I think he's trying to smile—an unnatural act for him.

The cameraman moves to his left, staying focused on Diana. As he circles, the camera catches the side of her face. Then he pans back. I realize she's in the hot tub with a man, and she's embracing him. The photographer moves farther to his left. He focuses on Diana. Then he focuses on the man she's kissing.

It's Joel.

Skipper turns up the lights. "You still convinced there was no hanky-panky between Diana and Joel?"

I don't answer.

"There's one other thing, Mike. We've decided to ask for special circumstances. We're going to make this a death-penalty case."

* * *

Mort's in an expansive mood as we drive toward downtown. He's also happy to get his cigars back. "In every case," he says, "there comes a time when you know whether it's a winner or a loser. Today, I think we came to an important point."

I'm not in the mood. "And what point is that, Mort?"

"The point where I'm pretty sure we're completely and totally screwed."

* * *

"He has a video of you and Diana kissing in the hot tub at Silverado," I say to Joel. We're at Rabbi Friedman's house the same afternoon. It's time to explain the facts of life. Thankfully, his father is officiating at a funeral, and his mother is at the grocery store. I add, as calmly as I can, that they've decided to ask for the death penalty.

"Shit," he says.

"We can't have any more surprises, Joel. They're going to blow a hole through our defense if you don't start telling me the truth."

"It was nothing. She got playful. We got a little carried away."

It rings hollow. "If you want to get something off your chest, now's the time. It won't get easier. They're going to use the video at trial. Tell me the truth. I need to know what was going on."

"We got carried away. That's it. I admit it. Okay? Diana and I were kissing in the hot tub. Are you happy now?"

"Does Naomi know about this?"

"No."

"You'd better tell her. It's going to come out. And it's better if she hears it from you."

"I know."

Something's going on. "What is it, Joel?"

"Naomi said she wants to take the kids down to her mother's in L.A. until the trial is over."

I don't blame her. "We need her. It can't look like she's abandoning you." I know how it feels to have a marriage shatter. When Rosie and I split up, the pain in my stomach was unbearable. I couldn't eat. I couldn't sleep. I blamed myself. She blamed herself. We were both a mess. And we didn't help each other through it. And I wasn't on trial for murder when it happened to me. "Can you talk to her?"

"I'll try."

"Good. Now tell me what was really going on between you and Diana."

"Nothing, Mike. I swear to God."

He's on the verge of tears. He's begging me to believe him. My gut tells me he's telling the truth. My brain tells me he may be one helluva liar.

CHAPTER 22

"I NEED YOUR HELP, DORIS"

"We're very confident."
— Skipper Gates. NewsCenter 4. Monday, February 16.

Doris smiles. "You haven't had much to time to fix up this place up, have you?"

Three weeks later, on Monday, February 16, at ten in the morning, Doris is getting another look at my office. Nothing much has changed since her last visit, except for the boxes of files and evidence for Joel's case.

"I always water your plant," I say.

"Good thing." She gives me a hug. She's tan and more relaxed than I've seen her in a long time. She scrunches her face. "The daily special next door must be kung pao chicken."

She's probably right. "How was your trip?"

"Great. I love the Bahamas. I've met a lot of people down there over the years. Bob had business with a couple of the bankers. They showed me a good time."

"How's Jenny?"

"Okay. Last semester. A lot of stress." She shows me photos from her trip. After a few minutes, she turns serious. "Mikey, why did you ask me to come down here today?"

"I need your help, Doris."

* * *

Doris takes a sip of bitter coffee. "If you want to understand Bob, you have to go back to his early years at the firm. Things were different. The firm was smaller. The legal profession was a lot less complicated."

Ah, the good old days.

She adjusts her collar. "They hired Bob right out of Harvard to work with Leland Simpson. I was Leland's secretary."

"What was he like?"

"A gentleman, although some people thought he was a greedy old son of a you-know-what."

I never met him. According to my sources, he was an elegant man from one of the wealthiest families in the city. Depending on who's telling the story, he may also have been racist, sexist and anti-Semitic.

She continues. "Leland tried to take Bob under his wing, but Bob thought he knew everything. He told me on his first day he was going to be running the place within five years. Leland had him pegged. He said we'd have to take him down a rung or two."

"Was Bob married?"

"Yes. His first, to his high-school sweetheart, Sue, who was pregnant with his first son, Robert III. The marriage lasted only a year or two. By the time the baby was born, they were already separated. She left him and went back to Wilkes-Barre. There was a rumor that she ended up in an institution."

If working with Bob was hard, I can't imagine what it was like living with him. "Did the divorce have any effect on him?"

"Not really. He used to say he was going to sleep with every unmarried woman in the Bay Area. There was no such thing as AIDS back then."

He was developing habits for the rest of his life.

"Things weren't going so well for him at the firm," she says. "To be honest, he was lazy. His career limped along for a few years. At one point, they were going to ask him to leave. Then he married Elizabeth Sutro, whose father was the presiding judge of the San Francisco Superior Court. He started getting introductions into some of the city's tonier circles. Leland decided it might be a good idea to keep him around."

"You don't want to offend the presiding judge."

"Something like that, Mike."

I find it difficult to picture Bob Holmes in black tie at social functions in Pacific Heights.

"Then Bob got involved with Leland's biggest client, Vincent Russo Sr. He was a doctor from Hillsborough who made a lot of money and invested it in real estate. Eventually, he gave up his medical practice to manage his investments. According to Leland, Vince senior predicted every trend in the real-estate business for twenty years. He practically invented the real-estate syndication business. He made a fortune."

"Which his son pissed away," I say. She knows more about Russo's business than I thought. "How did Bob get involved with Vince senior?"

"Right place at the right time. Vince senior had two in-house lawyers. Ron Dawson was a decent attorney, but not the brightest star in the galaxy. Joan Russell was really smart. When she got pregnant, she took six months off. Dawson was overwhelmed, so Vince senior asked Leland if he could borrow an attorney until she returned."

"So Leland lent him Bob?"

"Yes. Leland was happy to get Bob out of his hair. Instead of staying for six months, he stayed for three years. He spent his time sucking up to Russo and Dawson. They loved him."

She explains that shortly after Bob returned to the firm, Leland had a heart attack and died. Bob was the only attorney at the firm who had extensive contact with Russo and Dawson.

"Sounds like he had pretty good leverage," I observe.

She fingers the gold chain that holds her glasses. "I'll never forget Leland's funeral. Bob pulled me aside and said he had the firm by the 'short hairs.'" She makes little quotation marks in the air with her hands. "He told me he'd take care of me if I stuck with him. I thought it was disgusting. He got a couple of offers from other firms. He told Art if they didn't make him a partner, he'd take Russo's business with him to Pettit and Martin. So they rolled over.

Made him a partner two years early. Gave him a big office and his own secretary—me. And pretty much everything else he asked for."

"The monster was born."

"Something like that."

* * *

Doris and I have adjourned to the Chinese restaurant. I munch a spring roll. Doris chews a pot sticker.

"What happened with Bob and the former Elizabeth Sutro?" I ask.

"Their marriage lasted almost five years. He seemed happy. She was pretty and rich. They had three kids and bought a big house on Broadway. Servants and everything. The firm was paying him a fortune. They put him on X-Com."

"He was running the firm by the time he was thirty-five."

"Yes. But in the early years, he was much more businesslike. He instituted financial controls. We opened the overseas offices. Then he started to get on everybody's nerves. The old-timers resented him because he kept insisting they bring in more business. The younger partners resented him, too, because they thought he manipulated the compensation system. Every year, he demanded more money. Every year, they gave in to him. He targeted partners he didn't like. Cut their points. Some got fired."

I'm familiar with that scenario.

She sips her tea. "Things got nasty during his second divorce. He swore off sex for a short period. It was supposed to be a year, but it only lasted about a week."

"Then he found another girlfriend."

Wife number three was Elizabeth Jorgensen, the weekend anchor on Channel 4. Around the firm, she was known as Elizabeth II. A year later, she dumped Bob and ran off with the weekend weatherman.

* * *

It's almost one. The waiter brings us fortune cookies. We're up to wife number four, Elizabeth Ryan, or Elizabeth III, a litigator with Sheppard Mullin. She's always been polite to me, but I wouldn't mess with her.

Doris opens her fortune cookie. "You know Beth used to be married to Art Patton."

"I wasn't aware of that."

"Art wasn't happy when she married Bob."

I'll bet. "Is that when Art began his search for the perfect trophy wife?"

She doesn't answer. "Bob and Beth were married five years ago. They had three kids. Of course, he was sleeping around the entire time."

Give him points for being consistent. Sort of like a dog in perpetual heat, without the charm.

"About two years ago," she says, "Beth told him she'd had enough. She said she'd divorce him and take every penny. He was good for about six months."

A new record.

"Then he met Diana. He was infatuated with her."

I could understand why. After almost three hours, we've finally made it to the good stuff.

"Mike," she says quietly, "am I going to have to testify at the trial?"

Damn right you will. "I hope not. If it helps Joel, we may have no other choice. I'll try to keep you out of it if I can."

"I figured you'd say that."

"I know you and Bob were close, but I'm running out of time and leads. I need you to tell me what you know."

She takes a deep breath. "Bob and Diana had a torrid affair. He sent her flowers. They met at hotels during the day. They used to sneak off on business trips."

"How long was this going on?"

"From the time she started until the beginning of December. They were at it for a little over a year. That's when Beth found out.

It's a miracle she didn't figure it out sooner. Everyone at the firm knew about it."

Everyone but me.

"She hired a private eye. He caught Bob and Diana in bed. Beth told him she was going to file for divorce. I was there the night she confronted him. He begged her for one last chance. He broke it off with Diana."

"And?"

"Obviously, the reconciliation was unsuccessful."

Duh, Mike. She did, in fact, serve him with divorce papers. I ask the waiter for the check. "Doris, did you know Diana was pregnant?"

Her eyes dart away. "Yes, I knew."

"Do you have any idea who the father might be?"

"I don't know."

"Do you think it could have been Joel?"

"Come on, Mike. You know Joel. Not a chance."

* * *

At two o'clock, we're back in my office. "What was young Vince Russo like?" I ask.

"A pig. A sexist. A self-centered jerk."

"Don't sugarcoat it, Doris."

She doesn't smile. "He was a wild animal. He treated everyone like dirt. He cheated on his wives. He cheated his business partners. He's lucky he didn't end up in jail."

"Were he and Bob friends?"

"In a manner of speaking. Bob pretended to be friends with any client who paid him a lot of money. Bob hated his guts, but Vince didn't know it."

"Did they socialize?"

"They went on business trips together to the Far East. If chasing thirteen-year-old virgin barmaids in Thailand falls within your definition of socializing, the answer is yes."

"Do you think he may still be alive?"

"Wouldn't surprise me."

I move on to another subject. "Do you know anything about Bob's will?"

She nods uneasily. "I typed it. I'd rather not talk about it."

"I understand. But it's going to become a matter of public record. It will save me a lot of time if you can tell me the names of the beneficiaries."

She pauses. After more than twenty years of guarding Bob's secrets, she's uncomfortable revealing the terms of his most personal document. "A third to Beth, a third to the kids and a third to charity."

Sounds pretty straightforward. "Do you know if Bob was going to change his will?"

"Maybe. He asked me to print out a copy of his will the day before he died. He didn't ask me to make any changes."

"Did he have a lot of money?"

"I would think so. He kept his finances private."

No big surprise. "Do you know which charities were named in the will?"

"Actually, it's a charity down in the Bahamas called the International Charitable Trust. He donated a lot of money to it over the years."

That name keeps popping up. "Do you know what the International Charitable Trust does?"

"I'm not sure."

"Do you know how we can get in touch with them?"

"There's a banker in the Bahamas named Trevor Smith who handles everything. I'll get you his phone number."

It's time to play a hunch. Finding out the story behind the International Charitable Trust is going to the top of Pete's priority list.

CHAPTER 23

THE GRIEVING WIDOW

"My husband would have been touched by the great outpouring of love when he died."
— Elizabeth Holmes. Interview on NewsCenter 4.
Tuesday, February 17.

I summon my best priest-voice as I address Bob's widow. "I'm terribly sorry about what happened, Beth. I know there isn't anything I can say to change things."

The next morning, I'm sitting in the Versailles-like living room of the Presidio Terrace mansion Beth Holmes shared with Bob. Although six and a half million bucks doesn't buy as much as it used to in San Francisco, Presidio Terrace is about as tony as it gets. The turn-of-the-century homes are occupied by a U.S. senator and her investment banker husband, several Fortune 500 CEOs, a few tech entrepreneurs who hit it big, and a smattering of San Francisco aristocracy.

She lights a cigarette. "Thanks. You don't have to lay it on too thick. Everybody knows I served him with divorce papers."

As far as I can tell, she isn't overwrought with grief.

She's early forties, with unnaturally bleached-blond hair, leathery skin from the tanning machine, a slightly altered nose, several minor enhancements to her hips and, if I'm guessing right, breasts. If all of her bodily adjustments slip at the same time, she'll look like a rubber band shooting across the room. She's also one helluva commercial litigator. She reminds me of her ex-husband, Arthur Patton, minus the charm or the chins.

"I know this is difficult, but I was hoping you might be able to help us sort out what happened that night."

She smiles knowingly. "I find Skipper's version of the story a lot more convincing than yours."

At least we're starting on an even keel. "I understand you were at Bob's office that night."

"I wanted to see the look on his face when I served him with divorce papers."

"Couldn't you have waited until after the closing?"

"I *wanted* to deliver the papers in the middle of his stupid closing, while all his buddies were around. Especially that pimp, Vince Russo, and the little tramp, Diana. Sweet little Princess Diana." She mutters something under her breath that rhymes with the word "runt."

I take a sip of the iced tea from the crystal glass provided by her maid. "I realize it's none of my business, but you know I've got to ask. What happened between you and Bob?"

She takes a long drag on her cigarette. "The same thing that happened with you and Rosie."

I think she may have intended that as a cheap shot. "Was he seeing another woman?"

"For God's sake, Mike. Everybody knew he was shtupping Diana. When I found out about it at the beginning of December, I threw him out. He promised he'd make it up to me. Then he hopped right back in the sack again."

"With Diana?"

"Yeah. And with anybody else without a penis. He was like a rabbit."

"Why didn't you file divorce papers sooner?"

"I gave him one last chance. He behaved for a week. Then my PI caught him with another woman. I threw his ass out for good." She stubs out her cigarette in the crystal ashtray.

"Do you know if he was still seeing Diana at the end of December?"

"I don't know for sure."

"Do you know if he was seeing any other women?"

"I don't know that, either. My PI definitely saw him with little Diana in the beginning of December. And my PI saw him with somebody else after that. We couldn't ID her. It may have been a hooker, if my guess is right. He saw them at the Fairmont."

"Would you mind if I talked to your PI?"

"No problem." She turns to a servant who is standing by the door and speaks to her in Spanish. The servant leaves the room for a moment, then reappears and hands me a business card. It says Nick Hanson, Private Investigator. I recognize the name. I put the card in my pocket.

I change the subject. "We got a copy of Bob's will." A small lie. Actually, all I know about the will is what Doris told me. "It seems you may inherit quite a bit of money from him."

"It doesn't make up for all the crap, but it's not a bad consolation prize."

Interesting choice of words.

She plays nervously with her hair. "Charles Stern is handling everything. He's as dull as a parking meter, but he's good. A third of the estate goes to me, a third goes to the kids and the rest goes to some charity in the Bahamas."

"Do you happen to know the name of the charity?"

"It's called the International Charitable Trust."

Hello again. "Do you know anything about it?"

"Nope. Charles might be able to tell you something. Bob gave them a lot of money."

"Did it occur to you that if you split up, he might write you out of his will?"

"Yes."

"And you realize, of course, that his untimely death means your claim to one-third of the estate remains in place."

She pushes the phony blond bangs from her eyes. "I don't like the implication. I don't need the money. We can live perfectly well on my draw."

It's true, I'm sure. She must pull down at least a million bucks a year. Nice piece of change for a woman who's been described from time to time as trailer park trash from Texas. She may lack a certain amount of finesse, but she's made it on her own in the big boys' world.

I decide to try something else. "Was there any life insurance?"

"It's none of your business. But the answer is yes. There's a million-dollar policy for each of his kids and a five-million-dollar policy for me."

At least I know where the money's going. Of course, I'd assume the beneficiary on the five-million-dollar policy would have been changed after the divorce. And she may get nothing if Bob committed suicide. Life insurance policies contain a clause that says the beneficiary won't be paid if the named insured commits suicide within a couple of years after the policy is issued.

I ask her what she knows about Russo.

"He's an asshole. And a crook."

"I think we can all agree on that. We're still trying to find him. Some people think he and Bob may have had some investments together."

"Whatever Bob did with Russo was between the two of them. Bob never talked about it with me. And frankly, I didn't want to know. As far as I'm concerned, they were just two horny bastards chasing underage girls in Southeast Asia."

Not much left for discussion there. "Do you still see some people from the firm?"

"Charles Stern has been helpful. Art's been very supportive. It's nice when your ex still cares."

In many ways. "Do you think Bob was so distraught about the divorce that he decided to kill himself?"

She cackles. "Don't be ridiculous, Mike. He was a few hours from a three-million-dollar bonus. That's all he ever cared about. He changed wives more often than most people change socks. The only thing he was upset about was the fact that his little floozy, Diana, wasn't sleeping with him anymore. But he wouldn't have killed himself for it. Not a chance. Not with a three-million-dollar check waiting for him."

I'm sorry I asked.

She blows a smoke ring toward me. "You don't have to take my word for it. You can talk to his shrink. She's that nutcase up in Marin County with her own radio show. Dr. Kathy Chandler. Give her a call. If you can't get her office, try her on the radio."

* * *

"Mrs. Fink," I say, "I know this is difficult, and I appreciate your taking the time to see me."

Diana's mother, Ruth Fink, lives by herself in a cheerful bungalow at Twenty-second and Clement, about a mile from Joel's house. She's a heavyset woman in her late fifties with gray hair and lifeless eyes. Her kitchen cabinets are at least sixty years old and look as though they haven't seen a paintbrush in the last forty. There are two pictures of Diana in the living room. Unless someone told you it was the same person, you'd never know. The woman in the first photo weighs at least 250 pounds and has brown hair and a long, crooked nose. The second photo shows the trim, blond, sexy Diana that I knew. Joel was right. It was a rebirth.

"It's been very difficult," she says. "My husband died when Debbie was in her teens."

I'd forgotten that Diana was Debbie until her first year of law school.

"We managed to get by on my salary at the JCC and a few odd jobs that I picked up. We were lucky. We had enough life insurance to take care of most of the basics."

"Were you and Debbie close?"

"Yes, until she went to law school at UCLA. She got in with a different crowd. She changed." She glances at Diana's picture. "She became less attentive to her studies. She stopped coming home at the holidays. She became fixated on herself. And making money." She takes a sip of water. "Then she got married to that boy Billy. He was her instructor at the health club. I knew it wouldn't work out. She barely knew him. I tried to stop her. I'm sure it only pushed her toward him. The marriage lasted less than a year."

I think about Grace and wonder how I'll react when she brings home her first boyfriend. The kid better have an impressive resume.

"Mr. Daley, I just wanted what was best for my daughter. I wanted her to go to good schools and to get a good education. Is that so terrible?"

"Of course not, Mrs. Fink. That's what we all want for our kids."

"Toward the end, I hardly knew her. She started dating married men."

I keep my tone gentle. "Things don't always work out the way we hope. Did she ever mention Joel Friedman?"

She closes her eyes. "Yes, Mr. Daley. Diana was very fond of Joel. He was popular. I've known Joel and his father for years. I always thought Joel was a good boy. Now, I'm not so sure."

"Did Debbie have many friends?"

"Not really. She kept in contact with some of her friends from law school. The only people she ever mentioned from the office were Bob Holmes and Joel." She gives me a thoughtful look. "Did you know that she had resigned from the firm?"

"No."

"She had accepted a job in San Diego."

I wasn't aware of this. "Why was she leaving?"

"She wanted a fresh start. You knew that she was pregnant."

"I did. Why San Diego?"

"My sister lives there. I was planning to move down there, too. I thought it might be a good time for a fresh start for all of us. This house has a lot of memories."

"I see." Joel didn't mention that Diana was moving. "Mrs. Fink, I know this question is going to sound indiscreet."

She stops me. "I know what you're going to ask, Mr. Daley. The answer, I'm afraid, is I don't know who the father is."

"Thank you very much. You've been extraordinarily helpful."

CHAPTER 24

"I WOULD NEVER ASK YOU TO VIOLATE ANY CONFIDENCES"

"The only things in life that are certain are death, taxes and the need for tax lawyers."
— Charles Stern. Continuing legal education seminar.

The next morning I'm at the S&G office on a fishing expedition. Charles Stern has promised to give me copies of the firm's key-man life insurance policies. He's trying to appear cooperative. I could subpoena the firm's records. He knows it. I know S&G carried a life insurance policy on Bob. I'm trying to confirm how big the policy is. More important, it's a pretext to see if I can find out anything else about his will and finances.

I'm surprised he's agreed to see me. And I'm really surprised he's agreed to see me alone. Seems every time I show up at S&G, I'm greeted by the entire executive committee.

I accept his offer of coffee. He buzzes his secretary, and a cappuccino magically appears. There's something to be said for big-firm amenities.

His functional office has S&G's standard-issue executive furniture: industrial-strength rosewood desk, matching credenza, two guest chairs and a bookcase. Most of the power partners have custom-built furniture that they pay for themselves. Not Charles. He's too cheap for anything other than basic inventory. There's a gray sofa next to the door, which he pilfered when one of my partners was fired. The only picture on the wall is a *New Yorker* cartoon of an accountant hovering over a tax return. An antique adding machine sits on a small table beneath the cartoon. He once told me his father is the oldest living person still licensed to practice accounting in the state of New York. The bookcase holds a dozen black loose-leaf volumes. The gold lettering on the spine proclaims they're called the *CCH Standard Federal Tax Reporter*. Most people read the electronic versions of these reports. Not Chuckles.

His desk is immaculate. Not a scrap of paper or a speck of dust. I've always admired people who have a clean office. A state-of-the-art laptop sits on a small table next to his desk. It isn't turned on. It shows that he got the firm to buy him the computer. He isn't expected to use it.

He drinks coffee from a mug that bears the S&G logo. He's wearing his gray suit jacket. He straightens his tie and looks at me uncomfortably. "What can I do for you?"

"I was hoping you had a chance to put together the copies of the firm's insurance policies."

"I did." He buzzes his secretary and asks her to bring in a file marked "Insurance Policies." Charlotte Rogers is a middle-aged African-American woman who's been with Charles for about fifteen years. She's the lucky soul who gets to type his memos on billing procedures. She's reasonably pleasant about it. She appears with a large file folder almost as soon as he hangs up.

"Our malpractice policy is in there," he says. "I haven't the slightest idea why you'd want to look at it. I put in a summary of our medical policy. I can get you a copy."

I couldn't care less about the malpractice and medical policies. "Were you able to track down any life insurance policies?"

"There's a key-man policy on every partner. I've enclosed a summary of the terms. If you'd like the details, you can talk to our insurance agent."

"Hopefully, that won't be necessary." I'll see what I can get from the agent later. "How much life insurance do you carry on the partners?" This is, of course, something I should already know. I'm sure it was in a memo Charles sent out to the partners sometime in the last decade or so.

"It depends," he says.

"On what?"

"On how valuable the partner's practice is to the firm."

"I see." This means they probably had a ten-million-dollar policy on Bob and a five-thousand-dollar policy on me. "How big a policy did you carry on me?"

I get the hint of a grin. "The minimum. Fifty thousand."

More than I thought. "And the policy on Bob?"

"I think it was five million."

Not bad. Bob was worth only a hundred times more than I was. Bob would have said he was worth more. "Do you have any other policies on the partners?"

"No. We're starting the process of changing carriers. Brent Hutchinson is in charge of insurance issues."

Perfect. S&G's best bullshitter gets to spend his free time schmoozing with insurance salesmen. I wonder if some sort of harmonic convergence occurs when that much bullshit is jammed into one room. "Maybe I should talk to Hutch."

"I doubt he'll be able to tell you much. He was just getting started."

Hutch probably hasn't started at all. "I was hoping you might be able to help us figure out Bob's will."

He looks at his watch. "I'll do what I can." He hits the do-not-disturb button on his phone. He probably wishes he'd had a similar button installed on his brain. "I can't say much. Attorney-client privilege, you know. And I've got a meeting."

So many meetings. So little time. I glance at the picture of the accountant. The resemblance is striking. "I would never ask you to violate any confidences, Charles." The game begins. "I understand you're the executor of Bob's will."

"I am. It'll become a matter of public record as soon as it's submitted to the probate court. We've notified the beneficiaries."

He's being a little too forthcoming. This probably means there's nothing of consequence in the will. "I appreciate your honesty,

Charles. It's easier to do this informally. I was afraid Art was going to make me get a subpoena just to talk to you."

"He was just being careful. I'd rather tell you what I can. There's no point in turning this into something contentious."

Now I'm sure there's nothing important in the will. "Thank you, Charles."

"Besides, I like to help out my partners whenever I can."

I hadn't noticed this generous side of his personality when he and the other partners voted to fire me. "I understand his estate's divided into three parts. A third goes to Beth, a third goes to the kids and a third goes to some charity in Bermuda." I'm trying to set him up. I know the International Charitable Trust is set up in the Bahamas. I want to see if he'll correct me. And if he'll talk about it.

"Actually," he says, "the charity is in the Bahamas."

I pretend to make a note on my legal pad. "The Bahamas. What's the name of the charity?"

"What difference does it make?"

"Probably none," I lie. "I'm just trying to complete my file."

"It's called the International Charitable Trust."

"Does it benefit underprivileged kids or something?"

"Something like that."

You're a lousy liar. "Is it managed in the Bahamas?"

"Oh yes."

"You wouldn't happen to know who manages it, would you? I'm sure we could look it up, but it'll save me some time if you know. I'll bet there's a registry of charitable trusts."

"I really don't know very much about it."

I take it back. He's not just a profoundly lousy liar. "Actually, it's probably not important. I'm sure the money goes to widows and orphans." I shuffle my papers. "My investigator got a little information. Says here the trustee is First Bank Bahamas. A guy named Trevor Smith. I'll give him a call."

"I know Trevor. I've worked with him on some cases. I'd be happy to give him a call. I'll see what I can find out."

"I don't want to impose on you. I know you're busy. I'll call him."

"It's no problem—really. Let me save you the trouble."

How magnanimous.

"Bob checked it out," he says. "I'm sure everything is completely legal and aboveboard."

I'm convinced. "Does First Bank get a fee for acting as the trustee?"

"What difference does it make?"

"Just curious."

"I think they get a fee."

I'm *sure* they get a fee. "A large one?"

"I don't know. It's probably based on the amount of assets in the trust."

"I see. And do you know how much that fee might have been last year?"

His eyes dart toward the adding machine. "I really wouldn't be able to venture a guess."

Sure you would. "Are you involved in the administration of the trust?"

He squirms. "Technically, I hold the title of trust protector. It means I'm the administrative agent. It's just a formality. All the management is in the Bahamas. Bob asked me to act as trust protector in case they needed a signature in a hurry."

"Does S&G get a fee for the time you spend administering the trust?"

He tugs at his tie. "No, it doesn't."

S&G doesn't do much *pro bono* work. "If you're the administrative agent, how come S&G doesn't get a fee?"

He shifts in his chair. "I'm paid a modest fee for my efforts."

"I don't understand. If you're doing this trust administration on behalf of the firm, why doesn't the firm get the fee?"

"I do trust administration on my own time, and not on behalf of the firm. It's a liability issue."

"A liability issue?"

"Yes. This is a law firm. The services I provide to the trust fall into the category of fiduciary activities, which our malpractice policy doesn't cover. We notified our malpractice carrier when I was first asked to serve as trust protector. They wouldn't let me do it unless I agreed to do so in my individual capacity, and not in my capacity as an attorney in the firm."

Sounds like our malpractice carrier wants to insure just the right side of his brain. "So you did this at the insistence of our malpractice carrier?"

"I had no choice. I had to sign an agreement stating that I would indemnify the firm for any losses it incurs in connection with the activities of the trust." He gives me a "so there" look.

"You must collect a fairly hefty fee for this work—especially if you have to carry your own insurance and bear the risk of indemnifying the firm for any losses."

"My fee is modest. I did it as a favor to Bob."

And out of the goodness of your heart. "If you don't mind my asking, Charles, about how much was your fee last year?"

He tenses. "That's none of your business, Mike."

It's the answer I expect. "I understand. What happens to the trust now? Where does the money go now that Bob's dead?"

"I believe it's distributed among various charities in the Bahamas."

Of course. "Charles, do you happen to know what those charities are?"

"I don't recall, Mike."

Very persuasive, Chuckles. You're the administrator of a trust in which you don't know the beneficiaries. The fog is getting really thick. "Think you could find out for me?"

"Probably. It may take some time."

I'll hear from him the Tuesday after hell freezes over. "Maybe Trevor Smith can get me a list."

"I'll call him for you."

"That won't be necessary." I love to watch him squirm. "Charles, you know that Beth served Bob with divorce papers right before everything happened. Was he going to change his will?"

"Not that I'm aware of."

"Did you do the estate planning work for Vince Russo?"

"I did."

"Do you know the names of the beneficiaries of his estate?"

"I'm afraid that's confidential, Mike. I realize some people think Vince may have committed suicide. However, until a court declares him legally dead, his estate does not become a matter of public record. As a result, I'm not at liberty to discuss his situation with you."

"You haven't heard from Vince, have you?"

"No."

"Well, if you do, I'd appreciate it if you'd let me know."

"I promise."

I glance out the window. "Let me ask you one other thing, Charles. How's the firm doing?"

"Fine."

He'd never make it as a trial lawyer. "I'm sure the tragedy has taken its toll."

"It has." He tries to look solemn. "We've had some difficult times. But nothing insurmountable."

I look at the adding machine. "I saw in the paper you decided to let some people go."

"We did. It wasn't easy."

"Layoffs never are, Charles."

"They weren't layoffs. We do reviews this time of year."

I'm convinced. "By the way, could you ask your secretary to give me the phone number for Trevor Smith?"

* * *

"He's full of it, Mike," Rosie says.

Later the same evening, Rosie, Grace and I are eating at Spanky's, a burger joint in Fairfax, not far from my apartment. It's been Grace's favorite restaurant since she won a free sundae in a coloring contest a couple of years ago.

Rosie's reaction to my report on my discussion with Charles Stern is succinct. "I'll bet he knows everything there is to know about the International Charitable Trust. He's yanking your you-know-what."

Rosie's vocabulary switches from R to PG when Grace is around.

Grace's eyes open wide as she takes a long drink of her milkshake. She wipes her mouth with the back of her hand and says, "What's your 'you-know-what,' Daddy?"

I smile. "Ask your mother."

Rosie nods. "I'll explain it later, honey."

I turn back to Rosie. "I called Trevor Smith. He has a beautiful British accent. And he wouldn't tell me anything."

"Anything else?"

"He's going to be off the island, as they say, for at least the next four weeks. Meetings in Kuwait."

"Does he have an assistant who can help us?"

"She's going to Kuwait, too."

"What a surprise."

"I'm going to have Pete check it out. He's been looking a little tired lately. I think he may need a vacation."

"Any place in particular you have in mind?"

"I understand the Bahamas are very nice this time of year."

"When might he be going?"

"I think he might be able to clear his calendar about four weeks from now."

CHAPTER 25

"TERMINATED IN THE ORDINARY COURSE OF THE REVIEW PROCESS"

"We deeply regret that the media has chosen to characterize our personnel moves as 'layoffs.' While it is contrary to firm policy to discuss individual situations, the attorneys who were asked to leave were terminated in the ordinary course of the review process for performance reasons."

— Arthur Patton. *San Francisco Legal Journal.*
Thursday, February 19.

Wendy Hogan calls me the next morning. "I suppose you've heard?"

"Heard what?"

"There were layoffs at S&G. I got fired."

"Hell."

"They told the papers we were canned for performance reasons. It's chickenshit. We were laid off because there wasn't enough work and the firm is in financial trouble."

"Everybody knows what's going on at S&G."

"How am I supposed to find another job? We're the lepers of the legal community. Andy called last night. He said he's going to challenge our custody deal."

"He's an asshole. Your attorney will take care of it."

"He's on vacation."

I don't say anything.

"Mike, can you help me with this?"

I learned everything I know about divorce law when Rosie and I split up. "I'll see what I can do. Why don't you come down to my office and we'll talk."

What the hell. It isn't as if I'm busy preparing for a murder trial. Besides, I like her.

* * *

Wendy and I are eating Chinese takeout in my office.

"Pretty tight space," she says.

"You get used to it." I nibble on a pork bun. "Sounds like I need to find you a good divorce lawyer."

"I need a job."

Yes, she does. It helps to be employed when you're in a custody fight. Believe me, I know. When Rosie and I split up, I got the bright idea that I was better suited to have custody of Grace. Bad idea. It led to the nastiest fight in my life. Ultimately, at the suggestion of Rosie's mom and mine, I came to my senses. Then things started to get better. Wendy's ex-husband is a horse's ass. At the moment, however, he's an employed horse's ass.

"You're good at what you do," I say. "You'll find something."

"It's not that easy. The economy stinks. I don't have my own clients. Firms aren't hiring tax lawyers." She takes a deep breath. "Could you use some help? Maybe I could work on Joel's case."

How do I say this diplomatically? "We handle criminal cases around here. You know—we represent crooks."

"I represent people in the real estate business. They're crooks, too. Except for the fact that what they do is technically legal."

Touché. "I'd like to help you. But what I really need is another experienced defense attorney. Preferably one without Mort Goldberg's ego. It isn't that you aren't good at what you do. It's just that what you do isn't what we do. You wouldn't hire me to do an IPO."

"I can do research. I can interview witnesses."

This isn't a good idea.

"I'm in a tight spot," she says. "Maybe there's something else I can bring to the table. I've done tax planning for Bob and Vince.

Maybe I can help you with the investigation."

This is intriguing. "How much tax planning?"

"A lot."

"Slow down. The judge won't let you testify if you work for me. It confuses the jury."

"I know. I used to work for a superior court judge."

"I remember. There's something else. The stuff you know is probably privileged."

"Most of what I know is already a matter of public record. Besides, Bob is dead. In all likelihood, so is Vince." She takes off her glasses. "The privilege died with them. Who's going to complain? Their ghosts?"

Technically, that may not be entirely correct. Just because you die doesn't mean your lawyers can tell the world all your deep, dark secrets. "What about the beneficiaries under their wills?"

"What about them? The beneficiaries under Bob's will have been contacted. Nobody is going to complain. They'll notify the beneficiaries under Vince's will as soon as he's declared legally dead."

Without getting into the finer points of the potential claims of their respective heirs, I have to admit she may have a point.

"I won't tell you anything you couldn't find out yourself from public records. And you wouldn't have to hire me directly. I could start my own firm, and you could retain me as special counsel. My name wouldn't appear on the pleadings. I won't appear in court unless I'm called as a witness. What's wrong with that?"

"Nothing, I suppose."

She smiles. "We're making progress. As Bob Holmes used to say, good lawyers provide practical solutions to real-world problems."

Right. I've been in practice for a month and a half and I have a real-world problem—another mouth to feed, even if her name doesn't appear on my letterhead. "I can't afford to pay you much."

"I understand. At least I can tell a judge with a straight face I'm building my practice."

"All right. The Law Offices of Wendy Hogan are hereby hired as special counsel. You can help Pete with the investigation. Don't even think about asking for a retainer."

She's pleased. "Anything you say, Mike."

I finish my moo shu pork. "Do you know anything about an entity in the Bahamas called the International Charitable Trust?"

"What would you like to know? I did the legal work to set it up."

* * *

Wendy opens a fortune cookie. "The International Charitable Trust is something of a misnomer," she says. "It isn't really international. It was formed in the Bahamas by one guy—Bob Holmes. And it isn't the least bit charitable. Unless, of course, your favorite charity happens to be Bob Holmes. It's a tax dodge. I set up a similar trust in the Bahamas for Vince Russo called the Charitable Trust for Humanity."

My fortune reads, "You are about to embark on a great romance." Even the fortune cookies know I'm hard up. "You aren't violating anybody's attorney-client privilege here, are you?"

"What if I was?"

"Nothing. Just asking."

Her eyes sparkle. "Everything I'm about to tell you is a matter of public record. Of course, the public records in the Bahamas are a little trickier to track down."

I grin back. "So what were these two trusts all about?"

"We set them up so Bob and Vince would each have a place to park some of their hard-earned cash outside the U.S. in a hard-to-find, safe, tax-free place. Bob and Vince hated two things more than anything else: taxes and alimony. When you made as much money as they did, and when you got divorced as many times as they did, you paid a lot of taxes and alimony."

I can picture Bob and Vince swapping stories about who paid more to their respective ex-wives. Wendy explains that they wanted to find a place to stash their cash in a tax-free jurisdiction where it would be hard for their ex-wives to find. The Bahamas had everything they needed. Perfect weather. Established financial system. Excellent bank-secrecy laws. So Bob and Vince each formed a trust. First Bank Bahamas was the trustee. Trevor Smith handled all the arrangements. It's a standard tax scam. She says Smith is very smooth.

I take a gulp of water. "I spoke with him yesterday. He's very polished."

"And very slippery. Trying to get a straight answer from him is like trying to hold a gallon of water in your bare hands. They did all their investing through the trusts."

She's telling me a little more than I would have found out from the public records in the Bahamas. "Did you dream this up?"

"I had a little help from Chuckles."

It fits. "So Chuckles came up with this elaborate charade?"

"It's all perfectly legal, Mike."

"So it is." In this case, the word "legal" is spelled SLEAZY.

She confirms that Chuckles holds the title of trust protector, and First Bank is the trustee. "First Bank won't do anything without instructions from Chuckles. He gets a fee for his trouble. He got permission from X-Com to manage the offshore trusts on his own time. The firm decided it didn't want the fiduciary liability for managing somebody else's money."

"How big is his fee?"

"I bet he gets at least half a million bucks a year just from Bob's trust."

Nice work if you can get it. "What does he have to do?"

"Not much."

"What does it take to get money out of one of the trusts?"

"A signature from Chuckles, or, in the case of Bob's trust, a signature from Bob. Or, in the case of Vince's trust, a signature from Vince."

"So Vince could take money out on his own?"

"Sure. All he needs is an e-mail. He moved money in and out of the trust all the time. He could do it right now. Except, of course, for the fact that he seems to be quite dead."

Unless he's still alive. "Who gets the income from the trusts while Bob and Vince are alive?"

"It's distributed among a group of people who are called income beneficiaries."

"Do you know who they are?"

"Nope. It's a secret. The names of the income beneficiaries are listed in separate, confidential documents. Chuckles never let me see them."

"What happens to the trusts when Vince and Bob die?"

"The assets are sold, and the proceeds are distributed to a different group of people called the remaindermen. I don't know their names, either. It was the best kept secret in the Western Hemisphere."

Figures. "What happens to the fees paid to Chuckles when they die?"

"They stop. He can't prevent the trusts from liquidating. But he can probably slow down the process. If he does, he can collect his fees for a few more years."

Chuckles wouldn't have had any incentive to kill Bob if his death triggered the liquidation of his trust. "Do you know if Bob was planning any changes in his trust?"

"I think so. A few weeks before he died, he asked me to prepare a list of the steps to amend his trust. He didn't tell me what he had in mind, but I suspect he was thinking about changing the income beneficiaries and the remaindermen."

"That would make sense if Beth was an income beneficiary or a remainderman."

"Could be. He was also talking about changing the deal with Chuckles. He always complained that Chuckles made too much money in admin fees."

Interesting. "What about his will? Was Bob making any changes there?"

"He talked to Chuckles about it."

This is showing some promise. "Did he ever get around to amending his will or his trust?"

"Not that I know of. My guess is he died before anything could happen."

So close. Still, if we can figure out who gets the money from Bob's trust, we may be able to figure out who had motive to kill Bob. Unless, of course, he killed himself.

* * *

Later the same afternoon, Joel, Mort, Rosie, Pete and I meet in Rabbi Friedman's dining room. I've brought Wendy.

"I'd like to introduce you to the final member of our team. Wendy Hogan is taking a permanent leave of absence from S&G."

Wendy smiles uncomfortably. "That's Mike's way of saying I've been downsized, and I need something to help me pay the bills."

Mort smiles broadly. "Welcome to the Dream Team, young lady. I'm Mort Goldberg."

"I've heard a lot about you."

"It's all true."

I explain that she isn't a member of our firm. "For now, she'll be a consultant. Just like you, Mort."

He gives me a sideways look.

"Wendy is familiar with Bob's will and his investments. I've asked her to work with Pete to figure out how Bob's money gets divided up."

She smiles at Pete. "I think I may be able to enlighten you about the International Charitable Trust."

"Sounds good to me." Pete is uncomfortable. He likes to work alone.

"Wendy," I say, "I have another special task for you. You're a tax lawyer. You're good at money. I want you to figure out everything about the firm's finances. Moreover, you'll get to see why you'd never want to be a partner at a firm like S&G."

"I'll get right on it." She turns to Mort. "Could you help me subpoena some of the firm's financial records?"

Mort beams. "I'd love to, honey."

I'll have to remind him not to call her "honey."

* * *

"You know what you're doing with Wendy?" Rosie asks. We're standing on her back porch the same evening.

"Yeah. She's smart." I pause. "I'd like to help her. She's a good lawyer."

"She's a tax lawyer, Mike." She says it in the condescending tone that trial lawyers reserve for transactional attorneys.

"I know. But she's tenacious. I think she'll help."

"You like her, don't you?"

She could always read me. "Is it that obvious?" I've had a crush on Wendy for five years.

"Yes. And she's pretty."

"That, too." I drink my beer. "You aren't jealous, are you?"

"Don't let it color your judgment. Keep it professional. You're running a law practice, not a counseling center."

She's right. "I wouldn't have brought her in if I didn't think she could help us."

Her eyes glow in the moonlight. "I'm going to remember you said that. And she'd better keep her hands off my sex slave."

CHAPTER 26

HUTCH

"Syc-o-phant n. One who attempts to win favor or advance himself by flattering persons of influence; a servile self-seeker; a toady."
— World Dictionary of the English Language.

The next morning, I'm back at S&G. Anyone who believes substance will ultimately triumph over style hasn't met Brent Hutchinson. His career is an ongoing charade of teeth, blond hair and good looks. His office overlooking Alcatraz Island and the Marin Headlands is furnished with an antique roll-top desk and matching chairs. An oriental rug graces the middle of his floor. A picture of his cheerleader wife, Barbi, smiles at him from his spotless desk. Life is good in Hutchworld.

"So, big guy," he says, "how's the new firm working out?"

To Hutch, everyone is a "big guy." "So far, so good. I seem to have stumbled onto a big murder case."

"Cool."

Someday, a team of graduate students will do a dissertation on Hutch called "The Mind of the Sycophant." It will take up many volumes. "Hutch, I came to ask you for your help."

"Anything. I always try to help out my friends."

I wasn't aware that we were friends. "Charles Stern told me that you're the firm's new insurance czar."

He throws his head back and forces a phony laugh. "Insurance czar. I like that. I'm the chairman of our risk-management committee." He winks. "It's real exciting, Mike."

I wink back. "I'll bet."

The potential exposure for malpractice claims at a firm like S&G

is hundreds of millions of dollars. Why they've put a moron like Hutch at the head of the professional liability team is beyond my comprehension.

I keep my tone matter-of-fact. "I'm trying to sort out the life insurance policies on Bob. Does the firm carry key-man insurance on the partners?" It's the first rule of cross-exam—never ask a question unless you know the answer.

"We do. Charles sent a memo to the partners about it."

"I must have missed it." Or tossed it.

"We carry life insurance on all the partners. On guys like us, we don't carry much. I think the minimum's about fifty thou. We carry a lot more on the heavy hitters like Bob and Art." He gives me the Cheshire cat grin.

"How much?"

"In a couple of cases, over a million bucks."

"Do you know how much you're carrying on Bob?"

The grin disappears. "You know, Mike, now that you don't work here anymore, I'm really not supposed to talk about this stuff with you."

"But I'm still on the line for firm debts incurred while I was a partner. If you're going to collect a big piece of change on the key man insurance, I have the right to know about it." I'm amiable when I add, "If you'd prefer, I can come back with a subpoena." You pretentious little jerk.

His phony smile returns. "Let's not get excited. We're carrying five million on Bob."

It confirms what Chuckles told me. "Thanks, Hutch." That wasn't so hard, was it? "Charles said you're looking into changing the firm's carrier."

"That's true. We got some of the new policies in place right before the end of the year."

Really? I got the impression from Charles that Hutch was just starting the process. "Did the firm take out any additional life insurance on the partners?"

"Yes. We were trying to increase the policy levels for some of the more junior people. I got bumped up from fifty thousand to a half a million."

That's because you're worth so much. "Was the policy on Bob increased?"

"I don't recall. I can find out."

"Actually, Hutch, if you'd give me the name of the insurance agent, I can give him a call."

"It's no problem, Mike. I can find out." Affability reigns.

"I don't want to take any more of your valuable time, Hutch. Really, it's no big deal."

"His name is Perry Guilford. I'll have my secretary get you the number."

"Thanks." I move to another topic. "Skipper was kind enough to show me some of your cinematography from last year's retreat."

He's pleased with himself. "I thought it turned out pretty well."

Right. "There was some pretty inflammatory stuff in there."

"You know how it gets at the retreat."

"Yes, I do." It doesn't mean you should stick your camera into everybody's face. "Hutch, the judge asked me whether there's an unedited version of the tape. You know—without all the music from Law & Order. Any chance you saved the original?"

He scowls. He probably thinks I'm trying to compromise his artistic integrity. "I don't have the original. We used it to make the over dubbed version. Our methods are pretty rudimentary."

I'll say. The special-effects wizards at Industrial Light and Magic won't be worried. "Did you give Skipper everything?"

"Yeah."

"What else was on the tape?"

"Not much. I really don't remember."

He's lying. "Who else saw the tapes?"

"Chuckles and Art."

What a surprise. "Did they tell you to destroy part of the tape?"

"No."

He's still lying. "We can do this the easy way or the hard way. Now, tell me what was on the tape."

"I don't remember, big guy"

Sure.

Chapter 27

DR. KATHY CHANDLER

"To speak to Dr. Kathy Chandler, call 1-800-GET-HELP."
— KTLK TALK RADIO. Friday, February 20.

Dr. Kathy Chandler fancies herself the Bay Area's Dr. Frasier Crane. Of course, Dr. Crane has an imaginary degree from Harvard. Dr. Chandler, on the other hand, has an honorary doctorate in family counseling from Southwestern Texas City College and an honorary degree from the Great Pacific School of Broadcasting. More important, Dr. Frasier Crane only talks to imaginary patients. Dr. Kathy Chandler, unfortunately, talks to real people. Every weeknight from seven until ten, she dispenses bubblegum psychology on the live one, KTLK Talk Radio.

I must confess that her show is mildly entertaining. I listen to her sometimes on my way home from work. I think I'll appreciate it more if and when I get the lobotomy I keep promising myself.

Like many radio talk show hosts, she's always known as Dr. Kathy Chandler. She's never simply Dr. Chandler—or, God forbid, Dr. Kathy. And she always refers to herself in the third person, like ballplayers and politicians. "Dr. Kathy Chandler says to break up with your boyfriend," or "Dr. Kathy Chandler says your husband's no good," or "Dr. Kathy Chandler says your sex life could be a lot better." Makes you want to puke.

At three-thirty the same afternoon, I make the pilgrimage across the Golden Gate Bridge to the picture-postcard town of Mill Valley, where Dr. Kathy Chandler maintains her office in a turn-of-the-century building across from the old train depot, which is now an upscale bookstore and cafe. When I called to make an appointment, Dr. Kathy Chandler's receptionist told me she wasn't taking new patients. When I explained I was representing Joel Friedman, I was put on hold for only a moment before the sickly-sweet voice of Dr. Kathy Chandler found its way onto the phone and promised me an appointment. Ah, the smell of free publicity.

Dr. Kathy Chandler's second-floor office is decorated in earth tones, with gray-beige furniture, light wood end tables and two large ferns. Her receptionist looks as if she's been through at least a dozen twelve-step programs. There are self-help magazines on the tables and a life-size poster of Dr. Kathy Chandler on the wall, along with the KTLK logo. The same poster appears on Muni buses in the city.

Dr. Kathy Chandler's luxurious setup is different from the office of the shrink Rosie and I saw in our abortive attempts at marriage counseling. Chuck was a terrific guy, but I lost faith in him when I found out he was a fifty-five-year-old bachelor. He kept trying to get us to see the big picture. He never realized he was dealing with little-picture people.

The receptionist gives me a warm smile, and I take a seat between a suntanned woman hiding behind a pair of dark sunglasses, and a man I recognize as a local television personality. Dr. Kathy Chandler's clientele is pretty well-heeled.

At exactly four o'clock, the door opens, and I'm granted entry into the inner sanctum. Her office is furnished with more muted tones and ferns. Quiet music surrounds me. One of those tacky artificial waterfalls cascades behind Dr. Kathy Chandler's desk. In fairness, the whole thing is very soothing.

I feel like Dorothy waiting for the grand entrance of the Wizard. The door opens. I expect to hear trumpets. The posters on the buses don't do her justice. Dr. Kathy Chandler is about six feet tall and Cindy Crawford beautiful. I'm beginning to see why Bob Holmes paid a fortune to spend forty-five minutes a week with her.

She pushes her long blond hair away from her striking blue eyes. "I'm Dr. Kathy Chandler," she purrs.

"Michael Daley. I represent Joel Friedman."

"I know." The voice is pure caviar. She sounds better in person than she does on the radio.

"I understand Bob Holmes was a patient of yours."

"Yes, he was, Mr. Daley." She licks her lips. "It's a terrible tragedy."

"Yes, it is." Composure. "Dr. Chandler, how long had you been treating Mr. Holmes?"

"About three months."

"And how was his treatment going?"

She pouts. "Mr. Daley, you're a lawyer. You know I'm not permitted to talk about my patients. It's privileged." She blinks her big blue eyes and gives me a look that says she'd love to help me, but the big bad lawyers won't let her.

"I understand your concern, but the privilege ends when a patient dies." This isn't exactly true, but she isn't exactly a lawyer. "And it would be very helpful to understand the nature and extent of your treatment of Mr. Holmes."

The kitten-like facade disappears, and the claws come out. Her voice drops a half-octave. "Mr. Daley, it has always been my policy not to discuss the treatment of my patients with other people."

This is an interesting argument from a woman who gives free advice on the radio. "Dr. Chandler, I'd like to ask you a few questions. If you can't answer them, I can come back with a subpoena." And then you'll really have a lot to talk about from seven to ten tonight.

"Ask your questions. If I don't want to answer, I'll tell you so. And if I need to get my lawyer involved, believe me, I will."

I believe you, Dr. Kathy Chandler. "What were you treating Mr. Holmes for?"

"He had relationship issues."

No kidding. "And he was about to get divorced again."

"So I understand. I was working with Mr. Holmes on creating a foundation for solid relationships—and to temper his enthusiasm for extramarital activities."

"Were you aware that he was having an affair with Diana

Kennedy?"

"Oh, yes. That's where his treatment started. He and Ms. Kennedy had been seeing each other for about a year. When Mrs. Holmes found out at the beginning of December, she asked Mr. Holmes to leave. About the same time, Ms. Kennedy broke up with Mr. Holmes. He was quite upset."

"Did he try to reconcile with his wife?"

"Yes. The reconciliation was unsuccessful. He began seeing someone in late December. I assumed he had rekindled his relationship with Ms. Kennedy, but it may have been somebody new. He was terribly conflicted about it. He missed his last couple of appointments."

"Was he depressed?"

"In the clinical sense, no."

"Was he upset about the breakup with his wife?"

"Yes. But not terribly upset. He seemed to have expected it."

"Was he upset about the breakup with Ms. Kennedy?"

"Oh, yes, Mr. Daley. He was terribly upset about it."

"Are you aware of any attempts to reconcile with Ms. Kennedy?"

"No, Mr. Daley."

"Do you think it's possible Mr. Holmes attempted to reconcile with Ms. Kennedy and she rejected him?"

She pauses. "If you were my lawyer, you'd instruct me not to answer a hypothetical question."

"That's true. On the other hand, we have reason to believe that he did, in fact, attempt to reconcile with Ms. Kennedy. And we know that she was not agreeable to such a reconciliation because she had decided to leave the firm."

I wasn't aware of that."

It's put-up time. "Do you think Bob Holmes was so distraught about his pending divorce and his breakup with Diana Kennedy that he may have committed suicide?"

She laughs. "Mr. Daley, I'd been seeing Mr. Holmes for only about three months. He was an unhappy man with some serious relationship issues. But, in answer to your question, it is inconceivable to me that he was suicidal. He didn't display any of the signs. And if I'm called upon in court to testify, I'll say just that."

Then you're of no help to us. I'll see you on the radio, Dr. Kathy Chandler.

CHAPTER 28

"DID YOU COME TO GLOAT?"

"We are confident that we will be able to work out a deal with our creditors to continue our practice without interruption through the bankruptcy process. We will continue to provide the highest quality legal services to our clients during this difficult period."
— Arthur Patton. *San Francisco Chronicle.* Monday, March 2.

"Jeff Tucker, please," I tell the person at First Bank who answers my call on the morning of Monday, March 2. I'm studying the article in the *Chronicle* detailing the bankruptcy filing of my former law firm. I figure it might be a good time to get reacquainted with the bank's general counsel. As Jeff promised me a few weeks ago, the bank has foreclosed on S&G's equipment loans right on schedule.

"Who's calling, please?"

"Michael Daley."

My first reaction could be summed up by the words "Nyahh nyahh nyahh—you went bankrupt, and I got my capital back!" I realize this may not be the most mature reaction to the impending meltdown of my professional home for the better part of the last five years. Then again . . .

"Jeff Tucker speaking."

"It's Mike Daley."

"You heard about the S&G bankruptcy filing?"

"Indeed I did."

"I don't take any pleasure in any of this, Mike."

Sure you do. "Me neither." Heh heh heh. I'd give everything I own to see the look on Art Patton's face. "Jeff, do you happen to know if the loans were recourse or nonrecourse?"

If the loans were "recourse," the bank can try to collect from the partners and perhaps even the former partners. If the loans were "nonrecourse," the bank can seek repayment only from the assets of the firm. I learned this from Joel. It's all I know about commercial law: recourse—bad; nonrecourse—good.

"They're all recourse loans. Fully guaranteed by each of the partners."

Crap.

I can hear the smirk in his voice when he adds, "Since you were a partner at the time the loans were made and at the time of the default, you're still on the hook."

"Wait a minute. I left on December thirty-first. How do you figure I was still a partner at the time of default?"

"That's when the loans were due. You were still a partner. Ipso facto, you're still on the hook."

I hate lawyers who talk Latin. "But you extended the loan. I wasn't a partner when the extended due date came up."

"It wasn't an extension. We simply decided not to foreclose until the sixty-day grace period ended yesterday. All the S&G partners who were at the firm on December thirty-first are still on the hook. That includes you."

And you're an asshole. I'm sorry we didn't fire you sooner.

His tone is condescending. "The bank doesn't want to spend a lot of time and money suing the partners individually. If you're like most of your partners, all your money is going for alimony and fancy cars."

He's right—except in my case, there's no fancy car.

"I'm sure we'll end up cutting a deal with the firm. We'll probably take the firm's receivables and sell off some assets. We'll sue the partners individually as a last resort."

Maybe I'll ask Wendy to set up one of those sleazy tax shelters in the Bahamas to hide some of my assets.

* * *

At eleven o'clock the same morning, the reception area of Simpson and Gates looks considerably different. Only one receptionist is working the phone console. The double doors are closed. There are no fresh flowers. The Currier and Ives lithographs are gone. I'm guessing the artwork at First Bank headquarters has improved dramatically since yesterday.

Art Patton's secretary escorts me to his office. The long hallways look barren without the high-priced art. The plants are gone, too. She knocks and opens Patton's door. I'm surprised he's agreed to see me. Then again, it gives him a golden opportunity to yell at me. I suspect he'd rather do it in the privacy of his own office than in open court.

Art is standing behind his desk, bellowing into his phone. Something about the repossession of the computers. He motions toward a leather chair. I admire the view of the Golden Gate Bridge as he castigates some poor collection attorney.

He slams the phone down. He looks like a bulldog shaking himself after he's had a bath. "So," he snaps, "what the hell do you want? Did you come to gloat?"

As a matter of fact, I did. "Art, I take no pleasure in this. I think it's unfortunate." I look solemn and lay it on thick. "Some good people are going to lose their jobs."

It seems to disarm him slightly. His chins jiggle. "The bankruptcy filing was just a precaution. We'll still be here when the dust settles."

I'm not sure if he's trying to convince me or himself. "I hope you're right. I'm on the line for the equipment loans along with the rest of you."

He isn't mollified. "Besides your touching little speech about firm finances, why did you come to see me?"

"I wanted to talk to you about Joel's case."

"We've been through this. We've told the police everything we know. If we find out anything new, I'll call you." He picks up his phone.

"There are some things I'd like to talk to you about informally. If you insist on doing this the hard way, I can come back with a subpoena."

He hangs up. "What things?"

"It's a little ticklish."

He looks right at me. "You aren't going to start up again about that nonsense about a sexual-harassment claim, are you? It's bullshit. I have a good mind to file a lawsuit for slander against you for the stuff you brought up at the prelim."

The best defense is a good offense. "Two people are prepared to testify that you propositioned Diana at the retreat, and she rejected your advances." I watch him closely. He doesn't flinch. "One person said you touched Diana in the bar. Another said you asked her to go to bed with you at your party. When she refused, you followed her back to her room."

The pit bull appears. "That's bullshit. Who the hell do you think you are coming here and making these wild accusations? What's wrong with you?"

"I take it you're denying those accusations?"

"Damn right, I am."

"And you're prepared to testify to that effect in court?"

"Of course."

"Good. I'm glad we've eliminated any misunderstanding. Is it true that you and Beth Holmes have a social relationship?"

"I should throw you out of my office right now." He picks up the phone.

"Art, let me show you something." I hand him a photo of him entering Beth's house.

"That doesn't mean anything."

"Here's a picture of you leaving Beth's house the next morning. My investigator is prepared to testify that you spent the night."

The beady little eyes flare. "You little shit. You had me followed? Are you trying to blackmail me?" He grits his teeth. "Beth and I have had a social relationship for some time. It's one of the reasons for my divorce. My wife knows all about it."

"Did you know Bob was going to write Beth out of his will just before he died?"

"Wouldn't surprise me. She doesn't need the money. If you want to get up in open court and tell the jury that Beth and I were sleeping together, so be it. All it shows is that we were having an affair. She's my ex-wife. We still have feelings for each other. It doesn't have anything to do with your client's case."

Unfortunately, he may be right. "Didn't you and Bob invest in a restaurant together?"

"Yes, we did. Le Bon Vivant in Palo Alto."

"How was the business doing?"

"Great. Except in the restaurant business, you can be doing great, but it doesn't mean you're making any money."

I'm surprised he admitted it.

"We were thinking about closing it. I've lost all the money I intend to lose on that damn thing."

"I don't suppose you had a key-man policy on Bob for the restaurant?"

"No, we didn't."

* * *

When I return to the office that night, Wendy is sitting at a table in the hallway, studying copies of life insurance policies.

"You can sit in my office," I say.

"I like it better here. Your office smells like chow mein."

It does. "Find anything we can use?"

"Nothing yet. Bob's life insurance policies named Beth and the kids as beneficiaries."

"Keep looking."

"I will." She takes off her glasses. She's very pretty.

"Are you okay?" I ask.

"I guess so."

"Andy?"

"Yeah. We have a custody hearing a week from Tuesday. Will you come with me?"

I put my arm on her shoulder. "Sure."

She pulls back. "Thanks, Mike."

* * *

A moment later, I sit down in my office and dial a familiar number.

Pete answers on the first ring. "What do you need, Mick?" he rasps.

"Do you have any plans for the weekend?"

"You got Warriors tickets? The Lakers are in town."

"I've got something better. I need your help. How would you feel about doing a little *pro bono* work?"

"For whom?"

"Wendy."

A pause. "Sure, Mick."

"Thanks."

CHAPTER 29

"WE'RE MISSING SOMETHING"

"Pretrial motions are set for Monday, March 9. Except for Mort Goldberg, it seems the entire defense team is sound asleep."
— NewsCenter 4 Legal Analyst Morgan Henderson. Tuesday, March 3.

We're having an all-hands meeting in Rosie's office the next morning. We have a pretrial hearing on Monday, and it's time to add things up. We sit around the small conference table. Rosie drinks a Diet Coke and looks at our preliminary witness list. Wendy nurses a cup of coffee and studies her notes. Pete is going through an inventory of the evidence. Mort plays with an unlit cigar.

"Mort," I begin, "did you finish our motions to keep the Silverado videos out?"

"Yeah. We filed our papers on Thursday." He drums his fingers on the table. "It's going to be a close call. The videos have been heavily edited. We have a decent argument the potential inflammatory effect outweighs the probative value. I wouldn't bet a box of cigars we'll win."

Rosie agrees. "Even if she doesn't let them use the videos, they can always call Hutch to testify that he saw Diana and Joel kissing in the hot tub."

"There's nothing we can do about that," Mort says.

I turn to Wendy. "Did you find out anything more about Bob's finances?"

"Not much. He and Art Patton owned a restaurant in Palo Alto. There are no financial records available to the public."

"Art told me it's losing money."

"We haven't found any suspicious liens."

"Keep looking." I turn to Rosie. "Any surprises on their witness list?"

"Not really. They're loading up their list just the way we are. They've included you and Wendy to tweak us."

"We'll get around that. We included Skipper and McNulty on ours, right?"

"Turnabout is fair play. Judge Chen will never let them testify."

"I know. But it'll give us an opportunity to show the judge that Skipper was there that night."

Mort is pleased. "That discussion should be fun."

"Who else is on their list?" I ask.

Rosie flips though her notes. "People you'd expect. Roosevelt. Marcus Banks. Rod Beckert. Sandra Wilson. Art Patton. Charles Stern. Brent Hutchinson. Beth Holmes."

"Not surprising," I say. "A little testimony from the grieving widow to soften up the jury. Who else?"

"Dan Morris, Jack Frazier, Rick Cinelli and Homer Kim."

"Any surprises?"

"Your good friend Dr. Kathy Chandler is on their list, too."

"She was Bob's therapist. She'll testify that Bob wasn't suicidal."

"Is she a real doctor?"

"Depends on your definition of the word 'real.' She has an honorary doctorate from a mail-order college in Texas. Did you include all the S&G partners on our witness list?"

"Yeah. Just like you said."

"Good. And did you send out subpoenas to each of them?"

"Oh, yes," she says, smiling. "We served them yesterday."

"Let me guess. They were not particularly well received by some of my former partners?"

Her eyes gleam. "You could say that, Mike. I let Wendy have the pleasure of serving Art Patton, Charles Stern and Brent Hutchinson."

Wendy is triumphant. "Makes you want to become a litigator."

I'm not heartbroken about tweaking my former partners. "I bet Skipper is getting a few phone calls this morning." Lawyers hate to get subpoenas. And we really hate to testify.

"Mike," Wendy says, "I took the liberty of asking Rita Roberts and the NewsCenter 4 team to come with me to the S&G office when I served the subpoenas." She bats her eyes innocently. "I hope that was okay."

"Absolutely. The public has a right to know. By the way, did you find out anything more about the International Charitable Trust?"

"Trevor Smith is still in Kuwait." She grins. "I know his secretary. Her name is Felicity Smoot."

"You're kidding."

"No, I'm not. I told her I was following up on the trust so we could close the file. Evidently, Chuckles asked them to prepare a final inventory of trust assets so they can begin liquidation. For now, the trust is frozen."

"Were you able to confirm the amount of his fee?"

"Not yet. His deal isn't stated in the trust instrument. He has a separate administration contract that I haven't seen. I asked Felicity to send me a copy. We'll see if she does."

Not bad. "Did you have any luck identifying the income beneficiaries and the remaindermen?"

"Nope. Felicity didn't know. I didn't want to push her too hard. I thought it might make her nervous."

"You never want to make a banker nervous." I tap my pencil on my legal pad. "I'm surprised she talked to you. I'll bet Chuckles told her not to talk to anybody who doesn't work for S&G."

She gives me a conspiratorial grin. "Maybe I didn't tell her I'd left the firm."

Wendy has the makings of a fine criminal defense attorney. "When do you expect to hear from her?"

"Probably not until Smith gets back."

Swell. We'll be halfway through the trial. "See if you can find out when he's coming back. I want you and Pete to be there."

"An all-expenses-paid trip to the Bahamas? Cool."

"Think of it as a working vacation." I turn to Pete. "What have you found, Mr. Gumshoe?" Pete doesn't like being called Mr. Gumshoe. He doesn't joke around when it comes to business. Actually, he doesn't joke about anything.

"I ran an asset search on the custodian, Homer Kim. Seems his bank account recently became twenty thousand dollars fatter. Nice chunk of change for a guy who makes thirty-six grand a year."

"You think somebody paid him to testify?"

"I can't tell for sure. He doesn't look like the kind of guy who gets twenty thousand dollar bonuses. When we ran the search on his bank accounts, we saw one big deposit. It went out the next day. We don't know where the money came from or where it went. He's had some gambling problems."

"Stay with him," I say.

"There's something else. You remember Beth Holmes said her PI caught Bob with another woman at the Fairmont in December? Well, I talked to her private eye. She hired Nick Hanson."

Mort and Rosie burst into laughter. "Nick the Dick!" Mort shouts. "She hired Nick the Dick?"

Wendy's bewildered. "Who the hell is 'Nick the Dick'?"

Mort grins at Wendy. "Honey, Nick Hanson is a legend. He was the lead investigator for a defense lawyer named Nunzio Della Ventura. Nunz had a storefront office on Columbus Avenue in North Beach for fifty years. The prosecutors hated him. Nunz was quite a character. So's Nick."

"You have to see him to believe him," Pete says.

"That's right," says Mort. "He may be all of five feet tall. Quite the man about town. Always has a fresh flower in his lapel. You'd look at him and you'd be inclined to underestimate him. He's the most tenacious private eye I've ever met. He's in his eighties. Still a pistol. Still lives in North Beach. Still working every day."

"He's written several mystery novels based on cases he's worked on," I say. "One was made into a movie. I think Danny DeVito played him."

"I'll look for him next time I'm at the bookstore," Wendy says. "So, what did Nick the Dick find out about Bob?"

Pete clears his throat. "Nick saw Bob with a woman in a room at the Fairmont in late December. He couldn't ID her. He was in the building across the street. The drapes were partially closed, and the lights were dim. By the time Nick got to the hotel, she was gone. He took some pictures. He promised to let me see them."

"Will he testify?" I ask.

"Of course. This is a high-profile case."

Rosie looks puzzled. "How does that help us?"

"If it wasn't Diana, it undercuts Skipper's argument that Joel acted in a jealous rage."

"On the other hand," she says, "if it wasn't Diana, it may undercut our suicide argument. If Bob already had another girlfriend, he couldn't have been too distraught about his breakup with Diana. In that case, it doesn't seem logical that he would have killed himself."

As always, Rosie sees things with great clarity. "Unless," I say, "the mystery woman was just a rebound for Bob and she blew him off, too. Who knows? Maybe she was a hooker."

Rosie is skeptical. "Seems like a stretch to me."

It begs the obvious question. "Pete, can you talk to the staff at the Fairmont to see if you can get an ID on the woman?"

"I'm already working on it."

"Good." I look at my notes. "We're missing something. Any leads on Russo?"

"Maybe. You remember his car was found at the Golden Gate Bridge? His overcoat washed up at Fort Baker yesterday. He wasn't wearing it."

"Do you think he might still be alive?"

"It's possible. I talked to the cab companies in Sausalito. Marin Taxi had a pickup at the Vista Point at about three a.m. on December thirty-first. The dispatcher and the driver both confirmed the fare was taken to the international terminal at SFO. The driver said the passenger was a heavyset male in his thirties or forties, who paid cash. The driver couldn't identify Russo from a photo."

"You think it was Vince?"

"You bet your ass I do."

"Sounds like we may have to bring him back from the dead."

CHAPTER 30

"YOU CAN'T CROSS-EXAMINE A VIDEOTAPE"

"Judge Shirley Chen will hold a pretrial conference at ten o'clock to discuss scheduling and evidentiary issues. The trial starts in one week."
— NewsCenter 4 Daybreak. Monday, March 9.

March 9 is a day for the lawyers to argue about evidentiary issues, legal motions and scheduling. We'll also get our first taste of Judge Shirley Chen. The tenor of the trial will be set by the decisions she makes today.

Rosie, Mort and I park in the pay lot next to the Hall and lug our trial briefcases through the downpour. Skipper's Lincoln is parked illegally in front of the main entrance.

The news vans are out in force. Rita Roberts stands under an umbrella with the NewsCenter 4 logo. The wind is howling, but her hair doesn't move. I shrug when she asks for a comment. We push our way into the building, shake our umbrellas and walk through the metal detectors. It would be bad form to be late.

Judge Shirley Chen is in her mid-forties, although she looks younger. She began her career at S&G twenty years ago. It seems as if every judge in California started at S&G. She moved to the San Francisco DA's Office three years later. I tried two cases against her when I was a PD. I won one and I lost one. She was an ambitious prosecutor. She brings the same tenacity to the bench.

Her chambers are sterile. Her law-school diploma hangs on the wall, but her books and files are still in boxes. I'm reminded she's single as I notice there are no pictures of a spouse or children. There's a plaque from the San Francisco Women's Bar Association. There's a gavel from her alma mater, Hastings College of Law, which indicates that she was named distinguished alumna three years ago. There's a photo of her with the California attorney general.

Skipper and McNulty arrive a few minutes after we do. Everybody is decked out in their Sunday best. Skipper's navy blue pinstripe looks as if it was delivered earlier this morning from Wilkes Bashford. McNulty is wearing charcoal gray. We can't compete on clothing. Besides, the rain has taken the starch out of our best going-to-court clothes. Skipper plays with his MontBlanc pen. McNulty sits quietly.

"Let's get started," Judge Chen says.

We nod in unison.

Judge Chen looks at me. "First, let's talk about scheduling. May I assume, Mr. Daley, that your client hasn't reconsidered his position concerning the timing of his trial?"

"That's correct, Your Honor. My client does not intend to waive time." We're as ready as we're going to be.

She isn't happy. "Very well. We're scheduled to start one week from today." She looks at Skipper. "Mr. Gates, how many trial days would you estimate for the prosecution's case?"

"One moment. Your Honor." He and McNulty whisper to each other. Skipper turns back to the judge. "I don't think it will take us very long. If Mr. Daley is reasonable, we won't need a lot of time qualifying our witnesses as experts."

"How many trial days, Mr. Gates?"

"No more than ten. And perhaps substantially fewer. We think jury selection may take longer than our case."

She turns to me. "What about the defense, Mr. Daley?"

With a little luck, we won't have to present a lengthy defense. On the other hand, we may be here for weeks if they trot out a slew of experts. "No more than a week. Maybe less."

She seems pleased. "Very well, then. We'll begin jury selection one week from today."

"Your Honor," I say, "we presented several motions on evidentiary issues."

"I was just getting to that, Mr. Daley." She glances at Mort's papers. She says she'll give us some leeway in the jury selection process, called voir dire. She asks us for draft questionnaires to be given to the potential jurors. McNulty and Rosie have agreed on most of the major points. She reiterates Judge Brown's gag order with respect to the media.

"Your Honor," I say, "there are some matters regarding the prosecution's witness list."

"Let's keep this simple. Nobody in this room is going to be a witness at this trial. Period."

"Your Honor, we have a significant issue here."

"Let's not waste time, Mr. Daley. You know I'm not going to let any of you testify."

Skipper smiles.

Time to move on. "Your Honor, have you seen the security videos?"

Skipper's smile disappears. "Your Honor—,"

She stops him. "I'll tell you when it's your turn to talk, Mr. Gates."

"But, Your Honor—,"

"Mr. Gates, the rules here are simple. I get to interrupt you. You don't get to interrupt me. Are we clear?"

I like it. An early show of control.

Skipper nods submissively. "Yes, Your Honor."

"Good." She turns back to me. "I haven't seen the security videos, Mr. Daley."

"Mr. Gates was in the building that night. We can put the tapes on right now, if you'd like."

"I know he was there. The police reports said there was a reception for him at the office."

"He came back. He was in the building at one o'clock when Diana returned. He was there when Bob and Diana died."

Skipper shakes his head contemptuously. "Mr. Daley was there too, Your Honor. I'll withdraw his name from our list in the interests of justice."

I glare at him. "For God's sake, Skipper. You know I left at eight-thirty. I didn't come back at one in the morning at exactly the time you claim Bob and Diana died."

He turns to Judge Chen. "Your Honor, I resent Mr. Daley's implication."

I fire right back. "Your Honor, he's brought charges against my client for the murder of two people. I can prove he entered the building around the same time Diana Kennedy did. He has to be a witness. Frankly, I don't understand why he wasn't considered a suspect at the time."

A little over the top, but so be it. At least she's interested.

The judge is troubled. "Is this true, Mr. Gates?"

"Yes, Your Honor. I was in the office for a few minutes around one o'clock to pick up my briefcase. I didn't see or hear anything. My office wasn't even on the same floor as Bob's."

"He was there for almost an hour," I say. "It was a lot longer than just a few minutes."

Judge Chen's jaws are clenched. "This isn't good. The district attorney could be a witness." She looks at Skipper. "And you actually plan to try this case yourself?"

"Absolutely, Your Honor."

"If this doesn't beat everything." She turns to me. "Do you really need his testimony?"

"Absolutely, Your Honor."

She turns back to Skipper. "And I don't suppose you'd agree to let Mr. McNulty handle this case?"

"No, Your Honor. It's too close to the trial."

"And I don't suppose you'd be willing to testify about what you saw that night?"

"For obvious reasons, I would prefer not to. It confuses the jury if a lawyer is both an advocate and a witness."

"And what, if anything, did you see that night, Mr. Gates?"

"Nothing." He pauses. "And if you want me to testify to that effect, I guess I'm prepared to do so."

"I'm going to take this under advisement. I'll give you my decision by the end of the week. We also need to address the motion to quash the presentation of two video recordings of certain activities at the Simpson and Gates firm retreat in October of last year."

"Your Honor," I say, "I'd like to let my colleague, Professor Goldberg, make our presentation on this matter."

We've rehearsed this. I want Mort to play the part of the gray-haired sage on legal and evidentiary issues. Although I'd never say it out loud, the truth is that I trust him to speak for only a few minutes a day.

She gives me a knowing look. "I'm familiar with Mr. Goldberg's credentials. I was a student of his. It's my turn to see if he's prepared for class." She turns to Mort. "What do you have to say, Professor?"

He smiles. "Your Honor, may it please the court." His diction is a little slurred. The words "Your Honor" come out as a single word, which sounds like "yawner." "We have a potentially serious evidentiary matter concerning two videos from the Simpson and Gates firm retreat last fall."

"Mr. Goldberg, I've read your motion. Let's cut to the chase. If you don't have anything new to tell me, I'll rule based on your papers."

Mort acts as if he was expecting this. Give him credit. He doesn't fluster. "The prosecution would like to introduce into evidence a highly edited video of activities at the Simpson and Gates retreat. In addition, all of the original sound was edited out and replaced by the theme music from a popular television show. The events in the videos will be taken out of context. And it's all but certain that it will have an inflammatory and highly prejudicial effect on the jury."

Nice work, Mort. Concise. Direct. And you didn't use the words "kissing," "hot tub," "sex" or "affair."

The judge is skeptical. "Mr. Goldberg, isn't it true that the videos speak for themselves?"

Like all good lawyers, Mort pretends he's agreeing with her, while he's actually disagreeing. It's patronizing, but it works. "In general, Your Honor, that's true. On the other hand, when a video has been tampered with as this one has, or there is a substantial likelihood that it could be taken out of context, it could be unfairly damaging evidence."

"Mr. Goldberg, these videos show a man and a woman kissing. Coincidentally, the man is the defendant and the woman is the victim. Doesn't that speak for itself? A jury can figure out what was happening."

Mort uses his glasses to gesture. "Jurors are human. They see news stories about politicians having affairs. They think it's the truth if they see it on TV. It isn't a news flash that Mr. Gates is going to claim our client was having an affair with Ms. Kennedy. He has no evidence except for these videos. If he shows these heavily edited videos out of context, it will have an enormously prejudicial effect on the jury."

She looks at Skipper. "What do you have to say, Mr. Gates?"

"Your Honor, Mr. Goldberg is blowing this issue out of proportion. We believe the videos do, in fact, speak for themselves. The jurors will be free to draw whatever inferences they choose. That's what juries are supposed to do—figure out what happened. The defendant and Ms. Kennedy were caught on video kissing. It would be irresponsible to ignore it. We acknowledge that a part of our case will be to demonstrate that Mr. Friedman and Ms. Kennedy were having an affair. We believe the breakup led Mr. Friedman to murder two people. The video speaks for itself. It is what it is."

It is what it is. It's an effective legal argument.

It's Mort's turn. "Your Honor, you can't cross-examine a videotape. If Mr. Gates thinks he can demonstrate that Mr. Friedman and Ms. Kennedy were having an affair, let him bring forth witnesses at trial. Let us have an opportunity to cross- examine them."

Skipper and Mort volley back and forth for another ten minutes.

Finally, Judge Chen says she's heard enough. "Gentlemen, I find Mr. Goldberg's argument slightly more persuasive." She turns to Skipper. "Mr. Gates, if you want to introduce evidence of these tawdry events at the trial, you'll have to do so through witnesses who can be cross-examined by the defense." She's ruling in our favor, but sending a message. He can't use the videos, but he can call witnesses to testify about their contents. "For example, I see no reason why Mr. Gates couldn't call the individual who was operating the camera."

There's nothing we can do to prevent Skipper from calling Brent Hutchinson to testify that he saw Joel and Diana kissing—even if it was through the lens of his video camera. Of course, there's nothing to prevent us from going after him on cross.

Skipper isn't satisfied. "But Your Honor—,"

"I've ruled, Mr. Gates."

"Your Honor," I say, "there's one more issue. Mr. Gates has requested that this trial be televised. For obvious reasons, we're against it."

Skipper is mortified. "Your Honor, the public has a right to observe the criminal justice system."

And crown thy good with brotherhood, from sea to shining sea. "Your Honor," I say, "I'm only thinking of the interests of my client and the interests of justice. I don't want my client tried in the media. Mr. Gates's leaks have already contributed to a potentially irreversible tainting of the juror pool."

If you don't have a better argument, always invoke the interests of justice.

Judge Chen frowns. "I have mixed feelings. In my judgment, it is possible to televise a trial without turning it into a circus. Nevertheless, I'm inclined to agree with Mr. Daley."

Skipper strains to keep his tone even. "But Your Honor—,"

"I've ruled, Mr. Gates. I'll see you next week to begin jury selection. We're done."

This round goes to the good guys, but not by much.

* * *

Skipper and McNulty stop us outside the courtroom. "Nice work on your motions, Mort," Skipper says.

He waves an unlit cigar. "It's all part of the process."

"We'll get all the stuff from the videos into evidence at the trial. We were planning to call Brent Hutchinson anyway."

"At least we'll be able to cross-examine him," I say. "Hutch can be jumpy. He hasn't spent a lot of time in court lately."

Skipper laughs. "All the more reason for us to spend a little extra time in preparation."

Mort turns to McNulty. "You guys have any more evidence you'd like to share with us? I'm sure you aren't planning any surprises at trial."

"You've seen everything we have."

I ask if the results of the paternity test had come in.

"Not yet," Skipper says. "You aren't nervous, are you, Mike?"

"Nope."

"Good. I'm sure your guy is telling you the truth."

* * *

"It's a good result," Mort says to me as we're pulling out of the parking lot. "At least we got the videos out."

"Nice work," I say. "Let's go back to the office and call Joel with the good news." I pause. "What do you think that was all about in the hallway? You think they know something?"

He takes out a cigar. "Probably."

CHAPTER 31

"WHAT ELSE CAN YOU TELL ME, ROOSEVELT?"

"We have been asked to prepare papers to have Mr. Russo declared legally dead."
— Charles Stern. *San Francisco Legal Journal.*
Tuesday, March 10.

Tuesday, March 10. We take a break from our trial preparation to attend to an equally depressing matter: Wendy's custody hearing. Her ex-husband, Andy, has filed papers to revise their custody agreement. Wendy and I wait outside divorce court at ten a.m. We're joined by her attorney, Jerry Mills, a quiet, rational man in his mid-fifties. Wendy is nervous. I don't blame her. I haven't been in this hallway in five years. It brings back unpleasant memories. It was in this very corridor that I gave up on my lame-brained idea that I was better suited to have custody of Grace. I'll never forget the look of relief on Rosie's face. It was the only time during our divorce that she allowed herself to cry.

We're joined by Wendy's ex, Andy Schneider, a high-strung advertising executive in his late thirties with slicked-back hair. He's dressed in a flashy double-breasted suit and a designer tie. He's accompanied by his attorney, a fiftyish asshole named Craig Sherman, who bears an uncanny resemblance to a rattlesnake.

In my experience, divorce attorneys come in two species. Most are rational people like Jerry, who act more as counselors than adversaries. Some have a knack for defusing tense situations. The really good ones steer their clients toward counseling and sometimes salvage marriages. Then there are people like Sherman, who relish the role of barracuda. He represents only men. He has a picture of a shark on his business cards. If you're going to war with your ex-wife, he's your guy.

Sherman says, "You guys don't think the judge is actually going to believe this crap that Wendy has her own law firm, do you? We're going to call in child custody services to review this case."

Nice guy.

Mills looks at him. "We have an agreement, Craig. It's been approved by the court. It isn't going to change."

Sherman cracks his knuckles. "Sure, Jerry. I've had this judge modify custody orders for a lot less than this."

And you wonder why people hate lawyers. In reality, he's probably bluffing. In California, custody orders can be modified only if there is a significant change in circumstance. A change in one spouse's economic situation generally isn't enough.

Wendy glares at Andy. "You're an asshole. You aren't fit to take care of a hamster, let alone a six-year-old."

He tugs at his tie. "At least I've got a job."

I get between them. "It's time for court," I say calmly.

Andy winks. Wendy moves closer to Mills.

We turn toward the heavy double doors to the courtroom when Pete walks up, soaking wet. "Sorry I'm late."

Sherman looks at him. "I didn't realize we were going to have a family reunion."

"Craig," Pete says, "can I see you and Andy in private for a moment?"

"What the hell is this all about?"

"Thirty seconds," Pete says.

"Humor him," Andy says confidently.

Pete, Andy and Sherman walk down the hall out of earshot. Pete takes out a manila envelope and hands it to Andy. They huddle. They argue. Sherman gesticulates. Pete remains stone-faced. A moment later, the arrogance leaves Andy's face.

Wendy turns to me. "What's this all about?"

"I don't know."

A moment later, Pete, Andy and Sherman return. Sherman looks at Wendy, then he turns to Mills. "Jerry," he says, "we've decided not to pursue any changes in the custody deal. We're going to drop our motion." He turns to me. "You and your brother are assholes." He and Andy walk down the hall toward the elevators.

I turn to Pete, who arches an eyebrow. Wendy walks over and gives him a hug. He hugs her back uncomfortably. "I don't know what you gave them," she says, "but it worked."

Pete gives us a wicked grin and pulls out a stack of snapshots. "I took these last night." He starts flipping through the pictures, the way little kids flip through baseball cards. He provides a running commentary. "Here's Andy's executive assistant, Karen." It's a picture of an attractive woman going into a house in Pacific Heights. "Here's Andy going inside. Here's Andy taking off his clothes. Here's Karen taking off her clothes. The next few pictures are a little tough to see." He shuffles through them quickly. "Here they are rolling around on the floor."

Wendy is smiling. "We get the idea, Pete."

"It seems Karen is married to Andy's boss."

"I was not aware of that," I say.

"I'd say we're holding Andy's career right here in the palm of my hand."

Jerry Mills asks Pete for a business card. "You guys play in a different league."

* * *

Thursday, March 12. Four days before the start of jury selection. We've spent the last week interviewing witnesses, rehearsing my opening and working on jury selection strategy. The clock is ticking.

The process of preparing for trial is far more of an art than a science. You spend a lot of time honing your presentation. While the law professors and commentators like to talk about the pursuit of justice, when you cut to the chase, it's all theater. In a world of social media and 140-character messages, you can't just inform the jury; you have to entertain them and, if possible, dazzle them with special effects.

Unlike real theater, a trial attorney has to perform all the important roles: producer, director, lead actor, costume designer, special effects supervisor, production accountant and, perhaps most important, food provider. We have created an impromptu "war room" in the hallway just outside my office. Exhibit binders, easels, enlarged pictures, diagrams and charts are everywhere. My biggest worry is that our stuff will get soaked as we lug it from the parking lot to the courtroom.

Rosie, Mort and I spend the day with our jury consultant, Barbara Childs, who is an up-and-comer in a growing field. I've worked with her on a couple of cases. She's a little full of herself, but you have to be in her line of work. I take her suggestions with a grain of salt. We don't have the time or the resources to do a full mock trial.

At three in the afternoon, I walk past Wendy, who is pouring over some S&G financial records at a table just outside Rosie's office. "Find anything we can use?"

"Nothing yet." She looks at me. "Where are you going? I would think you might have a few things to do today."

"I thought I'd take the afternoon off. You know—conserve my strength for trial."

"Really, Mike. Where are you off to?"

"I'm going to take one more run at Roosevelt."

* * *

I meet Roosevelt in the back of a cop bar not far from the Hall. The cops and detectives respect each other's private space here. The place is run by a heavyset man named Phil Agnos. It's sort of a cross between a saloon and a halfway house for Greek immigrants. Phil is the only person permitted to handle the money. Every three weeks or so, there's a new young man with a toothpick in his mouth standing at the grill. Since the only English words he ever knows are "cheeseburger" and "double," your culinary options are limited. I opt for a single cheeseburger today.

Roosevelt is sitting in the back room, nursing a cup of coffee and reading the paper. A picture of Joe DiMaggio hangs on the wall behind him. He stands to greet me. "I was just reading about you in the paper."

"What are they saying now?"

"The usual. You're spending all your time on a hopeless disinformation campaign in a feeble attempt to find some technicality to get your client off. Typical stuff for a defense attorney."

"I knew they'd get my number sooner or later." I take a bite of my cheeseburger. "Have you guys found anything else?"

He sips his coffee. "Nothing I haven't told you already. Skipper has poor Bill McNulty living with two jury consultants. One of them told me Skipper has practiced his opening in front of two different mock juries."

"How are the test audiences playing?"

"Pretty well. For all his faults, the man has charisma."

Indeed. "What else can you tell me, Roosevelt? Anything else I can use?"

"Not a thing, Mike. You're doing everything you're supposed to be doing. Once you got the confession knocked out, it turned into a circumstantial case. It isn't an easy one."

For either side.

He wipes his glasses. "Why don't you ask for more time? Your client isn't rotting in jail. Why the rush?"

"He won't listen to reason. Anything new on Vince Russo?"

"Nope. His story went cold at the Golden Gate Bridge."

"Pete thinks a cab driver may have picked him up and driven him to the airport."

"That's more than we've found."

Great. Just great.

* * *

Mort calls me at the office at five o'clock the same afternoon. "I got an e-mail from the judge," he says. "She ruled we can't call Skipper as a witness at the trial."

"No big surprise there, Mort."

"Nope. I was surprised she didn't rule against us on the spot."

Four days until trial. On Monday, we start playing for keeps.

CHAPTER 32

OPENING CEREMONIES

"We are extremely confident."
— Michael Daley. NewsCenter 4. Monday, March 16.

"I'm scared to death, Rosie," I say. "I haven't been this nervous in a long time."

We're driving to Rabbi Friedman's house in a light rain on the morning of Monday, March 16. El Niño's giving us a small respite today, but the gray skies further dampen my mood.

She touches my hand. "First-day jitters. You're like a baseball pitcher. After you make it through the first inning, you'll be fine." We pull into Rabbi Friedman's driveway. She gives me a peck on the cheek. "Go get 'em. Once the trial starts, there's no looking back."

* * *

The rabbi meets us at the door. His expression is grim. Per my instructions, Joel and his dad are dressed in dark business suits, white shirts and subdued ties. Joel's mom and Naomi are wearing conservative clothes, no jewelry and minimal makeup.

I gather everyone in the dining room. "I know we've gone over this, but I want to remind you once more that trials are theater. It sounds paranoid, but you have to assume everything you say and do will be scrutinized by the jury. I want you to act normal, but be careful. An inappropriate gesture could have greater impact than you'd think."

The rabbi raises a hand. "Are we allowed to show any emotion?"

Generally, histrionics don't play well in the courtroom. "It won't hurt to shake your head every once in a while. I don't want you to draw unnecessary attention to yourselves. I want to keep the jury focused. And I don't want the judge to think we're trying to disrupt her courtroom. She's very businesslike."

Rosie looks at her watch. "Time to go."

* * *

Joel and Naomi hold hands in the back of Rosie's car as we drive to the Hall. He's stoic, almost serene. She's tugging her hair.

"It's going to be all right," I tell them.

Naomi whispers, "I know."

We pull into the pay lot next to McDonald's. Joel's parents take the spot next to us. They huddle under an umbrella while Rosie and I pull our trial cases out of the trunk.

Even though it's now raining steadily, reporters from the local stations are waiting for us on the steps of the Hall. The nerdy guy from CNN is here. The arrogant woman from Court TV who's been calling me an idiot for the last six weeks has left the comfort of her studio to insult me in person. A dozen police officers form a human barricade for us. The cameras and reporters follow us. It starts to rain harder. We're pelted with questions and rain as we push our way to the doors.

"Mr. Daley, is it true you're discussing a plea bargain?"

"Mr. Daley, is your client going to take the stand?"

"Mr. Daley, is it true you're going, to have a surprise witness?"

"Mr. Daley? Mr. Daley? Mr. Daley?"

As we reach the door, I turn back and face the nearest camera. Channel 7 will get the best footage tonight. Two dozen microphones are held up to my face.

"Ladies and gentlemen, we are extremely confident that Mr. Friedman will be fully exonerated of these outrageous charges." I turn and walk into the building. Reporters continue shouting questions to my back.

* * *

Mort meets us inside. We make our way through the metal detectors and up the elevators. Police mill around. Security is tight.

As I turn to open the wooden doors to Judge Chen's courtroom, I see Skipper's smiling countenance as he strides toward us, reporters nipping at his heels. If he's nervous, he isn't showing it. It's sound-bite time. I can't hear what he's saying, but I'm sure he's extolling the strength of his case and his faith in the justice system. I catch his eye. It's opening day. Let's play the National Anthem and start the game.

* * *

The windowless courtroom is packed. The hot, heavy air smells of mildew. Umbrellas and raincoats are strewn about. McNulty and two law clerks lug in four trial bags. Skipper and McNulty take their places at the prosecution table near the jury box.

Joel sits between Rosie and me at the defense table. Mort sits at the end. Mort has his game face on. He looks forward intently, eyes moving constantly. He's looking for any nuance or advantage.

The gallery is full. Naomi and her in-laws are in the first row, directly behind us. Diana's mother sits behind Skipper. The courtroom artists have their sketch pads poised. Reporters and onlookers crowd into the remaining seats.

* * *

Judge Chen's bailiff is an African-American woman named Harriet Hill. At precisely ten o'clock, she instructs us to stand. The judge hurries to her tall leather chair and nods to Skipper, and then to me. Her hair is pulled back tightly. She calls for order. The courtroom becomes silent. "Any last-minute issues?" she asks.

"No, Your Honor," Skipper and I say almost in unison.

"Good." She's trying to set a businesslike tone. "Let's get started."

* * *

To the great chagrin of the media, we will spend the next few days, and perhaps weeks, picking a jury. Like most trial lawyers, I believe cases are won or lost during jury selection.

Unfortunately, picking a jury is the most important and least scientific part of this enterprise. Jury consultants get paid hundreds of thousands of dollars to identify personality traits and biases gleaned from juror questionnaires that may not have been answered honestly. Some jury consultants claim they can help you pick a sympathetic jury simply by watching the body language of the potential jurors. At the end of the day, you go with hunches and gut instincts as much as demographics.

Picking a jury is more difficult than it used to be. In 1991, California voters passed Proposition 115, which gave judges, rather than the prosecutors and defense attorneys, the authority to question prospective jurors during the voir dire. Before Prop. 115, jury selection in a capital case could take months. With the judges asking the questions, the process goes much more quickly. Lawyers can still give the judge a list of questions we want asked—which the judge is free to ignore. Although Judge Chen has promised to give us some leeway, she reminds us that she'll be asking the questions.

Skipper has hired one of the jury consultants from the Simpson trial, who's appeared on CNN from time to time. My jury consultant, Barbara Childs, is a regular on Court TV. I suspect the battle of the consultants will end up about even.

The best thing about jury selection is that it tends to bore the media to tears. The judge asks the same questions of a large group of people for days on end. Occasionally, the lawyers get to stand up and make a speech to try to have a juror excused. After a few preliminaries, Judge Chen tells Harriet Hill to bring in the first panel of potential jurors.

* * *

Thursday, March 19. Three days later, we're still at it. The first-day media blitz has died down. Although the local TV stations are still sending reporters to monitor the proceedings, we've been relegated to the third page of the *Chronicle* and the fourth story in the local news broadcasts. We get a little more play on CNN every night. Everybody will be back once we've picked the jury.

We must select twelve jurors and six alternates. So far, we've managed to select nine jurors. I'm having a tougher time than Skipper. He's looking for people who hate lawyers. That includes about 99 percent of the population.

Skipper wants people who have had a bad experience with the legal system, who might take out their hostility on Joel. I'm trying to avoid anybody who's ever been arrested, divorced or sued. That doesn't leave much. I like his odds better.

According to my consultant, I should try to fill the jury with women, because they're more open-minded. On the other hand, they tend to turn quickly in cases where a woman is a victim, especially if the accused is a man. So much for statistics.

By three o'clock on Thursday, we've picked our twelve jurors and six alternates. Judge Chen has kept the process moving. We've finished sooner than I would have predicted.

The jury is a mixed bag. Eight women and four men. Two of the women are Asian, one African-American. One man is Asian, another Hispanic. Seven are married, and three have been divorced. Two are lawyers. The African-American woman is a supervisor for the phone company. I have a hunch she'll be one of the leaders. I tried to get her excused because she was divorced. Judge Chen ruled against me. There are two homemakers, a retired Muni bus driver, a data-entry clerk, a hotel worker and a CPA. I have no idea how they'll react.

After the last juror is seated, Judge Chen glances at her watch and turns to Skipper. "I trust you'll be ready to begin your opening statement tomorrow?"

"Absolutely, Your Honor."

* * *

Back at the office the same evening, Barbara Childs congratulates me for picking a terrific jury. Her words ring hollow. What else would she say? After she leaves, I get a more realistic view from Rosie and Mort.

"Could be worse," Mort says.

Rosie agrees. "We've done the best we could. It's a crap shoot

She's right. All the studies and empirical research go out the window when you're in a courtroom picking a jury. You never get used to it. Your client's life is in the hands of twelve strangers. You never know if you've picked twelve Mother Teresas or twelve Jack the Rippers.

"Which ones did you like the best?" I ask.

Mort clutches his cigar. "You should get a pretty good shake from the two lawyers. I think the accountant will be okay. Tough to tell with the rest of them."

Rosie adds, "I think the Asian women and the Hispanic man will be conscientious."

"Anybody you didn't like?"

"I wasn't happy with the phone company supervisor. She looks like she has a chip on her shoulder."

"I wasn't crazy about her, either," Mort says.

* * *

At eleven-thirty that night, I'm at home watching the legal analysts on CNN dissect our jury. The panel of eight "experts" sits in two rows of bleacher seats on one side of the studio, fielding questions from the strident woman with the bad hair and the wormy guy with the bad glasses. It looks like a pregame show for a football game. You know you've made the big time when your trial has its own graphics and theme song. The voice of James Earl Jones intones that we're watching coverage of "Special Circumstances: The Law Firm Murder Trial."

After voting 6-2 in favor of Skipper's jury selection acumen, the people in the bleachers turn to the TV monitor in the middle of the studio and begin a heated discussion with a jury consultant from the Menendez case, who seems to have a television studio in her home. It looks odd to watch the two hosts and the eight panelists talking to the woman's head.

"Mr. Gates clearly got the better of the jury selection process," says the disembodied head. "Asians are good prosecution jurors. They like order. On the other hand, the Hispanic man has probably had trouble with the law. I'm sure he'll be sympathetic to the defense."

It's disturbing to listen to these blatant stereotypes. She should know better. It was revealed in the voir dire that the Hispanic man is a senior vice president at Chevron who lives in the most expensive corner of the ritzy Seacliff neighborhood. He's a big contributor to the Republican party.

"The black woman," she continues, "will almost certainly favor the defense. I'm sure she's had friends or relatives hassled by the cops. She'll give the defendant a fair shake."

I'm not so sure. The woman's husband is a cop. If the disembodied head had been paying attention during the voir dire, she would have known this.

The host interrupts her. "Do you think the jurors will be predisposed against Mr. Friedman because he's a lawyer?"

The consultant smiles. "Absolutely. That's the wild card. Most people think lawyers get away with murder every day." Raucous laughter. They take another vote before they go to commercial. This time it's unanimous. The jury is clearly going to be on Skipper's side.

I flip to CNBC. Marcia Clark is lecturing on the strength of Skipper's case. I turn off the TV and run through my opening statement one more time.

* * *

Friday morning arrives with another driving rainstorm. The news vans are lined up on Bryant, and umbrellas blanket the steps of the Hall. We push our way through the crowd and march up to the courtroom. Reporters surround Skipper outside the door. We have barely enough time to take off our raincoats when Harriet Hill instructs us to rise. Judge Chen walks to her chair. She asks Harriet

Hill to bring in the jury. She greets them warmly, and says they'll have the privilege of hearing opening statements today. Then she turns to Skipper. "You may begin your opening statement, Mr. Gates."

He stands and buttons the jacket of his navy suit. He walks to the lectern and places a stack of note cards below the reading light. He doesn't look at them. The courtroom is silent. It's like the moment at the symphony when the conductor raises his baton. He nods to the judge and turns to the jury. He scans their faces for an instant. Then he turns back and addresses the judge.

"May it please the court, my name is Prentice Gates. I am the district attorney for the city and county of San Francisco. We are here today to address a serious matter. A matter of life and death."

The jurors shift uncomfortably. The phone company supervisor's eyes meet Skipper's. Judge Chen watches intently. I focus on the jury. Joel swallows.

Skipper leaves the lectern and walks slowly toward the jury. They size each other up. He takes his gold pen from his breast pocket and points toward enlarged color photos of Bob and Diana sitting on an easel in front of the jury box. "We are here today because of these two people. Robert Holmes and Diana Kennedy. I knew both of them. They were colleagues of mine. They were my friends."

I could stand up and object because he's supposed to stick to the facts in his opening. On the other hand, it's considered bad form to interrupt.

"We are in court because of that man sitting over there." He points at Joel. "We will show you evidence that the defendant knowingly and willfully, with malice aforethought, killed Diana Kennedy and Robert Holmes."

McNulty has coached him well. Skipper will always refer to Joel as "the defendant." It's easier for the jury to convict a nameless "defendant." I remind myself to refer to Joel by name.

Skipper spends twenty minutes expressing his outrage and

disappointment that a member of the legal profession and his former colleague took the lives of two respected attorneys. Skipper holds up his right index finger melodramatically. "I want you to remember these two pictures. Bob Holmes and Diana Kennedy can't speak for themselves. We can't undo the pain suffered by their families. But we can bring their killer to justice. We have to speak for them."

I stand and invoke a respectful tone. "Excuse me, Your Honor. Would you please remind Mr. Gates that opening statements should stick to the evidence? There will be time at the end for closing arguments."

"Please stick to the facts, Mr. Gates."

"Yes, Your Honor." He turns back to the jury. "Ladies and gentlemen, we are going to show you incontrovertible evidence placing the defendant at the scene of the crime." He spends twenty minutes describing the physical evidence. The jurors sit quietly. He's finding his rhythm. "In addition, we will present evidence that the defendant was having an affair with Diana Kennedy." Murmuring in the gallery. I glance at Naomi. Our eyes meet. "When the relationship soured and the defendant found out that Ms. Kennedy was romantically involved with Mr. Holmes, he became enraged. The defendant was also angry at Mr. Holmes because the defendant was passed up for election to the partnership at the Simpson and Gates law firm." He clears his throat. "Imagine. He killed another human being because he didn't make partner."

Rabbi Friedman looks down. Joel remains stoic.

"Finally," Skipper says, "I realize there are many people who aren't particularly enamored of members of the legal profession." A couple of jurors nod. "I want to make something clear. The legal profession is not on trial here. The defendant is. It's my job to show you enough evidence to give you the tools that you need to convict. I will give you those tools.

"You'll be hearing today from Mr. Daley, who is the defendant's attorney. It's his job to try to confuse you and put doubts in your mind. I'm saying this not as an indictment or criticism of Mr. Daley. It's just the way our system works."

That's not entirely true. He is, in fact, saying it as an indictment and a criticism of me.

"I ask you to use your common sense." He points to the photos again. "Above all, I want you to keep these pictures in mind. I need your help to find justice for Bob and Diana."

He makes eye contact with each of them. He walks past the easel and looks at the pictures of Bob and Diana. He unbuttons his jacket and sits down.

Judge Chen turns to me. "Mr. Daley, will you be making an opening statement today?"

We have the option of deferring our opening statement until after the prosecution has completed its case. If I wait, I can tailor my opening to address issues raised in Skipper's case. On the other hand, it may be several weeks before the jury hears me say anything of substance. We've agreed that if Skipper opens strong, I'll make our opening today. I glance at Rosie and Mort. They both nod.

"Your Honor, we'll be giving our opening statement today."

I stand up and button my jacket. I walk toward the jurors and look each of them in the eye. I move to the edge of the jury box. I like to start close to them.

I always start in a quiet, conversational tone. "My name is Michael Daley. I represent Joel Friedman, who has been unjustly accused of a terrible crime he didn't commit."

Skipper could leap up right now and demand that I stick to the evidence. Fortunately, McNulty's told him to stay in his chair. I'm going to take advantage of it while I can.

"Joel Friedman is an honest, hardworking man with a wonderful wife and two young children. His life has been turned upside down because he happened to be at the office doing his job on the night two people died. Imagine what it must be like when the police come to your house and arrest you in front of your wife, your parents and your children for two murders you didn't commit. What do you tell your wife? What do you tell your parents? What do you tell your kids?

"That's why we're here. Mr. Gates is absolutely right that this is a very serious matter. It is a matter of life and death. I need your help. I need you to sort out what happened. I need you to sift through the evidence so we can figure out the truth—together. In our system, Mr. Gates is required to prove his case beyond a reasonable doubt. That's a tough standard." I pause. "After you hear the evidence you're going to come to a simple conclusion. Joel didn't do it."

I get the hint of agreement from the accountant.

"You'll hear Joel was in the office that night. You'll find out he phoned Diana Kennedy and asked her to return to the office. You'll hear he left an angry voicemail message for Bob Holmes. All of these things are true." I describe the fingerprints on the gun. I argue that they got there when Joel unloaded it. I claim they can't prove he pulled the trigger.

"Mr. Gates is going to introduce circumstantial evidence to show that Joel Friedman and Diana Kennedy were having an affair. He's going to claim that she broke up with him and initiated a romantic relationship with Mr. Holmes. There was, in fact, no such affair between Joel Friedman and Diana Kennedy. It didn't happen."

I spend fifteen minutes trying to cast doubt on every piece of evidence, liberally using the words "shaky," "contrived" and "convoluted." I think the jury is with me. At the very least, they seem to be listening. I glance at Rosie, who blinks twice. It's my signal to wrap up.

"Ladies and gentlemen, Mr. Gates has suggested to you that my job is to obfuscate and confuse you. Let's be realistic. We all know that there are lawyers who will do just about anything to get their client off. I'm not that kind of lawyer. I will not lie to you. I will not attempt to confuse you. And I will not, under any circumstances, try to mislead you."

Actually, I'd try to obfuscate and confuse them in a New York minute if I thought it would help get Joel off. "I need you to keep an open mind and review the evidence. I know there's a lot of animosity directed toward lawyers. I ask you not to take out your feelings toward the legal profession against Joel Friedman. You don't have to look very far to find cases where justice wasn't served. I would ask you to help me try to make the system work. When we're done, I know you will agree that Joel Friedman is not guilty of these terrible crimes."

I sit down. The judge says we'll break for the weekend.

* * *

At nine o'clock the same evening, Rosie and I are watching CNN. The experts in the bleachers have proclaimed Skipper the hands-down winner of opening statements. "Daley should have waited until after the prosecution's case to give his opening," says the woman with the bad hair.

"Nah," says the disembodied head on the TV screen. "Gates has too much charisma. At least Daley got to the jury before the horse was out of the barn."

The prosecutor from Texas who always wears a Stetson in a hot TV studio also sides with Skipper. "They should have tried for a plea bargain," he drawls.

We flip to CNBC, where Marcia Clark is holding court. "If I were in Daley's shoes, I'd be begging the prosecution for a deal."

Thanks, Marcia. Rosie shuts the TV off.

"Was it that bad?" I ask her.

"You held your own. The prosecution gets to play its good cards first."

I hope she's right. It doesn't make me feel any better.

CHAPTER 33

LAYING THE FOUNDATION

"Keep your case short and sweet."
— NewsCenter 4 Legal Analyst Morgan Henderson.
Monday, March 23.

The sun makes a brief cameo appearance on Monday morning. By the time we reach the Hall, it's raining again. We push our way past the ever-present TV cameras.

We take our seats at the defense table. Joel asks, "Who do you think they'll call first?"

The conventional wisdom is that prosecutors build their case one piece at a time. They have to prove the defendant was there. They have to show he had opportunity. They have to demonstrate he had contact with the murder weapon. And they have to prove motive. Piece by piece. Block by block. If the blocks don't fit, the defendant walks. It's that simple.

"They'll probably start with the first officer at the scene and work their way through the physical evidence," I say. "It lays the foundation for their case."

Harriet Hill calls for order. Judge Chen takes her seat and looks at Skipper. "Are you ready to call your first witness?"

"Yes, Your Honor. The people call Officer Paul Chinn."

Not a bad place to start. Chinn was the first officer at the scene.

The young officer's uniform is freshly pressed. He walks to the front of the courtroom and is sworn in. Cops are trained to stay calm. Some are better at it than others. My dad used to hate going to court.

"Officer Chinn," Skipper begins, "were you the first officer to arrive at Simpson and Gates on the morning of December thirty-first?"

"Yes, sir. I arrived at eight-twelve a.m. I responded to a nine-one-one dispatch." His delivery is a little wooden, but the tone is straightforward. Juries pay close attention to the early witnesses. Then they start to get bored. Chinn says Chuckles met him in the lobby. Chuckles said nobody was in danger. Then he escorted Chinn to Bob's office, where Joel was waiting outside.

Skipper nods to McNulty, who places a drawing of Bob's office on the easel in front of the jury. Skipper has Chinn identify it as a diagram of the crime scene. Skipper turns to Judge Chen and requests that it be introduced as an exhibit.

"No objection, Your Honor," I say. I'm glad they've decided to use a diagram instead of the crime-scene photos. I'm sure those will come later.

"Officer Chinn," Skipper continues, "would you mind showing us where the bodies were found?"

Chinn walks over to the diagram. He uses a Bic pen to point to the places on the floor where the bodies were found.

Skipper walks him through a brief tour of the scene. Then he picks up a revolver wrapped in clear plastic from the evidence cart. "Officer Chinn, do you recognize this?"

"Yes. It's the weapon I found on the desk of Mr. Holmes."

At least he didn't call it the murder weapon.

Skipper has him identify three spent shell casings and the three unused bullets. "Where did you find the casings and the bullets?"

"On the desk."

"Do you know how the bullets got there?"

I'm up. "Objection, Your Honor. Calls for speculation. Officer Chinn has no personal knowledge of how the bullets made their way to the desk." It's good to get your first objection out of the way.

"Sustained."

Skipper rephrases. "Did the defendant explain how the casings and the bullets found their way to the desk?"

Chinn's tone is measured. "The defendant said he unloaded the gun. He directed me to the casings and the bullets."

"Did you see the defendant unload the gun?"

"No."

"Was the defendant acting suspiciously?"

"Objection. The question goes to the defendant's state of mind."

Well, not exactly, but I'm going to try to break up Skipper's rhythm.

"Your Honor," Skipper says, "I'm not asking Officer Chinn to read the defendant's mind. I'm simply asking for his observations of the defendant's behavior."

"Overruled."

Chinn looks at Joel. "The defendant was agitated and extremely upset."

Skipper is pleased. "And did you have any basis to conclude that the defendant may have had any involvement in the deaths of Mr. Holmes and Ms. Kennedy?"

"Objection. Speculative."

"Sustained."

I'm going to take my shots while I can. Skipper is going to get the hang of this sooner or later.

Skipper strokes his chin. "Officer, after you found the bodies, murder weapon, bullets and shells, what did you do?"

"Objection. There's no foundation for the characterization of the gun as the 'murder' weapon."

"Sustained." Judge Chen turns to the jury. "Please disregard the characterization of the revolver as the 'murder' weapon."

Sure they will. Skipper rephrases the question, leaving out the word "murder."

Chinn says he followed standard procedure; he secured the scene and called for reinforcements. He describes the arrival of the police and the paramedics, followed by the technicians from the medical examiner's office, the police photographers and the homicide inspectors.

"No further questions, Your Honor."

Not a bad direct exam for a guy who's never done it before. And not a bad performance by a young cop who's batting leadoff in his first big case.

* * *

"Officer Chinn," I say calmly, as I stand, "you said you found the revolver, the spent shells and the unused bullets on the desk of Mr. Holmes."

"Correct."

"And you testified that Mr. Friedman told you he unloaded the gun."

"Yes."

"Did he tell you why he unloaded the gun?"

"To protect the safety of the other members of the firm."

"That's an admirable goal, isn't it?"

"Objection. Speculative."

"Sustained."

I've made my point. "Officer, did you have any reason to disbelieve Mr. Friedman?"

Chinn looks helplessly at Skipper. "No."

"Did you see any evidence on his hands or clothing suggesting he had fired the gun?"

"It would have been very difficult to see any such evidence with the naked eye, Mr. Daley."

"I understand. But did you see any such evidence?"

"No, sir."

It's always a good sign when the witness starts calling you "sir." "Did you collect samples of tissue or clothing from Mr. Friedman to obtain evidence that he had, in fact, fired the gun?"

"No, sir."

"So you have no personal knowledge as to whether he fired the gun?"

Skipper stands. "Asked and answered, Your Honor."

"Sustained. Move along, Mr. Daley."

I was wondering how long she'd let me go. "Officer, you testified that you secured the scene."

"That's right."

"So nobody could have left the Simpson and Gates suite once you arrived, correct?"

"That's true."

"You secured the elevators?"

"Yes."

"And the stairs?"

"Yes."

I give him an inquisitive look. "You were the only officer at the scene when you arrived, right?"

His eyes dart toward Skipper. "Yes."

"Yet you were able to secure six elevators and two internal stairways all by yourself?"

"Other officers arrived right away. We secured the scene as soon as possible."

"What about the freight elevator?"

"We secured it."

"When?"

"When the other officers arrived."

"So, Officer, it is possible that any number of people could have fled the scene on the elevators or the stairs or the freight elevator before additional officers arrived, isn't it?"

"Objection. Speculative."

"Overruled."

Chinn looks troubled. "I suppose that's possible."

So far, so good. "Officer, you testified that Mr. Friedman was agitated and upset when you arrived."

"Correct."

"How long have you been on the force?"

"Three and a half years."

"How many times have you been the first officer at the scene of an alleged homicide?"

"This was the second time."

"How many dead bodies have you seen?"

"Objection," Skipper says. "I fail to see any relevance."

Judge Chen's tone has the first hint of impatience. "Overruled."

"I've seen three dead bodies," Chinn says.

I move closer to him. "Officer Chinn, in your experience, when you've arrived at the scene of the homicide, isn't it usually the case that the people are upset?"

"Yes."

"And the people who were most upset were the people who found the body, right?"

His tone is grudging. "Yes, sir."

"Wouldn't it be fair to say that Mr. Friedman's reaction was not unusual in the circumstances?"

Skipper should object. I'm asking him to speculate.

"That's fair," Chinn says.

Gotcha. "One last thing. When you arrived, you were met by Mr. Stern, who told you nobody was in danger."

"Correct."

"You arrived within minutes after Mr. Stern discovered the bodies. How did he know there wasn't a killer on the loose in the Simpson and Gates office?"

Chinn looks at Skipper and then at McNulty. "I guess he assumed nobody was in danger because he found the murder weapon on the desk of Mr. Holmes."

"Move to strike the word 'murder' from Officer Chinn's testimony."

"Sustained. The jury will disregard the characterization of the revolver as the 'murder' weapon."

I'm not quite finished. "Officer Chinn, isn't it possible that Mr. Stern knew that nobody was in danger because he knew Mr. Holmes had committed suicide?"

"Objection. Speculative."

"Sustained."

"Isn't it possible Mr. Stern knew that nobody was in danger

because he knew who the real killer was? And the real killer may have even been him?"

"Objection. Speculative."

"Sustained." Judge Chen taps her gavel to silence murmurs in the gallery. "If there are any other disruptions, I will clear this courtroom."

"No further questions," I say.

* * *

"You took him apart," Joel says.

We're taking a short recess after Chinn's testimony. We're in the consultation room behind Judge Chen's courtroom.

"He's a kid, Joel. He's just a table-setter."

"You made him contradict his story. That's good."

I get a more realistic view from Mort. "Nice cross. The jury seems to like you."

Rosie is always a voice of reality. "Still a long way to go."

* * *

After the recess, Skipper calls Sandra Wilson. She spends the next hour describing how she meticulously gathered every shred of evidence in Bob's office and Diana's apartment. Skipper is doing it by the book. He's confirming to the jury that there are no chain-of-custody issues. He's introducing the evidence he'll need later in the trial. He gets Sandra to describe how she handled and catalogued the revolver, the spent shells and the unused bullets. She confirms that the revolver was registered to Bob. She identifies the keyboard. I interrupt periodically. Realistically, I'm not going to win any battles with Sandra on the stand. There's no point in making an ass of myself while she's testifying. It will only annoy the phone company supervisor.

I ask a few perfunctory questions on cross. I want to get her off the stand as fast as I can.

* * *

After lunch, Skipper raises the stakes. Marcus Banks looks ready for battle as he strides to the front of the courtroom. After he's sworn in, Skipper picks up a meticulously labeled cassette tape from the evidence cart.

"Inspector," he says, "do you recognize this?"

"It's a recording of a message left on Diana Kennedy's home answering machine at approximately twelve-fifty-one a.m. on December thirty-first."

"And could you describe the contents of the message?"

"Objection, Your Honor. Hearsay."

"Overruled."

I'm not surprised. I know she's going to let them introduce the tapes into evidence. We've fought this battle and lost.

Banks keeps his tone measured. "The message was from the defendant. He asked Ms. Kennedy to return to the office."

Nice response. Straightforward. Non-inflammatory. I can see McNulty's influence. They're going to build their case carefully. They don't need theatrics—yet.

"Inspector, did the defendant sound agitated or upset in the message?"

"Objection. Asks for Mr. Friedman's state of mind."

"Sustained."

Skipper introduces the tape into evidence. He asks the judge for permission to play it to the jury. Judge Chen gives me an inquisitive glance.

"Your Honor," I say, "the defense renews its objection to having this tape entered into evidence." I'm stating it for the record so we can challenge her decision on appeal.

"We've been over this, Mr. Daley. Your motion is denied."

"The defense therefore requests that Your Honor instruct the jury to consider the fact that this tape is being played in the absence of context."

Skipper says, "Your Honor, we believe the tape speaks for itself."

Judge Chen looks at the jurors. "Ladies and gentlemen, you are about to hear a recording of a conversation between Mr. Friedman and Ms. Kennedy. You should consider the fact that you have not been given information concerning the context in which this recording was made."

Skipper hands the cassette to McNulty, who puts it into a tape player. The jurors focus on the tape player. The heated voices of Joel and Diana resonate in the courtroom. Joel closes his eyes. Naomi's lips form a tight line across her face.

The tape ends. Skipper turns back to Banks. "Were you able to identify the voices?"

"Objection. Inspector Banks has not been qualified as a voice-recognition expert."

"Overruled."

"The male voice was that of the defendant," Banks says. "The female voice was that of the victim, Ms. Kennedy."

They go through a similar exercise for the voicemail message from Joel to Bob. "Inspector Banks," Skipper says, "do you believe Mr. Friedman was angry enough at the time these tapes were made to kill two people?"

I'm up like a shot. "Objection, Your Honor. Speculative. State of mind."

"Sustained."

Skipper smiles. "No further questions."

I stand up immediately. "Inspector Banks, you weren't present when these telephone conversations were recorded, were you?"

"Of course not."

"So you don't really know why Mr. Friedman called Ms. Kennedy, do you?"

"It's obvious. He was angry at her."

"Inspector, are you aware that Ms. Kennedy and Mr. Friedman were working on a very large transaction?"

"Yes."

"And they were under a lot of pressure to close that deal the next morning?"

"Yes."

"And millions of dollars were riding on the successful closing?"

"Objection. Leading."

"Overruled."

It's okay to lead on cross. I'm now standing right in front of Banks. "Isn't it possible that Mr. Friedman called Ms. Kennedy because he needed help on the deal?"

"I don't think so."

"But it's possible, right?"

"I don't think so."

He isn't going to budge. "Inspector, let's talk about Mr. Friedman's voicemail message to Mr. Holmes. Are you aware that Mr. Friedman was told that he wasn't going to make partner that night?"

"Yes."

"Do you believe Mr. Friedman was upset about that?"

"Yes."

"If you'd worked for eight years to try to make partner, you'd probably have been upset, too."

He shrugs.

"Inspector Banks, you seem to have chosen to interpret Mr. Friedman's voicemail message to Mr. Holmes as a threat."

"It was. I think it's obvious."

"Have you ever worked in a law firm?"

"No."

"But you've spent a lot of time around lawyers, right?"

He smiles sardonically. "More than I'd care to."

"And you know a little bit about how lawyers think, right?"

"Objection, Your Honor. Can we get to the point?"

"Sustained." Judge Chen rotates her hands like a basketball referee making a traveling call. "Speed it up, Mr. Daley."

"Inspector, lawyers sometimes say things for effect, right?"

"Kind of like right now, right, Mr. Daley?"

Touché. "As a matter of fact, yes. Lawyers sometimes take

exaggerated positions as a negotiating tactic, don't they?"

"That's true."

"Isn't it possible, Inspector, that Mr. Friedman's voicemail to Mr. Holmes was, in fact, lawyerly posturing?"

"Not the way I heard it."

"Come on, Inspector."

Skipper stand and objects. "Your Honor, Inspector Banks has answered Mr. Daley's question."

The hell he has.

"Sustained."

I've gone as far as I can. "No further questions."

* * *

Joel is agitated in the consultation room during the break. "Couldn't you have nailed Banks?"

Mort sticks up for me. "Banks wasn't going to move an inch. Mike got him to look like a stubborn jerk. It's the best we could do."

Joel scowls. "Maybe Mort should take a few witnesses."

Mort looks pleased.

I hold up a hand. "The prosecutor always looks good at the beginning. We have to chip away a little at a time."

He tosses a crumpled paper cup into the trash and doesn't respond.

CHAPTER 34

"I AM THE CHIEF MEDICAL EXAMINER FOR THE CITY AND COUNTY OF SAN FRANCISCO"

"Dr. Beckert has testified at hundreds of trials."
— NewsCenter 4 Legal Analyst Morgan Henderson.
Monday, March 23.

At three o'clock, Skipper says in a clear voice, "The people call Dr. Roderick Beckert."

Beckert nods to the judge as he walks confidently to the front of the courtroom. The college professor tweed jacket hanging on the coatrack in his office has been replaced with a charcoal-gray business suit and a burgundy tie. He's the embodiment of authority.

Skipper stands at the lectern. He doesn't want to crowd Beckert. "Would you please state your name and occupation for the record?"

"Dr. Roderick Beckert." The hint of a smile. "I am the chief medical examiner for the city and county of San Francisco. I've held the position for twenty-seven years."

Skipper begins to run Beckert through his credentials. I stop him almost immediately and stipulate to his expertise. There's no point in giving Skipper twenty minutes of free time to wave Beckert's diplomas in front of the jury.

"Dr. Beckert," Skipper says, "did you perform autopsies on the bodies of Robert Holmes and Diana Kennedy on January first of this year?"

"Yes."

"And would you be kind enough to describe the results of those autopsies?"

He turns slightly toward the jury. "Of course, Mr. Gates." He says Bob and Diana died of gunshot wounds, his to the head, hers to the chest. Time of death between one and four a.m. He explains that Diana was two months pregnant, and that the unborn fetus also died. His tone is conversational, yet forceful. I let him drone on for a few minutes about body temperature, lividity and discoloration before I stipulate to his determination on the range for the time of death. The jury believes him. It isn't to our advantage to let him build empathy.

On cue, McNulty trots out a poster-size version of a photo Beckert showed me in his office. We tried to keep it out.

"Doctor Beckert," Skipper says, "what is this a picture of?"

"The left side of the head of the victim, Robert Holmes."

"Would you please describe the gunshot wound that killed Mr. Holmes?"

"Of course. Entry through the right parietal, just above the right temple. It severed the cerebral cortex and pierced the mesencephalon, or midbrain, before exiting through the left parietal lobe and the left parietal bone of the skull, just above the left ear. In other words, the gun was placed against the right temple and shot laterally through the head, causing instantaneous death as the bullet passed through the midbrain."

The courtroom is silent.

"Doctor, would you mind showing the jury the exit wound?"

"Of course." Beckert walks to the easel and points at the area just behind Bob's left ear.

"Dr. Beckert," Skipper continues, "was there another wound to the head?"

"Yes, Mr. Gates." Beckert points at Bob's left ear, just above the edge of the exit wound. "Right here, on the parietal bone, there's a small hematoma, or concussive injury."

"Objection," I say. "I can't tell what Dr. Beckert is pointing at."

Judge Chen says, "I'm afraid that I can't either. Doctor, I'm going to have to ask you to mark the wound more precisely."

"Of course." Beckert pulls a felt-tip marker from his pocket and he draws a circle on the picture. "Right here."

Judge Chen nods. "Thank you."

Skipper studies the picture. "Doctor, would you please describe the concussive wound in greater detail?"

"Certainly. Mr. Holmes suffered a blow to the head, which caused a hematoma, or bump, to the parietal bone of his skull. Based upon the swelling and the freshness of the wound, I believe he was knocked unconscious shortly before he died. It's similar to a blow suffered by a football player in a helmet-to-helmet collision."

"Is it possible he was killed by the concussive blow?"

"Unlikely. There was trauma to the skull, but not enough to kill a healthy male."

"Why would somebody have knocked him out before they shot him?"

"Objection. Speculative."

"Sustained."

"I'll rephrase. Doctor, do you have a theory as to why someone would have knocked Mr. Holmes unconscious and then shot him moments later?"

"Objection. Still speculative."

"Sustained."

"Doctor, does it appear to you that the killer was attempting to make this look like a suicide?"

"Objection. Speculative."

"Sustained." Judge Chen glares as Skipper. "Enough, Mr. Gates.

"No further questions, Your Honor."

* * *

I'm on my feet right away. "Dr. Beckert, can you show me this alleged concussive wound one more time?"

He points at the circle he drew a moment ago. "Right here."

"And you're one hundred percent sure that mark was caused by someone taking a heavy object and hitting Mr. Holmes?"

"Yes. One hundred percent sure."

"And it is not possible the wound was caused by the bullet that obliterated much of his head?"

"In my best medical judgment, no."

"Doctor, did you find any evidence of the object that you claim was used to strike Mr. Holmes?"

"I'm not sure I understand."

"If Mr. Holmes was hit with a piece of wood or metal, you may have found fragments of wood or metal or perhaps paint in the wound, right? Did you find any such evidence?"

"No."

"How is it possible that somebody hit Mr. Holmes hard enough to knock him unconscious, yet you found no evidence of the object?"

"Objection. Speculative."

"Overruled."

Beckert shakes his head. "He must have been hit with an object that didn't leave any traces."

"Doctor, you recall that the body was found on the floor."

"Correct."

"Is it possible the concussive wound was caused by Mr. Holmes hitting his head on his desk as he slumped to the floor?"

"No, Mr. Daley."

"Why not?" I'm taking a bit of a chance.

"Mr. Holmes died instantly from the gunshot wound. The hematoma was fairly well developed. If he'd hit his head on his desk after he'd been shot, there would have been no bump." He explains that bumps are formed by blood rushing to the injured area. When you die, your heart stops beating and your body is therefore incapable of pumping enough blood to create a bump. "Mr. Daley, you can hit a cadaver as many times as you'd like, but you can't generate a bump on its head. As a result, I concluded that Mr. Holmes was very much alive when he was struck on the head."

I'm sorry I asked. I pick up a copy of his autopsy report. "Doctor, do you recognize this document?"

"It's my autopsy report on Mr. Holmes."

I hand it to him. "You dictated this report as you conducted your autopsy, right?"

"Yes."

"Could you please turn to page fourteen."

He puts on his reading glasses and flips through the report. "I've found it, Mr. Daley."

"Does page fourteen describe the concussive wound?"

He studies it quickly. "Yes."

"Would you be kind enough to read the portion of the report that I highlighted?"

"Of course. 'Approximately three centimeters from the top of the exit wound, there appears to be a small concussive wound on the parietal bone of the skull. The wound appears relatively fresh.' "

"Those were your exact words, Doctor?"

"Of course."

"At the time you dictated your notes, were you looking at Mr. Holmes's head?"

Skipper stands, then sits down. He can't figure out a reason to object.

Beckert replies with a hint of irritation. "Of course I was looking at his head."

"When you were looking at Mr. Holmes's head, you described what 'appears' to be a 'small concussive wound' that is 'relatively fresh.' Yet, a moment ago, you testified that you were one hundred percent sure that it was, in fact, a concussive wound, and it was absolutely fresh. How did your tentative observation turn into such an absolute conclusion?"

"Mr. Daley, I've been a medical examiner for many years. You read my preliminary observations. I examined the wound more closely during my more detailed autopsy procedures. The size and depth of the concussive wound led me to conclude, unequivocally, that Mr. Holmes was struck on the head."

I glance at the jury. "How much time elapsed between the day you performed the autopsy and the day you issued your report?"

"About a week."

"And how many times did you look at the body again?"

"I didn't."

"You didn't? Yet, a week later, your view on the concussive wound seems to have changed."

"After reviewing the evidence, I became certain that there was, in fact, a concussive wound."

"And it certainly helps the prosecution's case if there's such a wound, right?"

Skipper and McNulty both stand. "Objection," Skipper shouts. "Move to strike."

"Sustained."

I turn back to Beckert. "Could you please read the portion of your report that I've highlighted on page nineteen?"

" 'Chemical residue was found on victim's right hand.' "

"What sort of chemical residue?"

"Gunpowder."

Judge Chen's eyes open wide.

I try to look perplexed. "There was gunpowder residue on his right hand?"

"Yes."

"How did it get there?"

Skipper pops up. "Objection. Speculative."

"Sustained."

"I'll rephrase." I turn back to Beckert. "Isn't it true that when a gun is fired, it emits chemicals, including gunpowder, traces of which can be found on the hands of the party who fired the gun?"

"Objection. Dr. Beckert isn't an expert on firearms or chemical substances."

"Your Honor, Dr. Beckert wrote the seminal textbook on forensic science. Surely he's capable of answering such a basic question."

"Overruled."

Beckert pushes his glasses to the top of his head. "Yes, Mr. Daley. When someone fires a gun, it is possible to find traces of gunpowder and other chemicals on his hand."

"Gunpowder traces are one of the first things the police test for on the hands of a person charged with a shooting, right?"

"Yes."

"So the gunpowder traces on the right hand of Mr. Holmes suggest it's possible that Mr. Holmes fired the gun that killed him."

"Objection. Speculative."

"Overruled."

Beckert answers in a grudging tone. "Yes, it's possible. However—I,"

"No further questions, Your Honor."

Skipper leaps up for redirect. "Doctor, in your best medical judgment, was Mr. Holmes unconscious when he was killed?"

"Yes."

"What about the gunpowder traces on his right hand?"

"Objection. Speculative."

"Overruled."

Beckert remains calm. "I believe Mr. Holmes was knocked unconscious by a blow to the head. I believe someone placed the gun in his right hand and caused Mr. Holmes to pull the trigger. It was a clumsy attempt to fake a suicide."

"Thank you, Doctor. No further questions."

I jump up once more and try for a tone of incredulity. "So, Doctor, it's your testimony that you think somebody sneaked up behind Bob Holmes, whacked him on the head, and, while he was unconscious, put a revolver in his hand and caused him to use the same hand to shoot himself. Is that about it?"

His tone is even. "Yes, Mr. Daley."

"You realize that nobody in their right mind would believe such a preposterous scenario."

"Objection," Skipper shouts.

"Sustained." Judge Chen gives me an icy glare. "Mr. Daley, I don't want any more grandstanding in my courtroom."

"No further questions."

CHAPTER 35

BUILDING BLOCKS

"Prosecutors build their cases one block at a time."
— CNN. Tuesday, March 24.

"Please state your name and occupation for the record," Skipper says.

"Edward O'Malley. Ballistics technician, SFPD."

Ed O'Malley takes the stand at nine o'clock the next morning. He's a forty-seven-year-old civilian scientist who is the department's ballistics guru. He works in a hermetically sealed area in the basement of the Hall. The cops refer to guys like Ed as white coats. He can determine with statistical precision whether a bullet was discharged from a particular weapon. His demeanor is studious. His tiny, rimless glasses perch on a large nose above a tidy gray mustache. His role in this play will be relatively short.

Skipper runs him through his resume, then picks up the plastic-wrapped revolver from the evidence cart and holds it up as if it's the Super Bowl trophy. "Mr. O'Malley, do you recognize this revolver?"

"Yes. That's the murder weapon."

I'm up immediately. "Objection. There's no foundation for Mr. O'Malley's characterization of this revolver as the 'murder' weapon."

"Sustained." Judge Chen sighs. "We're starting early today. The jury will disregard the characterization of the weapon." She turns to Skipper. "Try it again, Mr. Gates."

Skipper leads O'Malley through a detailed description of the revolver. He concludes that it was the weapon that fired the fatal shots. Skipper sits down.

There isn't an iota of doubt in my mind that the bullets were fired from this gun. Of course, this doesn't stop me from trying to plant a few seeds of doubt in the mind of the phone company supervisor. "Mr. O'Malley," I say, "how long have you been with the department?"

"Fourteen years."

"Ever been suspended?"

"Objection," Skipper says. "Relevance."

"Your Honor, Mr. Gates called this witness as an expert. His record is highly relevant."

"Overruled."

O'Malley glances at the clock. "I was suspended for a week eleven years ago."

"No further questions." The jury doesn't have to know he was suspended when he pled no contest to a DUI—which was, of course, unrelated to his credentials as a ballistics expert. Skipper doesn't seem to know about it. If he did, he might try to rehabilitate O'Malley on redirect. O'Malley glares at Mort, who has brought his integrity into question for the second time. Mort found out about O'Malley's suspension in a case five years ago. In that case, his client walked. I hope we get the same result.

* * *

"My name is Sergeant Kathleen Jacobsen. I'm an evidence technician with the SFPD. I've been with the force for twenty-two years."

Skipper stands at the lectern. "Do you have a particular area of expertise?"

"Fingerprints and other chemical and physical evidence."

Kathleen Jacobsen is a tall, gray-haired woman in her late fifties with a professional demeanor and a commanding aura. One of the first lesbians to work her way up the ranks, she's become a nationally known figure on evidentiary matters.

Skipper begins to walk her through her impressive resume: undergrad at USC, master's from UC-Berkeley. I stipulate to her expertise. She confirms she was the lead evidence technician in the investigation.

Skipper strolls to the evidence cart, picks up the revolver and parades it in front of the jury. "Are you familiar with this weapon?"

"Yes. It fired the shots that killed Mr. Holmes and Ms. Kennedy." Her authoritative tone is a prosecutor's dream.

Skipper is pleased. "Did you find any fingerprints on this weapon?"

"Yes. The defendant's." Her delivery is precise.

They go through the same exercise for the computer keyboard. She confirms that Joel's fingerprints were found on it, too. Skipper signals to McNulty, who turns on a projector. The suicide e-mail appears on the screen.

"Sergeant, could you please describe the message displayed on the screen?"

"It's an e-mail message generated from Mr. Holmes's computer at one-twenty a.m. on December thirty-first."

"Does that appear to be a suicide message to you, Sergeant?"

"Objection. Sergeant Jacobsen is an expert on evidence, not suicide."

"Overruled."

Jacobsen looks at the message. "I believe it was intended to look like a suicide message. However, it was obvious the message was a fake. We found the defendant's fingerprints on the computer keyboard. We believe the defendant typed the message."

"And why would he do that?"

"Objection. Speculative."

"Sustained."

"Wouldn't he have done so to make it appear that Mr. Holmes had committed suicide?"

"Objection. Leading."

"Sustained."

"No further questions, Your Honor."

He's made his point. McNulty turns off the projector.

I address Jacobsen in a respectful tone. "Sergeant, who was the registered owner of this gun?"

"The victim, Robert Holmes."

"He kept a loaded gun in his office?"

"So it seems."

"Sergeant," I say, "did you find any fingerprints on the weapon besides Mr. Friedman's?"

"Yes. We found smudged fingerprints belonging to the victim, Robert Holmes."

"On what part of the weapon did you find his fingerprints?"

"On the handle."

"And could you please show us where you found the fingerprints of Mr. Friedman?"

She says she found Joel's right thumb and right middle finger, ring finger and pinky on the handle. His right index finger was on the cylinder.

I hand her the plastic-wrapped revolver. "Sergeant, you didn't find Mr. Friedman's fingerprints on the trigger, did you?"

She glances at Skipper. Then she looks back at me. "We found smudged fingerprints on the trigger, Mr. Daley."

"I understand. But, you could not positively identify any of Mr. Friedman's fingerprints on the trigger, right?"

"Correct."

This helps. "And isn't it possible that Mr. Friedman's prints found on this weapon were generated while Mr. Friedman was unloading it, just the way he described it to Officer Chinn?"

Skipper could object, but it would undercut her credibility.

"It's possible," she says.

I pause to let her answer sink in. "And isn't it true that while you may have fingerprint evidence that Mr. Friedman touched this revolver, you have no evidence that he actually fired it?"

"Objection, Your Honor." Skipper's trying to stop the bleeding. "Argumentative."

"Overruled."

Jacobsen looks right at me. "That's true. I can say to an absolute certainty that Mr. Friedman held this revolver. I can't say to an absolute certainty that he pulled the trigger."

I take the computer keyboard from the evidence cart. "Would you please tell us which keys had Mr. Friedman's fingerprints?"

"All of the alphabetic keys."

"What about the numeric keys and the function keys?"

"We found his fingerprints on all of the numeric keys and three of the function keys."

I signal to Rosie. The suicide e-mail appears on the screen in front of the jury. "Sergeant, you and Mr. Gates contend this message was typed by Mr. Friedman."

"Correct. The defendant's fingerprints were found on the keyboard."

"Did you find the fingerprints of Mr. Holmes on this keyboard?"

"No, we didn't."

"Isn't it odd that you didn't find Mr. Holmes's fingerprints on his own keyboard?"

"Objection, Your Honor. Speculative."

"Sustained."

"I'll rephrase. Sergeant, based on your experience as a fingerprint expert, wouldn't you expect to find Mr. Holmes's fingerprints on his own keyboard?"

She frowns. "Probably, although we think he may not have been a secretor. In other words, Mr. Holmes didn't sweat profusely enough to give off a lot of fingerprints."

Sure. "But you've said you didn't find any at all."

"Objection. Asked and answered."

"Sustained."

I've made my point. "You said you found Mr. Friedman's fingerprints on all of the alphabetic keys. Did you stop to determine whether the e-mail used all of the letters of the alphabet?"

"No."

"May I ask why not?"

She looks straight ahead for a moment. "We were looking for his fingerprints. We didn't attempt to analyze the contents of the e-mail message."

"Would it surprise you to find out that the e-mail didn't use all of the letters of the alphabet?"

"It wouldn't surprise me."

"In fact, Sergeant, if you read the e-mail carefully, you'll find that it does not contain the letters J, K, Q, X or Z, or any punctuation marks other than periods, and no numbers at all. Yet you found Mr. Friedman's fingerprints on all of the alphabetic keys."

"Perhaps he typed the message several times, or made corrections or erased."

I move closer. "The fact is, you don't know. The fact is, you can't explain it. Isn't that right?"

"Objection. Argumentative."

"Overruled."

"Yes, Mr. Daley. We can't explain why his fingerprints were found on all the alphabetic keys."

Now we'll see if Skipper's awake. "Isn't it possible, Sergeant, that the reason his fingerprints were found on all the alphabetic keys is that somebody switched his keyboard with that of Mr. Holmes?"

"Objection. Speculative."

Judge Chen looks at me. "Unless you're prepared to bring evidence concerning this allegation, the objection is sustained."

"Withdrawn." We'll get back to this subject when it's our turn. "No further questions."

Judge Chen looks at Skipper. "Redirect?"

"Yes, Your Honor." Skipper picks up the wrapped revolver and hands it to Jacobsen. "Sergeant, could you please show us once again where you found Mr. Friedman's fingerprints?"

She points to various spots where fingerprints were found.

"Would you please grip the gun in the manner that would have generated these fingerprints?"

"Objection, Your Honor. There's no foundation."

"Your Honor," Skipper says, "Mr. Daley asked Sergeant

Jacobsen to describe the locations of the defendant's fingerprints. I'm just asking her to amplify her answer."

"Overruled."

Crap.

Jacobsen picks up the revolver in her right hand. She grips it in her palm with her right thumb, middle finger, ring finger and pinky. Her right index finger rests on the cylinder.

"Sergeant," Skipper says, "without moving your thumb or other fingers, would you please move your index finger down to the trigger?"

She holds up the gun so that the jury can see it. She easily moves her index finger from the cylinder to the trigger.

"What would you conclude from this demonstration?" Skipper asks.

"Objection. Speculative."

"Overruled."

Jacobsen nods at the jury. "I would conclude that the defendant could have created the fingerprints I've described while pulling the trigger of this weapon."

"No further questions."

I'm back in her face. "It's still your testimony that you could not find identifiable fingerprints of Mr. Friedman on the trigger, right?"

"Yes. The fingerprints on the trigger were smudged and unidentifiable."

"So, you can't prove he pulled the trigger."

"Objection. Asked and answered."

"Sustained."

"No further questions."

* * *

"The people call Richard Cinelli."

The bartender is sworn in and takes his seat on the stand. He pulls the microphone toward him. He likes talking to people. Before he's said a word, he's already connected with the jury.

Skipper walks him through the preliminaries. He was at work at Harrington's on the night of the thirtieth. He confirms that Joel and Diana came in about nine-forty-five. It was crowded. They ordered drinks and dinner.

"Around ten o'clock, Mr. Friedman and Ms. Kennedy had a disagreement," Cinelli says.

"Would it be more accurate to call it an argument?" Skipper asks.

Cinelli shrugs. "I'd call it a disagreement."

"But it could have been described as an argument."

"Maybe. She threw a glass of water in his face and she left."

"Was she upset?"

"Obviously."

"Did you hear anything they said?"

"Not much. I'm a bartender. I get paid to be discreet."

"But you did hear something, right?"

"Yes. Mr. Friedman told Ms. Kennedy that he'd get her for something. Those were his exact words. 'I'll get you for this.'"

"So he threatened her?"

"Objection, Your Honor. Speculative."

"Sustained."

"No further questions."

I walk over to Cinelli. "Do you know what they were arguing about?"

"No."

"You knew they were attorneys, right?"

"Yes."

"And you knew they were working on a big deal?"

"Objection. Foundation."

"Overruled."

"That's what I understand."

"Is it possible Mr. Friedman and Ms. Kennedy were arguing about work?"

Skipper stands. "Objection. Speculative."

"Overruled."

Judge Chen is treating us equally.

Cinelli nods. "Yes, Mr. Daley. That's entirely possible."

"No further questions."

* * *

"My name is Homer Kim. I'm a custodian at the Bank of America Building."

A nervous Kim is sitting in the witness chair late in the afternoon. He's uncomfortable in a new, ill-fitting suit.

"Mr. Kim," Skipper says, "you were at work at the Bank of America Building on the night of December thirtieth of last year, right?"

"Yes." His pronunciation is pretty good, but his tone is tentative. Kim says that he walked by Bob Holmes's office at approximately twelve-thirty in the morning.

"Was there someone in the office with Mr. Holmes?" Skipper asks.

Kim points at Joel. "Yes. Mr. Friedman." It's a wooden gesture that's been rehearsed. "Mr. Holmes and Mr. Friedman were having an argument. Mr. Friedman was angry at Mr. Holmes. Very angry." His eyes dart.

"Did you hear Mr. Friedman say anything to Mr. Holmes?"

"Objection. Hearsay."

Skipper explains he isn't trying to prove the truth of what was said.

"Overruled."

Kim gulps water from a paper cup. "Mr. Friedman said to Mr. Holmes, 'I'll get you for this.' " He gestures with his right index finger for emphasis.

"Did it sound like Mr. Friedman was threatening Mr. Holmes?"

"Objection. Calls for Mr. Kim to make a determination of Mr. Friedman's state of mind."

"Sustained."

"No further questions."

I move right in front of Kim. "How long have you known Mr. Friedman?"

He looks perplexed. "A couple years."

"Do you know him well?"

"No."

"And have you ever heard him raise his voice?"

He glances at Skipper, who shakes his head. "No."

"Mr. Kim, do you know what they were arguing about?"

"No." He sounds tentative.

"Is it possible they may have been arguing about work?"

"Objection. Speculative."

"Overruled."

"I don't know," Kim says. He glances at Skipper for help. Skipper closes his eyes.

"It's possible, right?"

Out of the corner of my eye, I see Skipper nod.

"Yes, it's possible."

"Mr. Kim, you've had some problems over the years with your finances, haven't you?"

Skipper's up immediately. "Objection. Mr. Kim's financial situation is irrelevant."

"Your Honor," I say, "Mr. Kim's financial situation is very relevant."

"I'll give you a little leeway, Mr. Daley."

"Mr. Kim," I continue, "isn't it true you've had some significant debts over the last few years?"

He looks desperately at Skipper. "Yes."

"You filed for personal bankruptcy last year, didn't you?"

"Yes."

"You've lost substantial amounts of money gambling, right?"

His shoulders slump. "I don't recall."

"You're under oath, Mr. Kim. I'd be happy to introduce the bankruptcy court filings into evidence." I turn to the judge. "Your

Honor, would you please instruct the witness to answer."

"Mr. Kim, I'm going to have to ask you to answer Mr. Daley's question."

"Yes. I have lost some money gambling."

"Mr. Kim, isn't it a fact that you received a check in the amount of twenty thousand dollars shortly before you agreed to testify in this case?"

"No."

"Isn't it true that twenty thousand dollars was deposited into your account at Bank of America on February twentieth of this year?"

"No."

"You're under oath. We can subpoena your bank records."

He looks at Skipper. "Yes. I received a bonus."

"And would you mind telling us who promised you the bonus?"

He looks around the room wildly. "Mr. Patton."

"Arthur Patton? The managing partner of the Simpson and Gates firm?"

"Yes."

"And why did Mr. Patton promise you a bonus?"

"He wanted to be sure I was available to testify at this trial. He said he wanted to bring Mr. Holmes's killer to justice."

His hesitant English is suddenly more fluent. "Mr. Kim, there was no argument between Mr. Holmes and Mr. Friedman, was there? You were paid to say there was, but there really wasn't."

"No. I mean, yes. There really was an argument. Mr. Friedman was very angry."

"No further questions, Your Honor."

CHAPTER 36

MY FORMER PARTNERS

"It is unfortunate we must testify in the murder trial of one of our colleagues."
— Arthur Patton. NewsCenter 4. Wednesday, March 25.

At six-thirty the following morning, I'm watching the news on Channel 4. Every day at this time, Morgan Henderson, a self-absorbed former federal prosecutor who now works for a big downtown firm, reports on the trial and gives a preview of today's attractions.

"Today should be very interesting," he drones. "District Attorney Gates is going to call several of his former partners to testify against Mr. Friedman."

I'm surprised he isn't giving odds.

* * *

"My name is Charles Stern. I have been a partner at Simpson and Gates for twenty-seven years." Chuckles looks stiff as he takes the stand at ten-fifteen.

Skipper's primed. No more idiot cops who couldn't get a legitimate confession. No more arrogant medical examiners and uppity lesbian evidence technicians who won't give him the answers he wants. He gets to put on *his* guys now. The Skipper Network is on the air.

He walks Chuckles through his resume. Chuckles gives clipped answers directly to Skipper. He never turns his eyes even slightly toward the jury. He confirms that he was at the office the night of the incident. He says he was preparing for a partners' meeting the next morning. He doesn't go into detail on the ceremonial reading of the Estimate.

"Mr. Stern," Skipper says, "did you attend a meeting with the firm's associates that evening?"

"Yes." The crow's-feet around his narrow eyes become more pronounced. "We had convened a meeting to discuss certain issues involving associate compensation and the partnership track."

The "royal we" doesn't fit Chuckles.

"Was the defendant there?"

He glances at Joel. "Yes."

"Could you tell us what happened?"

"We announced that we were extending the track to partnership by one year. The vote on Mr. Friedman was going to be postponed. Mr. Friedman became upset that my partner, Mr. Holmes, had not told him about our decision. He expressed his displeasure and stormed out."

"Did you see the defendant later that night?"

"Yes. He came to my office. He said he was going to read Mr. Holmes the riot act."

"Did his tone sound threatening?"

"Objection. State of mind."

"Sustained."

"Did the defendant appear very upset to you?"

"Objection. State of mind."

"Overruled."

Chuckles fingers his reading glasses. "Yes. He appeared very upset to me."

"Upset enough to kill two people?"

"Objection, Your Honor. Speculative."

"Sustained." The judge glares at Skipper. "The jury will disregard the last question."

Skipper turns back to Chuckles. "Mr. Stern, you and the defendant found the bodies of Mr. Holmes and Ms. Kennedy the following morning, did you not?"

"Yes." He says that he called 911 and went back to the partners' meeting.

Skipper picks up the revolver from the evidence cart. "Mr. Stern, do you recognize this weapon?"

"Yes. It belonged to Bob. We found it on the floor."

"Did you touch this revolver?"

"No."

"Did you see the defendant touch this revolver?"

"No."

Joel leans over and whispers, "He's lying."

Skipper asks Chuckles if he saw Joel unload the gun.

"No."

"Mr. Stern, is it possible that the defendant unloaded the gun while you weren't watching?"

"It's highly unlikely. We went to the partners' meeting together. We returned to Bob's office together. We were both there until the first officer arrived. If he unloaded the gun, I didn't see it."

"No further questions."

I'm up right away. "Mr. Stern, you said you were with Mr. Friedman the entire time before the police arrived."

"Yes."

"Officer Chinn testified that you met him in the lobby."

He shifts in his chair. "That's true."

"Mr. Friedman wasn't with you when you met Officer Chinn, was he?"

He takes a drink of water. "No."

"So you weren't with Mr. Friedman the entire time before the police arrived, were you?"

"I guess not."

"It's possible that Mr. Friedman may have unloaded the weapon while you were meeting with Officer Chinn, isn't it?"

"Objection. Speculative."

"Overruled."

Chuckles shakes his head. "I was with Officer Chinn in the lobby for only a few moments. I don't see how Mr. Friedman could have unloaded the gun so quickly."

I hold up the revolver. "Mr. Stern, you were in the military, weren't you?"

"Objection. Relevance."

"Your Honor, Mr. Stern has expressed an opinion as to how fast this particular weapon could have been unloaded. His background and experience with weapons is relevant."

"Overruled."

Chuckles clutches reading glasses more tightly. "I was in the Marines."

"And you're familiar with firearms, aren't you? In fact, you've shot this weapon, haven't you?"

He adjusts the microphone. "Yes. Mr. Holmes and I went to the range from time to time."

"You've unloaded this weapon at the range, haven't you?"

"Yes."

"How long did it take *you* to unload it?"

"A few seconds."

"A few seconds. And it took you more than a few seconds to meet with Officer Chinn, didn't it?"

"Yes," he says grudgingly.

Good. "Mr. Stern, you knew Mr. Holmes kept this revolver at his desk, didn't you?"

"For self-protection."

"Of course. And he kept it loaded, didn't he?"

"Yes."

"No further questions."

* * *

During the recess, I ask Joel when he unloaded the gun.

"Right after we walked in. He saw me do it. He's lying."

"Did anybody else see you?"

"No. We were the only people there."

* * *

"The people call Arthur Patton," Skipper announces.

Patton lugs his chins through the courtroom. He smirks at the jury as he's sworn in. He says he's the managing partner at S&G. He confirms he was there on the fatal night.

Skipper starts with an easy one. "Did you have occasion to see the defendant late that evening?"

"Yes." The avuncular Art has joined us today. His tone is sincere, meant to charm. "I saw him in the hall around twelve-thirty in the morning. He was walking into Bob's office."

"Could you describe his demeanor?"

"He was very upset." He describes his brief conversation with Joel. He looks toward the jury and scowls. "That's when he started shouting at Bob."

"Do you know what he was shouting about?"

"I believe he was expressing his unhappiness about the fact that Bob hadn't told him that the vote for his election to the partnership had been deferred." He pauses. "And I believe they were arguing about Ms. Kennedy. I heard her name mentioned several times."

"Mr. Patton, were you at the firm retreat at the Silverado Country Club last October?"

"Yes."

"Did you have an opportunity to see Mr. Friedman at about three a.m. on Saturday, October twenty-fifth?"

"Yes. He was in his condominium."

"Why did you have occasion to see him in the middle of the night?"

"There were loud noises coming from his room. I wanted to make sure he was all right."

"Was he alone?"

"No. There was somebody else in his room."

"Who was in his room at three o'clock in the morning?"

"Diana Kennedy."

"No further questions."

* * *

"Mr. Patton," I begin, "what time did you go home on the morning of December thirty-first?"

"Objection. Relevance."

"Overruled."

Patton answers in a forceful tone. "Around one-thirty in the morning."

"And you heard a discussion between Mr. Holmes and Mr. Friedman?"

"It was an argument."

"Was the door to Mr. Holmes's office open or closed?"

"Closed."

"You stood outside the door and eavesdropped on their conversation?"

"I wanted to help my partner. Mr. Friedman was upset."

"For all you know, they could have been arguing about work."

His voice fills with disdain. "I don't think so."

"But you aren't sure."

"I'm sure."

"Let's talk about the incident at Silverado. There was a party in your room earlier that evening, wasn't there?"

"Yes."

"And Ms. Kennedy was at that party, wasn't she?"

"Yes."

"Isn't it true, Mr. Patton, that you accosted Ms. Kennedy at the party?"

"Absolutely not."

"And you followed her to her room and attacked her?"

"I did not."

He sounds just like my daughter. "Isn't it true she went to Mr. Friedman for protection?"

"That's a lie."

"We'll see about that, Mr. Patton. No further questions."

* * *

A few minutes later, Skipper calls another old friend. Brent Hutchinson slithers to the front of the courtroom, a smarmy grin plastered on his pretty face. Whenever I see him, I want to punch his lights out.

"Mr. Hutchinson," Skipper begins, "we've known each other for some time, haven't we?"

"We were partners at Simpson and Gates. I still work there."

He looks like a cocker spaniel who wants to be petted.

Skipper smiles. "Mr. Hutchinson, you have a nickname around the firm, don't you?"

"Most people call me Hutch."

He sounds like Forrest Gump. Makes me sick.

"Would you mind if I call you Hutch today?"

"Sure." His grin widens. All this male bonding turns my stomach.

"Now, Hutch, you attended the firm retreat at Silverado in October of last year, didn't you?"

"Yes. We have our retreat there every year. It's a great time."

"Could you tell us about what happens at these retreats?"

"Objection. Relevance." This love-fest has to stop. Hutch is likable on the stand—if you're into handsome airheads.

"Overruled."

"We have attorney meetings and social events. We play golf and tennis."

"Did you attend a social gathering in the cocktail lounge at Silverado at approximately nine o'clock in the evening of Friday, October twenty-fourth?"

"Yes."

"Were Diana Kennedy and the defendant also there?"

"Yes."

"Would you mind describing what happened as Ms. Kennedy was leaving the party?"

He turns toward the jury and flashes his most sincere smile.

"Joel was sitting at a table near the door. Diana was at the bar. She walked toward the door. As she passed Joel, she stopped, leaned over and kissed him." His grin broadens.

Skipper smiles back. Good Hutch.

I look at Naomi. She stares at the floor. Joel doesn't move.

Skipper move closer to Hutch. "Did she kiss the defendant on the mouth?"

"Yes."

"Did she kiss him hard?"

"Objection. The witness has no personal knowledge of the intensity of the kiss."

"Overruled."

"Looked pretty hard to me," Hutch says.

A few snickers from the gallery.

"Hutch," Skipper says, "did the kiss appear to you to be a romantic one?"

"Objection, Your Honor. Speculative."

"Sustained."

Skipper gives the jury a conspiratorial wink. "Did it appear to you that the defendant enjoyed being kissed?"

"Objection. State of mind."

"Your Honor," Skipper says, "I'm not asking Mr. Hutchinson to make a determination as to whether he thought Mr. Friedman enjoyed the kiss. I'm simply asking him to describe what he saw."

"Nice try, Mr. Gates. The objection is sustained. Move on."

"Hutch, did you also see the defendant and Ms. Kennedy in a hot tub the next day?"

"Yes."

"Would you mind telling us what they were doing?"

"They were kissing again."

"They were kissing again? Could you describe how Ms. Kennedy was dressed?"

"She was wearing a bikini, but the top was unfastened."

Murmurs in the gallery. Judge Chen taps her gavel.

"Hutch," Skipper says, "was it a hard kiss?"

"Yes."

"And did it appear to you that the defendant was, for lack of a better term, kissing her back?"

"Absolutely."

"And how long did this go on?"

"About a minute. Then I thought it would be best if I moved on."

How sensitive.

Skipper flashes a knowing look at the jury, then he turns back to Hutch. "Did you see Ms. Kennedy and the defendant together at any other time during the retreat?"

"Later that evening, I saw them sitting in the same hot tub. I'm pretty sure they were both naked. However, it was dark and I was on my way to my room. This time, I didn't stop."

"No further questions."

* * *

"Mr. Hutchinson," I begin, "we've known each other for a long time, too, haven't we?"

"Yes." His teeth gleam. "We used to be partners, too."

"In addition to being called Hutch, you have another nickname around the firm, don't you?"

The smile disappears. "I'm not sure what you're talking about, Mr. Daley."

"Your other nickname is the Party Guy, isn't it?"

"Yes."

I grin. "Could you please tell us why they call you the Party Guy?"

He smiles sheepishly. "I guess it's because I like to party, Mr. Daley."

"Were you partying the night you saw Ms. Kennedy kiss Mr. Friedman at the bar?"

"I guess you could say that."

"And you'd probably had a glass of wine or two that night?"

"Probably."

"How many glasses of wine?"

"Several."

"More than two?"

"Probably."

"More than three?"

"Maybe."

"Enough so that you wouldn't have gotten behind the wheel of a car that night?"

"Definitely."

"So, when you saw Ms. Kennedy kiss Mr. Friedman, you may have been intoxicated."

"I don't think so."

"You just said you'd had at least four glasses of wine. Your memory of that night may be a little cloudy."

"Maybe."

"Now, let's talk about the incident on Saturday afternoon where you saw Ms. Kennedy and Mr. Friedman in the hot tub. Could you tell us where the hot tub was located?"

"Near one of the pools at Silverado."

"And you just happened to walk by the hot tub and you saw Ms. Kennedy kissing Mr. Friedman?"

"Not exactly. I was walking down a path that leads to the golf course."

"How far was the path from the pool?"

"I'm not sure."

"Ballpark figure, Mr. Hutchinson. Fifty feet? A hundred feet? The length of a football field?"

He darts a glance at Skipper. "Maybe the length of a football field."

"Really? From a hundred yards, you were able to see Mr. Friedman and Ms. Kennedy kissing?"

"Yes."

"And you're sure the top of Ms. Kennedy's bikini had been

unfastened?"

"Yes. I'm sure."

"You must have really good eyes, Mr. Hutchinson."

"Objection. Move to strike."

"The jury will ignore Mr. Daley's remark."

I leave it there. "I don't suppose you were standing in the same place when you saw them in the hot tub later that night."

"As a matter of fact, I was."

"So, late at night, from a hundred yards away, you were able to identify Mr. Friedman and Ms. Kennedy in the hot tub. You were also able to determine that they were kissing. And you were able to determine that they were naked. Is that about it?"

"Yes."

"Did they get out of the hot tub?"

"No."

"Were the jets on?"

"I think so."

"Weren't there bubbles in the hot tub?"

He's starting to look a little older now. "Probably."

I shoot a knowing glance at the jury. "If it was night and they didn't get out and the jets were on and there were bubbles in the hot tub, how in the world were you able to determine that they were both naked?"

He takes a deep breath. "I saw them. I could tell."

"It's your story, and you're sticking to it."

"Objection."

"Withdrawn. Mr. Hutchinson, you realize that what you've just told us is utterly preposterous, don't you?"

"Objection."

"Withdrawn. Next he'll say he saw them in a hot tub while he was flying over Silverado in a hot-air balloon."

"Objection."

"Sustained. The jury will disregard Mr. Daley's last remark."

"No further questions."

* * *

At eight o'clock the same night, I'm at my mom's house meeting with Pete. Mom's having one of her not-so-good nights. We sit at the dining room table. She clears Pete's plate and says to me, "You didn't finish all your carrots. Tommy. No dessert until you do."

"I will, Mama. Right away."

She walks into the kitchen.

Pete shrugs. "Sometimes she spends a little while in the sixties. Then she comes back."

"It's getting worse, isn't it?"

"Yeah."

"Look, Pete, if we need to get you some help . . ."

"Not yet, Mick. I'll let you know." He takes a drink of water. "How did things go at court today?"

"Not great. Have you found anything else on Russo?"

"The trail goes cold at the international terminal at SFO. One person said she thought he might have gone to Hong Kong, but nobody on the flight crew recognized his picture. If he's flying on a fake passport, he's going to be tough to find."

"Crap."

"We may not be the only people looking for him. He had some co-investors from Saudi. They're looking for him, too."

"What about the banker in the Bahamas?"

"Still in Kuwait. Longer than expected—he won't be back for another couple of weeks. Wendy and I are going to pay him a visit as soon as he is."

"Has Wendy been helpful?"

"Yeah. She's great." He looks at the picture of my older brother Tommy in his Cal football uniform, frozen in time at the age of twenty. Pete and Tommy look almost identical, except Tommy was taller and Pete has a mustache. "Mike, is she, well, seeing anybody?"

Unlike Rosie, who is all too familiar with my crush on Wendy, Pete doesn't have a clue. I'd like to tell him he's out of luck and that I have dibs. Instead, I say, "I don't think so."

"Do you think she'd have any interest?"

"I'm not sure. She's been divorced a couple of times. You'll never know if you don't ask." I decide to change the subject. "Did you get anything from Nick Hanson on the mystery woman at the Fairmont?"

"He hasn't been able to ID her. The people at the Fairmont couldn't, either."

We keep coming up empty. "Did Nick think it was Diana?"

"He's pretty sure it wasn't. The woman had longer hair. Nick's real good on details like that. He thinks it might have been a hooker."

"Does he have any other ideas?"

"Just one. But he said it was just a wag."

"A wag?"

"Yeah. W-A-G. Wild-ass guess. Guess who was making an appearance at the Fairmont that night?"

"The mayor?"

"Somebody more famous: Dr. Kathy Chandler."

"You think? No. It couldn't."

He smiles. "We shouldn't jump to any conclusions. I did some checking on Dr. Kathy. She's very single. She's had a little trouble with long-term relationships. She fits the description."

"Is there any hard evidence she was with Bob that night?"

"Nope. Like I said. It's just Nick's wild-ass guess."

At the moment, Nick the Dick's wild-ass guess is the only lead we have.

CHAPTER 37

"WAS YOUR MARRIAGE A HAPPY ONE?"

"In what promises to be an emotional moment, the widow of Robert Holmes will take the stand today."
— NewsCenter 4 Legal Analyst Morgan Henderson. Thursday, March 26.

The next morning is a Thursday. Skipper calls Beth Holmes to the stand. In lieu of her customary business suit, she's wearing a light blue dress with a gold chain and a small brooch. Today, she'll be playing the role of grieving widow instead of legal barracuda.

Her tone is subdued. "My name is Elizabeth Barnes Holmes. Robert Holmes was my husband."

Skipper has set up the photos of Bob and Diana in front of the jury. "How long were you and Bob married?"

"Five and a half years." She describes how she and Bob met, the children, the vacations to the Italian Riviera and the mansion in Presidio Terrace. The idyllic power marriage between power partners at power law firms. She doesn't mention her divorce from Art Patton.

Skipper tries to sound empathetic. "Was your marriage a happy one, Mrs. Holmes?"

"Yes. At least until recently."

"Then what happened, Mrs. Holmes?"

"He became distant. I began to suspect he was seeing another woman."

"Was he?"

"Yes. He was having an affair with Diana Kennedy."

Murmurs in the gallery.

Skipper remains a respectful distance from her. "How did you find out about the affair, Mrs. Holmes?"

"I hired a private investigator." She holds her head high. "I confronted Bob in early December. I told him he had to break off the affair, or I'd leave him."

"What happened?"

"He broke up with her. A few weeks later, my investigator found them together again. I decided to end our marriage. I was there when he was served on December thirtieth."

"Mrs. Holmes, was your husband upset when he was served with the divorce papers?"

"Objection. State of mind."

"Overruled."

"He took it pretty well."

"Do you think he was so upset that he may have been driven to suicide?"

"Objection. Speculative."

"Overruled."

"I think he was relieved when I filed the papers."

I glance at Diana's mother. She closes her eyes.

"No further questions," Skipper says.

* * *

"Mrs. Holmes," I begin, "what time was your husband served with divorce papers?"

"About five-thirty in the evening."

"Who was there?"

"A bunch of people in the main conference room."

"What was your husband doing when he was served?"

"I believe he was on the telephone."

"Wasn't he with his client and several attorneys? And weren't they in negotiations on a significant business transaction?"

"Yes."

"Isn't it a fact that he barely looked up when you and your process server walked in?"

"It took a few minutes to get his attention."

"So, it's not really surprising that he didn't react when he saw you, is it?"

"He knew what was going on."

"Did he look at the papers your process server handed him?"

"Briefly."

"Mrs. Holmes, isn't it true that your husband had very little reaction to the papers because he was concentrating on his deal and he expected you to file the papers?"

Skipper's up. "Objection. Argumentative."

"Sustained."

"Mrs. Holmes, did your husband carry any life insurance?"

"Objection. Relevance."

"Overruled."

She says Bob carried a five-million-dollar policy naming herself as beneficiary, and a million-dollar policy for each of the kids.

"Have you received the proceeds from the policies yet?"

"No. The insurance company is working on the claim."

I'm sure they're hoping it's ruled a suicide. "Did it occur to you that your husband might change the beneficiaries if you were divorced?"

"Objection. Speculative."

"Overruled."

"Of course, Mr. Daley." She gives me her best "big-firm evil litigator" look. "If you're suggesting I had some incentive to see my husband dead, you're out of your mind."

Out of the corner of my eye, I see the phone company supervisor nod. I've gone a little too far. I have to remember that she's the grieving widow. "Mrs. Holmes, do you know the names of the beneficiaries of your husband's will?"

"I get a third, the children get a third and the balance goes to a charity in the Bahamas."

"Did it occur to you that he may have decided to change his will after you got divorced?"

"Of course. I don't need the money."

"You said your investigator found your husband and Ms. Kennedy together in late December."

"That's correct."

"Where did that incident occur?"

"At the Fairmont Hotel."

"How did your investigator find them?"

"He was viewing their room from across the street."

"Did your investigator positively identify Diana Kennedy in the room with your husband?"

"He said the woman looked like Diana."

"But he wasn't able to positively identify the woman in the room with Mr. Holmes that night, right?"

"That's true."

"And it's possible that it wasn't Ms. Kennedy."

"It's possible. What difference does it make, Mr. Daley?"

I have what I need. "I'm sorry to make you relive these difficult times, Mrs. Holmes. No further questions."

CHAPTER 38

"HOW LONG HAVE YOU BEEN A PRACTICING THERAPIST?"

"KTLK's very own Dr. Kathy Chandler will be testifying today at the murder trial of Joel Mark Friedman. Dr. Kathy Chandler will be able to tell you about it during her regular time slot at seven tonight."
— KTLK Talk Radio. Thursday, March 26.

We're standing outside the courtroom at one o'clock when Dr. Kathy Chandler and her entourage arrive. She just finished an impromptu press conference in the corridor. She's surrounded by cameras as she and her handlers inch down the hall. She towers over most of the reporters. She flashes the smile that graces Muni buses all over town.

"Dr. Chandler, what are you going to talk about today?"

"Dr. Chandler, did Robert Holmes killed himself?"

"Dr. Chandler, was Mr. Holmes having an affair with Diana Kennedy?"

"Dr. Chandler? Dr. Chandler? Dr. Chandler?"

"I'm sorry, fellows," she purrs. "I don't want to be late for court. I'll talk to you after I'm done."

* * *

Skipper walks Dr. Kathy Chandler through her credentials, such as they are. I interrupt frequently. After the ordeal is concluded, Skipper says, "How long did you know Robert Holmes?"

She smiles. "I began treating him in September. I was his therapist for about three months."

"What were you treating him for?"

"I usually don't talk about my patients' problems." She bats her eyes.

"Your testimony is very important. If you're uncomfortable answering a question, let me know, and we'll talk it over with Judge Chen."

Who will be more than happy to lock you up for contempt. Then you'll have the honor of being the first person to initiate a radio broadcast from the new jail at the Hall.

Judge Chen addresses Dr. Kathy in a stern voice. "Doctor Chandler, let me simplify this for you. If there's a question I think you shouldn't have to answer, I'll tell you so. For now, unless I instruct you otherwise, I expect you to answer Mr. Gates's questions. Are we clear?"

The kitten disappears. "Yes, Your Honor."

"Good." Judge Chen nods to Skipper. "Please continue, Mr. Gates."

"Dr. Chandler, why did Mr. Holmes come to see you?"

"He was having relationship problems with his wife."

"What kind?"

I'd give everything I own to hear her say, "He was having trouble keeping his zipper zipped."

"Mr. Holmes was seeing another woman."

Skipper feigns empathy. "Oh, dear. Do you know who the woman was?"

"Diana Kennedy."

"Was Mr. Holmes still seeing Ms. Kennedy at the time they were murdered?"

"Objection. Move to strike the term 'murdered.' "

"Sustained. The jury will disregard the term 'murdered.' Try it again, Mr. Gates."

"Do you know if Mr. Holmes was seeing Ms. Kennedy on December thirtieth of last year?"

"I don't think so. He was pretty sure Mrs. Holmes was going to serve him with divorce papers. He had broken up with Ms. Kennedy. He said he was seeing somebody new. He was very uncomfortable talking about it."

"Did he mention the name of the woman?"

"No. It may have been Ms. Kennedy. It may have been somebody else. To be honest, he may have been making it up. Sometimes, you couldn't tell with Mr. Holmes."

Skipper nods understandingly. "Doctor, based upon your observations of Mr. Holmes in the final weeks of his life, did he appear distraught to you?"

"Objection. State of mind."

"She was his therapist," Skipper says. "I'm asking for her professional observations."

Judge Chen scowls. "I'll allow the witness to answer."

"No," Dr. Kathy says. "He didn't appear distraught. In fact, he was relaxed. I think he was relieved that he'd resolved his issues with Mrs. Holmes."

Oh, bullshit.

Skipper moves to the front of the witness box. "Did he appear emotionally disturbed?"

"Good heavens, no."

"Depressed?"

"No."

"Unhappy?"

"No."

Enough. "Objection. We can spend all afternoon trying to identify every range of emotion *not* exhibited by Mr. Holmes."

"Sustained. Move on, Mr. Gates."

"One final question. Did he appear at any time to you to be suicidal?"

"Absolutely not." Dr. Kathy smiles demurely at the jury.

"No further questions."

* * *

"Dr. Chandler," I begin, "I'd like to ask you a few more questions about your credentials. You got your degree from Southwestern Texas City College, right?"

"Yes."

"Is that an accredited school?"

"It depends on what you mean by the term 'accredited.' "

"I mean it in the conventional sense. You know—schools like Stanford, Cal, UCLA—they're accredited. Was Southwestern Texas City College accredited?"

"Not exactly."

"And your doctorate in family counseling is from the same institution, right?"

"That's correct."

"Did you actually attend classes there?"

She pauses. "Yes."

"But most of the courses were offered online, weren't they?"

"Yes."

She probably could have gotten any title she wanted if she paid them enough money. "And you got a master's from the Great Pacific School of Broadcasting?"

"Yes."

"Was that program also offered primarily over the Internet?"

"Yes."

"Not exactly Harvard and Yale, are they, Doctor?"

"Objection. Argumentative."

"Sustained."

"Dr. Chandler, how long have you been a practicing therapist?"

"Seventeen years."

"And how many years have you been doing your radio show?"

"Fourteen."

"You have one of the top-rated programs in your time slot, don't you?"

Her voice fills with pride. "Yes, I do."

"I'll bet your radio show takes up a lot of your time, doesn't it?"

"It's a very demanding job."

"How many hours are you on the air every day?"

"Three. From seven o'clock until ten."

"You must have a very busy schedule."

Skipper stands. "Your Honor, I fail to see the relevance."

"Mr. Daley," says Judge Chen, "get to the point."

"I will, Your Honor." I turn back to the good doctor. "Do you handle a full caseload?"

"Yes. I wouldn't be comfortable giving advice over the radio if I didn't maintain a private practice."

"How many patients do you see in a typical day?"

"Two or three."

"That's what you consider a full practice? That's ten or fifteen patients a week. If each of them gets an hour of your time, that's only one or two days' work."

"As I said, Mr. Daley, my radio show takes a lot of time."

"And you also write self-help books, don't you, Doctor?"

"Yes."

"Does that take much time?"

"Well, my publisher gives me a lot of help with those."

"Somebody helps you write your self-help books?"

"Yes."

She fails to see the irony. "Is it fair to say that you spend a lot less time seeing patients than most of your colleagues?"

"Most of them don't have a radio show."

No doubt. I look at Rosie. She shakes her head almost imperceptibly. I'm having fun tweaking Dr. Kathy Chandler. Unfortunately, the jury doesn't seem to care. "Doctor, have you ever had a personal relationship with one of your patients?"

The facade disappears and she turns serious. "No. That would be unethical."

"Isn't it a fact that your license was suspended several years ago because you had a sexual relationship with one of your patients?"

The claws come out. "It is true that my license was suspended. It is not true, however, that I had a relationship with one of my patients. A very sad and lonely man made some wild accusations. They were never proven."

"You arrived at a settlement, didn't you?"

"That's confidential."

I turn to Judge Chen. "Your Honor, I must ask you to instruct the witness to answer."

"Answer the question, Dr. Chandler."

She strokes her bangs. "We settled out of court." She glares at me. "Any other questions, Mr. Daley?"

"Yes. Isn't it true that your ex-husband was one of your patients?"

Her tiny nose twitches. "Yes."

"So it wasn't exactly true when you said you've never had a personal relationship with a patient."

"He was no longer a patient when we began our personal relationship."

I glance at the jury, then I turn back to her. "Just one more question. Were you having an affair with Robert Holmes, Dr. Chandler?"

Skipper screams his objection. "Your Honor, this is irrelevant and insulting to Dr. Chandler."

"Your Honor," I say, "we believe Dr. Chandler was having a sexual relationship with Mr. Holmes. It would clearly color her credibility. I would ask you to instruct her to answer."

Judge Chen bites her lower lip. "Dr. Chandler, I have to ask you to respond."

"The answer is no. I was not having an affair with Mr. Holmes."

I decide to go for broke. "Dr. Chandler, we have evidence that you and Mr. Holmes were having a sexual relationship in a room at the Fairmont in December of last year. Do you deny it?"

"Objection. There's no foundation for any of this."

"Your Honor, we are prepared to bring forth the private investigator hired by Mrs. Holmes. It would save us an extraordinary amount of time if Dr. Chandler answers my question."

Judge Chen turns to Dr. Kathy. "Answer the question, Dr. Chandler."

Her eyes are on fire. "No, Mr. Daley. I wasn't with Mr. Holmes."

"No further questions."

* * *

Joel's father is incredulous as we sit in the consultation room during the afternoon recess. "How does it help to attack Bob's widow? How does it help to attack his therapist? What were you thinking?"

"Rabbi," I say, "they called those two witnesses to demonstrate that Bob was a happy guy who didn't kill himself. They're undercutting our suicide argument. And it's working. We have to show that Beth Holmes is lying to protect her husband's reputation. And we have to show that Dr. Kathy Chandler is a bubblegum-spewing radio jockey. If you don't like the way I'm trying the case, you can get Joel another lawyer."

Mort speaks up. "We don't have time for this. Maybe it wasn't the greatest cross in the history of the legal profession. But we have to keep at it. They put on witnesses for a purpose—to get a conviction. We can't stop now because we're afraid we're going to hurt somebody's feelings."

Rosie holds up her hand. "Could you please be quiet for a moment. We aren't going to be able to deliver a knockout punch on every witness. We have to stay focused."

Joel stands up. "May I say something here? Seeing as how my ass is on the line, I'd appreciate it if you'd keep your petty squabbles to yourselves. If you guys screw up, I'm going to jail. So I don't want to hear anything else about who's doing a good job or a bad job. I don't want to hear you argue about strategy. I'm not interested in blaming anybody. We're wasting time. I don't want to see this again. Get your heads screwed back on and do your jobs."

I hate it when the client is right.

CHAPTER 39

"WE WERE WORKING ON A VERY BIG DEAL"

"Everybody wanted the Russo deal to close. It was good for the city."
— The Mayor of San Francisco. Thursday, March 26.

Jack Frazier, the pride of Continental Capital Corporation, looks like he's ready for a board meeting when he takes the stand at three o'clock. He's wearing the standard investment banker uniform. His shirt is so heavily starched, it could walk across the courtroom.

Skipper is wearing a subdued gray pinstripe today, with huge gold cuff links. "Would you mind telling us why you were at the Simpson and Gates office on the night of December thirtieth?"

Frazier gazes past Skipper's left shoulder. "We were working on a very big deal. My company was going to purchase a conglomerate called Russo International." He outlines the terms of the deal. "The closing was scheduled for the following morning."

"Was the deal going to close on schedule?"

"As far as I knew, yes. All the papers had been signed."

"Why didn't it close?"

"With the tragic deaths of Mr. Holmes and Ms. Kennedy, we couldn't proceed."

"Did you see Mr. Holmes that night?"

"Yes."

"Did he appear to be in a good mood?"

"Yes. He was looking forward to the closing."

"Did you see any signs that he may have been distraught?"

"Objection. State of mind."

"Sustained."

"I'll rephrase. Did Mr. Holmes appear distraught that evening?"

"No. Nothing out of the ordinary."

"No further questions, Your Honor."

* * *

I walk slowly toward Frazier. "There were problems with the deal, weren't there, Mr. Frazier?"

"There are always problems with big transactions."

"But this deal had more than its share, didn't it?"

"Not really."

"Isn't it true there was substantial doubt about whether your company would approve this deal?"

Frazier glances at his lawyer, Martin Glass, who's in the gallery. "No. The deal was approved."

"Isn't it true your board of directors had an emergency meeting that night to discuss pulling the plug?"

"They met that night. I don't know what they discussed."

Right. "Isn't it true your board would have voted against the deal if you hadn't been able to negotiate a forty-million-dollar reduction in the purchase price at the last minute?"

"It's true that I was able to negotiate a reduction in the purchase price. I have no idea whether the board would have approved the deal without the reduction."

I don't know why he's resisting. I'm just trying to show that Bob may have been stressed out. Frazier seems to be trying to justify the deal to his superiors. "Isn't it true that the seller, Vince Russo, was undecided about whether he would close the deal? And isn't it true that even though all the papers were signed, Mr. Russo told everyone he wouldn't make up his mind until morning?"

Skipper's up. "Objection, Your Honor. Argumentative."

They want to avoid mentioning Russo. "Your Honor, Mr. Russo was a key player in this transaction. Mr. Frazier has testified that the deal was proceeding according to plan. However, the evidence will suggest that Mr. Russo didn't want to close."

"I'll allow it."

I glance at McNulty, who is frowning. He realizes this is a significant ruling. It opens the door for me to blame everything on Russo.

I turn back to Frazier. "Isn't it true that Mr. Russo was waffling?"

Frazier looks toward Glass again. "I firmly believe he intended to close the deal."

"What time did Mr. Russo leave that night?"

"I don't know."

"Could you tell us what time Mr. Russo showed up the next morning for the closing?"

"He didn't show up. He seems to have disappeared."

"Did he call you?"

"No."

"Leave a message?"

"No."

"Try to get in touch with you?"

"Objection," says Skipper. "We get the idea."

"Sustained. Move along, Mr. Daley."

"What time did you leave the building that night, Mr. Frazier?"

"About one thirty-five."

"Was Mr. Russo still in the building when you left?"

"As far as I know."

"When was the last time you saw him?"

"Around one o'clock. He was talking to Mr. Holmes."

"About what?"

"Objection, Your Honor. Hearsay."

"Your Honor, I'm not trying to establish precisely what was said or the truth of what was said. I'm simply asking Mr. Frazier to report on the subject being discussed."

"Overruled."

"They were talking about the deal."

"Is it possible Mr. Russo told Mr. Holmes that he did not intend to close the deal?"

"Objection. Speculative."

"Overruled."

Frazier holds up his hands. "It's possible. I don't know."

"Was that the last time you saw Mr. Russo?"

"Yes."

"Isn't it possible, Mr. Frazier, that Mr. Holmes may have become distraught and killed himself after Mr. Russo told him that he didn't want to close the deal?"

Judge Chen looks at Skipper, who should object. I've just asked a highly speculative question.

Frazier pushes out a heavy sigh. "It was just a business deal. It wasn't worth committing suicide for."

Good point. "Isn't it possible that Mr. Russo's disappearance can be explained by the fact that he killed Mr. Holmes and Ms. Kennedy, and that he fled?"

"Objection. Speculative."

Look who woke up.

"Sustained."

I haven't taken my eyes off Frazier. "Isn't it true that you really didn't want the deal to close?"

"Of course not."

"Isn't it true you figured out that you couldn't make the profit margins on the deal that you had originally anticipated?"

He's indignant. "No."

"Isn't it true that if you killed the deal, you would have had to pay Mr. Russo a fifty-million-dollar breakup fee?"

"Objection. Relevance."

"Overruled."

Frazier is squirming. "Your Honor, the terms of the deal are confidential."

The judge isn't buying it. "Mr. Frazier, a moment ago you were trying to impress us with the enormous size of this deal. You can't have it both ways. Answer the question."

Another promising corporate career is heading for the Dumpster.

"The breakup fee was fifty million dollars," he says.

The suits in Stamford just got a severe case of indigestion. I try not to appear smug. "Just so everybody understands this, Mr. Frazier, if you pulled the plug on the deal, your company would have had to pay Mr. Russo fifty million dollars. Is that correct?"

"Yes."

"And if Mr. Russo pulled the plug, you wouldn't have owed him a penny, right?"

"Right."

"And you wouldn't have had to buy a company you really didn't want."

"We wanted the company, Mr. Daley."

"Right. You could have saved your company a fifty-million-dollar breakup fee and you could have avoided buying a company you really didn't want if you could have found a way to get Vince Russo to kill the deal. Isn't that about it, Mr. Frazier?"

"Objection. I don't believe there was a question there."

There wasn't.

"Sustained."

"No further questions."

* * *

Ed Ehrlich from the city attorney's office is next. "Mr. Ehrlich," Skipper says, "you were representing the city of San Francisco in connection with the Russo deal, weren't you?"

"Yes." He looks nervously through his thick glasses. A member of the board of supervisors is here to make sure he doesn't screw up.

"The city had agreed to provide financing?"

"Yes."

Good answer. Keep it short. Stick to the facts.

"When did you leave the Simpson offices that night?"

"Around ten o'clock."

"And did you expect the deal to close?"

"Yes." Skipper gets Ehrlich to say that Bob was in a good mood and was looking forward to the closing.

"No further questions."

I get in front of him right away. "Mr. Ehrlich, the mayor had some serious issues with this deal, didn't he?"

"There were some concerns about our ability to obtain sufficient funds to finance the deal."

"How serious?"

"Not serious.

"Yet you were prepared to move forward."

"Yes."

"And you believe Mr. Russo and Mr. Holmes were prepared to move forward?"

"Yes."

"You were aware that Mr. Russo had serious reservations about proceeding with the deal, right?"

A grudging nod. "I knew he had some issues."

"Isn't it true, Mr. Ehrlich, that the mayor had instructed you to do everything in your power to terminate the deal?"

He glances at the mayor's henchman. "No."

"Isn't it true that the mayor determined that the city didn't have sufficient funds to conclude the deal on the original terms?"

"There were cash-flow issues. But we wanted to close the deal and keep the jobs in the city."

I may have him cornered. "Mr. Ehrlich, where was the city going to get the money to finance the deal?"

"Sources in the San Francisco banking community."

"What was the interest rate?"

"Prime plus four."

"And what rate were you charging the buyer?"

"Prime plus one."

"So the spread was three percent?"

"Right."

"And how big was the loan?"

"A hundred million dollars."

"I see. The spread at three percent is three million dollars a year, right?"

"That's right."

"And how many jobs would you have saved for the city?"

"About three thousand."

"By my math, that's about a thousand dollars a job."

"I guess you could look at it that way."

"And it's your testimony that Bob Holmes was in a great mood?"

Ehrlich takes off his glasses. "He did not appear upset to me."

Add the city to the list of parties that look like idiots. "No further questions."

* * *

Dan Morris smiles confidently as he takes the stand. "I was present that evening," he replies to Skipper's first question. "The mayor asked me to assist with the closing. He wanted to be sure it got done."

"What time did you leave the office, Mr. Morris?"

"Around one-thirty-five." He says that Russo and Holmes were ready to close the deal. According to the political fixer, everybody was in a great mood.

"Did you have any indications from Mr. Holmes or Mr. Russo that they would not proceed with the closing?"

"None."

"No further questions."

I address Morris from my chair. "Isn't it true that the city couldn't afford the deal?"

"I'm not sure I understand the question."

"Isn't it true that the city didn't have enough money to fund the deal? And isn't it true that the mayor sent you and Mr. Ehrlich to the Simpson and Gates offices to try to torpedo it?"

"That's ridiculous. It was a good deal for both parties."

"If it was such a good deal for Vince Russo, why did he disappear?"

"Objection. Argumentative. Speculative. Foundation."

"Sustained."

"Did Mr. Russo appear agitated to you that night, Mr. Morris?"

He's smug. "He always appeared agitated."

"Do you have any idea why Bob Holmes committed suicide?"

"Objection. Move to strike the suggestion that Mr. Holmes committed suicide."

"Sustained."

"I'll rephrase." I look him right in the eye. "Come on, Mr. Morris. Level with us. Two people are dead, and another person has disappeared. Why did it happen? Why were so many people unhappy about this deal?"

"Objection. Speculative."

"Sustained."

"Certainly, you must have a theory, Mr. Morris?"

"Objection. Speculative."

"Sustained."

There's nothing else I can do. I've planted the seed with the jury. "No further questions."

CHAPTER 40

"I'VE BEEN A HOMICIDE INSPECTOR FOR THIRTY SEVEN YEARS"

"Gates is going to bring in his cleanup hitter, Inspector Roosevelt Johnson."
— NewsCenter 4 Legal Analyst Morgan Henderson.
Friday, March 27.

The next morning is Friday, and Skipper goes to his strength. "My name is Roosevelt Johnson. I've been a homicide inspector for thirty-seven years."

Joel tenses. Rosie eyes Roosevelt. Mort studies the jury.

"Inspector Johnson," Skipper says, "could you tell us what time you arrived at the Simpson and Gates offices on the morning of December thirty-first of last year?"

"Eight-thirty-seven." His tone is authoritative. The courtroom is silent.

"Would you please describe what you found?"

Skipper's approach is textbook. You lob open-ended questions to strong witnesses. This will allow Roosevelt to tell his story the way he's rehearsed it. I'm going to have to try to break up his flow.

Roosevelt clears his throat. He turns slightly toward the jury. He's going to tell his story to *them*. "The office was in a state of chaos and shock. Word had spread throughout the firm of the homicides."

I stand and try to sound respectful. "Your Honor, there's no foundation for Mr. Johnson's characterization of the events that day as 'homicides.' We must move to strike."

She turns to Roosevelt. "Inspector, please limit your testimony to factual matters. We'll determine whether the deaths of Mr. Holmes and Ms. Kennedy should be characterized as homicides."

"Yes, Your Honor."

She tells the jury to disregard his characterization of the deaths as homicides. She looks at me with a pained expression, as if to say, "Are you happy now?"

"Inspector," Skipper continues, "you were telling us what happened when you arrived."

Roosevelt describes his interviews with the police at the scene and his discussions with the paramedics and the technicians from the medical examiner's office. He confirms that Bob and Diana were pronounced dead at 8:22. "We knew this was an important case. We wanted to make sure we got everything right."

"Inspector Johnson," Skipper says, "what happened next in your investigation?"

"We interviewed witnesses and gathered evidence." He says the police obtained statements from everyone who was present that night. They talked to building security and impounded the security videos.

"Did you interview the defendant?"

"Yes. He confirmed he was at the office that night."

"Was he a suspect on December thirty-first?"

"No. Originally, we thought this case was a murder-suicide. It wasn't until later that we began to focus more closely on the defendant." He never mentions Joel by name.

"Inspector, when did you first begin to suspect the defendant may have been involved?"

Roosevelt says they became suspicious of Joel when they received the medical examiner's report and began to examine the physical evidence.

Skipper picks up the cue. "This would probably be a good time to turn to the physical evidence."

Rosie whispers in my ear, "We're going to take a pounding for a while."

Skipper picks up the gun and hands it to Roosevelt. "Do you recognize this weapon?"

"Yes. It's the weapon that fired the bullets that killed the victims, Robert Holmes and Diana Kennedy."

Time moves slowly for the next two hours. Skipper has Roosevelt describe every piece of physical evidence in detail. Ten minutes on ballistics. Fifteen minutes on fingerprints. Fifteen minutes on the message on Diana's answering machine. Ten minutes on the voicemail message to Bob. Ten minutes on the fingerprints on the computer keyboard. I object frequently, ferociously and, for the most part, futilely. We have a fundamental problem with the physical evidence. It all points toward Joel.

At eleven o'clock, they're still going strong. Skipper's on today. Roosevelt and the jury seem like old friends. Rita Roberts takes notes. Rabbi Friedman stares straight ahead. Naomi is stoic. At eleven-forty-five, Skipper asks Roosevelt to summarize his views on the physical evidence.

"We concluded the defendant fired the shots that killed the victims. In a clumsy attempt to cover up his crime, he typed a bogus suicide message on Mr. Holmes's computer."

Judge Chen looks at her watch. "This is a good time to break for lunch."

* * *

Joel ignores his sandwich in the cramped consultation room behind Judge Chen's courtroom. "We're getting killed, Mike."

Mort takes a bite of his corned beef sandwich. "You take some lumps when the prosecution presents its case."

I add, "We haven't had a chance to cross-examine Roosevelt yet."

Joel is unconvinced. Without a word, he puts his uneaten sandwich into the white paper bag and drops it into the trash.

* * *

The afternoon session doesn't start any better. "Inspector

Johnson," Skipper begins, "this morning, we discussed how Robert Holmes and Diana Kennedy were killed. We talked about the murder weapon. We listened to incriminating tapes. The defendant's fingerprints were found on a computer keyboard that was used to type a bogus suicide message."

Enough. "Objection. Mr. Gates is making his closing argument a little early."

"Sustained. Mr. Gates, do you think you can find a question to ask Inspector Johnson?"

"Yes, Your Honor." He continues to lecture. "This afternoon, we need to discuss why the defendant killed Mr. Holmes and Ms. Kennedy."

I interrupt again. "Your Honor, is there a question in there somewhere?"

"Let's get to it, Mr. Gates."

"Yes, Your Honor." He turns back to Roosevelt. "Inspector Johnson, do you have any reason to believe the defendant was angry at Mr. Holmes and Ms. Kennedy?"

"Yes."

"Angry enough to kill them?"

"Objection. Inspector Johnson isn't a mind reader."

"Sustained. Please, Mr. Gates."

He's undaunted. "Could you please explain why you believe the defendant was angry at Mr. Holmes?"

"Mr. Holmes was his mentor. Mr. Holmes had been assigned the task of telling the defendant he wasn't going to make partner. Apparently, he did not do so."

"That led to the agitated voicemail message?"

"Objection. Speculative."

"Sustained."

"I'll rephrase. Do you believe the defendant's voicemail message to Mr. Holmes related to the fact that Mr. Holmes failed to inform the defendant that he wasn't going to make partner?"

"Objection. Speculative."

"Overruled."

Roosevelt nods. "Yes. I believe the defendant's voicemail message related to the fact that Mr. Holmes failed to tell him he wasn't going to make partner."

Joel leans over and whispers, "Can't you object? You think I'd kill somebody because I didn't make partner?"

I signal him to be quiet. I whisper, "The jury's watching us."

"Inspector," Skipper continues, "are you aware of any reason why the defendant may have been angry with Ms. Kennedy?"

"The defendant told us Ms. Kennedy did not complete a set of escrow instructions for the Russo deal. He was upset because he had to complete the task himself."

"Isn't it odd that the defendant would kill Mr. Holmes because he didn't make partner, and Ms. Kennedy because she failed to complete a legal document?"

"Objection. Speculative."

"Sustained."

"Inspector, are you aware of any other reasons why the defendant may have been upset with Mr. Holmes and Ms. Kennedy?"

"We believe the defendant was having a romantic relationship with Ms. Kennedy, which she terminated to rekindle an earlier romance with Mr. Holmes."

"Move to strike. Foundation."

"Overruled."

Joel looks straight ahead. Rabbi Friedman is rocking back and forth in his seat. Naomi is staring into the back of Joel's head. Ruth Fink rubs her forehead.

Skipper can barely contain himself. After a week of forensics, guns, fingerprints, autopsy reports, computer keyboards and tape recordings, we've finally got some really juicy stuff for the jury. "Inspector," he says, "I want to be sure I'm clear on this. Are you saying that Ms. Kennedy, for lack of a better term, dumped the defendant in order to resume a romantic relationship with Mr.

Holmes?"

"Objection. Foundation."

"Overruled."

"Yes."

"Is it your belief that he killed Mr. Holmes in a jealous rage after Ms. Kennedy dumped him?"

"Objection. Speculative. State of mind. Foundation." The kitchen sink.

"Sustained." Judge Chen gives Skipper a sharp look. "Let's stick to the facts, Mr. Gates."

He doesn't seem to care. He's getting to all the sordid goodies now. "Inspector, let's take this one step at a time. What evidence do you have that Mr. Holmes and Ms. Kennedy were romantically involved?"

"Mrs. Holmes's private investigator discovered that Mr. Holmes and Ms. Kennedy were having a romantic relationship." He testifies that Beth stated she had found out about the affair in early December and told Bob she would file divorce papers if he didn't break it off. He terminated his relationship with Diana at that time.

"Yet on December thirtieth, Mrs. Holmes served divorce papers on her husband."

"The private investigator observed Mr. Holmes having a rendezvous at the Fairmont with a woman other than Mrs. Holmes."

"Was the private investigator able to identify the woman?"

"He wasn't absolutely sure. He said the woman may have been Diana Kennedy."

Skipper glances at the clock. "You also determined that the defendant was having a romantic relationship with Ms. Kennedy, did you not?"

"Objection. Foundation."

"Overruled."

"Yes. We interviewed several partners at Simpson and Gates who attended the firm retreat at Silverado last fall." He confirms Hutch's accounts of the hot tub incidents. He reiterates Patton's story about finding Diana in Joel's room at three in the morning.

Naomi looks at the floor. This is going to be the bloodiest cross-examination I've ever done.

Skipper asks, "Inspector, if the defendant and Ms. Kennedy were romantically involved, why would the defendant kill her?"

"Objection. Speculative."

"Sustained."

"Inspector, do you have a theory as to why the defendant killed Ms. Kennedy?"

"Objection. Speculative."

"Overruled."

Roosevelt takes off his glasses. "We believe Ms. Kennedy was the woman in the hotel room with Mr. Holmes. We believe she told the defendant that she had resumed her relationship with Mr. Holmes. And we believe she told the defendant that she no longer wanted to see him."

"Objection. Move to strike. There's no foundation for any of this."

"Overruled."

"So, Inspector, you believe that the defendant was so upset about the end of his relationship with Ms. Kennedy that he killed Ms. Kennedy and Mr. Holmes in a jealous rage?"

"Yes."

Joel starts to stand up. I grab his arm and pull him back into his seat. "Stay calm," I whisper.

Skipper spends the rest of the afternoon lobbing softball questions to Roosevelt, who keeps pounding out winners. He describes his interviews with Rick Cinelli and Homer Kim. I object frequently and, for the most part, inconsequentially. Skipper stretches out Roosevelt's testimony until four-thirty.

Judge Chen looks at her watch and says, "I think we should break here until Monday."

It's a bonanza for Skipper. The jury has all weekend to mull over Roosevelt's testimony.

CHAPTER 41

THE CROSS-EXAM OF A LIFETIME

"After Inspector Johnson's devastating testimony, Michael Daley had better be at the top of his game."
— NewsCenter 4 Legal Analyst Morgan Henderson. Monday, March 30.

We spend the weekend preparing for my cross-exam of Roosevelt. Mort keeps pounding on the idea that we have to give the jury a reason to think somebody else did it. Our best bet is Russo. As Mort leaves on Sunday night, he summarizes our defense succinctly. "When all else fails, blame it on the dead guy."

* * *

Monday morning arrives too soon. I'm watching Morgan Henderson give his daily sermon on Channel 4 at six-forty-five. "It might be a good idea to let Mort Goldberg handle Johnson's cross. Goldberg's an old warhorse. He has more capacity for all-out war than Daley does."

Thanks, Morgan.

The former talk-show host who now fancies himself a serious newsman furrows his brow under his blow-dried hair. "Who do you think's winning, Morgan?"

"The prosecution has scored a lot of points, but they haven't delivered a knockout blow."

"Any predictions?"

"It's looking pretty good for the prosecution. I wouldn't want to be wearing Michael Daley's shoes today."

Frankly, neither would I.

* * *

The reporters swarm around me today when we get to the Hall because they know I'll have a major speaking role. I utter the usual platitudes about my faith in the justice system. I can't ignore them, but I don't want to say anything that may get me in trouble. The judge watches the news, too.

* * *

The routine in court has become familiar. Joel takes his seat between Rosie and me. Mort sits at the end of the table. Harriet Hill asks us to rise. The judge takes her seat. The jury is brought in. Roosevelt is called back to the stand. The judge reminds him he's under oath. Then she turns to me and says, "It's your turn for cross-examination, Mr. Daley."

I walk to the lectern. "Good morning, Inspector." I turn to the judge. "May I approach the witness?" I want to appear respectful. She nods. I walk toward Roosevelt. As of this moment, the battle is now fully engaged.

"Inspector, I'd like to go over a few of the items you discussed on Friday in a little more detail."

Our eyes lock. "Of course, Mr. Daley."

I pick up the revolver from the evidence cart. I go over to the jury box and show it to them. Then I walk back to Roosevelt. "Inspector, you identified this revolver as the weapon that fired the bullets that killed Mr. Holmes and Ms. Kennedy, did you not?"

"Yes."

I hand it to him. "And you've testified that Joel Friedman's fingerprints were found on the revolver, right?" I'm trying to elicit one-word answers.

"Yes."

"When you arrived, Officer Chinn told you that Mr. Friedman had informed him that he had picked up the revolver and disarmed it, right?"

"That's true."

"So it's possible that Mr. Friedman may have gotten his

fingerprints on the revolver when he picked it up and disarmed it, isn't it?"

"Objection. Speculative."

"Overruled."

Roosevelt nods. "Yes, it's possible."

One small victory for the good guys. "Inspector, you've studied the lab reports on this gun, haven't you?"

"Yes."

"Would you mind showing us exactly where Mr. Friedman's fingerprints were found on this revolver?"

He asks to see the lab report. Rosie hands it to me, and I turn it over to him. She's marked Sandra Wilson's diagram of the fingerprints on the revolver. I direct him to the correct page. He puts his glasses on the top of his head. I turn to Rosie, who turns on her computer. The diagram appears on a screen in the front of the courtroom.

"Inspector, is this the diagram that you're looking at?"

"Yes."

"Would you please show us where Mr. Friedman's fingerprints were found on the revolver?"

He holds up the revolver and goes through the same exercise that Kathleen Jacobsen, the evidence technician, went through last week. He explains that fingerprints from Joel's thumb, middle finger, ring finger and pinky were found on the handle. He says the fingerprint from Joel's index finger was on the cylinder. He shows the jury how Joel was holding the gun.

"Inspector, could you please show us how Mr. Friedman would have fired the revolver with his hand in that position?"

"He couldn't, Mr. Daley. His finger wasn't on the trigger."

"Thank you, Inspector."

"But, Mr. Daley . . ."

"You've answered my question." I nod to the jury. "So you have no evidence that Mr. Friedman pulled the trigger."

"We have no identifiable fingerprints of Mr. Friedman on the trigger. That's all."

I'm not going to wage a war of semantics. Juries hate it. "Isn't it a fact, Inspector, that the locations of Mr. Friedman's fingerprints were consistent with the act of unloading the revolver?"

"Objection. Foundation."

"Overruled."

Roosevelt folds his arms. "Mr. Daley, I believe that Mr. Friedman left a smudged fingerprint on the trigger of this revolver when he fired it. On the other hand, his fingerprints were in a position that might have been consistent with the act of unloading it."

Good answer. "Thank you, Inspector. You're also aware that when a gun is fired, it emits a cloud of gas and particles of gunpowder fly into the air."

"That's correct."

I ask him whether any such traces were found on Joel's hands or clothing.

"No." He confirms Kathleen Jacobsen's testimony that they didn't test Joel's hands or clothing. "By the time he became a suspect, he had showered several times and his clothes had been cleaned. As a result, we would not have found traces of gunpowder or other chemical substances."

"So you decided not to do the tests because you thought you wouldn't find anything."

"Objection. Asked and answered."

"Sustained."

I've made my point. We hammer at each other for the rest of the morning and into the afternoon. I challenge the handling of the evidence and the phone messages. We argue about the fingerprints on the keyboard. At three o'clock I glance at Rosie, who tugs on her left ear. We have one more subject.

"Inspector, did you ever seriously consider any other suspects?"

"Yes. We ruled them out. Not enough evidence."

"For example, did you ever consider Vince Russo as a potential suspect?"

"For a brief time, yes. But we ruled him out."

"You knew that Mr. Russo had been at the Simpson and Gates offices that night, and that he was very upset about the deal that he was supposed to close the next day."

"Yes."

"He was so upset that he drove to the Golden Gate Bridge and has not been seen since."

"We're aware of the circumstances, Mr. Daley."

"He may even have jumped off the bridge."

"We don't know that."

"Yet you didn't consider him a serious suspect?"

"Objection. Argumentative."

"Sustained."

I'm blowing smoke. "Is it possible he fled because he killed two people?"

"Objection. Speculative."

"Sustained."

"You would at least acknowledge Mr. Russo had a substantial motive to commit this terrible crime, wouldn't you?"

"No."

"Come on. Inspector. Mr. Russo was very unhappy about this deal. By killing Mr. Holmes and Ms. Kennedy, he had an opportunity to disrupt the deal and flee the country."

"We have no evidence to that effect."

"You haven't found his body, have you, Inspector?"

"No."

"And it's possible, isn't it, that he may have faked his suicide and fled the country?"

Skipper's up. "Objection. This is all hopelessly speculative."

It certainly is.

"Sustained."

I'm just starting to speculate. "Inspector, there was evidence confirming that Mr. Russo was in Mr. Holmes's office that night, wasn't there?"

"Yes, Mr. Daley. We found his fingerprints on the desk of Mr. Holmes. However, we have no way of knowing what time he was in Mr. Holmes's office, and we did not find a shred of evidence suggesting he was involved. His fingerprints were not on the weapon or anywhere near the bodies of Mr. Holmes or Ms. Kennedy. As a result, we ruled him out as a suspect."

"Inspector, you were able to determine who was present in the building that night by reviewing the security tapes, right?"

"Yes."

"And you were able to rule out several individuals as suspects because the security tapes indicated that they left the building, right?"

"Correct."

Now, for some smoke and mirrors. "Inspector, are you aware that it is possible to get into the building without passing by the security desk in the lobby? In fact, it is possible to enter the building by the stairs or the freight elevator, isn't it?"

"The stairways and the freight elevators are kept locked."

"But it is theoretically possible for someone to have entered and exited the building via the stairways or the freight elevator without passing the security desk, isn't it?"

"Objection. Relevance."

"Overruled."

Roosevelt shrugs. "Yes, it's theoretically possible, but you would need a key to access those areas."

"But if somebody had a key, or a stairway door was propped open, it is possible somebody could have gotten upstairs and entered and exited the Simpson suite without passing by the guard desk, right?"

"I suppose that's true."

"And there are no security cameras on the stairways or the freight elevator, right?"

"Correct."

"So somebody could have entered the building, gone up the stairs or the freight elevator, killed Mr. Holmes and Ms. Kennedy, and left the same way, without ever being detected, right, Inspector?"

"Objection. Speculative."

"Overruled."

Roosevelt sighs. "Yes, Mr. Daley. That's theoretically possible."

I glance at Rosie, who nods. We have a final item on today's agenda. "Inspector, we've heard a lot of talk about the personal lives of Joel Friedman and Diana Kennedy."

"We certainly have."

"You've testified that you believe Joel and Diana were having an affair, which she terminated."

"That's correct."

"And you base your conclusion on the testimony of Mr. Patton and Mr. Hutchinson?"

"Yes."

"You realize Mr. Patton did not say he actually saw Joel and Diana in bed together."

"That's true."

"And you realize Mr. Patton saw Joel and Diana in the same room together immediately after he attempted to attack her?" A bit of a stretch, but I decide to go for it.

"Objection."

"Overruled."

Roosevelt looks right into my eyes. "We questioned Mr. Patton at length. We have no reason to doubt the veracity of his testimony."

"Mr. Hutchinson claims he saw them in a bar and in a hot tub. Yet Mr. Hutchinson admitted that he was intoxicated at the time. Surely, you must have doubted Mr. Hutchinson's testimony."

"We had no reason to question the truthfulness of Mr. Hutchinson's testimony, either."

Great. "Inspector, Mr. Hutchinson said he thought he saw them in a hot tub from a distance of about a hundred yards. He could have been mistaken. It was dark. He'd had a lot to drink. Other than the highly tentative testimony of Messrs. Patton and Hutchinson, you really don't have any evidence that Joel Friedman and Diana Kennedy were having an affair, do you?"

Skipper's up. "Objection, Your Honor. Speculative. Leading. Asked and answered."

All of the above.

"Sustained."

"No further questions."

* * *

Joel, Rosie, Mort and I sit in the consultation room behind the courtroom. I'm beyond exhausted.

"Nice work on cross today," Mort says.

"Thanks. Coming from a pro like you, it means a lot to me." A small lie.

Rosie's always a step ahead. "We'll move for dismissal tomorrow."

Joel perks up. "You think they'll really dismiss the case?"

Mort gestures with his cigar. "Maybe. Mike got Johnson to admit they have no hard proof that you fired the gun. He made a lot of points on motive. That's always been the weakest part of their case. They've never been able to prove conclusively that you and Diana were having an affair."

"That's because we weren't."

"We'll see tomorrow," I say.

* * *

Roosevelt is waiting for me by my car. "Nice work today."

I toss my trial bag into the trunk. "Thanks, Roosevelt. I'm sorry if I beat you up. Nothing personal."

He glances at the cars roaring by on the 101 freeway. "I hear they've found something. I don't know what it is. You're going to find out tonight, and it's going to come down tomorrow."

I pause. "You think he's innocent, don't you, Roosevelt?"

"I don't know." He motions toward the Hall. "It isn't up to me. The guy on the third floor is making the decisions."

I watch a police car drive by on Bryant. He's silent as a uniformed cop walks by us.

"I've got to run," he says. "It'll be my ass if anybody sees me talking to you." He turns and walks away.

"Thanks, Roosevelt," I call out to his back.

CHAPTER 42

THE FACTS OF LIFE

"District Attorney Prentice Gates says he'll call only one more witness tomorrow. Court watchers expect Friedman's defense attorneys to move for dismissal."
— KCBS News Radio. Monday, March 30. 6:00 P.M.

Rosie's secretary, Rolanda, hands me a manila envelope when I return to the office at six o'clock the same evening. Theoretically, she's supposed to be working just for Rosie. During the trial, she's been helping me, too.

"Thanks for sticking around," I tell her.

"You did a nice job on cross, today. Even the bitchy woman on CNN said so."

Small consolation. I tear open the envelope and pull out a stack of paper. "Skipper didn't call, did he?"

"No. But McNulty did. Said it was important. He left his cell number."

"Thanks." I rifle through the pages.

"What is it, Mike?"

I give her page 5 of the report. "Read this."

Her eyes get bigger. "The blood and DNA tests conclusively prove that Joel Friedman was the father of Diana Kennedy's unborn child. Oh crap."

"Yeah." I think Rolanda is going to go to law school after she finishes at State. "I'll call McNulty. See if you can get Mort and Pete to come down here. Rosie's on her way."

"I'll be here as long as you need me. You okay, Mike?"

Just great. We've built our defense on the proposition that my client wasn't sleeping with the victim and therefore had no motive to kill her. I've probably created enough doubts in the minds of the jurors to get an acquittal. And now I know he was lying all along. "I'll be okay. It's going to be a long night."

* * *

"Bill McNulty speaking." Even on a cell phone, his delivery is crisp.

"It's Mike Daley." My voice is hoarse as I cradle the phone in my shoulder.

"You get the lab results?"

"Yeah."

"We're going to introduce it into evidence tomorrow."

"I'm going to ask the judge for some time to study it and have our own experts look at it."

"She won't go for it. You pushed for the early trial date. You're going to have to live with it."

"If she doesn't give us some extra time, we'll appeal."

"We'll take our chances."

I'd do the same if I were in your shoes. "It doesn't change anything, Bill. You guys still can't prove your case beyond a reasonable doubt. You still can't show he pulled the trigger."

"We'll take our chances."

* * *

Pete arrives first. He glances at the report. "We got a problem," he understates.

"You know any good DNA guys?"

"A couple."

"I'll ask Mort, too." I rub my eyes. "We had them. We were going to move for a dismissal."

"They said on the radio your cross on Johnson was really good."

It was. "Anything new on the search for Russo?"

"Nothing. We've drilled a bunch of dry wells. They're supposed to be looking for him at border crossings. Fat chance."

* * *

Rosie is already here when Mort walks in. "So," he says, "turns out our client was the father after all."

I show him a copy of the paternity test. "Seems that way, Mort."

"You realize that we're completely and totally screwed."

Rosie snaps, "That's helpful. Got any other suggestions, Mort?"

"Easy, Rosie. I'm not throwing in the towel just yet. We've still got some cards to play."

"He's right," I say. "When in doubt, go back to the evidence. Point one. If we can put on a good enough expert to rebut Rod Beckert, we can argue it was a suicide. We could win the case right there."

Mort smiles. "Now you're thinking like a lawyer again."

"Your expert better be good in court."

"He's the best. Full professor at UCSF. And he's my brother-in-law, for God's sake. If he messes up, he's going to have to listen to me remind him at the Passover Seder for the next twenty years." He turns serious. "Wait till you see him in court. He's beaten Beckert. He can do it again."

Rosie's quiet. She's thinking.

"Point two," I say. "Even if the jury decides it wasn't suicide, they still can't show Joel fired the gun. Maybe he handled it, but they can't prove he fired it. Reasonable doubt right there."

Mort agrees. "Another perfectly legitimate argument."

Rosie still isn't biting.

"Point three. They've got a problem with the keyboard. Joel's fingerprints are all over it. But Bob's aren't. It doesn't make sense. If Joel was going to try to fake a suicide, why would he get his fingerprints all over Bob's keyboard?

"Point four. The paternity test will prove Joel and Diana had an affair. They're going to argue he killed her because she broke it off to get back together with Bob. If we can show that Bob and Diana weren't together at the end of the year, it blows a big hole through their motive."

Rosie shrugs. "It's tough to prove a negative, Mike."

"I know. But we've got to try." I look at Pete. "Are you thinking what I'm thinking?"

"The mystery woman at the Fairmont?"

"Exactly. If we can prove she wasn't Diana, we've got a pretty good argument that Bob and Diana never got back together. It's time to talk to Nick the Dick again."

"He'll testify," Pete says. "He has another book coming out this fall. It's free publicity."

I stop to think. "The one thing we haven't considered is the possibility that Joel isn't the father. We could argue the test results were flawed. How reliable are these tests, anyway?"

Rosie answers. "Ninety-nine percent."

Mort adds, "I know a guy at UC who's good. I can get him to confirm the test results. It'll take a little time, though."

"You guys got any better ideas?" I ask.

Mort says, "You forgot point five."

"Point five?"

"Yeah. If everything else fails, we'll use the S-O-D-D-I defense."

"SODDI?" Pete asks.

"Some Other Dude Did It. We need to give the jury a choice."

It may be our best shot. "Russo's perfect," I say. "He can't defend himself. If he didn't do it, why did he jump off the Golden Gate Bridge? Patton's a great candidate, too. He's a first-rate asshole, and he's been sleeping with the Widow Holmes. And he put the moves on Diana. We don't have to prove anything. We just have to suggest it to the jury to give them something to let them reach reasonable doubt. Hell, we should try to find a way to work in the fact that Skipper was there that night."

"You're stretching," Rosie says.

Mort tells her, "You'll see, Rosie. It'll work." Mort rubs his fingers around a cigar. "What should we do first?"

"Rosie, I need you to prepare papers to get things delayed until we can find our own expert and do our own tests. Mort, I want you to call your guy at UC. Pete, I want you and Wendy to go to the Bahamas right away and see what you can dig up before Trevor Smith gets back. Before you leave, I want you to set up a meeting for me with Nick Hanson. And I need you to pound on a few more witnesses to see if we can nail Art Patton. And anything you can get on the whereabouts of Vince Russo would be greatly appreciated."

"What are you going to do tonight?" Rosie asks.

"I need to talk to our client about the facts of life."

* * *

"We need to talk," I say to Joel.

He's standing in the doorway of his father's house at nine-thirty that night. He seems to be in a pretty good mood. Then I remember that the last time we spoke, we were suggesting that we may be able to get the case dismissed tomorrow.

He smiles. "Whatever you need, Mike. Great job on cross today."

"Thanks." My eyes dart. "Your mom or dad around?"

"No. They're at an Israel Bond dinner."

"Good." We walk into the living room and sit down. The TV is tuned to CNN. "Something's come up. It's serious."

His smile vanishes. His eyes bore in on mine. I look right back into his. He turns off the TV.

I thought things went pretty well today," he says.

"They got the results back on Diana's baby."

The color leaves his face. "And?"

"I think you know."

He rubs his eyes. "It's me, isn't it?"

"Yeah."

He folds his hands and looks out the window. In my family, such news would have been met with twenty minutes of histrionics, followed by another half hour of assignment of blame. When you're the rabbi's son, you aren't allowed such luxuries.

"Are they sure?" he asks.

"Ninety-nine percent."

He nods. "I was afraid of that."

"Did you know?"

"Diana said it was possible."

"I see." But I really don't.

"What am I going to tell Naomi?"

"You might start with the truth." I realize my tone is harsh.

He swallows. "You don't understand." He walks into the kitchen. I follow him. He pulls a glass from a cabinet and fills it with water. He leans against the refrigerator, and I lean against the counter. We're barely five feet apart. There's a look of desperation in his eyes.

"Explain it to me," I say. "If you want me to defend you, I have to understand."

"You can't."

"Maybe not. But I can try."

He blinks back tears. "You don't know what it's like being the rabbi's son. You live in a fishbowl. Everything gets blown out of proportion. If you get sent home from school, you aren't just another little kid getting in trouble. You're the rabbi's son getting in trouble. If you aren't dressed perfectly for services, it's viewed as a poor reflection on the rabbi and on the entire Jewish community. People notice."

He looks away. It's hard to believe he's the same guy who was working on a billion-dollar deal a few weeks ago.

"Naomi is more fragile than she lets on," he says. "She's been on antidepressants. I didn't mean to sleep with Diana, Mike. It just happened. And it only happened once. It was stupid. And I have to live with it."

"You're a defendant in a murder trial. You can't dwell on the fact that the Jewish community may find out about your relationship with Diana. You have to tell Naomi and your parents tonight. They're going to introduce the lab report in open court tomorrow. I can't stop them."

"I'm completely screwed." The stress overwhelms him. He dissolves into tears. He knocks his glass of water off the counter. I put my arm around his shoulder. The sobs are long and loud. "What am I going to tell her?" he repeats several times.

For a guy who thinks he has all the answers, I'm speechless.

I hear the front door open. Rabbi Friedman says, "Joel, are you still up?"

Joel has miraculously regained his composure. His parents find us in the kitchen. We stand in silence for a moment.

"What is it?" Joel's mother asks.

Joel looks at me. Then he turns to them. "Something's come up. We need to talk."

* * *

"How did he react?" Rosie asks later that night. We're watching the news in her living room.

"Not well," I say. "He broke down. He's humiliated. His marriage is falling apart."

She closes her eyes. "Did he tell Naomi?"

"They were talking when I left. They were both crying. She wasn't as angry as I thought she'd be. I don't think she has the energy. She looked so sad."

"And his parents?"

"He told them, too."

"How did they take it?"

"Stoic. It's the way they are. Do you think I should have stayed there, Rosie?"

"Probably not. You have to deal with some things in private."

"Would you stop by Naomi's on your way in tomorrow? She's going to need support. It might be better if it comes from you."

"Sure." She turns off the TV. "What are you going to do in court tomorrow?"

Beats me. "We have two choices. We can ask for a continuance and get Mort's expert to challenge the validity of the paternity test."

"Medical science isn't perfect."

"Paternity testing is pretty close. I'm sure he's the father."

"What's the other choice?"

"We stipulate that Joel is the father. We get to the truth quickly without a lot of hysterics."

"Why would we do that?"

"To avoid pissing off the jury with three weeks of expert testimony on the unreliability of paternity tests that we know are accurate."

"Tough choice. What does Joel want to do?"

"He wants to stipulate. He's ready to come clean."

"You think he's lied about anything else?"

"I don't know what to think anymore."

* * *

I'm lying awake at one o'clock in the morning when my phone rings.

"Mike, it's Naomi." Her voice cracks. She's been crying.

"Hi."

"I just don't know what to do."

"You don't have to decide tonight."

"I can't believe he lied to me."

I have no answers for her. "Maybe we should talk about it in the morning, Naomi."

She tries to catch her breath. "I can't go to court tomorrow. It will be too humiliating."

"I understand."

"No, you really don't."

"I know things will be tough for you. But it would help us if the jury sees you there."

"I don't know if I can."

"Let's talk about it in the morning. We'll stop by on our way in."

Five minutes later, the phone rings again. "It's Rabbi Friedman." He clears his throat. "This isn't good news."

"No, it isn't."

"How reliable are these tests, Michael?"

"Very."

"What would you suggest?"

"We're going to ask for more time to let our expert review the evidence. The judge may not give it to us. At the very least, we'll find another expert and blow some smoke at the jury." I regret saying it as soon as I've said it.

"You mean you think we should lie?"

"No. It's my job to get the jury to reasonable doubt. If I have to trot out an expert for three weeks of testimony, that's what I'll do."

He clears his throat. "This is very difficult."

"Maybe we should talk about it in the morning."

CHAPTER 43

"THE PROSECUTION RESTS"

"District Attorney Prentice Gates is expected to call his final witness today."
— KCBS News Radio. Tuesday, March 31. 7:40 A.M.

It's pouring when I reach Rabbi Friedman's house at seven-thirty the next morning. Joel and his parents are ready to go. Nobody says a word about last night.

"Michael," the rabbi says, "we don't want to be late for court."

"May I have a word with Joel in private?"

"Of course."

I pull Joel into the kitchen. "You okay?"

"As okay as I'm going to be."

"What about your parents?"

"They're pissed off, but they're still my parents. They're embarrassed and they'll probably kill me after the trial is over. Until then, they're going to play out their roles."

This helps. "What about Naomi?"

"That's tougher. She doesn't want to go to court this morning. She may take the kids down to her mother's in Southern California until the trial's over."

"One step at a time."

We gather our umbrellas and raincoats. As Rabbi Friedman opens the door, I see Naomi and Rosie walking up the steps under an umbrella. Even though it's raining, Naomi is wearing sunglasses.

"What are you all looking at?" she snaps. "It's time to go to court."

Joel tries to give her a hug, but she pulls away. "We have a lot to talk about when the trial's over," she says to him.

Rosie takes her arm and says, "It's time to go to court."

I give her hand a quick squeeze as we walk down the steps toward our cars.

* * *

"Your Honor," I begin, "the prosecution just provided some new and potentially inflammatory evidence. We need some time to review it."

We're sitting in Judge Chen's chambers. I asked for a meeting before the jury was brought in.

Judge Chen isn't in a particularly gregarious mood. She turns to Skipper. "What's this all about, Mr. Gates? It's a little late to bring in new evidence."

He smiles confidently and hands her a copy of the lab report. "Your Honor, we just got this." He clears his throat, but he's still grinning. "The defendant was the father of Diana Kennedy's unborn baby."

Judge Chen puts on her reading glasses and studies the report.

"Your Honor—I," I say.

She holds up her hand. "Let me look at this, Mr. Daley."

Rosie remains silent. Mort studies the judge. Skipper and McNulty exchange satisfied looks.

After what seems like an eternity, Judge Chen puts down the report. "This is serious. These tests are very reliable."

Skipper agrees vigorously. "Very reliable, Your Honor. Close to one hundred percent."

"Thank you, Mr. Gates."

"Your Honor," I say, "we received this information just last night. We haven't had an opportunity to review it with our expert. And we certainly haven't had an opportunity to conduct an independent test."

"That could take weeks," Skipper says. "They pushed for the early trial date. We're ready to conclude our case. We can't wait six weeks while their experts redo the paternity test. We'll lose the jury. They're going to come back with the same results, anyway."

The judge looks at me. "Mr. Daley, you knew this was a possibility when you asked for an early trial date."

She's right. I've made a significant blunder. I believed my client when he told me he didn't have an affair with Diana Kennedy. "In the interests of fundamental fairness, we request that you give us a few weeks to examine the report and consult with our expert." When all else fails, I try fundamental fairness.

"I'm not putting this jury on ice for a month."

"Judge Chen, you have to give us a couple of days."

"I don't have to give you anything."

"I know. But all I'm asking for is just a few days."

She turns to Skipper, who's whispering to McNulty. "Mr. Gates, it's Tuesday. I was planning on a couple of short trial days this week so I can attend to some other business. Would you object if we recess until Monday?"

"I see no purpose for this delay."

"Mr. Gates, it looks like the rain may stop for a while this afternoon. Why don't you and Mr. McNulty go out and hit some golf balls?"

Skipper gets the message. "I guess we might be in a position to adjourn until Monday."

"Thank you. We're done."

Skipper and McNulty dart out the door.

As I'm packing my trial case, the judge gives me a knowing look. "He lied to you about Diana, didn't he?"

"Yes."

"There isn't much I can do about it, you know."

"I know."

"Mike, I know you'll be tempted to try to get me to declare a mistrial so you can start over and retool your case. I won't let it happen. Understood?"

"Yes."

"See you Monday."

* * *

We spend the rest of the week trying to fill some of the holes in our case. On Thursday, Mort's DNA expert from UCSF confirms what we expected. The paternity tests were conducted by a reputable lab. Unless we can demonstrate that there were some shenanigans, it's virtually certain that Joel was the father. Pete and Wendy leave for the Bahamas on Friday.

I have one bright spot on Friday. I take Nick Hanson out for lunch at Caffe Sport in North Beach. At eighty-something, he's still a character. He assures me that he'd be delighted to testify, as long as we agree to pay him for his time at his standard hourly rate.

* * *

I spend all day Saturday and most of Sunday working with our medical expert, Dr. Robert Goldstein, on his testimony to rebut Rod Beckert. At seven o'clock Sunday night, Rosie, Mort and I regroup in our office. Joel has agreed to stipulate that he's the father. I phone Skipper with the news. He's pleased.

Within fifteen minutes, McNulty e-mails a draft stipulation. We quickly agree on the language.

Mort inspects a fine Cuban cigar. "It's the best we can do. We'll get the issue off the table as quickly as we can."

I'm not so sure.

* * *

Rosie and I are driving home on Sunday night. As we head northbound on the Golden Gate Bridge, I turn to her and say, "How did you get Naomi to come to court?"

"She's tougher than you think. I told her she and Joel have big issues, but that it would help Joel if she waited until after the trial."

"You think they'll be able to hold it together after this is over?"

"Tough to predict. They're going to have to make some changes." She looks out the window.

I've learned there are times when I shouldn't ask too many questions. We drive in silence.

* * *

On Monday morning, Judge Chen is pleased when we inform her in chambers that we've agreed to stipulate about the paternity test. We've just saved a couple of weeks of trial time. She has Skipper read our stipulation to the jury as soon as they're brought in. Although there are a few raised eyebrows among the jurors, there isn't much reaction. They're getting tired.

"Mr. Gates," the judge says, "do you have anything further at this time?"

"No, Your Honor." He turns toward the jury. "The prosecution rests."

"Very well." She speaks to the jury. "The prosecution has completed its presentation. We're going to take a short break while the attorneys discuss some legal issues." She nods to Harriet Hill, who leads the jury out. As soon as they're gone, she turns to me. "Mr. Daley, I presume you'd like to make a motion?"

"Yes, Your Honor. The defense moves that all charges be dropped as a matter of law."

This is routine. The defense always moves for dismissal at the end of the prosecution's case.

"On what grounds?"

"The prosecution has failed to prove its case beyond a reasonable doubt."

Skipper stands. "Objection."

"Sit down, Mr. Gates." She turns to me. "Mr. Daley, your motion is denied. The defense should be prepared to call its first witness tomorrow morning."

CHAPTER 44

THE BRAIN TRUST

"After two weeks of damaging testimony from the prosecution's witnesses, Friedman's attorneys will begin their defense. I hope they have a few rabbits in their hats."
— NewsCenter 4 Legal Analyst Morgan Henderson.
Monday, April 6.

"Have you heard anything from Pete and Wendy?" Joel asks me.

"The banker isn't back in town yet, but Wendy was able to sweet-talk his secretary into giving her copies of the correspondence in the file. She's e-mailing it to us tonight."

We're meeting in Rabbi Friedman's dining room at two o'clock the same afternoon. Joel is tense. Rabbi Friedman is in a contemplative mood. Mort fingers a cigar. Rosie is drinking iced tea.

"Who goes first?" Joel asks.

"We'll start with our medical expert, Dr. Goldstein."

Rabbi Friedman glances at Mort.

"He's good," Mort says.

I agree. "I worked with him on his testimony. If he can persuade the jury it was a suicide, we can go home."

"And if he can't?" Joel says.

"We'll attack the physical evidence. If we have to, we'll show the jury that Russo and Patton had more motive and opportunity than you did. If things get tight, we'll put some of my former partners on the stand and deflect the blame over to them."

"What about me?" Joel asks.

"What about you?"

"When do I go on?"

"We'll see how it goes. If things are going well, you don't."

"I want to testify, Mike. "I *need* to testify."

Over my dead body. "We'll decide later."

Mort clears his throat. "There's something I'd like to bring up." He looks at Rabbi Friedman and then he turns to Joel. "I wanted to discuss this privately with Joel, but it doesn't appear that I'll have a chance. Let me explain the situation."

Rosie scowls. "What situation, Mort?"

"After we got the results of the paternity test, I decided to talk to the DA."

What? I lean across the table. "You didn't have the authority, Mort."

"Hear me out. In light of the test results, I thought it would be in Joel's best interests to feel out the DA about a possible deal." He looks at Joel. "I think we should explore all options."

Rosie's eyes are on fire. My heart races, and I struggle to keep my tone measured. "Why didn't you tell me you were going to the DA?"

"Because I knew you wouldn't agree to it."

"We would have discussed it. We would have consulted with Joel. Then we would have made a decision."

"I doubt it."

"Bullshit. You should have told us."

"I talked man-to-man with Skipper. He thinks his case is shaky enough that he's willing to let Joel plead to voluntary manslaughter. It takes the death penalty off the table. And he's willing to recommend a fairly lenient sentence."

Joel glares at Mort, then his father, then he turns to me. "Seeing as how I'm on trial, maybe you guys would be interested in my opinion."

Mort interrupts him. "I was doing it for your own good."

"You think I'm guilty."

"I didn't say that."

"How could you possibly think I might agree to a plea bargain?"

"Look at their case. You're an admitted adulterer. You're an admitted liar. How big a leap is it for the jury?"

Joel's tone fills with anger. "You're right. I am an adulterer. I'm not proud of it. I lied about it. I'm not proud of that either. But I am not a murderer. If the jury wants to convict me for something I didn't do, so be it. But I'll be damned if I'm going to admit to something I didn't do. Period."

"Give it some thought," Mort says.

"I've given it all the thought that it deserves. No deal."

"Okay." Mort reaches for his briefcase.

"There's one other thing, Mort. Your assistance on this case is no longer required. You're fired."

* * *

Rosie and I are sitting in her office later the same evening to talk about strategy. The hallway is lined with binders, charts and exhibits. It looks like the backstage area of a theater.

"Well, Rosita," I say, "just you and me again."

"Just like old times at the PD's office."

"We've got them right where we want them."

She grins. "You've never been at a loss for self-confidence."

"I just hope we don't have any more surprises. And I sure wish Pete would find Vince Russo."

CHAPTER 45

OUR TURN

"Friedman Defense Begins Today."
— San Francisco Legal Journal. Tuesday, April 7.

I knock on Rosie's door at seven the next morning.

"Come in," she says. "You won't believe this."

Grace is eating a bowl of Froot Loops at the kitchen table. She's happy to see me. I say hi to Rosie's mom, who has been logging overtime with Grace during the trial. We'll have to do something nice for Sylvia.

Rosie leads me into the living room where the TV is tuned to Channel 4. Morgan Henderson is delivering his daily analysis. "The defense will begin its case today," he intones.

"So what?" I say.

Rosie turns up the volume.

Henderson looks solemnly into the camera. "As we reported earlier this morning, Professor Mort Goldberg resigned from the defense team last night. His office said his departure was the result of 'philosophical differences.' "

"Philosophical differences my ass," I say.

"Just wait," Rosie says.

Henderson smiles at the morning anchorwoman, who bats her eyelashes. "Susan, I am pleased to introduce the newest member of our legal team here at NewsCenter 4." His grin widens. "We are joined by Professor Morton Goldberg, who will be providing commentary on the trial for the duration."

"For the love of God," I say.

"Unbelievable," Rosie says.

The camera shifts to a beaming Mort, who is in a separate

studio, fiddling with an earpiece. "Is that you, Morgan?"

Henderson looks at his monitor. "Uh, Professor Goldberg will join us in a moment."

The picture stays on Henderson, but Mort's voice is heard. "I'm ready, Morgan."

They're going to have to decide who's going to play Laurel and who's going to play Hardy.

"Mort," Henderson says, "what are your thoughts on the beginning of the defense's case?"

The camera shifts to Mort. The lights reflect off his glasses. "You know, Morgan, I want to remind our viewers that I've just terminated my association with the defense team for philosophical reasons. I have to be careful not to divulge any client confidences."

"Can you believe this?" Rosie says.

I rub my temples. "At this point, I'll believe anything."

Henderson turns serious. "Without divulging any confidences, how do you feel about the defense's case, Mort?"

"The defense has a lot of ground to cover, Morgan. Michael Daley is a very good lawyer. I'm sure justice will prevail."

How insightful. "Turn it off," I say.

Grace looks at me. "Are you okay, Daddy?"

"Yeah, sweetie. Everything's fine." Daddy has a slight case of indigestion.

* * *

It's overcast, but not raining, when we reach the wall of reporters at the Hall.

"Mr. Daley, are you going to consider a plea bargain?"

"Mr. Daley, is it true Mr. Goldberg was fired?"

"Mr. Daley, does Mr. Friedman's affair change your defense?"

"Mr. Daley? Mr. Daley? Mr. Daley?"

I feel like screaming, "Shut up!" I try to look composed as Rosie and I push our way inside to meet Joel and his parents.

"Naomi is in the bathroom," Joel says. "She'll meet us upstairs."

Rabbi Friedman glances at me. "It's up to you, Michael."

"We'll just keep going. Rabbi."

Skipper comes over as soon as we take our seats. "I understand we have a change in the lineup."

"Yeah."

He grins.

Joel leans over and whispers, "You ready?"

"You bet." I don't have time to think of all the things I would have done differently. With hindsight, I might have deferred our opening statement until now. "Now we get to tell our side of the story."

* * *

Before the jury is called in, Judge Chen turns to me. "I understand there's been a change at the defense table."

"Yes, Your Honor. Mr. Goldberg won't be with us."

"Very well. Let's proceed." She instructs Harriet Hill to bring in the jury. I didn't expect her to stop the trial just because Mort's gone. He hasn't said a word to the jury, anyway.

* * *

"Please call your first witness, Mr. Daley."

"The defense calls Dr. Robert Goldstein."

Mort's brother-in-law, Bob Goldstein, is a professor at UCSF Medical Center. His appearance might be described as the anti-Mort. He's in his late sixties, with a full head of gleaming silver hair and dazzling blue eyes. He glides his six-foot-four-inch frame across the courtroom with the grace of a senior squash champion. His double-breasted gray suit matches his hair. A tasteful white kerchief sits in his breast pocket. He looks like he'd be right at home in a boardroom or a country club. The Rolex and gold cuff links suggest he's very successful and probably very rich. Pound for pound, he can hold his own with Skipper in the charisma derby.

He's sworn in and takes his place on the stand. He casually adjusts the microphone. He knows his way around a courtroom, and he knows how to work an audience. Mort says he isn't the kind of doctor you'd call if you're sick. He's the kind you'd call if you need him to testify.

He states his name for the record. He smiles at the jury. "I'm a full professor of Pathology and Trauma Surgery at UCSF Medical School."

I begin taking him through his credentials. We get through his undergraduate degree at Stanford and his medical degree from Johns Hopkins when Skipper interrupts us. "We'll stipulate to Dr. Goldstein's expertise."

Goldstein smiles. The two lawyers on the jury nod.

I hand him copies of Beckert's autopsy reports. "Dr. Goldstein, are you familiar with the autopsy reports prepared by Dr. Roderick Beckert with respect to Mr. Robert Holmes and Ms. Diana Kennedy?"

"Yes. I have reviewed both reports."

Skipper starts to stand, then he sits down. He's jumpy today.

"Would you be kind enough to tell us whether you agree with Dr. Beckert's conclusions?"

"Objection. There's no foundation for this."

"Your Honor," I say, "Mr. Gates just stipulated that Dr. Goldstein is, in fact, a medical expert. He did not object when I asked Dr. Goldstein whether he had reviewed the reports. Certainly, he can't object when I ask Dr. Goldstein for his opinion as to the conclusions in those reports. Why else would I call him to the stand?"

Judge Chen isn't buying into this completely. "I'll overrule the objection for now. But Dr. Goldstein better be prepared to explain his conclusions."

"He will." I turn back to Goldstein. "You were going to tell us your views on the autopsy reports."

"I have known Rod Beckert for many years. We are colleagues on the UCSF faculty. I respect him."

You also have more titles than he does, Bob, but don't lay it on too thick.

"In the case of the autopsy of Ms. Kennedy," he continues, "I think Rod got it absolutely right." He explains in medical and layman's terms that she died of gunshot wounds to her lung and heart.

"And the autopsy report on Mr. Holmes?"

He grimaces. "That's where I have a problem with Dr. Beckert's conclusions. There's no doubt Mr. Holmes died from massive trauma from a gunshot wound to his head. However, I have very serious doubts about Rod's conclusion that Mr. Holmes was knocked unconscious prior to the shootings. In fact, I believe Rod was wrong."

I glance at the jury. They seem to like him. "Would you mind explaining your conclusions. Doctor?" I'm taking a chance. It may be better to lead him with short, precise questions. On the other hand, at our rehearsal—I mean our trial preparation—he explained complicated concepts in terms that I could understand.

"Of course. I wonder if we could look at the autopsy photos."

Rosie sets up the easel and puts an enlarged picture of the left side of Bob's head in front of the jury. Dr. Goldstein turns to the judge and asks whether he can stand by the picture so he can point out certain items. He speaks to her in a tone that suggests they're old friends. She agrees.

He buttons his suit jacket as he walks to the easel. He takes a gold pen out of his pocket. He speaks directly to the jury. "Ladies and gentlemen, we're looking at an autopsy photo of the left side of Mr. Holmes's head. For reference, here's the edge of the skull." He makes a circular motion with the pen.

Goldstein nods to the jurors. As I instructed him, he speaks to the phone company supervisor. "Madam, can you see the photo?"

"Yes."

"Can everybody hear me? I hate using microphones."

They nod. Mort was right. This guy is smoother than fine scotch.

He turns to the photo and draws an imaginary circle above Bob's left ear. "This is called the parietal bone. Here's where the bullet came out. We call it the exit wound. Although we don't have a picture of it here, the entrance wound was, as you know, in the right parietal bone, just above the right temple."

He's striking a nice balance between knowledgeable and folksy. The accountant is looking receptive.

"Everybody with me so far?" he asks.

The jurors nod.

Skipper stands. "Your Honor, would you please instruct Dr. Goldstein not to ask questions of the jury? This isn't his anatomy class at UC."

Judge Chen is annoyed. "If that was an objection, I'll sustain it." She turns to Goldstein. "Please limit yourself to answering Mr. Daley's questions without questioning the jury."

"Yes, Your Honor."

I say, "Dr. Goldstein, you were describing the exit wound."

"Yes." He describes the wound in detailed medical-ese. Then he interprets in language Grace could understand. "As you can plainly see, the trauma to the head was massive."

"Were you able to make a determination about the accuracy of Dr. Beckert's conclusion that the wound may not have been self-inflicted?"

"Objection, Your Honor. He's leading the witness."

No, I'm not. "Your Honor, that wasn't a leading question." Skipper is trying to break Goldstein's rhythm.

"You're right, Mr. Daley. Overruled."

Goldstein says, "In my judgment. Rod was wrong. I believe the wound was self-inflicted."

Murmurs in the gallery. This shouldn't be a news flash. Did they think my medical expert was going to agree with Beckert? I ask Goldstein to explain his conclusion.

"I am certain Mr. Holmes fired the gun." He says that gunpowder residue was found on Bob's right hand. "There's no other way he could have gotten gunpowder on his hand, unless, of course, he happened to fire another gun the same day."

"Isn't it possible that someone may have placed the gun in his hand while he was unconscious and caused him to fire it? Wouldn't that generate the same chemical residue on his hand?" I'm trying to mitigate Skipper's argument that somebody knocked Bob unconscious, placed the gun in his hand and caused him to pull the trigger, making it look like a suicide.

"Yes, but that assumes Mr. Holmes was unconscious at the time the gun was fired."

"Was there any evidence that Mr. Holmes was unconscious?"

"No." He pauses. "I have all the respect in the world for Rod Beckert. But this time around, I think he's flat wrong."

I pretend to study the picture of Bob's head. I'm actually glancing at the jury. I was hoping I'd get a little more than halfhearted reactions. "Could you please explain why you believe Dr. Beckert's conclusion was wrong?"

"Certainly, Mr. Daley." He says that Holmes wasn't under the influence of drugs, and the amount of alcohol in his system was so small he couldn't have been prosecuted for a DUI. As a result, he ruled out the possibility that he was rendered unconscious by the use of any chemical substance.

He turns back to the photo. "Consequently, it seems the only way Mr. Holmes could have been rendered unconscious would have been through a blow to his head." He points to a spot above the exit wound. "This is the area where Dr. Beckert claims there was a concussive wound. In fact, the blow to the skull, if there was such a blow, wasn't nearly as traumatic as Dr. Beckert says. It certainly wasn't enough to render him unconscious."

I look skeptical. "How can you be sure, Dr. Goldstein?"

"It's less than a quarter of an inch in diameter. There was no significant contusion. More important, Dr. Beckert took X-rays of Mr. Holmes's head. There was no skull fracture or concussion. It was probably caused when the head hit the desk after he shot himself." He pauses. "Let me put it this way. If he was a football player and he sustained such an injury, he wouldn't have left the game. Based on my best medical judgment, it is my opinion that he fired the gun and that he took his own life."

Perfect. "Dr. Goldstein, you understand that Dr. Beckert concluded that the injury could not have been sustained after the shooting because the hematoma, or bump, could not have formed after the shooting."

"In general, that's true. A hematoma cannot form once the heart stops beating because it cannot pump blood to the injured area. However, in circumstances such as this where there is a wound to the head, the heart may continue to beat for seconds or even minutes after the shooting. As a result, it is likely that the hematoma was caused when Mr. Holmes bumped his head on the desk after he'd shot himself."

"No further questions, Your Honor."

* * *

Skipper is up like a shot. "Dr. Goldstein, you didn't examine the body, did you?"

"No."

"And you didn't have an opportunity to question Dr. Beckert, did you?"

"No."

"And isn't it likely that Dr. Beckert's exam was more comprehensive than yours?"

I've warned Goldstein to deflect hypothetical questions.

He smiles. "Of course, Mr. Gates. Dr. Beckert had the body in front of him when he performed the autopsy. I've been working off photos and X rays."

"Wouldn't it make more sense in this context to rely on Dr. Beckert's description of the wounds than yours?"

"Objection. Speculative."

"Sustained."

Skipper doesn't fluster. "I'll rephrase. Don't you think Dr.

Beckert's descriptions of the wounds would be more reliable than yours given the fact that he was observing the body as he performed the autopsy?"

"Objection. Still speculative."

"Sustained."

Surely he's going to do more than just ask Goldstein to agree with Beckert. On the other hand, if he gets into hand-to-hand combat, Goldstein will probably hold his ground. If I were in Skipper's shoes, I wouldn't push too hard. The jury understands Goldstein is our hired gun.

They joust for twenty minutes. They argue about the blow to the head. Goldstein doesn't give an inch.

"Dr. Goldstein," Skipper finally says, "are you being paid to testify today?"

"Yes I am."

"And how much are you being paid?"

Goldstein looks at me. This is a standard question. If Skipper can't shake him, at least he can try to show that we've bought his medical opinion, which, of course, we have.

Goldstein's tone is matter-of-fact. "Seven hundred fifty dollars an hour." He adds, sarcastically, "Plus two dollars to ride the streetcar each way."

A smattering of laughter breaks out in the gallery.

"How many hours have you spent on this case?"

"Counting today, about fifty."

Skipper nods melodramatically. "So, they were able to buy your medical opinion for about forty thousand dollars?"

"Objection. Argumentative."

"Sustained."

"No further questions, Your Honor."

As Goldstein steps down, Joel whispers, "That went pretty well, didn't it?"

I nod. Thanks, Mort. I hope you get good ratings tonight.

* * *

Our next witness is Dr. Greta Hudson, a dignified African-American woman who is a professor at USC. She used to be one of the top evidence techs in the FBI crime lab. We decided to go out of town for our expert on guns and fingerprints to make it tougher on Skipper's team to learn much about her.

I start by asking her if she's a medical doctor.

"No. I'm a Ph.D. in criminology. My area of expertise is forensics and, in particular, the gathering and analysis of physical evidence. I've written extensively on the subject of fingerprints. I'm also an expert on certain types of firearms, including revolvers."

Just the way we rehearsed it. We spend a few minutes going over her credentials before Skipper stipulates to her expertise.

In response to my question concerning Bob's position when he was shot, she explains that the trajectory of the bullet and the blood-spatter patterns on Bob's desk indicate that he was sitting at a ninety-degree angle to his desk. He slumped to the floor, possibly banging the left side of his head against his desk.

"Dr. Hudson, were you able to determine whether Mr. Holmes or Ms. Kennedy was shot first?" If Bob died first, it doesn't look like a suicide.

"Yes." She explains that the tattooing at the entrance wound indicates that the barrel of the gun was placed against Bob's head. In such circumstances, a vacuum is created when the gun is fired, which sucks a minute amount of blood into the barrel. "If the last shot fired from the gun killed Mr. Holmes, there would be traces of his blood in the barrel. If the gun was fired again to kill Ms. Kennedy, the traces of blood would have been cleared out, and no traces of his blood would have been found."

Here goes. "Were any traces of Mr. Holmes's blood found in the barrel?"

"Yes. As a result, I concluded that the last shot fired from this weapon was the shot that killed Mr. Holmes."

Good answer. I hand her the revolver. "Dr. Hudson, have you

reviewed the police and lab reports concerning this weapon?"

"Yes."

"In particular, did you review the fingerprint analysis prepared by the crime lab?"

"Yes."

Rosie puts a diagram showing all sides of the revolver on the easel in front of the jury. I ask Dr. Hudson to give the jury a summary of the fingerprint report.

Skipper objects. "Your Honor, the report on this weapon has already been entered into evidence. Surely we don't need Dr. Hudson to restate the entire report."

Actually, I want her to do just that—and to put our spin on it. "Your Honor, if Mr. Gates has a problem with Dr. Hudson's analysis, he can take it up on cross-exam."

"Overruled."

Dr. Hudson asks Judge Chen for permission to leave the stand. Then she uses her pointer to show Joel's fingerprints, noting that only unidentifiable, smudged fingerprints were found on the trigger.

I hand her the gun. "Dr. Hudson, would you show us how you believe Mr. Friedman gripped this weapon?"

"Objection. Speculative."

"Overruled."

She holds the handle with her thumb, middle, ring and pinky, carefully avoiding contact with her index finger. She holds it up for the jury to see. "This is as close as I can get."

"What about your index finger?"

She places her right index finger on the cylinder. "The index finger was on the cylinder."

"Could you explain why Mr. Friedman's index finger may have been on the cylinder?"

"Objection. Speculative."

"Sustained."

"I'll rephrase. Dr. Hudson, how do you open this revolver?"

"You press against the cylinder with your finger."

"And Mr. Friedman's right index fingerprint was found on the cylinder, was it not?"

"Yes."

"If he was unloading the weapon, he would have gotten his fingerprint on the cylinder, right?"

"Objection. He's leading the witness."

Yes, I am.

"Overruled."

"Yes, Mr. Daley. Mr. Friedman's fingerprint was in a place that is consistent with the act of unloading this weapon."

Good. "One final question, Dr. Hudson. Were any identifiable fingerprints found on the trigger of the gun?"

"No."

"So, in your opinion, is there any conclusive evidence that Mr. Friedman fired this weapon?"

"No."

"No further questions."

* * *

Skipper tries in vain for the next hour to trip her up. He's in a tough spot. He can't simply ask her if she thinks it's possible that Joel fired the gun. She'll say there's no evidence that he did, or she can say that anything's possible. Neither will help him. He tries to get her to admit that Joel could have left smudged fingerprints on the trigger when he shot the gun. She says there's no evidence to prove it. She holds her ground.

Finally, he asks her how much she's being paid for her testimony. This time, the bill is only twenty grand. Skipper sits down in frustration.

CHAPTER 46

"YOU'RE THE HEAD COMPUTER GUY, RIGHT?"

"Daley's presentation has been a little wooden."
— NewsCenter 4 Legal Analyst Morton Goldberg. Noon.
Tuesday, April 7.

"How many more witnesses, Mr. Daley?" Judge Chen asks.

We've just started. "Two for sure, maybe three or four. The defense calls Eric Ross."

Whispering in the gallery. "Who's he?"

Skipper looks at McNulty. They pour over our witness list. Ross has been head of information systems at S&G for five years. Skipper never spoke to him. He probably never knew how to turn on his computer.

Ross is sworn in. He's in his early thirties and uncommunicative. His eyes dart through thick wire-rimmed glasses. He's wearing his only suit. Somebody should inform him that wide lapels are out. His mustache twitches. He doesn't make eye contact.

"Mr. Ross, we've known each other for a while, right?"

"Objection. Relevance." Skipper is buying time.

"Overruled."

Ross nods. "We knew each other when you were at our firm."

"Right. And what's your job?"

"I'm the head of information systems." His delivery is stiff.

"In layman's terms, what does that mean?"

"I'm in charge of firm-wide information and technology systems."

"Firm-wide information and technology systems," I repeat. "For those of us who are technologically challenged, that means you're the head computer guy, right?"

He's annoyed. I'm treating him like he's the cable guy. "I guess you could say that."

"So you're in charge of keeping track of all the firm's computer stuff, right?"

"Computer stuff?"

"Yeah, you know—hardware, software—computer stuff."

"Yeah." His irritation is showing. Just the reaction I want. "Actually, I'm most concerned about the hardware. You know—the machines."

He has no idea where I'm going. "Mr. Ross, as the head computer guy, you're in charge of keeping track of the equipment, right?"

"That's right."

"And Simpson and Gates is a big firm, so you've got a big job, right?"

"Objection." Skipper's voice fills with sarcasm. "Your Honor, we're happy to stipulate that S&G is a large firm and Mr. Ross has a lot of computers to keep track of. What's the point?"

"Overruled. I presume this is leading somewhere, Mr. Daley?"

"Yes, Your Honor. Mr. Ross, how many computers do you keep track of at S&G?"

"Firm-wide?"

"Firm-wide."

"You want an exact number?"

"Ballpark's fine."

He sits up a little taller. "I'd say about three thousand."

"That's a lot of computers, isn't it?"

Skipper stands again. "Your Honor, please?"

She glares at me. "Mr. Daley."

"Yes, Your Honor." I want to play with him for another question or two. "Now, of the three thousand computers, how many have keyboards?"

He looks at me like I'm out of my mind. "Keyboards?"

"Yes, Mr. Ross. Keyboards."

"All of them, of course." He may as well have added "you moron." "You can't use them without keyboards."

"That's what I figured. Do you keep a list of all the keyboards?"

"Basically, they're all the same. Some are a little newer."

"I understand. But do you make a list of all the people who have keyboards?"

"As a matter of fact, I do. When a new person comes to the firm, they're issued a computer and a keyboard." He pauses. "But . . ." He stops.

"Mr. Ross? Did you want to add something?"

"Well, sometimes people switch keyboards without telling me. The action is better on the new keyboards."

Imagine. People taking each other's keyboards. "Is it a problem when people switch keyboards?" It's probably a felony in his mind.

"Not really. It just makes it more difficult to keep track of everything."

"I see. How often do you update the list?"

"Whenever a new keyboard is issued."

"Do you take an inventory of all the keyboards from time to time?"

"Once a year, but we don't always get around to it. Sometimes we're too busy."

Too busy to count keyboards? "When did you take the last inventory?"

"Right before the end of the last year."

"That's great, Mr. Ross." Rosie hands me a thirty-page printout. I give copies to Skipper and Judge Chen. "Your Honor, the defense would like to have this keyboard inventory entered into evidence. This list was provided to Mr. Gates before the beginning of the trial." Along with three dozen boxes of Simpson and Gates records that we subpoenaed, but never had any intention of using.

Skipper and McNulty look at it. It's a list of names and serial numbers.

Judge Chen turns to Skipper. "Any objection?"

Skipper looks at McNulty and shrugs. "I don't think so."

I hand the list to Ross. "Can you please tell us what this printout is?"

"It's the inventory we took in December. How did you get a copy?"

"We're very resourceful." It's nice to know all the time Wendy spent pouring over mountains of S&G records was not in vain. "Can you tell us what's described in this list?"

"The first column has the serial number. The second column shows the first initial and last name of the employee to whom each keyboard is issued."

"Including attorneys?"

"Yes."

"Can you please look at the serial number of the keyboard opposite the name JFRIEDMAN?"

"Sure."

"And would you please confirm that JFRIEDMAN refers to the defendant, Joel Friedman?"

"Yes. He's the only Friedman in the firm."

"Would you please read the serial number opposite his name?"

He studies it. "7-1-4-5-8-1-1-2-6-3."

I walk over to a large flip chart I've set up just for this exercise. "Would you mind reading that number again?"

"Sure."

He repeats it, and I write it in big block numbers on the chart. I walk over to the evidence cart and pick up the keyboard found in Bob's office. It's wrapped in clear plastic. I walk back to Ross and hand it to him. "Mr. Ross, can you see through the plastic?"

"Yes."

"Good." I walk back to my chart. "Can you read the serial number on the back again?"

"7-1-4-5-8-1-1-2-6-3."

I write the numbers on the flip chart directly below the identical numbers that are already there. The jury seems interested. My little grandstand play seems to be working. I pause to look at the two rows of identical numbers. "Mr. Ross, are you aware that the keyboard you are holding was taken from the office of Robert Holmes on December thirty-first?"

Skipper's up. "Objection. The witness has no basis to answer that question."

"Mr. Daley," Judge Chen says, "could you rephrase?"

"Yes, Your Honor." I turn back to Ross. "Would it surprise you to find out that the keyboard you're holding was found in the office of Mr. Holmes on December thirty-first?"

He looks helplessly at Skipper. "Uh, no, I didn't know that. I mean, yes, it would surprise me."

"Yet the keyboard you're holding is inventoried as belonging to Joel Friedman."

"Uh. Yes it is." His mustache twitches furiously.

"Why was Mr. Friedman's keyboard in Mr. Holmes's office on the morning of December thirty-first?"

"Objection. Speculative."

"Sustained."

"I'll rephrase. Do you have any idea how Mr. Friedman's keyboard got into Mr. Holmes's office, Mr. Ross?"

"No, I don't."

"Did you move it?"

"No, sir. I didn't."

"Well it didn't get up and walk next door, did it, Mr. Ross?"

"Objection."

"Withdrawn. No further questions."

* * *

Skipper confers with McNulty before he approaches Ross. He hands Ross the inventory list. "Mr. Ross, what is the date in the upper right-hand corner of the printout?"

"December first of last year."

"Was this inventory updated after December first?"

"No, sir. We have too many other important things to keep us busy."

I'll bet you do. I see where Skipper's going.

"So, Mr. Ross, this inventory means that on December first, the keyboard in your hands was sitting on Mr. Friedman's desk, right?"

"Right."

"And it could have been moved from Mr. Friedman's desk to Mr. Holmes's desk at any time after December first, right?"

I decide to slow down the train. "Objection. Speculative."

"Sustained."

"I'll rephrase. Do you have any way to account for the whereabouts of this keyboard after December first?"

"No, sir."

"No further questions."

I ask for a brief recess.

* * *

Joel, Rosie and I caucus in the consultation room.

"We may have a problem," I say to Joel. "There's a thirty-day window when the keyboard could have been moved from your office to Bob's."

Rosie says, "I say we go with what we've got. The jury already knows the keyboard was moved."

I agree with her. When we return to court, I tell Judge Chen that we will have no more questions for Ross.

"I'm inclined to adjourn for the day," she says. "How many more witnesses do you have?"

"Two or three. We should have the case in the hands of the jury by the end of the week."

I glance at Skipper. I'm hoping he'll spend all night preparing to cross-examine Joel.

* * *

Pete calls from the Bahamas that night. "They're expecting a storm in the morning," he says.

"Any luck tracking down Trevor Smith?"

"He's back the day after tomorrow. See if you can stall until then."

"We will. Time's getting short."

CHAPTER 47

NICK THE DICK

"A good dick has to wear out a little shoe leather."
— Private investigator Nicholas Hanson. *San Francisco Chronicle*. Wednesday, April 8.

The next morning, at precisely nine-fifteen, I stand and say in a clear voice, "Your Honor, the defense calls Nicholas Hanson."

The doors in the back of the courtroom open. Nick the Dick—all four feet ten of him—comes strutting down the center aisle. He's wearing a charcoal Wilkes Bashford pinstripe with a burgundy tie. A matching kerchief sits in his breast pocket. A small red rose adorns his lapel. His three-thousand-dollar toupee has been carefully groomed. He nods to the press. He looks like the president walking down the center aisle in the House of Representatives before the State of the Union.

The secret weapon just arrived.

The courtroom breaks out in a combination of laughter and chaos. Judge Chen bangs her gavel. I hear McNulty mutter, "For the love of God."

Joel leans over and whispers, "Is this for real?"

"The fun's about to start."

Nick stops in front of the bench and acknowledges Judge Chen, like they're old friends. "Hello, Your Honor. It's been a long time."

A very long time, indeed. They've never met.

She can't help herself and she smiles. "Hello, Mr. Hanson. I believe you're familiar with our procedures."

"Indeed I am." When Harriet Hill asks him if he swears to tell the truth, he replies, "Indeed I do." He climbs into the witness box and casually adjusts the microphone. He pours himself a glass of water and beams at the jury.

I've been waiting for this moment for weeks. I stand at the lectern and let him bask in the spotlight. "Good morning, Mr. Hanson."

"Good morning, Mr. Daley," he chirps.

He'll be eighty-three next month. I should look so good. "Would you please state your occupation for the record?"

"I'm a private eye."

"How long have you been a private investigator?"

He closes one eye and looks up, as if he's running an imaginary calculator in his head. "I've been doing this since I was seventeen. I guess that means almost sixty-six years."

"You've worked in San Francisco the entire time?"

"Indeed I have. Born and raised in North Beach. I played a little ball with the DiMaggio boys when we were kids."

The accountant looks impressed. If Joe DiMaggio was the Yankee Clipper, maybe Nick was the San Francisco Dinghy.

"Mr. Hanson, did Elizabeth Holmes retain your services in the fall of last year?"

"Indeed she did." He talks out of the corner of his mouth, like Sean Connery. "She wanted me to put a tail on her husband. She thought he was sleeping around."

Just the tone I was hoping for. Polished. Professional. Dignified. "Were you able to determine whether Mr. Holmes was in fact having an extramarital affair?"

He turns to the jury. "Indeed he was."

"And how were you able to make this determination?"

"How do you think? I followed him all over town."

The jurors are eating this up. "And you found him with another woman?"

"Indeed I did."

"Where was that?"

"In the woman's apartment at the Golden Gateway."

"When was that?"

"On December first of last year."

Skipper has seen enough. "Your Honor, I must object to this line of questioning. I fail to see the relevance."

I hold up a hand. "Your Honor, Mr. Hanson was retained to investigate the possibility that Mr. Holmes was having an affair. The prosecution has suggested that Mr. Friedman acted in a jealous rage because Mr. Holmes had rekindled his relationship with Ms. Kennedy. We're about to show you that Mr. Holmes had terminated his relationship with Ms. Kennedy in early December. By the end of December, there was nothing for Mr. Friedman to be jealous about."

"Overruled."

"Mr. Hanson," I continue, "are you sure he was having a sexual relationship with this woman?"

"I can show you some pictures, if you'd like."

Skipper leaps up. "Your Honor!"

Judge Chen turns to Nick. "That won't be necessary."

"I understand, Your Honor."

I'm standing a respectful distance from the stand. "Mr. Hanson, were you able to identify the woman?"

He nods to the jury. "Oh, yes. It was Diana Kennedy."

"So, on December first, you saw Mr. Holmes and Ms. Kennedy engaging in sex at Ms. Kennedy's apartment?"

"Indeed I did."

"And you reported this to Mrs. Holmes?"

"Yes."

"And what did she do?"

"She paid me."

Judge Chen beats back a smile.

"Didn't she also confront her husband with the pictures you provided?"

"Yeah. I think she laid it on him pretty thick."

I'll bet. "Did Mrs. Holmes ask you to do anything else?"

"Yeah. She wanted to be sure he stayed on the wagon, if you know what I mean."

"I take it she wanted you to keep Mr. Holmes under surveillance to be sure that he didn't continue his relationship with Ms. Kennedy?"

"Or anybody else." He grins. "Except for Mrs. Holmes, of course."

"Of course. Mr. Hanson, did you continue to observe Mr. Holmes?"

"Yeah."

"Did he 'stay on the wagon,' as you've put it?"

"Your Honor," Skipper says.

"Sit down, Mr. Gates."

Nick shakes his head. "No, Mr. Daley. Sadly, Mr. Holmes fell off the wagon."

More grins in the gallery. I can see how this guy writes mysteries. "Oh, dear," I deadpan. "When exactly did he fall off the wagon, Mr. Hanson?"

"On December twenty-eighth."

"Would you mind telling us what happened?"

"Sure." He clears his throat. "Mrs. Holmes told me that Mr. Holmes was going to attend a dinner at the Fairmont. On a couple of occasions, he'd met Ms. Kennedy there. He had a room in the tower where they used to go for, uh, recreation. When I heard he was going to be at the Fairmont, I got a room across the street at the Mark Hopkins. It had a direct view into the room where Mr. Holmes liked to hang out. I ordered room service, set up my telephoto camera, and waited. At eleven-forty-five, he came back with a woman."

"You're sure Mr. Holmes was in the room with a woman?"

"Oh yeah."

"And you're sure the woman was not Mrs. Holmes?"

"I'm sure about that. I was talking to Mrs. Holmes on my cell the entire time. She wasn't happy."

"What were Mr. Holmes and the woman doing?"

"The hokey pokey."

"I beg your pardon?"

He looks at the judge. "Am I allowed to say this in court, Your Honor?"

"Please be discreet."

"Of course." He shrugs. "For lack of a better term, Mr. Daley, Mr. Holmes and the woman were engaging in oral sex."

I try not to move a muscle until the roar dies down. Judge Chen pounds her gavel. Skipper shouts his objections. The jurors are smiling.

Judge Chen points her gavel at me. "Mr. Daley, you've made your point. Move along, please."

"Yes, Your Honor." I turn back to Nick. "Were you able to identify the woman in the room with Mr. Holmes?"

"No. It was dark. She left quickly. I ran across the street to try to identify her, but by the time I got up the elevators, she had already left."

I have trouble imagining Nick running anywhere. "Can you describe the woman?"

"Yes. Young. Slender. Long hair."

"Mr. Hanson, you're aware that Diana Kennedy had short hair, aren't you?"

"Yes. As a result, I concluded that the woman in the hotel room was not Diana Kennedy."

"Mr. Hanson, did Mrs. Holmes ask you to follow Mr. Holmes during the entire month of December last year?"

"Yeah. I was on him like a glove."

"And from December first through December twenty-eighth, did you ever see Mr. Holmes and Ms. Kennedy together again, other than at work?"

"No."

"Did you take any nights off during that period?"

"No. For what Mrs. Holmes was paying me, I would have stayed up for six months straight."

"No further questions."

* * *

Skipper's cross ends quickly. First, he questions Nick's eyesight. It's twenty-fifteen. Then he questions how Nick determined that Bob and the woman were having oral sex in a dark room. Nick says he has a powerful telephoto lens and offers to describe their every move in intimate detail. Skipper decides not to pursue it. He suggests that an eighty-two-year-old man might not be able to stay up all night watching Bob Holmes for an entire month. This irritates the retired bus driver on the jury. Nick explains that he and his three sons and four grandsons work in shifts. Unbeknownst to Bob Holmes, there was a set of Hanson eyes on him virtually every waking moment in the month of December. Another set of Hanson eyes chased Diana Kennedy. Skipper finally sits down in frustration. The jury is entranced with this diminutive PI.

Nick marches triumphantly down the aisle and out of the courtroom.

* * *

Rosie and Joel are all smiles in the consultation room during the break.

"Cherish the moment," Rosie says. "You may never get a chance to examine him again."

Joel shakes his head. "I wouldn't have believed it if I hadn't seen it with my own eyes."

"We've got some good momentum now," I say. "We need to keep pushing."

CHAPTER 48

"TOEING THE PARTY LINE"

"Michael Daley is expected to call witnesses who were at Simpson and Gates on the night two attorneys died."
— NewsCenter 4 Legal Analyst Morton Goldberg. Wednesday, April 8.

Jeff Tucker slithers to the stand after lunch. I stand in front of him. "You used to work at Simpson and Gates, didn't you?"

"Yes. Currently, I am general counsel of First Bank."

"Was your bank involved in the sale of Russo International?"

"Yes. We were one of Mr. Russo's lenders."

"Were you going to have a continuing relationship with Mr. Russo's company after the closing?"

"No. Our loans were being paid off. We were delighted with the result."

I'll bet. "Mr. Tucker, you met with Mr. Russo at Simpson and Gates on the evening of December thirtieth, didn't you?"

"Yes. My superiors asked me to check on the deal. I had no reason to believe it wasn't going to close."

"Did Mr. Russo appear upset?"

"Mr. Russo always appeared upset. He was particularly nervous that night."

"Was he unhappy about the deal?"

"Yes. He wanted to keep his company. He thought he could manage it back to profitability."

"So Mr. Russo didn't want the deal to close."

"I didn't say that."

"Let's not argue about semantics. Is it fair to say that Mr. Russo was unhappy about selling his father's company, and that you had doubts as to whether the deal would close?"

"That's fair."

That covers it. "Mr. Tucker, did you talk to Mr. Holmes that night?"

"Briefly. He was agitated. He said he couldn't predict what Vince would do."

"It's possible that Russo pulled the plug before he disappeared, isn't it?"

"Yes."

"And it's possible that Russo killed Bob Holmes and Diana Kennedy, isn't it?"

"Objection. Speculative. No foundation."

"Sustained."

"No further questions." I've made my point.

* * *

The parade continues throughout the afternoon. Ed Ehrlich swears that the deal was going to close. He assures us the city was 110 percent in favor of the closing.

Dan Morris is even more reassuring. And far more polished. Morris tells us he was certain that the deal was going to close. "The only way it wouldn't have closed was if Vince Russo changed his mind."

"Is it possible that he did so?"

"Anything's possible, Mr. Daley."

The afternoon concludes with testimony from Jack Frazier, who agrees with everyone who preceded him that Russo was going to close the deal.

"Mr. Frazier," I say, "you testified earlier that you negotiated a forty-million-dollar reduction in the purchase price at the last minute."

"I did."

"Wasn't Mr. Russo quite upset about it?"

"He was quite upset. At one point, he stormed out of the

conference room. He interrupted a cocktail party for Mr. Gates."

"So it's possible Mr. Russo may have been so upset he decided to terminate the deal?"

"I'm not sure. I mean, I guess so. But the fact is, I really don't know. He seemed ready to close the last time I saw him."

"What time was that?"

"Around one o'clock."

"And what time did you leave?"

"Mr. Morris and I left together at one-thirty-five."

"No further questions, Your Honor."

* * *

Joel is beside himself in the consultation room at the end of the day. The trial is nearing its conclusion, and he is wearing down. "I thought the idea was to make them believe it was a suicide," he says. "If that doesn't work, I thought we were going to blame Russo."

I'm exhausted. My patience is short. "We have to do everything indirectly. We can ask these witnesses to speculate about what happened. The other side has the right to object. We can't just ask them if they think Bob committed suicide. We have to give them a bunch of reasons why Bob would have been suicidal. We've shown the jury that Bob had a lot on his mind: a divorce, a deal that was imploding, a girlfriend who was leaving him and a bonus that he wasn't going to get. That's as far as we can go."

Rosie interjects in a calmer tone, "We have the same problem with Russo. Nobody saw him do anything. His fingerprints weren't on the gun. There's no evidence connecting him to the scene. All we can do is show he had opportunity and perhaps a lot of motive. That may be enough to get us to reasonable doubt and get an acquittal."

Joel stares at the gray steel table. "That's all we're trying to do at this point, isn't it? We're trying to punch holes in their case to generate enough doubt in enough members of the jury to get me off."

"Yes."

"I want to testify. I want to set the record straight."

"Let's see how things go in the next few days. We don't have to make a decision until we've finished with the other witnesses."

* * *

Rosie and I sit in her office at eight o'clock that night. She's finishing her cashew chicken. I'm drinking a Diet Dr Pepper. I haven't been hungry for days.

"You think Joel is starting to crack?" she asks.

"Maybe. Yeah. Probably." Time for a reality check. "You think we've got enough for reasonable doubt?"

"Hard to say. If you're on the jury, you're looking at an adulterer who lied about his relationship with one of the victims. They've heard enough to conclude that she dumped him. They know he was angry at Bob. They may even decide that Bob stole his girlfriend. His fingerprints were on the murder weapon and the keyboard. He left a threatening voicemail for Bob, and he made a threatening phone call to Diana. He had a fight with her at Harrington's. He may have even lured her back to the firm. All we've shown so far is that they couldn't positively identify his fingerprint on the trigger. And that his keyboard somehow walked from his office to Bob's."

"Our experts were good. They made a decent case for the suicide theory."

"True, but they were also expensive hired guns who we paid to say what we wanted them to say. The jury will discount their testimony."

She's right, of course.

The phone rings. Rosie puts Wendy on the speaker.

"It's pouring in Nassau," she says.

"Have you been able to talk to Trevor Smith?"

"Delayed again. He won't be back until Sunday. We'll be waiting for him." She pauses. "Have you put Chuckles on the stand yet?"

"Not yet. Why?"

"I was looking through the correspondence I got from Smith's

SHELDON SIEGEL

secretary. And I went down to the office of public records. I'm going to e-mail you some stuff."

A few minutes later, I'm putting on my jacket.

"You going home?" Rosie asks.

"Not yet. I'm going to play a hunch."

CHAPTER 49

"IT JUST SHOWS WHAT A LITTLE PLANNING CAN DO"

"The Guilford Insurance Agency. Life. Health. Peace of Mind."
— Brochure for the Guilford Insurance Agency.

At nine o'clock the same evening, I'm meeting with Perry Guilford, S&G's insurance agent. His office is in a high-rise on Market near Van Ness, a few blocks from City Hall. My walk through the homeless encampment on the Civic Center Plaza was treacherous. The streets are mean in this part of town, especially after dark.

Guilford's reception area has piles of brochures on variable annuities. They promise life, health and peace of mind.

"Mr. Guilford, I'm Mike Daley."

"Perry," he rasps. His age and waistline are right around fifty-five years and inches, respectively. His jowls measure right up there with Art Patton's, who is, coincidentally, his ex-brother-in-law from Guilford's first marriage. His toupee is flattering in a pathetic sort of way.

"Fair enough, Perry. It's Mike. And I appreciate your taking the time to see me."

His jowls jiggle as he laughs. "I'm sorry I've been hard to get hold of. Brent Hutchinson said you'd be calling. Anything I can do to help a member of the firm. Anything." He pats his ample gut and takes a gulp of Coke Classic. My arteries are hardening just looking at this guy.

"Actually, Perry, I left the firm at the end of last year and started my own shop. I was hoping you could help me get my insurance situation squared away."

He's pleased. Fresh meat. "Great, Mike. Anything I can do to help you. You know I handle all the insurance for S&G. It's my biggest account. I handle a couple of the other big law firms in town, too. I'm sure I can take care of you."

"Let me tell you what I have in mind." I explain that I've purchased malpractice insurance through the state bar. He says he might be able to get me a better deal. I tell him about Grace. He describes various whole life policies. I haven't a clue what he's talking about. I figure if I let him talk, he may wear himself out.

At the one-hour mark, he isn't slowing down. We're on our third diagram. Insurance agents can't sell anything without drawing pictures. The last one looks like a basketball court, with a half-court line and two free-throw lines. I'm lost when we start on variable annuities.

An hour and fifteen minutes into this torture, I ask him to prepare a written estimate of everything we've talked about. After he reminds me for the sixth time that he isn't in insurance just for the money, I decide it's time to see if I can get any useful information.

"Helluva thing over at the Simpson firm, eh, Perry?" I say.

"Unbelievable, Mike. Helluva thing. Were you there that night?"

"Yeah. Helluva thing."

"You know, they'd really be in the soup if they hadn't planned ahead." He shuffles his papers. "It's a good thing they had life insurance on Bob Holmes."

"It just shows what a little planning can do, right, Perry?"

"Right. That's why you need to plan now, Mike. You want to take care of little Mary if anything ever happens to you."

"Grace."

"Right. Grace. Five years old."

Close enough. "Did you handle Bob's life insurance?"

"Yeah. And between us girls, it's a damn good thing. I talked him into buying some extra coverage. Didn't cost much. Got his wife a five-million term policy, and each of the kids got a million." He frowns. "I was talking to Art about it. Helluva thing."

"Yeah. And it was a damn good thing you got the firm to take down those key-man life insurance policies. Hell, without those, they'd really be in the soup."

"No kidding. Art was telling me you guys were going to get a fat fee for Vince Russo's deal. Now, he says you guys may not get anything. Helluva thing."

"Looks that way, Perry. Maybe I should take down some more life insurance. How much was the firm carrying on Bob?"

"They were carrying five million until December. Lucky for them, I talked them into taking down bigger term policies on some of the heavy hitters right before all the excitement. The policy on Bob went effective only a couple weeks before the end of the year. Hutch is going to look like a hero."

Hello? "Yeah, Perry. Sure is a good thing they got that big policy in place when they did. Do you recall how much the policy was for?"

He laughs. "Hell, you should know. The damn thing's worth twenty fucking million, Mike. Biggest policy I've ever sold. Art says it's going to save his ass."

Twenty million? "Perry, another client of mine was asking about key-man insurance. Do you have a copy of the key man policy on Bob?"

"If my secretary were here, I'd be able to pull it up for you. I'm lost without her."

"Maybe you can messenger it to me in the morning? The client's in sort of a hurry."

Big smile. "Sure, Mike. First thing."

I give him my business card. "Perry, how soon can you get those quotes to me?"

"End of the week sound all right?"

"Perfect."

* * *

"There was a twenty-million-dollar life insurance policy on Bob?" Rosie says.

There's something wildly erotic about talking life insurance with a naked woman. I've stopped by her house on my way home. Grace is asleep. Dave Brubeck's on the stereo. She rubs my back with her thin hands.

"Yeah. Twenty million. It all goes to the firm." I turn over and kiss her ear. "Does any of this strike you as a little odd?"

"How's that?"

"I'm not sure. Something just doesn't feel right."

She runs her fingers through my hair. "Maybe this will feel better."

CHAPTER 50

"EXACTLY WHAT DOES THE ADMINISTRATIVE PARTNER DO?"

"Friedman Defense Grasping at Straws."
— San Francisco Legal Journal. Thursday, April 9.

The following morning, a subdued Chuckles sits uncomfortably on the witness stand, gulping water.

"Exactly what does the administrative partner do at a large law firm?" I ask him.

He responds with a sour look. "The administrative partner handles all aspects of day-to-day operations." He gestures with his reading glasses. "Finances. Personnel. Facilities. Computers."

"Sort of the glue that holds the firm together as an institution?"

He almost smiles. "Why, yes."

"How many years have you been administrative partner?"

His voice fills with pride. "Eleven. I sit on the executive committee, too."

I glance at the accountant, who nods with admiration. "Could you please tell us about the current financial situation at the firm?"

"Objection," Skipper sings out. "Relevance."

"Overruled."

"Your Honor," Chuckles pleads, "this information is highly confidential."

"I don't expect you to reveal how much money each of your partners makes. Answer the question, Mr. Stern."

"We have filed for bankruptcy protection. We are in the process of reorganizing our finances and negotiating with our creditors."

"Thank you, Mr. Stern," I say. I leave out, "You condescending ass." "Mr. Stern, you were at the Simpson and Gates offices on the night of December thirtieth, weren't you?"

"Yes."

"What time did you go home?"

"Two a.m."

"When was the last time you saw Mr. Holmes?"

"About twelve-thirty."

"Did you see Mr. Friedman together with Mr. Holmes or Ms. Kennedy after that time?"

"No."

I bore in. "Did you see anyone else there that night?" Let's see who he's willing to implicate.

He looks at the clock. Then he rattles off the names of Vince Russo, Art Patton, Ed Ehrlich, Dan Morris, Jack Frazier and Martin Glass. "Of course, I don't believe any of them had anything to do with the tragedy."

Of course not. "Mr. Stern, did you see Mr. Gates at the office that night?"

His eyes dart toward Skipper. "Why, yes. It was his last day at the firm. We had a reception for him."

"But did you see him later that evening?"

He looks helplessly at Skipper. "I saw Mr. Gates at about one in the morning. He was in our suite for a few minutes."

I walk over to the evidence cart and pick up a copy of Bob's will, which I hand to Chuckles. "Do you recognize this document?"

"Yes. It's the will of Mr. Holmes. I prepared it. It is a matter of public record."

"Would you mind turning to page thirty-four?"

He puts on the reading glasses. He flips to the correct page.

"Would you please tell us the names of the beneficiaries?"

He glares at me over the top of the reading glasses. "I'll have to refresh my memory."

He could recite all eighty-nine pages by heart. "Take your time."

He pores over the will, pausing briefly to lick his index finger to turn the pages. Finally, he says a third goes to Beth, a third to the kids and a third to the International Charitable Trust. He takes off his glasses.

"Mr. Stern, you're aware that Mr. Holmes was served with divorce papers on December thirtieth."

"Yes."

"Did Mr. Holmes ever ask you to prepare an amendment to this will to change the beneficiaries?"

"No."

Rosie hands me three copies of a document. I hand one to Skipper, one to the judge and one to Stern. "Your Honor, we'd like to introduce this document into evidence."

"Any objections, Mr. Gates?"

He's speed-reading. "I don't think so, Your Honor."

I turn back to Stern. "Do you recognize this document, Mr. Stern?"

"Yes." He takes a drink of water. "It's a draft of an amendment to the will."

"Really? Did you prepare this amendment?"

"No. One of my associates prepared it."

"At your instruction?"

"Yes."

"Which associate prepared this document?"

"I believe it was Ms. Wendy Hogan."

"I see." You never know what may turn up in somebody's files after they leave the firm. "Could you please tell us what this amendment purports to change?"

"The beneficiaries."

"Really? When was this amendment prepared, Mr. Stern?"

"In December of last year, I believe."

"Why did Mr. Holmes asked you to prepare this amendment?"

"Presumably because he intended to change the beneficiaries."

"Did he identify the new beneficiaries?"

"No."

"Any hints?"

"Objection. Asked and answered."

"Sustained."

"Did he tell you which of the beneficiaries were going to be replaced?"

"Yes. His wife."

"If he proceeded in the manner that you've just suggested, Mrs. Holmes stood to lose a substantial sum of money on the death of Mr. Holmes."

"Yes, she did."

I shift focus. "Could you please tell us what you know about the International Charitable Trust, Mr. Stern?"

"It's a charity organized in the Bahamas by Mr. Holmes."

"It does good things for mankind?"

"Yes."

"What sorts of good things?"

"The annual income of the trust is donated to various charitable causes. Schools, day-care centers, community centers, that sort of thing."

Hookers, drug dealers, that sort of thing, too. "And the charities that receive funding every year are called the income beneficiaries, right?"

"Yes."

"Will the income beneficiaries also divide the trust assets now that Mr. Holmes has died?"

"No. The remaining assets, or corpus, of the trust are divided among various designated individuals called the remaindermen."

"Could you tell us which charities received the most money last year?"

"I don't recall."

"Schools? Day-care centers? Community centers?"

"I'm not sure. I don't recall the names of the income beneficiaries. The trustee would know."

"Could you tell us the names of the remaindermen?"

"I'm afraid I don't know. That information was confidential. The trustee in the Bahamas was the only person who knew their names."

Sure. "Mr. Stern, did you assist in setting up the trust?"

"Yes."

"Yet you don't know the names of the income beneficiaries or the remaindermen?"

"That's true."

That's bullshit. "Why did you choose to set up the trust in the Bahamas?"

"Mr. Holmes enjoyed vacationing there. He became involved in various causes. Ultimately, he wanted to retire there. And, to be perfectly honest, the tax laws were favorable."

The accountant perks up. "When you set up the trust, you investigated the income beneficiaries very carefully, right?"

"Actually, the trust administrator in the Bahamas handled it. I'm not involved in the day-to-day management."

"I see." He's tap-dancing around my questions. Rosie hands me another document with a fancy seal of the Commonwealth of the Bahamas. I hand copies to Skipper, the judge and Stern. I ask that it be introduced into evidence. Skipper doesn't object. "Mr. Stern, do you recognize this document?"

"It's the charter for the trust. It sets forth the rules of governance. It names First Bank Bahamas as the sole trustee."

"It also names the income beneficiaries and the remaindermen doesn't it?" I'm setting him up. I know the names of the income beneficiaries and the remaindermen are set forth in a confidential addendum which I've not yet seen.

"Well, no. That information is in a separate document. It's confidential."

"And do you now recall the names of the income beneficiaries and the remaindermen?"

"As I said before, I don't know."

Sure. "There are two individuals who serve as the so-called trust protectors, aren't there?"

"Yes. They have the authority to take action on behalf of the trust and change the trustee. The trust protectors are Mr. Holmes and myself."

Now, we're getting somewhere. "As trust protector, I presume you would know the names of the income beneficiaries and the remaindermen of the trust?"

"I'm afraid not, Mr. Daley. As I said, that information is in a separate document. Under the laws of the Bahamas, it's confidential."

You're also lying. "You mean to tell us the trust protector doesn't know who gets the money when Mr. Holmes dies?"

"That's true. It's all handled in the Bahamas."

"So even though you are the attorney who set this thing up, you don't know who gets the money?"

"Objection. Asked and answered."

"Sustained."

I glare at Stern. "Do you get a fee for acting as trust protector, Mr. Stern?"

"Yes."

"How much?"

"Objection. Relevance."

I turn to the judge. "It is relevant, Your Honor. Unless Mr. Stern wants to tell us that he doesn't know how big his fee is, either."

"That's enough, Mr. Daley. The objection is overruled. Answer the question, Mr. Stern."

"It depends on the value of the assets in the trust at any given time."

I arch an eyebrow. "You get a percentage of the value of the assets?"

"Yes."

"What percent?"

"Your Honor," he implores. "This is highly confidential."

"Answer the question, Mr. Stern, or I'll hold you in contempt."

"Five percent," he mutters.

"Mr. Stern, how much was your fee last year?"

He looks at the judge. She stares him down. "About four hundred fifty thousand dollars."

"Four hundred fifty thousand," I repeat. "If my high school arithmetic is correct, this means the trust had about ten million dollars' worth of assets. Is that about right, Mr. Stern?"

"That's about right."

"Your Honor," Skipper says, "I fail to see the relevance."

"Mr. Daley, are we going to see a point anytime soon?"

"Yes." Here goes. "Mr. Stern, isn't it a fact Mr. Holmes was unhappy about your fee?"

"I don't know what you're talking about, Mr. Daley."

"Mr. Holmes thought your fee was excessive."

"No, he didn't."

I turn to Rosie, who hands me three copies of a letter. I hand one copy to the judge, one to Skipper and the other to Stern. I introduce it into evidence. "Do you recognize this document, Mr. Stern?"

"I don't recall."

"Let me refresh your memory. It's a letter dated September third of last year addressed to a Mr. Trevor Smith at First Bank in the Bahamas. You were copied."

He shrugs.

"Would you please read the sentence I've highlighted, Mr. Stern?"

On go the reading glasses. " 'I believe that the fees paid to the trust protector are extravagantly high. I would like to terminate the services of Mr. Stern at the end of this year.' "

"Who signed the letter?"

He takes off the glasses. "Mr. Holmes."

"Mr. Holmes wanted to fire you."

He clears his throat. "From time to time, he expressed some reservations about the amount of my fee. I don't believe he intended to implement the terms of this letter."

"What happens to your fee now?"

"It is paid until the trust is liquidated."

"When will that happen?"

"It will probably take two or three years."

"So, the death of Mr. Holmes will result in your receiving an additional million or million and a half dollars. Isn't that right, Mr. Stern?"

"I have no choice, Mr. Daley. I have a contractual obligation to act as trust protector. When the trust was put in place, my fees were tiny. Over the years, the assets have grown substantially. It's not my fault that it turned into a very favorable contract for me."

"And if Mr. Holmes had lived, he would have terminated your deal, and you would have lost a million and a half dollars."

"As I said, Mr. Daley, I don't believe he intended to terminate my services."

"That's terribly convenient, isn't it, Mr. Stern?"

"Objection."

"Sustained."

Rosie hands me a legal-size document. I hand it to Chuckles. "Mr. Stern, you're familiar with this life insurance policy, aren't you?"

He puts on his reading glasses. "Yes."

"It's called a key-man life insurance policy, isn't it?"

"Yes."

"It was taken out by Simpson and Gates, wasn't it? And the firm paid the premiums."

"Yes. That's how key-man insurance works. A business buys life insurance on important members of the management. In our case, we took down this policy on the life of Bob Holmes. We had similar policies for all of our partners."

"And would you mind telling us how much this policy was worth to the firm?" I've set the trap. At least I hope so.

He looks at Skipper. "Two and a half million dollars."

I pause. "Mr. Stern," I say, "I believe you've misread the policy value. Would you mind looking at the policy again?"

He flips open the policy. He adjusts his reading glasses. He stops cold. He takes off the reading glasses and looks at me.

"Mr. Stern? Would you mind telling us how much the policy was worth?"

"Twenty million," he whispers.

"Twenty million," I repeat. "That's even more money than Bob Holmes had in that hokey trust you set up for him in the Bahamas."

"Objection."

"Sustained. Let's stop the editorial comments, Mr. Daley."

I don't stop. "Mr. Stern, if the firm had a twenty-million-dollar policy on Mr. Holmes, how come it filed for bankruptcy?"

"The insurance company hasn't paid us yet. These things take time, Mr. Daley."

"Then the firm's financial difficulties will be resolved?"

"We think so, Mr. Daley."

"When was this policy issued?"

He puts on his reading glasses and glances at the cover page. "December fifteenth of last year."

"Mr. Stern, you've read this policy carefully, haven't you? You were a partner in a big law firm, after all."

There's only one possible answer. "Yes, Mr. Daley."

"Would you please turn to page six?"

He shuffles through the pages. "Yes, Mr. Daley."

"Would you please read the heading on page six?"

" 'General Provisions.' "

I face the jury. Without looking at Stern, I say, "Would you please read the title of the fifth paragraph in the right column?"

" 'Ownership and Control.' "

"No, Mr. Stern. The following paragraph. It's entitled 'Suicide Exclusion.' "

His voice is barely a whisper. " 'If the Insured, whether sane or insane, dies by suicide within two years from the issue date, we will pay no more under this contract than the sum of the premiums paid, minus any contract debt and minus any partial withdrawals.' "

Well-done. I finally turn to face Chuckles. "Mr. Stern, that section is what is customarily known as a suicide clause, isn't it?"

"Objection. Foundation. Mr. Stern isn't qualified as an expert on insurance."

"Overruled."

"It's a suicide clause," Stern says.

"In layman's terms, what does it mean?"

"If the insured commits suicide within the first two years, the insurer doesn't have to pay."

"And, if it was determined that Mr. Holmes committed suicide, what would it mean for the firm?"

"We wouldn't get the twenty million dollars."

"Just so we're all perfectly clear on this, Mr. Stern, if the death of Mr. Holmes is determined to be a suicide, you guys will lose the twenty-million-dollar insurance payment."

"That's right." His lips barely move.

"You might say the firm has twenty million reasons to hope the death of Mr. Holmes is not declared a suicide."

"Objection."

"Sustained."

"No further questions." Thanks, Perry. I'll buy a million bucks of life insurance from you.

* * *

Skipper is up immediately. "Mr. Stern, we saw each other briefly at the Simpson and Gates office at one o'clock in the morning on December thirty-first, didn't we?"

"Yes."

"And we had a brief conversation, didn't we?"

"Yes."

"And I told you that I had returned to the office to pick up my briefcase, right?"

I go for the quick tweak. "Objection, Your Honor. Hearsay. Mr. Stern cannot testify as to what Mr. Gates said. If Mr. Gates wants to testify about what he said, we're perfectly happy to permit him to do so."

The judge can't resist a grin. "Sustained."

Skipper gathers himself. "Mr. Stern, did you see me leaving the office with my briefcase?"

"Yes."

"Did I say anything to you?"

"Objection, Your Honor. Hearsay."

"Sustained."

Skipper frowns. "Mr. Stern, do you have any reason to believe that I was in the office for any purpose other than to collect my briefcase?"

"Objection. Speculative."

"Sustained."

Skipper spends five minutes asking Chuckles perfunctory questions about the insurance policy and the firm's financial condition. Chuckles swears that the firm is in solid financial shape, and doesn't need the proceeds from the policy to survive. He's unconvincing. The damage is already done.

* * *

We're back in my office at eight o'clock the same night. "You don't think it was Stern, do you?" Rosie asks.

"He had about a million of his own reasons to do it. And the firm had twenty million reasons. He sounded like a lying ass to the jury."

The phone rings. It's Pete. "I have somebody who wants to talk to you," he says.

I punch the speaker button so Rosie can hear. A nasal male voice shrieks, "Who the hell is this?"

"Who the hell is *this*?"

"Vince Russo."

CHAPTER 51

"HE CAME TO VISIT HIS MONEY"

"The bank secrecy laws of the Bahamas are among the finest in the world."
— First Bank brochure.

Wendy's voice is triumphant. "You'll never guess who we ran into at the bank today."

I play along. "Elvis Presley?"

"Close. We found Vince at Trevor Smith's office. He came to visit his money. Pete and I followed him back to his hotel. He's got a little cottage at the Graycliff. It's very nice."

Indeed. The finest hotel in Nassau.

"Anyway," she continues, "it's a little tough finding a room down here, so Pete and I are bunking with Vince. He was just telling us about his trip."

Dear God. "Wendy, listen to me. Don't hurt him. What you're doing may be somewhat illegal."

"Don't worry. We ordered room service. The foie gras is delightful. Pete takes off the handcuffs when he has to eat or pee. We offered to call the cops. Seems Vince is a little nervous about that. It kind of fouls up the part of his story where he wanted everyone to think he committed suicide."

Either we've just got a huge break or we're all going to jail. "You guys going to be there for a while?"

"Of course. We just ordered champagne." I hear a cork pop. "Mike, are you doing anything this weekend?"

"I think I may need to take a little trip. The stress is getting to me."

"Anyplace in particular?"

"I understand the Bahamas are nice this time of year."

"Our cottage is called Yellow Bird. Tell the concierge you're with Mr. Kramer's party."

I hang up. I look at Rosie. "I need you to go to Judge Chen tomorrow and tell her I was called out of town on an emergency. See if you can get her to put things off until Monday."

"What if she asks for details?"

"Tell her we found Russo."

* * *

At nine o'clock that night I'm on the phone. "Roosevelt, I need your help."

"I'm not supposed to be talking to you, Mike."

"Duly noted."

He chuckles. "What do you need?"

"Got any plans for the weekend?"

"The usual."

"How would you feel about an all-expense-paid trip to the Bahamas?"

"Sounds pretty good to me."

CHAPTER 52

"TECHNICALLY, YOU'RE DEAD"

"With long beaches, friendly people and perfect weather, the Bahamas have been a tourist mecca for over two hundred years."
— Bahamas travel brochure.

Fourteen hours later, at two in the afternoon Bahamas time, Roosevelt and I get out of a cab in front of the Graycliff, the dignified three-story Georgian mansion across the street from the Government House in Nassau. No matter where I go, it seems to be raining. Our connecting flights through Chicago and Miami were late, and we flew through a hailstorm to Nassau. I'm exhausted, but Roosevelt's stamina is remarkable.

The Graycliff was built as a private residence about two hundred years ago. With only nine guest rooms in the main house and four suites by the pool, it's a slice of nirvana in the middle of town. Although it's been a long time since the Beatles stayed here, it's still very popular among rock stars, businessmen and politicians.

When we walk into the lobby, our disheveled appearance attracts the attention of the concierge. "May I help you, gentlemen?" He sounds like Sir John Gielgud and bears a striking resemblance to John Cleese.

I nod. "Yes, please. We're here for an important meeting with Mr. Rus—Mr. Kramer. I believe he's in Yellow Bird."

He eyes us suspiciously. "We've been instructed not to disturb Mr. Kramer and his colleagues."

"They're expecting us. If you'll explain to his assistant that Mr. Daley and Mr. Johnson from the San Francisco office have arrived, I'm sure they'll have you show us to his suite."

"One moment, please." He picks up the antique phone. He nods several times. I hope he's talking to Wendy or Pete and not to the local police. "Right this way, please."

As we walk through the garden, I decide to speak the local language—money. "I trust you have access to a local banker. It may be necessary to set up an account here so we can wire some money to various locations around the world."

Roosevelt gives me the eye. I'm laying it on pretty thick.

The concierge looks straight ahead. "It can be arranged, sir." He pronounces the word "sir" as "suh."

"I trust you have Internet access?"

"Of course, sir."

"Excellent. What's your name?"

"Burton, sir. Duncan Burton."

Perfect. "Thank you for your assistance, Duncan."

"Of course, sir."

* * *

The Yellow Bird cottage is next to the pool where Winston Churchill once swam. The drapes are drawn as Duncan leads us to the door.

Duncan asks, "Will you be staying with us tonight, sir?"

"I'm afraid not. We'll be taking the red-eye."

"Very good, sir."

I love this guy. "Duncan, we'll be in negotiations all day. Would you please tell the hotel staff that we're not to be disturbed?"

"Of course, sir."

"Thank you." I slip him three crisp hundred-dollar bills. "Remember, Duncan. We mustn't be disturbed."

He almost smiles. "Please let me know if there is anything we can do to assist you, sir."

I glance around the garden and knock on the door. Pete opens it immediately.

"Come in," he whispers. He darts a quick look around the pool area before he shuts the door and fastens the bolt. "Anybody follow you?"

Roosevelt shakes his head. "No, Pete. This isn't a James Bond movie."

He grins sheepishly. "I'm out of my element."

You could have fooled me.

The sitting room in the Yellow Bird is furnished with period pieces from the Georgian era. A light blue sofa sits next to a tall chair with a paisley pattern. A ceiling fan circulates warm air. The window air conditioner detracts only slightly from the ambiance. A TV and an Internet connection are the only signs of the contemporary world. Trays containing the remains of dinner and breakfast sit by the door. An empty champagne bottle rests on the antique side table.

Wendy walks in from bedroom and smiles. "What took you so long?"

"We ran into a small hurricane. Where's our guest of honor?"

"Watching TV. He didn't want to miss his cartoons."

"Is he pissed off?"

"You could say that."

"How did you find him?"

"We got lucky. We saw him coming out of First Bank. We followed him here."

"How did you get in?"

Pete grins. "You don't want to know."

"Has he said much?"

"Nothing you would repeat to Grace. He said he's going to sue us for everything we're worth. Fortunately, that isn't a lot."

Roosevelt turns serious. "You guys could be arrested for kidnapping."

Pete holds up a palm. "I don't think he's going to complain. We offered to let him use the phone. He refused. He's gone to a lot of trouble to convince everybody that he's dead. He'd have to call the cops to bring charges." Pete lowers his voice. "Seems a couple of his investors from the Middle East are unhappy about some money they lost on one of his deals. He thinks his life may be in danger."

"You didn't hurt him, did you?" I say.

"No," Pete says. "We had a little shoving match. I pushed him. Wendy kneed him in the balls. Lifted him off the floor. He was doubled over for a couple of minutes."

"He tried to grab me," Wendy says, "so I drilled him."

Fair enough. "Let's go see our little friend."

We walk into the bedroom. The TV is tuned to CNN. The unshaven Russo is dressed in khaki pants and a maroon polo shirt. He's sitting at a table eating a muffin and drinking coffee. I notice he's using only his right hand. Then I see his left hand is handcuffed to the table.

"Mr. Russo, my name is Michael Daley. I'm Joel Friedman's attorney."

"I know."

"This is Inspector Roosevelt Johnson of the San Francisco Police Department. He's the lead investigator in the case involving the deaths of Robert Holmes and Diana Kennedy."

"Are you the one who sent this goon to kidnap me?"

"He's a licensed private investigator. He's also my brother. You're lucky that he found you before somebody else did. A bunch of bankers are looking for you. So are your investors and a couple of bounty hunters." Probably a few ex-wives, too.

He pushes the muffin away. "I have nothing to say to you." He strains to fold his arms before he realizes that he can't.

I hand him a legal document. "This is a subpoena that requires you to appear at Mr. Friedman's trial." Roosevelt and I got Judge Chen to issue it on our way to the airport. It's also a bluff. A California subpoena isn't binding in the Bahamas. "I may have to get some dispensation from the judge to permit you to testify."

"Why is that?"

"Technically, you're dead. But I think I can persuade the judge to the contrary."

"And if I don't cooperate?"

Pete hands him a card with English writing on one side and Arabic writing on the other. "This gentleman is looking for you. He's asked us to call if we find you."

"Read my lips. Fuck you."

"Mr. Russo," Roosevelt says, "I've come to ask you to voluntarily return to San Francisco so we can sort this out."

"Why the hell would I do that?"

"If you have nothing to hide, you shouldn't have any problem returning with us." He eyes him closely. "We'd be happy to buy you a ticket. You don't have anything to hide, do you, Mr. Russo?"

"Of course not."

"Good. Now, we can do this the easy way or the hard way. The easy way means you'll get on a plane with us and we'll go back to San Francisco together."

"And the hard way?"

"I'll call the local police. They'll want to know why a dead man checked into this lovely hotel under an assumed name. I'll ask them to detain you. I'll swear out a complaint that you're a flight risk. We'll begin extradition proceedings. You'll be spending a fairly long time in jail here in Nassau."

"Are you charging me with something?"

"Not yet. But you're a suspect. Which reminds me," he adds, "this would be a good time to read you your rights." He clears his throat and recites the Miranda warnings "Mr. Russo, we're prepared to call your lawyer right now. He can meet us at the airport."

Russo glares at Roosevelt. "I didn't do anything. It isn't a crime to go on a vacation."

"All the more reason for you to cooperate."

"I want to talk to my lawyer."

Wendy takes out her cell. "Who do you want me to call?"

"Arthur Patton."

* * *

Patton bellows at me through Wendy's cell phone. "Who the hell do you think you are? You can't detain him. It's kidnapping."

"He's here voluntarily," I say. "I can call the local cops."

"Let me talk to Johnson."

I hand the phone to Roosevelt. He listens for a moment. He says "Uh-huh" a few times. Then he says, emphatically, "No deal. Look, if you're going to be an ass, we'll call the local cops. I'm sure they'd be delighted to make up a bed for Mr. Russo for the next six months while you argue about his extradition." He winks at me. "By the way, we've made sure all his assets down here are frozen. I think all his assets up your way are already frozen, so you may be doing his legal work *pro bono*." He listens for a minute. "Uh-huh. Okay." He has Pete unshackle Russo. He hands the phone to Russo and turns to me. "I think reason is about to prevail."

I call the concierge. "Duncan, it's Mr. Daley. I need you to make some travel arrangements for us.

"Very well, sir."

* * *

Our plane leaves Nassau at six o'clock Friday night. We connect through Chicago. When we get off the plane at O'Hare, we're met by three cops. At first, I think they're going to arrest Russo. Or me.

Then I realize Roosevelt has called in a favor from a friend in Chicago PD. He doesn't want Russo to make a break through the mobs at O'Hare. With the help of Chicago's finest, we negotiate the United terminal. Our flight to San Francisco is delayed two hours.

* * *

Art Patton and three San Francisco police officers meet us at the gate at SFO. Art isn't taking any chances. He's brought Rita Roberts with him. As soon as we're off the plane, he turns to Rita's camera and demands that we release Russo.

Roosevelt glares at him. "Mr. Russo accompanied us voluntarily from the Bahamas."

"Then he's free to go?"

"After he's answered some questions at headquarters."

"I'm instructing him not to answer any questions."

"Fine. You can talk to him down at the Hall."

* * *

I haven't ridden in a paddy wagon in years. My head is throbbing as Roosevelt, Russo, Patton and I sit in silence in the back of a van, with two other officers.

Patton talks to Roosevelt. "Vince doesn't have to talk to you."

Roosevelt yawns. "I know. But I'm sure he has nothing to hide."

"You got that right," Russo snaps.

Patton holds up his hands. "Vince, we'll talk about this downtown. I don't want you to say anything right now."

Russo pouts. "Understood."

* * *

"Are you going to charge Russo?" I ask Skipper.

"With what? It isn't a crime to park at the Golden Gate Bridge. Last time I looked, it's legal to travel to the Bahamas."

We're sitting in a consultation room down the corridor from where Patton has been meeting with Russo for the last hour. Roosevelt drinks coffee. McNulty studies the sports section in the *Chronicle.*

"How about murder?" I say.

Roosevelt looks up. "How about murder, Skipper?" he repeats.

"There's no evidence pointing toward Russo."

"Yes, there is," I say. "He was at the scene. He faked his own suicide. He fled the country. He was traveling under an alias. What else do you want?"

"What's the motive?"

"He didn't want the deal to close. He had to create a diversion to get out of the country."

Skipper is skeptical. "If he didn't want to close, he could have just said so. He didn't have to kill two people. Besides, there isn't a single shred of evidence he pulled the trigger. We can put him at the scene, but we can't tie him to the murder weapon."

That much is true. There isn't any physical evidence to convict Russo. I turn to Roosevelt. "I need him to testify. You can't let him leave the country again. I'll put him on the stand on Monday."

"He isn't going anywhere."

There's a knock on the door. A uniformed deputy reports that Patton and Russo want to talk to Roosevelt.

"Mike," Roosevelt says, "I have to ask you to wait here."

"I understand."

* * *

I sit in the cramped consultation room by myself in the middle of the night. The Hall has an eerie, deafening quiet at this hour. My body is overwhelmed by fatigue and jet lag. I sit in never-never land—not quite asleep, but certainly not awake.

My mind starts playing tricks on me. I see Grace's face. I'm at the Hall of Justice in the middle of the night. I should be home taking care of her.

I hear footsteps in the hallway, and I see a uniformed policeman walk by. I think of my dad. So proud of his uniform. So proud he put the bad guys away. A good cop. He did what he thought was right. Hard to imagine he's been gone for five years. So little time to know his first grandchild, Grace. He was so proud of her. And she won't remember him. Sometimes, I think I never really knew him. Sometimes I think I knew him too well. He was a good dad, but somewhat distant. I think of my older brother Tommy, who went to war to please him. And my younger brother Pete, who became a cop to show him. And for a brief moment, I think of myself. I became a defense attorney to spite him. I think of my sister, Mary, who pleaded with him to take early retirement, just so she could stop worrying about him.

I think of my mom, who raised four kids on a cop's salary. How she stayed up every night, waiting for him to come home. How she wouldn't sleep until she heard his car door slam. How she counted the days until his retirement. And how she nursed him when they discovered the cancer only a few weeks later. Five years of caring for him through all that pain. She worried about all of us. Now she lives in a world of confusion that she doesn't understand and I can't imagine.

I think about Rosie, the only woman I've ever truly loved. And our mutual realization that we're incapable of living together. I feel the pain of our separation all over again. I wonder whether I'll ever find the same kind of love again. I hope I'll never feel the pain again.

I worry about Grace. I wonder where she'll be in another ten years. Or another twenty, for that matter.

I think about my friend and client Joel. His less-than-perfect marriage. His relationship with his father, which isn't that different from my relationship with mine. I wonder whether he'll have a chance to repair the damage to his life that's been inflicted on him— and that he's inflicted upon himself.

I think about our special circumstances. It may be the fatigue or the stress—or both. I realize I'm crying. And I wonder if it's all worth it.

"Mike?" Roosevelt is standing in the doorway of the consultation room, his hands in his pockets.

"Huh? Sorry, Roosevelt. I must have dozed off."

"Patton and Russo want to talk to you."

"Are you going to arrest him?"

"No."

"Will he testify?"

"I think so."

"Keep it under your hat, Roosevelt."

"I will. I can't make the same promise for the DA."

"Understood." I look at him. "Roosevelt?"

"Yes?"

"Thanks."

CHAPTER 53

"DID YOU HAVE A NICE TRIP?"

"In an unexpected twist, local financier Vincent Russo, Jr., has been located in the Bahamas. He will testify at the murder trial of Joel Mark Friedman later today."
— KCBS NEWS RADIO. Monday, April 13. 6:30 A.M.

The traffic on Bryant is terrible on Monday morning. The news vans are lined up two-deep. Word got out about Vince Russo's resurrection. The gallery is packed.

I stand at the lectern and say, "The defense calls Vincent Russo, Jr."

Judge Chen watches Russo slither into the courtroom in his dark blue suit. He's sworn in. He takes the stand. He's sweating. He gulps water from a Styrofoam cup. I can smell his aftershave. His diamond ring gleams. His cuff links look like gold golf balls.

Judge Chen says, "We weren't sure we were going to see you, Mr. Russo."

"I've been out of town."

"Please proceed, Mr. Daley."

"May we approach the witness, Your Honor?" I want to get right in his face.

"Yes, Mr. Daley."

I button my jacket as I position myself directly in front of Russo. I turn slightly so the jury can see his facial expressions and mine. "Mr. Russo, you were in the Simpson and Gates offices on December thirtieth, were you not?"

His slitty eyes wander. "Yes."

"You were working on a deal involving the sale of your company, right?"

"Yes."

"The sale was supposed to close on the morning of December thirty-first, right?"

"Objection, Your Honor. He's leading the witness."

Yes, I am. "Request permission to treat this witness as hostile."

"All right, Mr. Daley."

"Thank you." It's okay to lead hostile witnesses. I turn back to Russo. "The deal didn't close, did it, Mr. Russo?"

"No."

"Why not?"

"Because I said so. I didn't want Continental Capital Corporation to take over my father's company. It would have been disrespectful to his memory." So there.

"Instead of showing up for the closing, what did you do?"

"I decided to take a little vacation. Most recently, I was in the Bahamas."

I flash a sarcastic grin. "Did you have a nice trip?"

Skipper stands up, but doesn't say anything.

"As a matter of fact, I did," Russo says. "Right up until this weekend when you insisted that I return to San Francisco."

"Mr. Russo, let's talk about the night of December thirtieth."

He feigns indignation. "Whatever you'd like, Mr. Daley."

"You finished negotiations by about nine o'clock?"

"Yes." He tries to sound nonchalant.

"Then you went out for dinner with Mr. Holmes, didn't you?"

"Yes. We went to Tadich Grill. I'd recommend it."

"And you returned to the office around eleven-fifteen?"

"Yes."

"And everything was ready to go by about twelve-thirty?"

"Yep. Everything." He takes a swallow of water.

"You had a meeting with Mr. Holmes around twelve-thirty, didn't you?"

"Yes."

"What did you discuss?"

"A lot of things. Our plans for New Year's. Our kids. His latest divorce."

"Did you talk about the deal?"

"Yes. I told him I wasn't going to proceed with the closing. I decided I would keep my company or take my chances in bankruptcy."

"Or go to the Bahamas. How did Mr. Holmes react?"

"He was unhappy. He said I should sell the company. And he told me if the deal didn't close, Simpson and Gates was going to go bankrupt." He smirks. "You can't run a successful business worrying about whether your lawyers are going to be able to pay their bills."

Or an unsuccessful business like yours, Vince. "Mr. Russo, were you aware Mr. Holmes was going to receive a bonus in connection with the closing?"

"Yep. Three million bucks."

"And you realize that by pulling the plug, Mr. Holmes was going to lose his bonus."

"Like I said, you can't spend your life worrying about how much money your lawyers make."

Legitimate point. "Did Mr. Holmes appear upset when you told him you weren't going to close?"

"Objection. State of mind."

"Your Honor, I'm just asking for an observation of Mr. Holmes's demeanor."

"Overruled."

"Yes, he was very upset. Really honked off, if you know what I mean."

I do. "Was he upset about his divorce?"

"Not really."

I should have left well enough alone.

"Actually," he continues, "he was far more upset about the fact that his girlfriend dumped him."

"That would have been Diana Kennedy?"

"No, Mr. Daley. His relationship with Ms. Kennedy was long

over. Old and cold. Dead as a doorknob."

We get the idea.

He looks at the jury. "He was upset because his new girlfriend dumped him."

I look frantically at Rosie. I'm going to have to break the cardinal rule of cross-examination and ask a question for which I don't know the answer. "Mr. Russo, do you know the name of this new girlfriend?"

"No. It was his little secret. It was somebody we knew. He said he'd tell me when the time was right. He never did."

"Mr. Russo, did Mr. Holmes give any other indications that he may have been upset that night?"

"Objection. State of mind."

"Overruled."

"Are you asking me if he was suicidal, Mr. Daley?"

"In a word, yes."

"The answer, in a word, is maybe. He was very upset about the deal. He was angry about losing the bonus. And he was particularly upset about his girlfriend. But not *that* upset."

"Mr. Russo, what time did you leave Mr. Holmes's office?"

"Around one o'clock."

"Did you see Diana Kennedy before you left?"

"No."

"And Mr. Holmes was still alive when you left?"

"Very much so."

"So, Mr. Russo, just so we're straight, you didn't happen to kill Bob Holmes and Diana Kennedy that night, did you?"

"Of course not. Bob was still alive when I left him. I didn't see Diana."

"And you didn't see anybody else kill them, did you?"

"Nope."

"Did you hear any gunshots?"

"Nope."

"What time did you leave the building?"

"Around one-forty-five."

"After you left the Simpson and Gates office, you abandoned your car at the Vista Point at the Golden Gate Bridge, right?"

"I intended to retrieve it the next day." He looks up. "I was too tired to drive."

Right. "And you left your wallet in the car, didn't you?"

"I forgot it."

"And your keys."

"I forgot them, too."

"And you decided to leave the country."

"It isn't a crime to go on vacation, Mr. Daley."

"No, it isn't, Mr. Russo. Where did you go?"

"First, to New Zealand. Then Thailand and Greece. Then the Bahamas."

"Where you were checked into a fancy hotel under an assumed name."

"I always travel under an assumed name. I don't like to draw attention to myself. Americans are often targets in other parts of the world."

"Mr. Russo, you realize that reasonable people might interpret your actions as an attempt by a desperate man to flee the scene of a crime?"

"Objection."

"Sustained."

"Come on, Mr. Russo. Let's tell the truth today. You killed Bob Holmes and Diana Kennedy, didn't you?"

"No."

"And you fled the country."

"No."

"And you went to the Bahamas to collect a bunch of money that you kept hidden there."

"No."

"Your Honor," Skipper interrupts. "Is this harassment of Mr. Russo really necessary?"

"Your Honor," I say, "this man is lying. It's evident to everyone in this room that Mr. Russo killed Mr. Holmes and Ms. Kennedy and fled the country."

"Objection. Move to strike. Mr. Daley is out of order."

"Sustained. The jury will disregard Mr. Daley's last remarks." Judge Chen motions to me. "Sidebar."

We approach the bench. She puts her hand over her microphone. "Mr. Daley, if you're trying to get a mistrial, you'll be disappointed.

"Out of the corner of my eye, I see Rosie close her eyes. "No further questions, Your Honor."

* * *

Joel is disappointed with my direct exam of Russo. "I thought you were going to nail him," he says.

"Did you think he was going to confess?"

"Maybe."

"This isn't Perry Mason. He was better coached than I thought. And he held up better than I thought he would."

"I want to take the stand."

"We'll talk about it after Patton testifies."

CHAPTER 54

"WHAT DOES THE MANAGING PARTNER DO?"

"The managing partner of a major law firm is like the chairman of the board of a Fortune 500 company. Every big business needs leadership. And you have to have a vision."
— Arthur Patton. *San Francisco Legal Journal.*
Monday, April 13.

"You are the managing partner of the Simpson and Gates firm, aren't you, Mr. Patton?"

"Yes, I am."

Art Patton has squeezed himself into the uncomfortable wooden chair in the witness box. He's dressed carefully today. The red suspenders are at home. His chins jiggle. His eyebrows form a line right above the tiny wire-rim glasses that sit against the bulbous nose and mask the tiny eyes.

I feed him an easy one. "What does the managing partner do, Mr. Patton?"

"The managing partner of a major law firm is like the chairman of the board of a Fortune 500 company. Every big business needs leadership. And you have to have a vision."

"Your vision seems to have led the firm into bankruptcy."

"It was a protective filing. The firm continues to operate. We will remain fully functional while we are sorting out our obligations to our creditors."

The accountant doesn't seem convinced. It's time to talk about something Art understands: money. "Mr. Patton, the firm maintained a key-man life insurance policy on Mr. Holmes, right?"

"Yes."

"And you knew the firm had a twenty-million-dollar policy on the life of Mr. Holmes?"

"Of course."

I face the jury. "And you knew, of course, that the policy has a so-called suicide clause, right?"

This is ticklish. If he admits he knew about the suicide clause, he would have to acknowledge that the firm stands to gain twenty million dollars if he can show Joel killed Bob and Diana. If he says he didn't know, I'll have the pleasure of chastising him in open court for not having read the policy carefully—very unlawyerlike for an attorney of his stature.

"Mr. Daley, it's a standard clause in every life insurance policy. I never gave any particular thought to the suicide clause. I am much more concerned with the loss of Mr. Holmes. We'll certainly miss his contributions, but we're a large firm with many productive partners."

It's a good response. Now for some fun. "Mr. Patton, you have an ongoing social relationship with Elizabeth Holmes, don't you?"

"We're friends."

"Would it be fair to say you're more than just friends?"

"Objection. Mr. Patton's social life is not at issue here."

"On the contrary, Your Honor, his social life very much is at issue here."

"Overruled."

"Mr. Patton, would it be fair to say that you and Mrs. Holmes are now 'an item'?"

"I don't know what you mean."

"You and Mrs. Holmes have a romantic relationship."

"We're just good friends." He's starting to turn red.

I keep my tone measured. "I'm prepared to introduce evidence that you and Mrs. Holmes have spent more than a few nights together in the last few months. And I'm prepared to introduce pictures of you and Mrs. Holmes together on a beach in Mexico. I'll ask you again, Mr. Patton. Do you and Mrs. Holmes have a romantic relationship?"

"All right. Yes. We have a romantic relationship. What's the big deal? We used to be married."

"How long has this romantic relationship been going on?"

He looks away. "A couple of months."

I was hoping he'd say a couple of years. "Mr. Patton, are you aware that there was a five-million-dollar life insurance policy on Mr. Holmes naming Mrs. Holmes as the beneficiary?"

"Yes."

"And your former brother-in-law, Perry Guilford, is the firm's insurance agent, right?"

"Yes."

"And he was also the insurance agent for Mr. Holmes, right?"

"Yes."

"Mr. Patton, isn't it true that your former brother-in-law told you that Mr. Holmes was going to change his life insurance policy after he and Mrs. Holmes separated? And isn't it true that your girlfriend, Mrs. Holmes, was going to be removed as a beneficiary of that policy?"

"I haven't the slightest idea what you're talking about, Mr. Daley."

I'm convinced. "You're friends with your partner, Charles Stern, right?"

"Yes."

"Are you aware that Mr. Holmes had asked Mr. Stern to draft an amendment of Mr. Holmes's will when his marriage was on the ropes?"

"Yes."

"Were you aware that as soon as Mrs. Holmes filed for divorce, she was going to be written out of the will?"

He takes off his glasses. "Once again, Mr. Daley, your jump in logic is nothing short of remarkable. I had no idea what the will said before Mr. Holmes died. It was none of my business. If you're suggesting that I had some financial motivation to kill Mr. Holmes, you're crazy."

"That is exactly what I'm suggesting, Mr. Patton. If Mr. Holmes committed suicide, the firm was going to lose twenty million dollars. And you will be forever known in the legal community as the managing partner who presided over the dissolution of what was once the largest and most profitable law firm on the West Coast."

"Objection. Mr. Daley has started his closing argument a little early."

"Sustained."

"Mr. Patton, how much money will the firm get from the life insurance policy if they can pin this crime on Mr. Friedman?"

"Objection. Argumentative."

"Sustained."

"Mr. Patton, how much money will the firm receive from the life insurance policy on Bob Holmes if it is determined that it was not a suicide?"

"Twenty million dollars."

"And how much money was your girlfriend, Mrs. Holmes, supposed to get under the terms of the will that Bob Holmes was about to change just prior to his death?"

"Objection."

"Overruled."

"Five million dollars."

"And how much money was Mrs. Holmes supposed to get from the life insurance policy that he was about to change just prior to his death?"

"Five million dollars."

"So, Mr. Patton, isn't it fair to say that you had about thirty million reasons to hope Mr. Holmes died of murder, and not suicide?"

"Objection. Argumentative."

"Sustained."

"Come on, Mr. Patton. You had a chance to save the firm. You had a chance to help your girlfriend. You'd look like a hero. What more could you want?"

"Your Honor," Skipper wails. "Move to strike."

"Sustained."

Patton is starting to foam. "Look, you little jerk. I'm going to haul you into court and sue you for slander. These preposterous, unsubstantiated charges . . . "

"Your Honor," I say calmly, "would you please instruct the witness to answer questions and not make speeches."

"Please, Mr. Patton."

"Yes, Your Honor."

I'm not quite finished. "Mr. Patton, what was your relationship with Diana Kennedy?"

"She was an associate at our firm."

"Was she a good lawyer?"

"Yes. She got very good reviews for her legal work."

"And did she get good reviews in bed?"

"Objection."

"Sustained. Mr. Daley, please."

"I'll rephrase. Mr. Patton, isn't it true that you thought Ms. Kennedy was very attractive?"

"Everyone thought Ms. Kennedy was attractive."

"Isn't it a fact that you asked her out on several occasions?"

"No. That would have been inappropriate."

"Really, Mr. Patton? Your colleague Mr. Holmes apparently came out the other way on that particular moral dilemma."

"I wasn't privy to Bob's private life."

"But you were attracted to her, weren't you?"

"She was a professional colleague. Nothing more."

Sure. "Mr. Patton, isn't it true that you asked her to sleep with you at the firm retreat last year?"

Skipper leaps up. "Your Honor, for God's sake."

"Your Honor," I say, "it's a relevant question."

"Overruled. The witness will answer."

"I did no such thing," Patton says.

"Isn't it true she left your party at the retreat because you wouldn't leave her alone?"

"Absolutely not."

"And you followed her back to her room and attacked her."

"No."

"Mr. Patton, isn't it true the firm has had to pay four multimillion-dollar settlements to female associates who have accused you of sexual harassment?"

He glares at me. Then he looks helplessly at Skipper.

"Isn't it true, Mr. Patton?"

He mutters through clenched teeth, "The firm has settled various cases involving unsubstantiated charges. We decided that we didn't want the publicity or the trial costs."

Right. I glance at the phone company supervisor. Then I get right back into Patton's face. "Isn't it true that Ms. Kennedy made a claim against you for sexual harassment? And that you were negotiating a substantial settlement with her?"

"No."

"Isn't it true she threatened to go to the newspapers if the firm didn't agree to her demands?"

"No."

"Mr. Patton, if you don't start telling the truth, I'll call witnesses who will."

"These accusations are entirely without merit."

"Mr. Patton, isn't it true that you killed Diana Kennedy because she threatened to expose your pattern of sexual harassment to the media? And isn't it true you killed Bob Holmes because he threatened you with expulsion from the firm because you are a sexual predator? And so that the firm and your girlfriend could collect the insurance money?"

Patton eyes the jury. "No, Mr. Daley. That is not true."

I look at Rosie. She closes her eyes. I look at the ceiling and exhale melodramatically. "No further questions."

CHAPTER 55

I NEED HER TO CALMLY ASSASSINATE ALL OF THE PROSECUTION'S KEY WITNESSES

"The defense is battling uphill. Daley has done a decent job so far."
— NewsCenter 4 Legal Analyst Morton Goldberg.
   Tuesday, April 14.

"My name is Doris Charlotte Fontaine."

"What was your relationship to Robert Holmes?" I ask.

"I was his secretary."

At ten-thirty the next morning, Doris is dressed in her finest schoolmarm attire: a navy blue dress, a decorative pin and a minimal amount of makeup. Her glasses hang from a gold chain around her neck. I want her to project the embodiment of the voice of reason. In the simplest terms, I need her to calmly assassinate all of the prosecution's key witnesses. And I want Skipper to look like an arrogant ass if he interrupts her.

"Ms. Fontaine, could you please tell us how long you worked for Mr. Holmes?"

She smiles politely. Nice touch, Doris. "Twenty-two years. From the day he started."

"You must have been very close."

Skipper starts to stand, then stops. Good idea. It's too soon to be combative.

"We were. We'd been through a lot together."

"It's unusual to see such loyalty." I remind myself not to let things get too thick. "Ms. Fontaine, could you please tell us where you were on the evening of December thirtieth?"

"I was in the Simpson and Gates office assisting Mr. Holmes on a closing."

"How many people were working on the deal?"

"About fifty."

"When did you go home?"

"Around eight o'clock. We were having a going-away party for Mr. Gates that evening." She looks at Skipper. "I stopped by for a few minutes. I live out in the Avenues. I got home around nine."

She's hitting the right notes. The jury seems to like her. "Ms. Fontaine, could you please describe Mr. Holmes's mood that night?"

"Objection," Skipper says. "State of mind."

"Your Honor, I'm not asking for a medical determination. I'm asking her to describe her observation of his mood, based upon her many years of working with him."

Judge Chen gives Doris a smile. "Overruled."

Doris says Bob appeared extremely upset that night. "The deal wasn't going well. We weren't sure Mr. Russo would authorize us to proceed with the closing. Bob was worried about his bonus."

"Ms. Fontaine, is there any other reason why Mr. Holmes may have been upset?"

"Yes. Mrs. Holmes served him with divorce papers." She says he was surprised and repeats that he was very upset.

"Do you know what caused the breakup of their marriage?"

"Mr. Holmes was seeing another woman."

"Do you know the name of the other woman?"

"Diana Kennedy."

So far, so good. "You've testified that Mr. Holmes was surprised and distraught when the papers were served. Didn't he expect it?"

"He tried to reconcile with his wife because Ms. Kennedy had broken off their relationship."

"So, after Ms. Kennedy dumped him, he tried to reconcile with his wife?"

"Yes. It didn't work out. In late December, Mrs. Holmes's investigator caught him with another woman."

"Was it Ms. Kennedy?"

"No. It was a different woman. That's when she decided to file the divorce papers."

* * *

A half hour later, we are still discussing Bob's love life. "Ms. Fontaine, are you sure Mr. Holmes and Ms. Kennedy were no longer seeing each other on December thirtieth?"

"Yes, Mr. Daley. I was always aware of the women in his life. From time to time, Mr. Holmes asked me to cover for him."

"You mean he asked you to make up stories so Mrs. Holmes didn't find out about his affairs?"

"Yes."

"Can you identify the woman he was seeing in late December?"

"He never mentioned her name."

"Could it have been Diana Kennedy?"

"No."

"Was it Dr. Kathy Chandler?"

"I don't know."

"Were you aware that Joel Friedman and Diana Kennedy had been romantically involved in the fall of last year?"

"No."

"It's been suggested Mr. Friedman and Ms. Kennedy were still involved in late December."

"I don't know."

"It's also been suggested that Ms. Kennedy informed Mr. Friedman on December thirtieth that she was seeing Bob Holmes. Do you have any knowledge of that?"

"I don't."

"Ms. Fontaine, would it surprise you to find out that several witnesses in this courtroom have suggested Mr. Friedman killed Mr. Holmes because Ms. Kennedy dumped Mr. Friedman in favor of Mr. Holmes, and he was jealous?"

"Objection. Speculative."

"Overruled."

Doris tugs at her hair. "Yes, Mr. Daley, that would surprise me. Ms. Kennedy's relationship with Mr. Holmes was over. There was nothing for Joel to be jealous about. Diana broke up with Bob in the beginning of December."

* * *

"Ms. Fontaine," I say a little later, "let's talk a little bit about Vince Russo's deal."

She explains that Russo wasn't happy about selling his father's business. "There was great doubt as to whether it would close. Ultimately, it didn't and Mr. Russo disappeared."

"Was Mr. Russo distraught on the evening of December thirtieth?"

"Objection. State of mind."

"Sustained."

"Ms. Fontaine, how long have you known Mr. Russo?"

"About ten years."

"Did he spend a lot of time at the S&G offices?"

"Yes. He was in the office at least twice a week."

"Based upon your knowledge as an acquaintance of Mr. Russo, did it appear to you that he was distraught on the evening of December thirtieth?"

Skipper starts to stand, but McNulty stops him.

Doris nods. "Yes. He appeared very unhappy about selling his company."

"Could you please describe Mr. Russo's behavior that night?"

"Erratic. At one point, Mr. Russo stormed out of our main conference room while he was screaming at Mr. Holmes. He was angry because he had been told that the purchase price for his company was going to be reduced by forty million dollars."

"Is it fair to say Mr. Russo was extremely upset?"

"Yes."

* * *

Rosie, Doris, Joel and I are eating sandwiches in the consultation room.

"You're doing great," Rosie says to Doris. "You've created a plausible argument for suicide. You've cast doubt on the jealous-rage theory. And you've established motive for Russo."

Doris shrugs. "It's easy with Mike asking the questions."

She's right. "We've got about another hour, Doris. I need you to slay one more dragon for me this afternoon. Just follow my lead and keep the answers short."

"Did you hear anything from Pete?" Rosie asks.

"He said the banker in the Bahamas won't reveal the names of the income beneficiaries or the remaindermen of the International Charitable Trust. Wendy is looking for a judge."

Joel changes the subject. "When do I get to testify?"

"We'll talk about it later. If everything goes well today, we won't need you."

"But I want to."

"We'll talk about it later."

* * *

We begin the afternoon session at one o'clock. "Ms. Fontaine," I begin, "are you acquainted with a man named Arthur Patton?"

"Yes. He is the managing partner of Simpson and Gates. I've known him for many years."

"Are you familiar with an incident involving Mr. Patton and Ms. Kennedy at the Silverado Country Club in October of last year?"

"Yes."

"How did you become aware of this incident?"

"The firm conducted an internal investigation."

"How did you become aware of the internal investigation?"

"My boss, Mr. Holmes, was in charge of the investigation. He told me about it. Mr. Friedman was interviewed in the course of the investigation. He told me about it, too."

"Why didn't you come forward with this information when the

police first questioned you?"

"They didn't ask me. And it was a confidential, internal investigation. The matter was closed."

"Can you tell us about the nature of the investigation?"

Skipper stands. "Your Honor, I must object. Any testimony that Ms. Fontaine is about to give on this investigation is inadmissible hearsay."

It's a legitimate objection. I glance at the jury. The phone company supervisor seems perturbed. "Your Honor, rather than argue the merits of this objection, we would like to handle this issue in a different manner. We would like to introduce into evidence a memorandum prepared by Mr. Holmes which was dated December fifteenth of last year and was addressed to the Simpson and Gates executive committee." Rosie hands copies of a memo to Skipper and to the judge. "This memorandum sets forth the official findings of a special investigative committee appointed by the Simpson and Gates executive committee with respect to the so-called Silverado Incident."

Skipper is on his feet. "Objection. Irrelevant. This is highly inflammatory. It is an internal memorandum that is privileged communication. Furthermore, we have no basis to verify its authenticity. Finally, this information has not been provided to us by the defense."

I hold up my hand. "We produced this memorandum several weeks ago, Your Honor." I don't mention that it was included with the boxes of S&G financial records that we never planned to introduce into evidence.

Skipper glares at McNulty. Somebody on their side missed it.

I'm still talking. "In addition, if Mr. Gates is concerned about the authenticity of this memorandum, I am prepared to call Mr. Stern and the head of the firm's labor law department to verify that they got a copy of it. If Mr. Gates were permitted to testify, he would acknowledge that he has seen a copy of it."

Judge Chen is irritated. "The bailiff will take the jury out. I want to see all the attorneys in my chambers. Now."

* * *

We meet in chambers. Skipper tries to sound incredulous. "What kind of stunt are you trying to pull?"

This isn't the right tone in chambers. Judge Chen interrupts him. "Be quiet, Mr. Gates. Let me see that memorandum." She puts on her reading glasses. Skipper, McNulty, Rosie and I sit in silence. She scans it quickly and then studies it carefully. "Mr. Daley, where did you get this?"

"From Ms. Fontaine."

"How do you know it's authentic?"

"She typed it. She'll swear to it under oath."

"Your Honor—," Skipper says.

She cuts him off. "It will be your turn in a minute." She looks at the memo again. She turns to Skipper. "Mr. Gates, I happen to find Mr. Daley's argument persuasive on this point. Do you have anything to say?"

He glances at McNulty, then turns to the judge. "There is no foundation proving its authenticity. It could have been cooked up on Doris Fontaine's word processor. It isn't signed. We don't have an original. Before you destroy Art Patton's career, you should consider the ramifications."

I place my palms on the desk. "Your Honor, if he's accusing us of manufacturing evidence, he's crazy. Doris will swear under oath the document is authentic. I'll swear under oath we obtained it through legitimate means. If I'm lying, you can have my ticket to practice law right now. Our request is legitimate and our evidence is good. And if Skipper thinks it's tainted, he can argue it to the jury. Let them decide whether we made this whole thing up. We'll take our chances."

"Your Honor, with all due respect to Mr. Daley and his ticket to practice—,"

The judge holds up her hand. "Mr. Gates, have you ever seen this memo?"

"I don't recall," he stammers.

"I've heard enough. The objection is overruled. The memo comes in. Now all of you get out of here."

* * *

Skipper sits on his hands and seethes while Doris and I go through every detail in the memo in front of the jury. By the end of the afternoon, Art Patton's reputation is destroyed. There is a lesson somewhere in this. The memo reveals Diana had, in fact, reported Patton's advances to the head of the firm's human resources department, and had threatened to sue the firm for sexual harassment. According to witnesses, Patton had propositioned her at the party in his room. She rejected him and returned to her room. He followed her. Diana said Patton then grabbed her from behind and pinned her to her bed.

He tried to muffle her calls for help. She managed to free one of her legs and kicked him in the groin. She ran to Joel's room. About five minutes later, Patton knocked on Joel's door and found Diana there.

Patton claimed it was all a misunderstanding.

The report says Patton had been sued for sexual harassment on four occasions, and that the firm settled all four lawsuits. The firm also received a dozen other claims that did not lead to formal legal action. In each case, Patton claimed he was misunderstood. In his mind, it was all a problem of perception.

The other members of X-Com ordered him to have counseling and fined him two hundred thousand dollars. His points were reduced. He was told he would be expelled from the firm if another incident ever took place.

"Ms. Fontaine," I say, "were there any other developments after this memorandum was issued?"

"The day before Christmas, Ms. Kennedy gave her resignation to Mr. Holmes. She had accepted a job in San Diego."

"What does this have to do with Mr. Patton?"

"When she tendered her resignation, she told Mr. Holmes and Mr. Patton that she had retained a lawyer. She was going to sue the firm and Mr. Patton for sexual harassment. Mr. Holmes told me he was going to begin procedures to have Mr. Patton expelled from the firm."

"Did Ms. Kennedy ever initiate legal action against Mr. Patton?"

"No, Mr. Daley. She died before she had time to do anything."

"Ms. Fontaine, would it surprise you to know that Mr. Patton has testified that he had never propositioned Ms. Kennedy?"

"Yes."

"Was Mr. Patton telling the truth, Ms. Fontaine?"

"No. Mr. Patton is a liar."

"No further questions."

* * *

That night, we spend two hours at Rabbi Friedman's house arguing with Joel about whether he should take the stand. The conventional wisdom says you never let your client testify unless you absolutely must. A good prosecutor will turn a defendant's story around in a nanosecond. In a circumstantial case such as ours, the entire trial could turn on Joel's demeanor.

"Mike," he pleads, "I don't want to hide behind my lawyer."

"It's too risky. Skipper could tie you in knots."

"I'm not going to spend the rest of my life wondering if my testimony could have made the difference. I want to tell my story to the jury."

And maybe piss your life away. We spend an hour going over his testimony, just in case. As I'm leaving, he begs again for a chance to take the stand.

"Let me sleep on it, Joel. We'll make a final decision in the morning."

* * *

I spend the night consulting my most trusted consigliere. I'm inclined to put Joel on the stand for just a few questions. Rosie is dead set against it. Her instincts are usually better than mine. Randy Short, my mentor from the PD's office, says I should follow the conventional wisdom.

I make a final phone call at eleven-thirty. "Mort, it's Mike."

"Long time no talk."

"How's life as a TV star?"

"Not all that it's cracked up to be. I have to be up in a few hours for the morning news."

"The price of fame."

"Beats working for a living." He chuckles. "What's up?"

"I wanted a gut reaction from you."

"My gut is listening."

"You think I should put Joel up on the stand tomorrow?"

Silence. I picture him sitting in his bathrobe, fingering a cigar. "That's a two-cigar question."

"I know."

I hear his asthmatic breathing. "The conventional wisdom says no."

"I know."

"The conventional wisdom isn't always right."

"I know that, too."

He pauses. "I'd put him on. But I'd get him off in a hurry. Just a few questions. Get a good, forceful denial and get him the hell off."

"Thanks, Mort. I'll be watching you in the morning."

CHAPTER 56

"JUST KEEP EVERYTHING SHORT AND SWEET"

"In what court observers are describing as a reckless gamble, Joel Mark Friedman will take the stand in his own defense today in what might be described as the legal profession's equivalent of the 'Hail Mary' pass. Michael Daley should be sued for malpractice."

— NewsCenter 4 Legal Analyst Morgan Henderson. Wednesday, April 15.

"You ready?" I ask Joel the next morning.

He's pacing in the consultation room. "Yeah."

"You don't have to do this, you know."

"I know."

"And you understand my reservations?" A standard lawyerly CYA question.

"We've been through it. I'm going to testify. It's my life."

It's your funeral. "I'll be with you all the way."

"What would you do if you were in my shoes?"

"I'd listen to my attorney."

"I knew you were going to say that."

"Just keep everything short and sweet. I want you off the stand in no more than five minutes. Skipper can cross-examine you only on stuff that we've talked about. I don't want to open the whole case. I want you to tell everyone you're innocent, and sit down. Got it?"

"Got it."

* * *

The courtroom buzzes. The gallery is packed. Naomi sits between Rabbi and Mrs. Friedman in the first row.

Skipper has given V.I.P passes to three big campaign contributors. The gossip columnist from the *Chronicle* is here. It's the biggest local news event since the Niners were eliminated from the playoffs in January. We rise as Judge Chen enters the courtroom. Harriet Hill brings in the jury.

"Mr. Daley," Judge Chen says, "will this be your last witness?"

"Yes, Your Honor. The defense calls Joel Friedman."

Joel looks lawyerly. His hair has more gray than it did four months ago. His features are drawn, if not gaunt. Yet his eyes are clear. I've told him not to drink any water unless he has to. It makes you look nervous.

"Mr. Friedman, you were assisting Robert Holmes on a deal for Vince Russo on December thirtieth of last year, weren't you?" I like to start with an easy, leading question.

"Yes, Mr. Daley."

I ask Joel to provide a brief summary of the deal. We talk about his dinner with Diana at Harrington's. He says she left because they got into an argument about the deal. He says he returned to the office and Diana went home.

"Mr. Friedman, what did you do when you got back to the office?"

"I assembled the final documents for the closing. The papers were signed by twelve-thirty. I went to see Mr. Holmes. I explained to him that the escrow instructions that Ms. Kennedy was working on had not been completed and that I was going to finish them. Mr. Holmes was in the middle of a heated discussion with Mr. Russo. Mr. Holmes instructed me to call Ms. Kennedy and tell her to come back to the office."

"And it was that telephone call from you to Ms. Kennedy that was recorded on Ms. Kennedy's answering machine?"

"Yes."

"Did you see Ms. Kennedy after she returned to the office?"

"No."

"Mr. Kim, the custodian, testified that he heard you and Mr.

Holmes having an intense conversation about twelve-thirty on the morning of the thirty-first. Do you recall that discussion?"

"Yes. We were talking about the closing and certain issues involving my career."

"What career issues?"

"I was told that I was not going to make partner."

"And were you upset about that?"

"Yes."

"And did you convey your feelings to Mr. Holmes?"

"Yes, I did."

"And what was his response?"

"Objection. Hearsay."

"Sustained."

"Let's try this another way, Mr. Friedman. On the evening of the thirtieth, were you given an indication that you would be put up for partner the following year?"

Skipper stands. He's trying to figure out which objection applies.

Before he can speak, Joel says, "Yes, I was promised that I would be put up for partner the following year."

"And did Mr. Holmes promise to support your election to the partnership the following year?"

"Objection. Hearsay."

Judge Chen looks perplexed. "I'll allow it this time, Mr. Daley. Then I want you to move on."

"He promised to support me," Joel says.

"Mr. Friedman, could you please tell us what happened the following morning?"

Joel describes how he and Chuckles got the keys to Bob's office from Doris's desk. After they found the bodies, he went to the bathroom and threw up. When he returned, he opened the gun and took the three remaining bullets out. "I had shot the gun at the range. It was sensitive and unreliable. I disarmed it so that nobody would be injured. I thought it was the right thing to do."

"Could you describe your relationship with Diana Kennedy?"

"Yes. We were colleagues. And we were friends." He pauses. "And, for a very brief period of time, we were lovers. It's not something I'm proud of."

"How long did your affair with Ms. Kennedy last?"

"One night during October of last year." He looks at Naomi. "I'm embarrassed. I've let my family down. I've let myself down." He looks appropriately contrite. "I'm sorry, Naomi."

"Did you know she was pregnant?"

"Yes, I did. She told me in early December."

"Were you aware that you were the father of her baby?"

"No. She told me that I wasn't the father. I guess she was wrong."

"Were you aware that Diana had decided to move to San Diego?"

"Not until the night of the thirtieth. She told me when we were having dinner at Harrington's."

I need to be careful. "Joel, some people might think that your argument with Diana at Harrington's may have had something to do with the fact that you were the father of her baby and she was leaving town. Some might suggest that she dumped you and demanded support for the baby. Is that what really happened that night at Harrington's, Joel?"

"No, Mr. Daley. Diana and I were arguing about work. Our relationship was over long before the evening of December thirtieth."

"One final question. Let's put all of our cards right on the table. Did you kill Robert Holmes and Diana Kennedy?"

"No, Mr. Daley. I did not."

I glance at the phone company supervisor. No discernible reaction. "No further questions."

* * *

Skipper can't wait. "Mr. Friedman, do you recall having a conversation with Inspector Roosevelt Johnson on January eighth?"

"Objection, Your Honor. Mr. Gates is attempting to introduce into evidence matters that were not addressed in direct exam."

"I'll tie it together," Skipper pleads.

Judge Chen grimaces. "Overruled. But I want to see some direct relevance right away."

"Thank you." Skipper turns back to Joel. "Do you remember the conversation with Inspector Johnson?"

"I had lots of conversations with Inspector Johnson."

Don't get cute, Joel. Just answer the questions.

"Mr. Friedman, let me refresh your memory. According to Inspector Johnson's police report, you had an interview with him at the Hall of Justice. Do you recall the meeting?"

"Yes, I do."

"And do you recall that Inspector Johnson asked you whether you had ever had a sexual relationship with Ms. Kennedy?"

"Yes, I recall that he asked."

"And how did you respond?"

"I told him we had never had a sexual relationship."

Skipper is pleased. "We later found out that you were the father of her unborn child, didn't we?"

"Yes."

"So, Mr. Friedman, when Inspector Johnson asked you about your relationship with Ms. Kennedy, you lied, right?"

It's pointless to object.

Joel casts his eyes downward. "Yes."

"What other things have you lied about, Mr. Friedman?"

"Objection. Argumentative."

"Sustained."

I twist in the wind for the next forty-five minutes as Skipper cross-examines Joel. Joel admits that the fight at Harrington's was a big one. Joel acknowledges that his voicemail message to Bob sounded ominous. Joel admits that he didn't tell the cops about his phone call to Diana until he was confronted with the tape. I object every three or four questions to break up Skipper's rhythm. The jury is riveted. Naomi stares at the floor. Rabbi Friedman sits with his hands folded. I second- and third- and fourth-guess my decision to put him on the stand.

Joel acknowledges his affair with Diana. His explanation is credible. When you're the father of two kids and the rabbi's son, you don't necessarily want to admit adultery. He explains his love-hate relationship with Bob.

After a seemingly endless string of questions, Skipper gets right in Joel's face. "Mr. Friedman, as Mr. Daley so eloquently said, let's put our cards on the table. Let's admit what really happened that night. We'll all feel better about it."

Here we go. Stay the course, Joel.

"Mr. Friedman, what really happened that night is that Diana Kennedy dumped you at Harrington's. She told you she didn't want to see you again. And she told you she was going to resume her relationship with Bob Holmes. Isn't that the truth?"

Joel looks Skipper right in the eye and his tone is even. "That's not true."

"And you went back to the office that night and got into a big fight with Bob Holmes. Oh, it may have started out as a fight about business, but eventually it turned to a fight about Ms. Kennedy. Turns out she was two-timing you. She was sleeping with Mr. Holmes."

"That's not true, either."

"Come on, Mr. Friedman. We've seen you lie when things get tough. You lured her back to the office and you killed both of them with Mr. Holmes's gun. And you tried to make it look like a suicide. Except you got sloppy. You left your fingerprints on the keyboard. And you didn't realize your message to Ms. Kennedy had been recorded. Isn't that the truth, Mr. Friedman?"

"No, Mr. Gates, that is not the truth."

"You did it, Mr. Friedman, didn't you? You'll feel better if you get it off your chest."

Joel takes a deep breath. "It is not true. I did not kill Bob Holmes and Diana Kennedy."

"You're lying again, aren't you, Mr. Friedman?"

I leap up. "Objection, Your Honor."

"Sustained."

"No further questions."

* * *

My redirect is brief. I want to leave the jury with a final impression of a calm, collected Joel. I ask him to reiterate once more that he did not kill Bob and Diana. Then I sit the hell down.

At eleven-thirty Judge Chen looks at me. "Any more witnesses, Mr. Daley?"

"No, Your Honor. The defense rests."

"We'll hear motions right after lunch, and we'll begin closing arguments first thing in the morning. We're adjourned."

* * *

Late that night, Rosie and I are watching CNBC in her living room.

"I can't understand why Daley put him on the stand," intones Marcia Clark.

"It was a terrible mistake," says Morgan Henderson, who has left the comfort of the NewsCenter 4 studio for an appearance on CNBC.

"I should have left well enough alone," I say to Rosie. "I never should have put him on the stand. It was too risky."

"He did okay. At least he got it all off his chest. That's good."

"I don't think the jury bought it."

"They're tough to read. I just can't tell."

"Want to hear my closing one more time?"

"Sure."

* * *

The following day, Skipper and I spend the morning engaging in the legal profession's version of hand-to-hand combat. We line up toe-to-toe and deliver our closing arguments. The commentators will describe it as a classic matchup: the charismatic DA against the eloquent defense attorney. Skipper rants for the better part of two hours. He pounds the lectern. He prances like a gazelle. He points at Joel as he describes each piece of evidence. The theatrics are effective. The jury follows his every move.

I speak for less than an hour. I keep my tone measured. I can't compete with histrionics, so I have to try for empathy. The courtroom is a blur of jurors' faces. I attack each piece of evidence. I plead with them to believe Bob killed Diana and then committed suicide. I remind them that somebody could have entered and exited the S&G suite by the stairs or the freight elevator without being filmed by the security cameras. Finally, I tell them that if they insist on concluding that somebody killed Bob, they have far better choices than Joel. With glib self-assurance, I try to deflect the blame toward Vince Russo, Chuckles Stern and, above all, Art Patton. I remind them Art had at least thirty million reasons to kill Bob.

At a quarter to twelve, I thank them and tell them that Joel's life is in their hands.

* * *

When all is said and done, I'm not a big believer that you win cases in closing arguments. If the jury isn't already predisposed to vote your way, your goose is probably cooked. We take a brief lunch break and Judge Chen charges the jury. At two o'clock, she pounds her gavel and sends them to the jury room.

After four long weeks of trial, it's out of my hands.

CHAPTER 57

"I OVERREACHED. I JUST KNOW IT"

"We have great faith in this jury and we are confident Mr. Friedman will be acquitted."
— Live interview on Channel 4 with defense attorney Michael Daley. Thursday, April 16.

I'm jumpy as we're driving back to the office. "I overreached, Rosie. I just know it."

"You're overreacting. You did fine."

I'm looking for any wisp of comfort. Some lawyers walk out after closing arguments firmly convinced they were so good they could have persuaded the pope to convert to Judaism. I remember all the things I should have said differently, or didn't say at all. "You've got to admit I overreached a little."

"You did fine," she repeats. "They were listening, and they were with you. I could see it."

"You never can tell with juries."

We park in the pay lot across the street from the office. News vans are lined up on Mission Street. I know most of the reporters by name. Rosie and I push through them. I mouth appropriate platitudes about the strength of our case.

Rolanda hands me a stack of phone messages as soon as we get inside. I sift through them quickly. One catches my eye, and I head for my office.

* * *

I dial 1, 809, and the seven-digit number. You don't need to dial 0, the international access code, to call the Bahamas. The person answers in an elegant British accent. I recognize the voice of Duncan

Burton, the concierge at the Graycliff.

"Ms. Hogan has left for the airport," he says. "You can reach her at the following number." It's Wendy's cell.

I can barely hear her when she answers.

"It's Mike. Where are you?"

"O'Hare. We just got in from the Bahamas. Our plane for San Francisco leaves in a few minutes. How are things?"

"It's up to the jury."

"You ought to go back to the Bahamas when you can spend more time."

"Maybe when I have a lot of money to hide. Did you find anything?"

"The good news is we finally got Trevor Smith to talk. We found out who gets the money from the International Charitable Trust. The bad news, I'm afraid, is the information won't help you much. If you were looking for a magic bullet, I don't think it's here."

"Try me. Who gets the money?"

"Bob's kids."

"That's it?"

"Yeah. And one other person. Jenny Fontaine. Kind of a thank you to Doris, I guess."

"Bob always had a soft spot for Jenny. Is it divided up evenly?"

"Not exactly. Jenny gets a third of the money. The other kids share the rest equally."

"Interesting."

"Yeah, I guess. Any of this going to help you, Mike?"

"I doubt it. It's too late to introduce any of it into evidence. I can't imagine Bob's kids or Jenny were involved."

"Yeah." Silent disappointment at the other end of the line.

"Look, Wendy, I didn't expect you to break the case. You really helped a lot, okay?"

"I guess."

"When will you be home?"

"Tonight."

"Good." I look through the bars on my window. I hang up the phone as Rosie walks in.

"Find out anything good from Wendy?" she asks.

"How did you know it was Wendy?"

"You have that 'I wish Wendy would realize how big a crush I have on her' look."

"It's that obvious?"

"Uh-huh."

"You're not jealous, are you?"

"Nope." She smiles. "I'm not giving up my boy toy without a fight."

* * *

A few minutes later, Rosie and I are sitting in my office. My TV is tuned to NewsCenter 4. Morgan Henderson and Mort Goldberg are arguing about whether I should have put Joel on the stand. They've already declared Skipper the hands-down winner of closing arguments.

Henderson is explaining how I botched Joel's defense and what a horse's bottom I am. "He never should have let his client get up on the stand. Friedman should have hired a real lawyer."

"Forget it," Rosie says. "The only people whose vote counts right now are locked up in a closed room. And they aren't talking to anybody but each other."

* * *

At four o'clock Rolanda walks into my office. "They just called. The jury's in.

CHAPTER 58

"WHAT SAY YOU?"

"It's a complicated case. The jury will be out for several days, or maybe even a week."
— NewsCenter 4 Legal Analyst Morgan Henderson. Thursday, April 16.

"That's quick," Rosie says.

The jury was out for less than two hours.

"I don't like it," I say, more out of superstition than conviction. I know attorneys who never change their shoes while a jury is out. I never predict a positive outcome. Then again, I never predict a negative one, either. I turn to Rolanda. "What time?"

"Five o'clock."

"I'll call Joel."

* * *

I can't leave it. "What do you think, Rosita?"

"Too hard to predict."

We're in Rosie's car, driving toward the Hall. The announcer on KCBS solemnly intones that the verdict will be read at five.

We turn onto Bryant. I look at the auto-body shops and bail bondsmen. "I know I'll regret saying it out loud, but I just can't see how they can vote to convict." Even superstitious people have moments of weakness. And moments of wishful thinking, perhaps.

Rosie nods. "Juries are funny. They make decisions for different reasons. I had one jury vote to acquit because they didn't like the way the prosecutor dressed. In this case, they might vote to convict just because Joel is a lawyer. Or they may not like guys who cheat on their wives. You just never know."

* * *

A dozen news vans are parked bumper-to-bumper on the north side of Bryant in front of the Hall. At least two dozen reporters from the local and national media have staked out spots on the front steps and are broadcasting live. Satellite trucks line the south side of Bryant. One enterprising bail bondsman is renting his driveway to a cable station for a thousand bucks a day.

The horde surrounds Rosie and me as we walk through the police line toward the front entrance to the Hall.

"Mr. Daley, how do you think the jury's going to decide?"

"Mr. Daley, doesn't it seem like the jury was out for a very short time?"

"Mr. Daley, do you plan to appeal?"

"Mr. Daley, do you think your client got a fair shake?"

"Mr. Daley? Mr. Daley? Mr. Daley?"

We push our way inside. Joel and Naomi are waiting with Rabbi and Mrs. Friedman by the metal detectors. Naomi gives me a hug. "This is it," she says.

"Everything's going to be all right."

Rabbi Friedman and I shake hands, but we don't speak. We take the elevators. They seem even slower than usual.

We huddle outside the courtroom. "Listen," I say, "no matter what happens in there, we'll have no comment today. There'll be plenty of time to talk to the reporters."

As we're about to walk into the courtroom, Rosie touches my arm and motions down the hall with her eyes. "Check this out, Mike."

I see Skipper and his entourage. McNasty is at his side. A few reporters follow them. For some reason, Art Patton and Charles Stern are with him. Moral support from his old partners, I suppose. They look grim. I get an uneasy feeling in my stomach.

"What do you make of that?" she whispers.

"Beats me."

Skipper sees me and nods. Chuckles's face is unreadable. Patton looks daggers at me.

We walk into the courtroom. The bailiff escorts us to the defense table. Naomi and the Friedmans sit in the front row of the gallery.

"Mike," Joel says, "I guess this is it. What do you think?"

"They haven't been out very long. That's usually a good sign."

"What's your gut?"

I look him in the eye. "Innocent." There's no point in telling him the truth. I just don't know.

* * *

We take our places. The court reporter is already seated. We rise for the judge. She recites we're on the record. She asks Harriet Hill to bring in the jury. Time slows down.

Joel looks at the jury as they walk in. They aren't looking at him. Not a good sign. Naomi is wearing her sunglasses. Rabbi and Mrs. Friedman hold hands.

Rosie sits perfectly still. I'm glad she's here. My stomach churns.

Judge Chen turns to the jury. "Have you reached a verdict, Madam Foreperson?"

The phone company supervisor stands. "Yes, we have, Your Honor."

We watch the ceremonial passing of the paper from the phone company supervisor to Harriet Hill to the judge. She looks at the verdict impassively. No discernible sign either way.

"Will the defendant please rise."

Joel, Rosie and I stand. So does Skipper. McNulty stays seated. Out of the corner of my eye, I see Naomi and the Friedmans. Their eyes are closed.

Here we go.

Judge Chen turns to the jury. "What say you?"

I can hear myself breathing.

The phone company supervisor takes a deep breath. "Not guilty on all counts, Your Honor."

Pandemonium in back of me. Reporters sprint to the door. Joel falls back into his chair.

Judge Chen pounds her gavel. "The jury is excused with the court's thanks. The bailiff is instructed to release Mr. Friedman at once. We're adjourned."

Joel turns to me with a bewildered look. "Does that mean what I think it means?"

"Yeah. It's time to go home, Joel."

* * *

When a client is acquitted, the defense lawyer becomes an extraneous observer in a matter of seconds. Joel, Rosie, Naomi and I get together in the front of the courtroom for a group hug. Naomi is sobbing. Then Joel climbs over the rail and hugs his parents.

The reporters have already left the courtroom. I give Rosie a big hug of her own. "Thanks," I manage to say. I barely notice the tears in her eyes. I feel the tears in mine. I pause for a moment before I gather my papers. "What the hell just happened?"

"You won, Mike."

Skipper strides toward me, the three-million-dollar smile plastered on his face. He shakes my hand forcefully. "Nice job, counselor."

"Yeah. Thanks, Skipper." Let's go out for a beer sometime.

He turns and addresses the gallery. "Obviously, we're disappointed with the result. However, we believe in the system, and we must accept the jury's verdict. I'll be holding a press conference in my office in twenty minutes." I tune it out.

I turn and see Bill McNulty sitting at the prosecution table in stone-cold silence. He's looking straight ahead. His hands are folded. He's shaking his head.

CHAPTER 59

MY LAST CONFESSION

"We still have faith in the criminal justice system."
— Skipper Gates. Anderson Cooper 360. Thursday,
   April 16.

There are no victory laps or trips to Disneyland for victorious defense attorneys. A few get interviewed by Anderson Cooper. Some get book contracts. Most are held up to universal scorn and are cited as the reason for the collapse of the justice system and, by extension, the moral fabric of our society.

I seem to be one of them. As Rosie and I drive from the Hall to Joel's house for an early-evening celebration, the Monday-morning quarterbacks on the radio are already proclaiming I'm a social pariah. "In local news, in a stunning conclusion to the trial of the decade, accused double murderer Joel Mark Friedman was found not guilty. District Attorney Prentice Gates expressed his disappointment with the verdict, but said he would abide by the result. Friedman's attorney, Michael Daley, said he was pleased and had no further comment. KCBS news time is six-ten."

Rosie turns off the radio. "Enough. This case will be held up as a textbook example of what's wrong with the justice system."

"And the American way of life. Actually, Rosie, I doubt anybody will be thinking about it in a couple of days."

"You're probably right. Did the judge have anything to say?"

"Skipper and I talked to her for a few minutes. She said it was the most disgusting display she had ever seen in a courtroom. It seems she isn't real fond of lawyers who hide evidence and bring witnesses back from the dead. It violates her sense of fair play." I smile. "She said she hopes she'll never see any of us again."

"You're running out of judges, Mike."

"I know. Well, you know the old saying. 'So many judges, so little time.' "

Rosie grins. "Actually, I thought she did a good job."

"She did. She's going to be a good trial judge."

"Did you interview the jurors?"

After a trial is over, the lawyers are permitted to ask the jury about the case and how they reached their decision.

"Briefly. They thought it was a suicide. They didn't buy Beckert's theory that Bob was knocked unconscious."

"What did they think about you and Skipper?"

"They said Skipper was arrogant. And they thought I was whiny."

"Sounds about right. What about Joel?"

I give her a thoughtful look. "They were impressed that he had the guts to get up on the stand." I look out at City Hall. "And they didn't really believe a word he said."

"Why?"

I grin. "He's a lawyer."

She chuckles. "Did you get anything out of Skipper or McNasty?"

"Not much. Skipper was extolling the beauty and wisdom of the criminal justice system. McNasty kept saying he couldn't believe it."

"He's such a jolly guy."

"He may be a sourpuss, but at least he's an honest one."

"You're not going soft on prosecutors, are you?"

"I'd take a hundred Bill McNastys ahead of Skipper Gates anytime."

We drive in silence north on Van Ness and turn west onto Geary and head toward Joel's house. We're reversing the route I took in January when I made my mad dash to the Hall the night Joel was arrested. It was only four months ago, but it seems like years.

We find a parking space in front of Joel's house. You know the stars are lining up right when you find a place to park on the street on a weeknight. It's warm and the sun is still out. Winter may be ending.

The news vans are parked in every driveway on Joel's block. The neighbors will be furious.

Rosie pushes me toward Rita Roberts. "Say something nice to Rita about Joel and your renewed faith in the criminal justice system."

Rita sticks the microphone in my face and asks me how it feels. I utter banalities about how pleased I am that justice has been served, that a good and innocent man was set free and how the criminal justice system worked. I also prattle on about how proud I am to be a lawyer.

I take the obligatory gratuitous swipe at the press for attempting to try the case in the media. I ask them to respect Joel and Naomi's privacy, and give them an opportunity to put their lives back together. Rita nods solemnly. To me, it sounds like "blah blah blah justice, blah blah blah legal system, blah blah blah media, blah blah blah privacy." Rosie grabs my arm and we push our way toward the door.

The party is already in full swing when we enter. Joel gives me a hug and puts a beer in my hand. Naomi kisses me. Alan and Stephen come running down the hallway. Alan leaps up and gives me a bear hug. Doris has a glass of champagne in her hand, and we toast each other. High fives and more hugs. The owners of David's Deli on Geary are members of Rabbi Friedman's temple. They have sent over huge trays of corned beef, pastrami, roast beef and turkey. Naomi gives me a sandwich and I devour it. I'm hungry for the first time in weeks.

I see my mother in the living room. Her eyes sparkle. "I'm proud of you, Michael."

I'm glad she's having a good day. "Thanks, Mama. It means a lot to me."

About thirty people jam into Joel and Naomi's living room to watch the early news. There's wild applause when the announcer gives the verdict. I get an odd feeling when I see myself on TV. Rosie screams, "Mike, you look like shit." Roars of laughter.

I see myself talking to Rita Roberts. Then I'm talking to the serious reporter from Channel 5. The anchors on Channel 7 joke that I must be having a great day. I watch myself on three different channels. Then I catch Mort interviewing Skipper on Channel 4.

"So, Mr. Gates," Mort says, "do you feel like Marcia Clark?"

"I don't know what you're talking about, Mr. Goldberg. We're disappointed with the result, but we respect the process and the jury system."

Mort rolls his eyes. I watch him spar with Skipper for five more minutes before I leave the throng in the living room and make my way to the back porch, where I find Joel sipping a beer.

"Getting some air?" I say.

"Yeah." He pauses. "By the way, thanks for everything. I don't know if I would have made it without you."

"You're welcome. You would have been okay, one way or another."

He isn't persuaded.

I look out at the small patio. The garden has fallen into a state of disrepair. "Joel, if you wouldn't mind, I'd like to ask you something. Man to man, attorney-client, just you and me."

"Sure."

"Was justice served today?"

He takes a long draw from his Anchor Steam. He looks me in the eye and doesn't blink. "Yeah, justice was served today."

"I thought so. I just wanted to be sure. How are you and Naomi doing?"

"One day at a time, Mike."

"Maybe you could get some counseling."

"That's probably a good idea."

"I know some people who might be able to help you."

"I thought I'd call Dr. Kathy Chandler." A pause. "Just kidding. Give me a few days, I'll call you."

I wonder if he will. I take a deep breath of the unseasonably mild air. "Thought about what you'd like to do next?"

"I haven't given it much thought. I've had a lot on my mind. I think maybe I'd like to try teaching."

"You'd be good at it."

"Maybe. Naomi thinks I should write a book."

"Really? A law book?"

"Nah. I've always wanted to write a novel. Legal thriller. You know. John Grisham."

I laugh. "Forget it. It's harder than it looks. And every lawyer I know is writing a novel. It's been done to death."

He grins. "You're probably right. What about you and Rosie? You guys are so good together. You're more married than most married people. Why don't you try it again?"

Tough question. No good answer. "We talk about it every once in a while. I think we finally figured it out. We work great together. We love each other very much. We have a great time when we're together." And, Lord knows, the sex is terrific.

"There's a big 'but' coming, isn't there?"

"Yes. Do you know people who are really nice, but when they get together with somebody in particular, they become obnoxious jerks?"

"Yeah."

"Well, the same concept sort of applies to Rosie and me. We're nice people and we get along great. But when we try to live together, we lose it. I can't explain it. We're fundamentally incompatible. And we take it out on each other. She's careful about money. I don't have a clue. I'm neat. She's not. She likes everything to be scheduled. I don't. We drive each other crazy."

"Maybe the status quo isn't so bad after all, Mike."

"I guess. One of these days, she's going to find a guy and I'm going to get really jealous."

"Maybe not for a while. You never know. People change."

Rabbi and Mrs. Friedman walk onto the back porch. They each give Joel a hug. Then, to my surprise, they each give me a hug.

"Michael," says Rabbi Friedman, "thank you for all that you've done." He clears his throat. "I'm sorry I may have underestimated you. You're a fine attorney."

"I'm glad everything worked out, Rabbi."

* * *

At seven-thirty, Wendy and Pete walk up the steps and enter to another round of wild cheers. They're exhausted. Wendy comes right over to me and gives me a big hug. "You did it Mike!" she shouts.

"We did it, Wendy. And we couldn't have done it without you."

Pete's beaming. "You son of a bitch. We heard it on the radio in our cab."

"How did you get the banker to talk?"

Wendy says, "Pete's very persuasive. He held him by his ankles from the window of his office. It's on the tenth floor."

"You're kidding, right?"

"Yes, I'm kidding."

"You didn't hurt him, did you?"

"No."

I don't want to know the details.

Wendy beams. "And Mike, there's one other thing. Guess what? Pete and I have spent a lot of time together the last couple of months. We've decided to get married."

Wow. Crap. Great. I think. How do you tell a woman her taste in men still leaves a lot to be desired? How do I tell my brother I had dibs on Wendy? I know these people too well. I feel too close to them. I know all their flaws. There's no purpose pointing them out now.

Wendy shows me the engagement ring they bought in Nassau. "That's great, you guys," I say. "I'm very happy for you." I raise my hand and shout at the top of my lungs that Pete and Wendy have an announcement to make. Wendy holds up her ring finger, and the room bursts into cheers. I see my mother in the corner of the room, her face glowing.

* * *

At eight-fifteen, I'm on the back porch. The sun has gone down and a cool breeze is beginning to blow. After two beers and a glass of champagne, I'm getting lightheaded.

Doris smiles. "You did a helluva job, Mikey. I knew you'd find a way."

"I couldn't have done it without you, Doris. Like always."

"You're a helluva lawyer."

"Thanks. Now will you come work for me? I might be able to afford you now."

"I'll let you know."

We look out into the evening sky. "So, Doris, let me ask you something."

"Anything, Mikey. It's your night."

"You won't get mad at me, will you?"

"Of course not."

"Good. Well, there are a couple of things I've been wondering about for a while now. Maybe you can help me piece them together."

She drinks her champagne. "Sure."

"Well, for one thing, could you explain how you managed to get back upstairs after you ran your security card through the scanner and made sure the security camera showed you leaving? That was the key, right? To be certain that you had witnesses who saw you leave."

She sets her champagne flute on the railing. "I don't know what you're talking about."

I don't say anything. I feel my jaws tighten. I wait.

The silence finally gets to be too much for her. She fingers her glasses. "I could lie to everybody but you, Mikey. You figured it all out, didn't you?"

"I think so."

"When?"

"Just this afternoon. When I found out Jenny was going to get the money from the International Charitable Trust. Bob was trying to amend the trust. That's when I realized there was a big financial stake for Jenny in all of this. It gave you a motive."

"Are you going to turn me in?"

I take a deep breath. I think of the day she came by and gave me the hundred-dollar retainer check that's hanging in a frame in my office. "No, Doris. I can't. I'm your lawyer, and you're my client. Everything we say is privileged." I look directly into her eyes. "It doesn't mean I'm happy about it."

She's trying to hold back tears. "Good," she whispers.

There's a lump in my throat. "You killed two people, Doris."

"I know." Tears roll down her cheeks.

We stand in silence for a few minutes, staring at the trees in Joel's backyard. I think of Doris's daughter, Jenny. I think of Diana Kennedy and her mother. I realize I'm standing next to a woman who has murdered two people, and there isn't a damn thing I can do about it. The pain at the bottom of my stomach is excruciating.

I can't stop thinking about Diana's mother. And Joel. And Naomi and the kids. Lives forever changed. Finally, I manage to say, "You framed Joel. How could you do that to an innocent man?"

She grimaces. "I didn't mean to. I didn't know I had. That's not what was supposed to happen."

I wait.

"It was such a perfect plan, Mike. I'd read up on investigative techniques, planned it all out carefully. I thought of everything to make it look like suicide. Bob's fingerprints on the gun. A close shot, so there'd be residue from the gunpowder on his hands and shirt and tattooing around the entrance wound. Typing the suicide e-mail on his computer. I didn't miss a thing. And it would have worked, except for Joel. I couldn't have predicted all the things that pointed toward him."

True enough. "You were willing to ruin his life for something he didn't do."

"I know. I'm truly sorry about that—believe me. But I was trapped. Hell, if he hadn't made such an ass of himself when he called Diana that night, they probably wouldn't even have brought charges. And then he went and picked up that damned gun—how could I have guessed anyone would do something that stupid?"

She's right about that. I even think she means it when she says she's sorry. But it doesn't change anything, and I still can't put it together. She's watching me uneasily.

"It was always supposed to be a suicide," she says. "That's the way I planned it. And even with Diana turning up, it would have worked if it hadn't been for Joel. It was such a standard script. She and Bob were sleeping together, and he was a jilted lover. Plenty of reason for him to kill her and then himself."

"Were they sleeping together?"

"For a while. But she'd dumped him."

I need to backtrack. I've got the *how*—some of it, at least—but the *why* is missing. It doesn't make sense. No matter how much of a bastard Bob was, Doris had endured him for twenty-two years. What could have brought her to decide on murder—cold-blooded murder? And it isn't as if she did it on impulse. She'd organized it like a military campaign: reading up on it, getting all her ducks in a row. Nothing can alter the atrociousness of two deliberate killings, but I think somehow it will help if I can only understand why.

That's going to take a while. I know Jenny's got to be at the heart of it but I'll wait on that. Best to begin with the timing.

I say, "How long did you plan all this?"

"Several months. I didn't pin down the time when I began, but I knew I had to do it."

"And that night Beth served Bob with the divorce papers, the time had come? You figured he might change his will? Maybe write Jenny out of the trust?"

"Yes." She's crying now.

Okay, I have the when. I decide to fill in the rest of the how. "How did you get back upstairs?"

"I took the freight elevator. There's no security camera there. After I made sure everyone saw me leave at eight. I went downstairs to the Catacomb and took the freight elevator up to the new construction area on forty-nine. I waited there until one in the morning. I figured everyone else had probably left by then."

"How did you know Bob would still be there?"

"I didn't—I just took a chance he might still be finishing up on Russo's deal. If there was anyone else around, I wasn't going to do anything. I'd have just gone home."

"And after you went to Bob's office, then what?"

"I told him I came back to work on his bills. I started giving him a back rub, like I always do—did. Then I hit him on the side of the head with one of those heavy Plexiglas bookends on the shelf behind his desk. You know: the ones with the scales of justice on them that say, 'Justice, Equality and Mercy.' I'd put on gloves so there'd be no fingerprints. He just sat slumped over in his chair after I hit him, quiet as a baby.

Then I put the gun in his hand and brought it up to his right temple, and I was set to make him pull the trigger . . ."

"And Diana walked in."

Her shoulders sag. "And Diana walked in and fouled everything up." She swallows. "She was in the wrong place at the wrong time. It happened in a flash—I didn't even stop to think, I just aimed at her and shot. And then I went back and made Bob shoot himself."

The bloody photos of the bodies flash before my eyes. I shake my head trying to get rid of them. I can't.

She's keyed up too, remembering. "I was shaking all over. I couldn't keep my hand under control. The gun was jiggling when I pressed his finger against the trigger. I wanted to get a clean fingerprint on it, but I didn't. I was too upset about Diana. I meant to press his finger on it again but I had to finish everything up—type the e-mail with my gloves on, wash the bookend to get rid of any traces of blood—and I forgot about it."

The smudged fingerprint—I have all the *how* now, except for all the keyboard evidence that pointed toward Joel.

"What about the keyboard?" I ask. "Was it Bob's?"

"How do I know? I assumed it was. It must have been."

"Then how did it get switched?"

She says she doesn't know for sure. "Art and Charles were certainly eager to pin it on Joel. Maybe one of them switched them or got someone else to do it."

"You didn't move it?"

"Swear to God, Mike."

"Well, you almost pulled it off. If it hadn't been for Joel."

"Yes. If Joel hadn't screwed it up, it would have gone down as a murder and a suicide. And that's what I wanted: the suicide verdict on Bob." Then she says "suicide" again, so emphatically that I'm startled. "That's what mattered most."

Well, sure, I think—that would have ended it then and there, unlike a charge of murder, which never closes until it's solved. But so what? Doris was never under suspicion. It was Joel who was the unwitting victim of that foul-up, but she was clean. Why is she so fixated on suicide? I'm at a loss.

"Doris, what difference does it make now? Sure, the official cause of death is murder, and that means they can reopen the investigation at any time, but I don't think you're in any danger. I've told you everything we've said here is privileged."

"I know that." She sounds impatient. "You don't understand. That's not the reason the suicide verdict was so important." Her eyes are on fire. "Don't you get it, Mike?"

"Get what?"

"It's the key-man policy. The suicide clause. I wanted Bob dead—Christ did I ever!—but I wanted the whole damn firm wiped out too. Just as dead as he was. Stone-cold dead."

I'm stunned. The venom in her voice is palpable. I don't understand it. Sure, Bob treated her terribly for years. And there's Jenny to protect. But killing two people because she hated him? Bringing down the firm because she hated him? It doesn't make sense. All I can manage is a barely audible, "Why, Doris?"

"Because I hate them all—every last one of them. They're all scum. I knew they were in trouble. I wanted to be sure there was nothing to save them. I didn't want them to get the twenty million from the key-man policy. I hope they all go to the poorhouse and rot in hell."

I keep trying to bring some semblance of reason to all of this. I can't. I tell her she may get her wish about the firm. After the verdict, Skipper said Art told him they were going to shut down because they'd lost too many partners—but there's still a chance of their getting the insurance money.

"The official cause of death is still murder," I remind her.

"It isn't a perfect world, Mike. They'll be fighting with the insurance company until hell freezes over, anyway."

"I still don't get it. Why do you hate them so? Even Bob—you put up with him for more than twenty years. I know he treated you like dirt, but murder? Even to protect Jenny's share of the trust, how could that justify killing him in cold blood?"

"It wasn't the money, Mike. I couldn't kill for money. You should know that. It's Jenny."

"Jenny?"

"Bob was sleeping with her, Mike."

Dear God. A married man more than twice her age preying on the daughter of his secretary. Bob was an even fouler bastard than I thought. But I still find myself thinking why the leap to *murder*?

She's crying now. "I begged him to stop. I begged him over and over, and he refused." I can hardly hear her for the sobs. "Oh, Mike, I had to, don't you see? He was Jenny's father."

What the hell? "Did he know?"

"Of course he knew. From the very beginning. That's why he left all that money in the trust for her."

"And Jenny?"

"I never told her. I didn't think she had to know." She's trying to pull herself together. She takes a deep breath. "I asked him to stop, and he wouldn't. He was infatuated. He wouldn't even acknowledge he was doing anything wrong. My God, I even went to Art Patton. He wouldn't believe me. He said I was making it all up. I got so furious I threatened him. I said I'd reveal things that would bring down the whole damn firm—and he . . . he *sneered* at me, Mike, as if I was a piece of dirt. He said he'd crush me."

She looks at me imploringly. "What was I supposed to do? What else could I do? What would you have done if it were Grace? I did what I had to do, and I'd do it again. Twenty-two years ago I made a mistake when I slept with Bob. He controlled my life. I wasn't going to let him control Jenny's. Destroy it. No way. So I did it."

I realize Jenny was the new girlfriend that Bob talked about, the woman Beth's investigator had seen at the Fairmont. I know *why* now, and I feel sick. We stare into the backyard and hear the joyous voices of the party behind us.

"You going to turn me in?" Doris asks.

I'm prepared to shred my state bar card right now and lose my license. But I won't. "Nope. You're a client. I can't do it."

"Thanks, Mikey."

* * *

"What are you thinking about?" Rosie asks.

At eleven o'clock the same night, Rosie and I are sipping champagne on her back porch in Larkspur. Naomi gave us a bottle as we were leaving. I glance at the full moon.

"Nothing, Rosie."

"You're a lousy liar."

"Sometimes the legal system just sucks everything out of you. And sometimes, it just sucks."

She smiles at me. "Don't beat yourself up on this one. Your client is free. He didn't do it, and now he's back home with his kids. What's so bad about that?"

"Nothing, I guess. I'll probably get to fulfill my lifelong dream of being the first lawyer to grace the cover of a Wheaties box."

I get a chuckle. "You're upset, though."

"It's the way I'm drawn."

"Why do you always do this to yourself? The system got the right result this time. That's not so bad. Half the time it puts away the good guys or sets the bad guys free. This isn't figure skating. You don't get style points. Your client ended up in the right place. So for once in your life, take what you can and enjoy it."

"Okay, Rosie. But just for tonight. Tomorrow I get to go back and be my usual guilt-ridden, tortured self."

"It's a deal." She drinks her champagne. "There's more to all of this than you're telling me, isn't there?"

I remain silent.

"He didn't do it, did he?"

"He didn't do it. That's all there is to it."

"It wasn't a suicide, was it?"

"I'm not talking."

"What's it going to take to get it out of you?"

"I'm not talking."

"I can be very persuasive."

"I know."

"Let's try this. I'd like you to become a full partner in the firm."

"Sounds pretty good so far. I'll have my people talk to your people and we can set up a meeting to discuss terms." We can use the settlement agreement from our divorce as the model form for our partnership agreement.

"Good. Oh, by the way, matrimony is out of the question in these negotiations."

"Absolutely."

"Now that we're partners, everything you say to me is completely confidential within the confines of our firm."

"I like the sound of that. Our firm."

"I thought you would. It's what we should have done from the start."

"I know."

"Now, about your little secret."

Well, you see, Rosie, my former secretary—the one I've been trying to get to come to work for me—murdered two people in cold blood, and is going to get away with it—scot-free. She probably had a good reason to kill Bob, but she killed Diana just because she was in the wrong place at the wrong time. But, hey, don't worry— she hasn't killed anybody else in the last four months, and she promised me—pinky swear—that she'd never do it again.

"It's going to take more than a partnership to get it out of me."

"What did you have in mind?" She pours the rest of her champagne into my empty glass.

"If I didn't know better, I'd say you're trying to get me drunk and take advantage of me."

"You could say that."

Her dark brown eyes reflect the moonlight. I remove the elastic band that holds her hair in a tight ponytail. I pull her close. "Where's Grace?"

She kisses me softly on the mouth. Her warm breath smells of champagne. "Staying with her grandmother."

I smile. "Well, a second ago you said that for tonight, I should just take what I can and enjoy the moment."

"After all, you won your big case, but you didn't get your trip to Disneyland." She begins to unfasten the buttons on my shirt. "I've got another trip in mind."

"Is there a technical legal term for this?"

"Yes. Victory sex."

"Victory sex. It has a nice ring to it."

THE END

ACKNOWLEDGMENTS

During the day, I'm a corporate and securities lawyer. When I began to write a book about a murder trial, I realized that I needed a lot of help. I'm very lucky that I know many wonderful and generous people. I have to say a lot of thank-you's, so you'll have to bear with me.

To my extraordinary editor, Ann Harris. Your thoughtful work and dedication helped make this book a lot better than the draft that found its way to your in-box. Thanks very much.

To Margret McBride, the finest literary agent in the business, and the gang at the Margret McBride Literary Agency: Kris Sauer, Donna DeGutis, Sangeeta Mehta, Rachel Petrella and Faye Atchison. Thanks for all your hard work. You've made my life a lot easier. Special thanks to my colleague, Chris Neils, who introduced me to Margret.

To my generous and talented writing instructors, Katherine V. Forrest and Michael Nava. This book simply would not have happened without you.

To the Every Other Thursday Night Writers' Group: Bonnie DeClark, Priscilla Royal, Gerry Klor, Meg Stiefvater, Kris Brandenburger, Anne Maczulak, Liz Hartka and Janet Wallace. I'll look forward to seeing your work in bookstores in the very near future.

To criminal defense attorney David Nickerson, who helped me figure out the ins and outs of criminal procedure. If you ever get in trouble, David's your man.

To Inspector Sergeant Thomas Eisenmann and Officer Jeff Roth of the San Francisco Police Department, who helped me with police procedural issues. If Tom or Jeff arrests you, not even David will be able to get you off.

To Dr. Gary Goldstein and Dr. Dan Scodary, who taught me about the anatomy of the human brain. If you ever get sick, they're your guys.

To my friends and colleagues at Sheppard, Mullin, Richter & Hampton LLP, who have been wonderfully supportive of my literary efforts, and who have relaxed the firm's stringent billable-hour requirements from time to time so that I could meet my publishing deadlines. I am proud to work with you, and I'm glad you're my friends. Unlike some of the lawyers portrayed in this book, you embody all of the ideals that are honorable about our profession. In particular, my heartfelt thanks to Randy Short, Bob Thompson, Joan Story, Lori Wider, Becky Hlebasko, Donna Andrews, Phil Atkins-Pattenson, Julie Ebert, Geri Freeman, Kristen Jensen, Tom Counts, Ted Lindquist, Bill Manierre, Betsy McDaniel, John Murphy, Tom Nevins, John Pernick, Joe Petrillo, Maria Pracher, Ted Russell, Rick Runkel, Ron Ryland, John Sears, Mark Slater, Bill Wyatt, Bob Zuber, Aline Pearl, Terry Meeker, Kathleen Shugar, Sue Lenzi, Nancy Posadas and Donna Luksan. Special thanks to my secretary, Cheryl Holmes, who read every word of this book, helped me scout locations in San Francisco, and has put up with me every day for more years than either of us cares to admit. Thanks also to Jane Gorsi for her incomparable editing skills.

To my friends who read early versions of this manuscript, who (as we lawyers are fond of saying) include, without limitation, Rex Beach, Jerry and Dena Wald, Gary and Marla Goldstein, Ron and Betsy Rooth, Alvin and Charlene Saper, Angele Nagy, Polly Dinkel and David Baer, Jean Ryan, Sally Rau, Bill Mandel, Dave and Evie Duncan, Jill Hutchinson and Chuck Odenthal, Tom Bearrows and Holly Hirst, David and Petrita Lipkin, Pamela Swartz, Cori Stockman, Allan Zackler, Ted George, Nevins McBride, and Al and Marcia Shainsky. Special thanks to Maurice Ash, who quietly sat next to me on the Larkspur ferry for the better part of two years while I composed on my laptop.

Thanks to Charlotte, Ben, Michelle, Margie and Andy Siegel,

Ilene Garber, Joe, Jan and Julia Garber, Terry Garber, Jan Harris Sandler and Matz Sandler, Scott, Michelle, Stephanie, Kimmie and Sophie Harris, Cathy, Richard and Matt Falco, and Julie Harris and Matthew, Aiden and Ari Stewart. Family matters.

Finally, thanks to my wonderful, beautiful, supportive wife, Linda, the love of my life, my soul mate and best friend, who reminds me every day that extraordinary things can happen when you believe in yourself. I'll love you forever and ever. And thanks for buying me the computer.

Last, thanks to the joys of our lives, our twin sons, Alan and Stephen, who were very understanding when Daddy had to stay up late or miss a few days of vacation to edit his book. You make every day a celebration. And thanks for letting me use the computer.

ABOUT THE AUTHOR

Sheldon Siegel is the New York Times best-selling author of the critically acclaimed legal thrillers featuring San Francisco criminal defense attorneys Mike Daley and Rosie Fernandez, two of the most beloved characters in contemporary crime fiction. He is also the author of the thriller novel *The Terrorist Next Door* featuring Chicago homicide detectives David Gold and A.C. Battle. His books have been translated into a dozen languages and sold millions of copies worldwide. A native of Chicago, Sheldon earned his undergraduate degree from the University of Illinois in Champaign in 1980, and his law degree from the Boalt Hall School of Law at the University of California-Berkeley in 1983. He specializes in corporate and securities law with the San Francisco office of the international law firm of Sheppard, Mullin, Richter & Hampton LLP.

Sheldon began writing his first book, *Special Circumstances*, on a laptop computer during his daily commute on the ferry from Marin County to San Francisco. A frequent speaker and sought-after teacher, Sheldon is a San Francisco Library Literary Laureate, a member of the national Board of Directors and the President of the Northern California chapter of the Mystery Writers of America, and an active member of the International Thriller Writers and Sisters in Crime. His work has been displayed at the Doe Library at the

University of California at Berkeley, and he has been recognized as a Distinguished Alumnus of the University of Illinois and a Northern California Super Lawyer.

Sheldon lives in the San Francisco area with his wife, Linda, and their twin sons, Alan and Stephen. He is a lifelong fan of the Chicago Bears, White Sox, Bulls and Blackhawks. He is currently working on his ninth novel.

Sheldon welcomes your comments and feedback. Please email him at sheldon@sheldonsiegel.com. For more information on Sheldon, book signings, the "making of" his books, and more, please visit his website at www.sheldonsiegel.com

Find Sheldon online at:

E-mail: sheldon@sheldonsiegel.com
Website: www.sheldonsiegel.com
Facebook: www.facebook.com/sheldonsiegelauthor
Twitter: @SheldonSiegel

Enjoy the first chapter of the next
Mike Daley/Rosie Fernandez Novel (#2)

INCRIMINATING EVIDENCE

Chapter 1
"WE HAVE A SITUATION"

"The attorney general is a law enforcement officer, not a social worker."
— Prentice Marshall Gates III, San Francisco District
   Attorney and Candidate for California Attorney
   General. Monday, September 6.

Being a partner in a small criminal defense firm isn't all that it's cracked up to be. Oh, it's nice to see your name at the top of the letterhead, and there is a certain amount of ego gratification that goes along with having your own firm. Then again, you have to co-sign the line of credit and guarantee the lease. You also get a lot of calls from collection agencies when cash flow is slow. In this business, founder's privilege extends only so far.

Unlike our well-heeled brethren in the high-rises that surround us, the attorneys in my firm, Fernandez and Daley, occupy cramped quarters around the corner from the Transbay bus terminal and next door to the Lucky Corner Number 2 Chinese restaurant. Our office is located on the second floor of a 1920s walk-up building at 553 Mission Street, on the only block of San Francisco's South of Market area that has not yet been gentrified by the sprawl of downtown. Although we haven't started remodeling yet, we recently took over the space from a defunct martial arts studio and moved upstairs from the basement. Our files sit in what used to be the men's locker room. Our firm has grown by a whopping fifty percent in the last two years. We're up to three lawyers.

"Rosie, I'm back," I sing out to my law partner and ex-wife as I stand in the doorway to her musty, sparsely furnished office at eight-thirty in the morning on the Tuesday after Labor Day.

Somewhere behind four mountains of paper and three smiling photos of our eight-year-old daughter, Grace, Rosita Fernandez is already working on her second Diet Coke and cradling the phone against her right ear. She gestures at me to come in and mouths the words "How was your trip?"

I just got back from Cabo, where I was searching for the perfect vacation and, if the stars lined up right, the perfect woman. Well, my tan is good. When you're forty-seven and divorced, your expectations tend to be pretty realistic.

Rosie runs her hand through her thick, dark hair. She's only forty-three, and the gray flecks annoy her. She holds a finger to her full lips and motions me to sit down. She gives me a conspiratorial wink and whispers the name Skipper as she points to the phone. "No, no," she says to him. "I expect him any minute. I'll have him call you as soon as he gets in."

I look at the beat-up bookcases filled with oatmeal-colored legal volumes with embossed gold lettering that says *California Reporter*. I glance out the open window at the tops of the Muni buses passing below us on Mission Street. When we were in the basement, we got to look at the bottoms of the very same buses.

On warm, sunny days like today, I'm glad we don't work in a hermetically sealed building. On the other hand, by noon, the smell of bus fumes will make me wish we had an air conditioner. Our mismatched used furniture is standard stock for those of us who swim in the lower tide pools of the legal profession.

Rosie and I used to work together at the San Francisco public defender's office. Then we made a serious tactical error and decided to get married. We are very good at being lawyers, but we were very bad at being married. We split up almost seven years ago, shortly after Grace's first birthday. Around the same time, I went to work for the tony Simpson and Gates law firm, and Rosie went out on her own. Our professional lives were reunited about two years ago when I was fired by the Simpson firm because I didn't bring in enough high-paying clients. I started subleasing space from Rosie. On my last night at Simpson and Gates, two attorneys were gunned down in the office. I ended up representing the lawyer who was charged with the murders. That's when Rosie decided I was worthy of being her law partner.

I whisper, "Does Skipper want to talk to me?"

She nods. She scribbles a note that says "Do you want to talk to him?"

Prentice Marshall Gates III, known as Skipper, is the San Francisco district attorney. We used to be partners at Simpson and Gates. His father was Gates. He's now running for California attorney general. His smiling mug appears on billboards all over town under the caption "Mr. Law and Order." Two years ago, he won the DA's race by spending three million dollars of his inheritance. I understand he's prepared to ante up five million this time.

I whisper, "Tell him I just came in and I'll call him back in a few minutes." I'm going to need a cup of coffee for this.

Skipper is a complicated guy. To my former partners at Simpson and Gates, he was a self-righteous, condescending ass. To defense attorneys like me, he's an opportunistic egomaniac who spends most of his time padding his conviction statistics and preening for the media. To the citizens of the City and County of San Francisco, however, he's a charismatic local hero who vigorously prosecutes drug dealers and pimps. He takes full credit for the fact that violent crime in San Francisco has dropped by a third during his tenure. Even though he's a law-and-order Republican and a card-carrying member of the NRA, he has led the charge for greater regulation of handguns, and he sits on the board of the Legal Community Against

Violence, a local gun-control advocacy group. He's an astute politician. It's a foregone conclusion that he'll win the AG race. The only question is whether he'll be our next governor.

Rosie cups her hand over the mouthpiece. "He says it's urgent."

With Skipper, *everything* is urgent. "If it's that important, it can wait."

She smiles and tells him I'll call as soon as I can. Then her grin disappears as she listens intently. She puts the chief law enforcement officer of the City and County of San Francisco on hold. "You might want to talk to him."

"And why would I want to talk to Mr. Law and Order this fine morning?"

"Mr. Law and Order just got himself arrested."

* * *

My new office isn't much bigger than my old one downstairs. My window looks at a hole in the ground that will someday evolve into an office building across the alley. At least I don't have to walk up a flight of stairs to the bathroom.

I stop in our closet-sized kitchen and pour coffee into a mug with Grace's picture on it. I glance at the mirror over the sink. My full head of light brown hair is fighting a losing battle against the onslaught of the gray. The bags under my eyes are a little smaller than they were a week ago. I walk into my office, where my desk is littered with mail. I log on to my computer and start scrolling through e-mails. Finally I pick up the phone, punch the blinking red button, and say in my most authoritative tone, "Michael Daley speaking."

"Skipper Gates," says the familiar baritone. "I need your help ASAP. We have a situation."

I haven't heard the euphemism "We have a situation" since I left Simpson and Gates. We used to refer to this as Skipper speak. When somebody else screwed up, Skipper called it a fuck-up. When he screwed up, it was a situation.

"What is it, Skipper?"

"I need to see you right away."

Nothing changes. I'm still going through my e-mails. We aren't the best of pals. He led the charge to get me tossed out of the Simpson firm, and we've had our share of run-ins over the last couple of years. It comes with the territory when you make your living as a defense attorney. San Francisco is a small town. We have long memories and unlimited capacity for holding grudges. "Where are you?"

"The Hall of Justice."

"In your office?"

"In the holding area. They're treating me like a prisoner."

"What happened?"

Silence.

"Skipper?"

He clears his throat. "We had a campaign rally at the Fairmont last night." He always refers to himself in the royal we. "It ended late, so I decided to stay at the hotel. When I woke up this morning, there was a dead body in my room."

These things happen. "How do you suppose it got there?"

"I don't know."

"What do you mean?"

"Just what I said. It wasn't there when I went to sleep last night."

With Skipper, the line between reality and dreamland is often pretty fluid. He isn't exactly lying. Well, not on purpose, anyway. He spends a substantial part of his waking hours in a parallel reality. This is a very useful skill if you're a lawyer or a politician.

"Do you know who it was?"

"Uh, no."

"Did you call security?"

"Of course. They called the cops."

"What did they say?"

"They arrested me." He may as well have added the words "you idiot."

I stop to regroup. "Skipper, why did you call me?"

"We need to deal with this right away. We have to start damage control. This isn't going to help me in the polls."

I'll say. A dead body is serious. "You know how the system works. You should hire somebody you trust. There are plenty of defense attorneys in town. I may not be the right guy for you."

"You *are* the right guy. Notwithstanding our history, I called you for a reason. You're a fighter. You have guts. You'll tell me what you really think." He pauses. "And unlike most of your contemporaries in the defense bar, you won't try to cut a fast deal or turn this case into a self-serving infomercial."

I'll be damned. A compliment from Skipper Gates. "All right. I'll be over right away."

Rosie walks in. "So, did you get lucky?"

"Maybe. Looks like we may have a new case."

"No, dummy. Mexico. Did you get lucky in Mexico?"

Rosie. Ever the pragmatist. First things first. "No, I didn't get lucky." I'm probably the *only* guy at Club Med who didn't get lucky. "I'm still all yours."

She's pleased. "Well, then you *did* get lucky." She glances at my notes. "What's Skipper's story?"

I take a sip of bitter coffee. "Nothing out of the ordinary. A dead body wandered into his room in the middle of the night. The cops think he had something to do with it becoming dead."

"Have they identified the victim?"

"Not yet. The cops think it might have been a hooker."

"How did she die?"

"They think it was suffocation." I arch an eyebrow. "By the way, it wasn't a she."

End of Chapter 1 of
INCRIMINATING EVIDENCE
Read more at: www.sheldonsiegel.com.
Sheldon Siegel's novels are available in print and e-book.

ALSO BY SHELDON SIEGEL

Mike Daley/Rosie Fernandez Novels
Special Circumstances
Incriminating Evidence
Criminal Intent
Final Verdict
The Confession
Judgment Day
Perfect Alibi
Felony Murder Rule
Serve and Protect
Hot Shot
The Dreamer

David Gold/A.C. Battle Novels
The Terrorist Next Door

Connect with Sheldon

Email:	sheldon@sheldonsiegel.com
Website:	www.sheldonsiegel.com
Amazon:	amazon.com/author/sheldonsiegel
Facebook:	www.facebook.com/SheldonSiegelAuthor
Goodreads:	goodreads.com/author/show/69191.Sheldon_Siegel
Bookbub:	bookbub.com/authors/sheldon-siegel
Twitter:	@SheldonSiegel

SHELDON SIEGEL

CPSIA information can be obtained
at www.ICGtesting.com
Printed in the USA
FSHW021325060121
77456FS

9 780999 674796